CHASE MARTIN

A Roar of Strength

Tundavik

T undavik Vandes walked the dirt path between empty patches of ground. A brown barn jutted out of the once golden fields. The manor behind him was made of the wood chopped from the forest that once surrounded Ruwy. Banners rippled from the windows in the cold winter breeze, the sigil was of a hundred trees encircling an iron seat. Peasants and farmhands who would have broken their backs working the harvest were all gone as winter set in. The land deserted except for the slaves. They cared for the animals and cooked for the manor; planted winter rye and cabbage. The cracking of a whip could be heard on occasion. Reports of slaves rebelling along two of the Three Rivers worried those who lived along the River Arner. Lord Delan wanted none of that.

The barn was weathered like it had been out there for thousands of years. It smelled of mildew and the door creaked on its hinges, sending sheep fleeing to the pasture. Moans escaped from the worker's quarters in the back of the barn. Tundavik couldn't believe people were able to sleep so near the smells of sheep shit.

He opened the door and saw Burt, an older farmhand, with his lips wrapped around Sir Mar's cock. Tundavik knocked and Burt jumped for a pillow for cover. "It's alright." He pursed his lips at the naked knight. "Not to rip you away from your pleasure, but I think it's time we left."

He had come with Mar to Ruwy a week ago. The knight's face dropped when he was told where he was going, the seat of his family, but the Eastlands was between the Lands of Asara and the Flewthlands. They had to get to Storyah. Lord Blume would listen to their pleas for aid, and Tundavik would do anything to get more men to fight this war.

Mar wobbled to his clothes and slipped on his gray trousers and tunic. He patted Burt's bare ass and said, "It's been fun. Maybe I'll stop by next time." The farmhand blushed. "My father always knew how to pick them." He winked.

Mar slipped his boots on as they walked back up the dirt path. The manor looming overhead as a winter storm cast shadows from the west. "What made you want to leave today? Why not yestermorn like I wished? Why come at all?"

Tundavik kicked some pebbles off the path. A cluster of houses was near the river, the barn behind them, the manor ahead. "A safe place during a war is a good thing. Even if it is with your parents."

"Mar?" A voice shouted from along the Arner, near the homes and shops of peasants. A man on horseback in glistening plate armor with two guards wearing surcoats with the symbol of Ruwy kicked his horse to fly over the barren fields. "I cannot believe it's you." He jumped to the ground and embraced Mar. His hair was darker than Mar's and he was a head taller but his eyes the same gray. "Brother." He kissed Mar's cheeks.

"It's good to see you Reren." Mar pulled away. "Mother said you were off scouting."

"Making sure no slaves rebelled or armies marched north. We wish to stay out of this war as long as possible. Let the young Duke Adyn lead the rest of the Eastlands to their death. Not Ruwy." He embraced a stiff Mar again. "Why are you here? I believe the last time, oh, a decade ago, you promised on Veltoora that you would never step foot north of the Arner."

"Times changed." Mar looked to Tundavik. "Lord Vandes," Mar introduced and Tundavik winced at the title 'lord,' but he nodded a hello at Reran who returned the favor.

"How do you do?" Reran asked.

"Traveling is hard," Tundavik said, "We've been in Ruwy for a week resting."

"Travels?" Reran said. "Has my brother finally decided Eotros is where he is meant to be?"

"We're going to Storyah," Mar said pointing to the north-east. "You don't want the war to come this far north, but I do. We're off to treat with the Duke of the Flewthlands. Ask for support."

"Support for whom?"

"Hurvir's son, the rightful heir."

Reran laughed even though no one else did, then his face became one of worry. "After everything that happened in Vikry when the Rainvealandians invaded you wish to fight another war?" Reran rubbed his mare's snout. "Never thought I'd see it."

"We're going to say goodbye to mother and father and be out of Ruwy by nightfall. If Lord Blume does give us an army, I'll try my best to keep them along the coast."

"Thoughtful." Reran said with sarcasm as he turned to the wooden manor. "Well, they'll want to see me too. Shall we?"

Reran and his guards led the way to the manor, their horses kicking dirt from the path into Tundavik's eyes. Groomsmen took the mares and the group entered the seat of Ruwy. Candles lined the walls. Shadows pulled them into corners and dark rooms. House slaves bowed as Reran went by, guards straightened their backs. *The future heir, and Mar the second son.* They entered the great hall, but there was nothing great about it, not like the Crossing or Gereduss. It reminded Tundavik of the keep in Ritaeum, his old home. Dark and feeling like you've entered a forest. The ceilings were low, and the iron seat wasn't even on a dais, it was at the same level as the commoners who would come to complain.

Delan and Memi, Mar's mother, were sitting at a table to the side. Reading and writing letters. A single window behind the seat let in the scattered sunlight from behind the storm clouds. Mar's parents did a double take when they saw the group. Memi running to Reran and kissing his face all over.

"It's been weeks since we last heard from you." She lightly slapped his head. "We were worried you were sucked into battle."

"No battle mother." He embraced her. "But sending messengers gets dangerous in times of war."

"I see you found Marlen." Delan said as he embraced his heir. "I thought Veltoora was going to crack open and swallow us all when he arrived."

"It was a good surprise." Reran said. Mar had sunk behind the guards. "No news along the Arner either." Reran said. "The slaves were going about their usual business and I only heard tales of battles near the Byway and Winterlake."

"We had news from Redington." Delan said. "Apparently

Ultiir's forces are carrying out executions on rebels." Mar cleared his throat. Probably thinking the same as Tundavik. Sir Raimund had gone to Redington weeks ago, and he hadn't returned. Mar's best friend. Possibly dead. *Would Raimund be stupid enough to fight alone? Be killed as a rebel.* "I never thought that man had it in him. Always the quiet one watching his brother destroy the kingdom. Turns out he's more like Hurvir than even he thought."

"Enough about the war," his wife said, "we're lucky that no fighting has made its way to Ruwy. Both Marlen and Reran are here and Meret had graced us with another winter. Shall we celebrate?"

"My lord and lady," Tundavik said, "your son and I think it's best we left tonight. We've come to say goodbye and thank you for your hospitality."

"No need Lord Vandes." Delan said, "Seeing our son once more is all the thanks we need." Mar huffed.

Memi nodded and said, "Just one more night. The cooks are making goose, and I know how much our Marlen loves a good goose."

"Fine." Mar said hidden behind the guards.

***

The two geese were golden brown, filling the dining hall with the smells of honey and orange. Bread was passed around the table to be smothered in jam. Candied fruit littered the center of the table. Cooks and slaves bustled around the room, filling goblets with wine and wiping away messes. Delan sat at the head of the table with his wife and Reran to the side, another chair had to be found for Mar to join them. Tundavik made sure to sit near Mar and away from the household staff who conversed about finances and harvests and the ever-looming threat of war. It seemed like Ruwy was completely untouched by war, even the food was in abundance. *If the Flewthmen join me the feasts will surely stop. Eventually all Delan and Memi will have is roots.*

"And where is your wife?" Mar had to shout to Reran over the noise of the instruments being played on a small stage.

Reran drank his wine and said, "When news of the war spread I sent Luxe and Orson to Coaston in Maera."

"Orson?"

"My son." Reran said with a bright smile. "He has seen five summers. I guess you never would've seen him have you?" He brushed his brown hair from his face.

"He is as handsome as his father and is going to be just as strong." Memi said.

Mar played with his thumbs. Tundavik passed yellow butter to Mar for his bread. "You've been away a while," he said to the knight.

"Never imagined Reran as much of a father," he said as quiet as he could over the noise, "but I guess someone has to continue our family lineage."

His father must've heard that because he said, "We'll be lords of Ruwy until the end of time," and drank his wine with a laugh.

The night continued with more food and drink. Mar requested wine and ale and fermented horse milk from Eotros. The doma came in before dessert to preach the importance of Mother Meret and to give her offerings for blessing winter upon the world. Delan offered an extra goose to the cookfire much to Mar's dismay. Tundavik ate some candied ginger before slices of custard tart were brought.

Mar hiccuped instead of eating. Watching his brother laugh with his parents about jokes and stories Mar wasn't there for. His eyes started to lower as the night drug on. Tundavik wanted to leave as well. The band had stopped to eat after playing a rather lousy rendition of 'The Joy of Lady Hart.' The doma was still preaching about Meret. The staff picked at their teeth and complained about the Lands of Asara dragging all of Viguran into war.

Tundavik leaned over his plate, getting close to Lord Delan. "My lord. I know it's been some time since we talked last about the war, but it would bring me and Mar great pleasure if you joined our side. Fought for the lawful heir."

"Did I not tell you that I want Ruwy to stay out of this war?" The lord wiped his mouth of custard. "We've not enough men, slaves are feeling mutinous, and Lord Rely has never shown me kindness. I will support no one, even if my son supports the bastard." Mar stood and went toward the door, Burt the farmhand was stuffing his face when the knight found him and they disappeared outside together. "My son has always had peculiar tastes. If Reran wished to fight for Devro then perhaps we could talk."

Reran stared at his plate. "I feel the same as my father, I've already sent my wife and son away. I know how dangerous it can get."

Tundavik wanted to roll his eyes but didn't want to completely turn them away. "Then we'll be gone before you wake." Tundavik excused himself, hearing Memi wishing for Mar to stay.

His room was on the second story, as big as a closet. It was worse the first night when Mar slept in the room as well, but once the knight found someone to fuck, the room grew in size. The world was dark. Pitter patter of rain hit the roof and windows. Tundavik shivered as he crawled into bed and went to dream.

***

The forest was flooded by purple light from pools on the floor. The trees dead. The land barren. A manor twisted and destroyed by roots crashing through the ground. A throne carved from a tree trunk rose into the sky and Tundavik knew where he was. Ritaeum. His old home was darker than he remembered. There wasn't a star in the sky as a thick mist shrouded everything. Shadows crawled near his feet grabbing at his ankles.

A voice boomed like thunder. "You must find Ryobas. He who rides Nardal. Time is fleeting." The woman appeared in front of him. Bumps on her skin in swirling and snaking patterns. "The fall of the world is here. Nhamcaryn must be stopped. You must find the children. You must find Ryobas."

Again he saw a great tree. Larger than any mountain he had ever seen. People below cried out for help as the tree began to fall. Then Tundavik realized the people were not humans, but elves. They ran as the limbs and leaves came crashing down, splitting the earth in two. Thousands upon thousands of elves dying. Screaming.

The world went even darker. The woman gone in a puff of smoke. The elvish screams vanishing. Fire roared overhead, blinding Tundavik, burning the trees and the shadows below. Tundavik couldn't scream as he was engulfed in flames.

***

His brow was sticky with sweat once he woke, his heart pleading for peace. The sun had just begun to rise. The bedchamber soaking the light. Tundavik grabbed his head as he stood, wishing for the throbbing to stop. Wishing for whatever this woman wanted to stop. To stop hearing her voice as he slept. To stop seeing Ritaeum. His old home. The place where his family was massacred by the king.

Out the window guards and knights were running every which way, the common people shouting and pointing into the woods, horses rearing with excitement. Lord Delan and Memi were surrounded by swords. A barn was burned. *Was my dream real? Did fire rain down from the heavens?* Sheep surrounded the barn on the edge of newly planted cabbage fields. *Mar*, he thought as he whipped out of bed and down the stairs.

"What's happened?" Tundavik asked anyone who would listen once he got outside.

"The slaves," a cook said, "they attacked at night, burned the barn with men inside, fled into the woods."

"How could you let this happen?" Delan yelled at a master with a whip at his side." I told you to keep these slaves in line. How did they know about the revolts?"

"Some think slaves from the south came and rescued them."

Delan backhanded the master. "You best join the hunting party or I'll send you to the slaves along Sayer's River. I hear they're treating any masters they find very honorably," his voice dripped with anger.

Tundavik raced to the barn, through the crowds of guards and peasants and workers. The remaining slaves were chained together, a few lay dead beside them. Swordsmen watching their every move. Embers and ash floated into the air from the barn. Empty buckets littered the field. Dead sheep and charred human bones were among the rubble.

His headache returned, but not from his dreams, but for Mar. Devro would be devastated if the knight was dead. Raimund was already … missing. Tundavik couldn't bear to think that the knight was dead. The bastard would go mad if both his protectors were gone. Dropping to his knees, he buried his hands in the soot, trying to keep the tears from falling.

"Worried about me?" Mar said from behind. "At least I know you care."

Tundavik shoved the knight. "Where were you? Is Burt dead?"

"We were in the town last night. I'm not an animal who always sleeps in barns. Surprised you slept through the commotion," Mar said as he kicked debris, "the screams of burning men traveled for miles. Almost all of Ruwy was awake to see the slaves disappear."

Tundavik rubbed his head. "Bad dreams."

Mar squinted his eyes before saying, "Bera and Brun are in town, I was able to grab them during the chaos."

Tundavik didn't even think about the horses. Luckily the slaves didn't steal them too. "You don't want to stay and help?"

Mar swatted the idea. "I don't care much for Ruwy or my father's manor. If it can't survive without slaves then should it exist at all?" Mar took him to the horses, a young girl was feeding them sugar cubes and singing a song about horse riders.

"Are the slaves going to come back and murder us all?" The girl asked. "My mother said slaves are as savage as a wild bear."

"I don't think you have much to worry about." Mar said. "Thanks for helping." He gave her a coin before sending her away. "I hear Storyah calling us." He said as he climbed atop Brun whom he was watching while Raimund was … away.

"Sure you don't want to say goodbye?" Tundavik asked.

Reran popped out behind a stone bakery. "He doesn't have a choice. I haven't seen you in a decade and you're just going to run away after the night we just had? Mother will be devastated."

"She'll get over it. She has you and your son to make her happy."

"They do love you Mar." Reran said and shrugged. "They may not show it much, but they do. A decade alone with them has shown me that."

"Don't let Ruwy fall to war." Mar said with no emotion as he climbed atop his horse. His eyes looked sad as he told his brother, "Keep your family safe."

Reran stepped in front of Brun so Mar couldn't run away. "I will talk to father, try to make him see reason. Ultiir usurped the throne, killed his last surviving brother, I don't need you getting any ideas." Reran laughed and patted Mar's leg. "Make sure it isn't ten years before I see you again. You'd love Luxe and Orson."

"And they'd love me too." Mar snickered. He kicked Brun and Tundavik followed on Bera. They left behind the people of Ruwy gawking at the burned barn and wondering why slaves would revolt. Off to Storyah.

Aveline

"Safe travels Princess." A man at the gate bowed after Ivlin, the pocked-face guard showed their passes at the Gate of the Steppe in the eastern part of the city of Rowan.

That was a sign Aveline needed to raise her hood. The blue-gray cloak protected her from the peasants who meant her harm. The same ones who had destroyed the palace and the domaton and the Royal Chancellery, the ones who had children and bred hatred into them. As they rode along the newly cobbled conquest road, she couldn't help but wish she were on the western road. The palace was her home, but the western parts of the city was where she came alive. She didn't fear the peasants as much as her father or brothers. She knew a few of them. Had learned from them. Even the ones who wished nothing more than to see King Bartel's head desecrated by a mob enjoyed her company. She drank with them, smoked with them, played games with them. She missed it so very much. The formalities of court always bored her.

Even as the stench of the city filled her nose, she couldn't help but feel at home. Rowan was her favorite city in the world and nothing could change that. Zoell, another guard, saw Aveline's smile and rolled her eyes. "Wait until I bring you to Moon Bay, my Princess, there you'll be surely amazed."

"She'd be amazed at pig shit if it were shiny enough the way she looks at this city." Bert, her eldest guard, said.

They traveled the conquest road which had gotten considerably busier as Aveline grew. New manses and farms for the city's elite sprang up like weeds outside the city. Highborns looking for fresher air and larger lots to look down upon the poor. Inside the walls, the road had become overcrowded with people from the countryside looking for work. The road was where King Artin made his procession into the city to be crowned king. The same road her father took eight hundred years later to quell the flames that had killed Artin's kingdom. Now she took the road. But for nothing. Only arriving back from the kingdom of North Ferga. Her father would be disappointed the marriage didn't work out, but why would a princess marry a lower born lord? A Northerner at that. She always knew her father had a soft spot for Northerners from spending his childhood there in hiding while the kingdom fought, but a marriage? He almost had a heart attack when she suggested she marry a Rainvealandian prince, but he wouldn't hear her objections about going North for the winter.

To the west, jagged hills and rocks emerged from the flatness to create the River Marches which would eventually give way to the greater Gorthair Marches. Her father had told her how the smell of Rowan had changed for the worse after the flames. The whole city smelled of rot and burning wood. Before it smelled of roses and cherries. She didn't believe a city this big could ever have smelled good, but it was a nice thought.

Her guards protected her on all sides, but tried to make it look as if they just happened to be riding beside her. *Nothing more suspicious than someone being guarded by five people,* she thought with a raised brow. The conquest road ended at the river. The Bruthak churning below. Carrying both the life and filth of the city through her heart, cutting Rowan into two.

They crossed a bridge, almost too crowded to move, near Brissa's Point, named for her aunt, where the River Crom flowed into Bruthak. From atop the bridge she could see Amalia's Rest near the domaton. The spot where her grandmother was put on trial by the People's Chamber for crimes against Rowan and hanged. Her body thrown into the river. This city and its people had caused her family so much harm, yet still she smiled at the sights of children playing, bakers kneading, crazed fools proselytizing about the end times. The Fragrance Guild wore their blue robes and gold masks and wafted perfume about the center of the city. From the domaton to the palace.

The marble palace rose over the shops and homes. A striking white. Almost blinding her as the sun reflected off its walls and columns. There were more guards and knights around the palace gates then when she left. Winter was a hard time for some, and storming the palace for warmth and food seemed like a good idea. *Did father ever make the farmers' tax lower? I guess I'll find out if they burst into my room to steal me and my jewels.*

The crowd outside the palace gates scowled when Ivlin presented the pass and the guards bowed. *If only the guards knew that was a bad idea.* Once behind safety, Aveline dropped her hood and heard more hissing, she didn't turn to look at them. The last thing they wanted was to see her eyes. Eyes that would close tonight in the warmth of a bed stuffed with feathers and wrapped in the nicest wools in the known world.

"Back so soon?" Mari, her handmaid asked, emerging from the doors of the palace. Aveline towered over her atop her horse. "My Princess," she bowed and Aveline could tell she hated doing it.

"I guess I couldn't bear to be away for so long, and there was a bit of an accident involving Raff." She dismounted her horse, remembering poor Raff's cracked head against the stone from his fall. The red mess of blood matting his black hair. "My body is as stiff as a tree. I've ridden enough to last a lifetime. And the snow was dreadful. From North Ferga to the Sylvastist. You'd think the world ended north of the Therirock. Too quiet. I actually missed the rains of Rowan." Groomsmen found their way to her and her guards' horses before taking them to the stables.

Zoell kissed her spotted mare goodbye and said, "I think we need to visit some Telemese bathhouses."

Ivlin smelled himself, his tunic with sweat stains under the arms. "I could bathe for a month and still not get the stench of Heller off my clothes."

"Would you like it if I drew you a bath?" Mari asked Aveline.

"Nothing would please me more." Dern the Third said. "Will a beautiful lady such as yourself be joining me?" Dern gave a small bow, showing off his bald and scarred head, and reached for Mari's hand but she pulled it away, much to the joy of Aveline and her other guards.

Bert slapped Dern's back as he laughed. "For that you'll need Lady Indy's house."

Aveline finally said to her handmaid, "That would be great."

Her guards all parted, Bert and Dern off to a brothel to tell of their adventures fighting imaginary monsters in the North, Ivlin and Tomas disappearing to their quarters, Zoell to practice her swordplay. Commoners watched it all from the gates of the palace. *Just let me take a bath,* she thought as she imagined the horde of people spilling over into the palace.

Aveline and Mari passed below the elven-etched columns and into the palace with bowing servants and those who had come to court. Mari told her why they came. A few peasants who complained of the price of wheat. Envoys from Viguran to discuss politics. The lords of the Sunrise and Sunset, Darry and Rean, arguing about the kingdom.

"Welcome back, Princess." Aida, another handmaid bowed.

"Get water ready for a bath." Mari told her. "Miss your handmaids?" She asked Aveline with a drop in formality. The North was full of 'princess this' and 'princess that.' She was happy to be back around someone who didn't care about her title.

Aveline chuckled. "How could I not? Raff's hospitality was sorely lacking, and Erbat, his father, was no better." They came to a great door to the throne room. The iron handle called for her. "I should speak with my father before disappearing into my chambers."

Mari cleared her throat. "Not to be rude, but your father would think you've been sleeping in stables. You may scare away the peasants and their children."

"That bad?" Aveline sniffed herself and grimaced. "Fine."

***

Aveline lay naked in the tub. Mari and Aida trying to clean the filth off her. Mari rubbing her hair, the other her feet. Candles lit the small room. The scents of lavender and rose wafted through the air. The water had already been replaced with how brown it had turned.

"I did miss this." She tilted her head back and closed her eyes, a chill ran down her spine as the warm water hugged her.

"Did the Hellers even know what a bath was?" Aida asked.

"They're not complete savages, but being a princess comes with perks, and the North didn't seem to care if I were a goddess from their Vatya herself." She shivered as if she were still in that barren, cold land. "I had to wash myself. Which wasn't so bad, I've done it before, but I missed your touch." Mari squeezed her fingers on Aveline's head. "And only Mari knows the best way to clear my hair of tangles."

She let the candle wicks die down and another bucket of hot water be poured over her before saying, "I think we're finished. Aida can you find me a dress suitable for an audience with my father, it doesn't need to be perfect, I'm sure he wouldn't mind if I showed up in rags. Maybe something of mother's." Aida curtsied and went on her adventure.

"A towel?" Mari walked by the tub and Aveline pulled her closer and kissed her.

"This is what I missed most. Your soft lips." They laughed as they continued to kiss. "I didn't find Raff knew how to pleasure a woman."

Mari pulled back like she was slapped. "You promised you wouldn't."

Aveline laughed and kicked her legs up, water sloshing. "I would never," she squeezed Mari's hands, "trust me." Her handmaid couldn't help but smile. Aveline pulled Mari's hand into the water and between her legs. She tried not to splash hot water onto the floor.

***

They lay naked on Aveline's bed. She drew a finger over Mari's breasts. "We've taken too long," Mari said. "Aida will be quite suspicious if we don't unlock the door and get you dressed." She began to move but Aveline held her close.

"I haven't seen you in months. The world can wait a bit longer." Aveline kissed Mari's sweet lips. "Tell me what the world of Rowan was like while I was away. Meet anyone?"

"Worried about new handmaids?" Mari gave a sly smile. "There is no one but you." She pushed the princess' mahogany hair back. "The king was said to miss his children immensely, I didn't see much of him. Always coughing and sweating that one. Prince Bertin made it safely to Vaandet, but hasn't been heard from since. 'No reason to worry,' they say. Little Baldewin has written back and Blis has given reports of his exceptional fishing skills. Apparently he caught a great shark, teeth as large as your leg."

"Baldewin?" Aveline laughed. "My brother has a hard time catching flicker bugs."

"There's a war in Viguran." Mari said and Aveline stopped laughing. "Believe it or not it isn't against the Rainvealandi-ans. Each other. King Hurvir died. Your cousins fight one another. The Council wishes for your father to do something, the Chancellors wish for him to stay out of it. Obviously he hasn't done anything, and winter is here."

"Devro leads an army?" Aveline sat up. "Just a few months

ago he was celebrating with Bertin about fucking every whore in Gereduss."

"It's just what I hear."

Mari had a way about her that got anyone to talk. Rumors could fly all day in the washer rooms, but Mari would be the first to know. She just had to find the right knight or page to spill his secrets. If she wasn't a handmaid she would make a good spy. But Aveline didn't need a spy. "And who is winning?"

"Redington fell to Ultiir and Devro couldn't even take some small town named Riverton. The Councilors think Ultiir will win."

"Which would mean Devro's death." Aveline sighed remembering when he was younger than Baldewin and missing his father. She would muss up his hair. He absolutely hated that. "Well, at least father has kept us out of it. It's been only a decade since the last of the flames were extinguished."

"Is the king going to be happy about Raff dying?" Mari moved closer. Her feet intertwining with Aveline's. "There will be many lords and chancellors happy about this, expect many offers of marriage."

"If they haven't realized by now I'm not interested then the Four help them."

"It if means they become royalty, I don't think they'll care." Mari shook her head.

Aveline chewed on her cheek as if she were in deep thought. "They'd probably let me fuck you as long as I gave them children. That or murder you."

"And how do you think they'd do that?" Mari giggled.

"Poison. Push you off a cliff. Trample. So many gruesome ways that we shouldn't even talk about it." Aveline wore a smile and slightly tickled Mari. The warm bed shaking. Mari grabbed Aveline's hands and pushed them down.

"But you would protect me. My knightly princess." Mari said as she straddled Aveline, bending to kiss her lips. "You would never let anything happen to me."

"Never." Aveline returned the kiss, forgetting her father and the lords that all wanted to wed and bed her and the handmaid who would be waiting outside the door. Wishing so much for this moment to last forever.

There was a knock on the door. Aida said, "my Princess. I need to speak with you."

Aveline pushed a chuckling and blushing Mari off to find her robe made of the finest wool in Rowan. "Can't it wait?"

But there was no answer, only the jangling of keys and the turning of the knob. Mari dashed for her clothes and Aveline tried to slip the robe on quicker, but a gaggle of knights and guards and servants were outside her room staring at Aveline and Mari's nakedness. The princess felt her cheeks go red. Sir Delmar, one of her father's household guards, closed the door behind him and Aida. If Delmar had an ounce of emotion in his rigid steel body, Aveline would believe he had been crying.

"My Princess," the knight bowed, "I bring my most sincere apologies for barging into your room like this." He took a deep breath. "Your father, the King, is dead."

Raimund

His eyes opened as the wagon jolted. Raimund tried to stretch to wake himself more, but the ropes on his legs and wrists kept him bound. "Look at that snow." A young man, almost big enough to have a wagon to himself, said as he peered over the others' shoulders. Raimund could see the snow from his view as well. Everyone could. They didn't need some boy to tell them, they were all shivering. *Even me*, Raimund thought, *even I'm cold. Without Valkyr I am useless.*

He had lost his sword, Valkyr, and the red stone inset on the hilt. With it his power was gone too. With his sword he could make towers of fire and vanquish his enemies in ash, not that he ever did, but now all he could do was maybe light a match without a spark. He hadn't tested it since the incident in Raior. He hadn't even made it to Redington when pirates from the Nokys stole him. *I couldn't even save anyone.* None of the people in his iron-barred wagon had been one of the people he had seen in Raior, he had no idea where any of those people were taken, the innocent victims stolen by pirates. What hell they were sent. Slavery, sex houses, human sacrifice? He also had no idea where he was going.

But he knew he was in the North.

The air smelled crisper, it reminded him of this childhood. The mountains packed with snow that grew all around the wagon made him wish his parents were still alive. They would play in the snow. Throw it at each other. Chase each other. Until that winter where the fire engulfed them.

"I've never seen such beauty," the fat man said. He was the only one speaking the common language, the rest of the captives spoke the northern language of Heller. Raimund was out of practice, but he knew the others laughed or cursed at the fat boy. There were only six of them in the wagon. Two guards up front driving the horses through the winding passes of the mountains and the forests. The man next to Raimund had a long scar across his face from what was probably a deep wound. Across from him sat a man with no arms. The other two were twin robbers and rapers from the Glybelm, matching in every way, from the way their faces were twisted to the tattoos swirling down their arms.

"We've nothing like this in the West," the fat boy said.

"Zamni die urva!" The man with the scar shouted.

"What did he say?"

Raimund shook his head and said, "he told you to 'shut up' in a not so polite way."

"Oh," the young one said with a defeated face. "I was just tryin' to find the good in this."

"Why are you here anyway?" Raimund asked to an angry grunt from the scarred man. "You don't look like a criminal like the others do."

"Neither do ya, but I was on some ship from the West, I'm from there you see, and apparently the captain was tryin' to sell slaves in the North." The boy shuddered. He wasn't much younger than Raimund, but his face was that of a child's. "I've never been so scared in my life. Our jailers took us around the North until they dropped me off around here somewhere. Now, I don't know where we're going."

"Do you know where?" Raimund asked in Heller to the other men. None of them answered, only one of the twins shook his head.

"What'd you do?" The fat one asked. "These others scare me half to death, but not you. You seem nice. Caught sailing on a slaver ship?"

"No." Raimund sat silent after that, not wanting to get angry with himself for failing. He was supposed to get money and mercenaries from Redington, instead he got captured by a bunch of northern pirates.

"Don't wanna tell me? Because we're strangers? I'm Potter, what's your name?"

"Raimund."

"Now we're not strangers anymore so you can tell me."

Raimund looked into Potter's eyes. Not sure if this boy could help him or not. "It was only pirates, nothing special. I tried to get rid of some in Raior in Viguran and failed. They scooped me up and sold me to the highest bidder."

Potter's mouth was agape. "Real pirates. That's amazing … well not so amazing for you, but I've never seen no pirates before."

"Wouldn't the ship you were sailing on be considered pirates in the North? Selling slaves is illegal of course."

"Right you are," he nodded then smiled. "Guess I am a real life pirate."

Raimund and Potter both laughed with each other while the others stared at them with annoyed faces. They shivered as a gust of wind pierced through the iron cage, Raimund thought he could see frost forming on the bars.

The world was starting to get dark, much quicker thanks to the mountains blocking the sun. Raimund wished with all his might that Valkyr would find its way to him just for the night so he could stay warm. But it was useless. The guards whipping the horses to go faster were wearing black cloaks of fur, reminding him of Whitehall. *How's everyone doing now that I'm not there. Winning battles? Dead?* He prayed they weren't dead.

A roar shook through the earth. He expected the mountains to start crumbling. The drivers stopped the wagon as the horses reared and kicked and whinnied. The scarred men had been woken from a snoring slumber. *"Potvoryn,"* he said.

"The what?" Raimund asked. "I've never heard of that before and I lived in Irto for decades."

"Potvoryn is the beast of the Noest. He flies down from the peaks and finds his victims. Usually men to grow stronger. He leaves women and children alone unless he is starving."

"Stop with the myths, Liznar," one of the twins said. "you'll scare the fat one," he laughed and tried to poke at Potter who had no idea what was being said.

"No myth, Vojak," Liznar said. "And we all should be scared. Unsuspecting travelers get eaten all the time. Dangerous roads in the winters."

"I'd believe in the wailing woman of the Kormat before your nonsense." The man with no arms spat. "At least I've seen her."

Raimund rubbed the bridge of his nose. He didn't have time for superstitions. He had to figure out a way to get back to Viguran and his people. *"You're my people,"* he remembered Mar had said. And now Mar probably thought Raimund had died in Redington or drowned on Sayer's River or got caught up in the slave revolts. *I have to get back home.*

A gust of wind. Another. Then another. Not natural. The wind hitting them in a rhythm. Like the flapping of wings. Then a growl rattled the cage and sent the horses into a frenzy, but they couldn't run anywhere. One of the horses was pierced with thick, long talons and lifted into the sky, the wagon going with it.

The guards had fallen off into the snow, but the prisoners weren't so lucky. Raimund fell against the door on the back of the wagon and everyone else fell atop him. The wagon and horses was at an angle with the ground, Raimund could see the guards below screaming in terror as the sunset lit their faces with pinks and oranges. A talon gripped the other horse, ceasing the cries and screams as it was drug into the air. A vortex of snow and twigs and leaves surrounded the wagon. Blood and guts and bone from the horses was covering them, entrails dumping on them. The men grunted and yelled out and tired to move but the beast that held them in their talons wasn't letting up.

Raimund could do nothing. The ground was twenty feet below, and the amount of weight on him made him think he was going to break every bone in his body. He wrapped his fingers around a bar and concentrated all his might on it. He wasn't trying to break it. He wanted to burn it. As his fingertips flickered red, he smiled. Even without Valkyr and the sunstone a small part of him was still lit with fire. Touched by the gods. He was an éithrio, and that would help him get back home.

The bar didn't burn. It broke.

Whatever beast had hold of them decided to drop them. So

they fell. And fell. Until they crashed into the ground, pieces of horse falling with them.

Raimund could hardly see, hardly breathe, he felt like dying in the Noest Mountains, far away from civilization. The no-armed man was dead beside him, his lungs and head both pierced from the cold, iron bars. The twins were trying their best to stand with tied wrists and ankles. Liznar was lucky. His ropes had come undone and he raced toward the forest, but that's where his luck ended. The winged beast cast a shadow over them and a huge paw, with bird-like talons extended, grabbed Liznar by the back and threw him into the air, and caught him with a beak. Liznar's blood and guts spilled from the monster's mouth as his screams were silenced.

That's when Raimund knew he couldn't die here.

He rubbed his face in the snow, trying to clean it from the blood so he could see and crawled forward with his shoulders and chest as best he could. The twins were fighting to stand, but the beast landed with all it's might and got to work feasting. Raimund finally saw the monster in its full glory. It looked like a great eagle that soared over the mountains, and a large cat from the southern reaches of Adedor. He had never seen a griffin before. Didn't think they still existed.

The griffin put its paw on one twin while tearing the flesh and meat from the other. Both brothers were screaming and crying and cursing but it was use. When the monster was done with one it went to the other. Potter, his body splayed over some rocks, would've been next, but the guards caught the griffin's eye as they shouted and ran.

The griffin lurched its body into the hair, large wings carrying the large cat-like body over the snow and whacking a guard with a paw while it's beak dove into the other. A guard's sword had flung near Raimund and he saw his chance while the beast was distracted. He crawled to it and positioned the sword between his legs, the blade facing the rope, and began to furiously move his legs up and down. He also thought about fire. How the rope could burst into flames and he could be gone even quicker.

And just like that the rope fell apart. He didn't have time to figure out if it was the sword or his magic or an act from the gods, he had to flee. Using his knees to lift himself, he stumbled for a moment. The blood rushing back into his legs. But he managed a trot, still sore from the fall and the exploding wagon.

Raimund ran towards the woods just like Linzar had, but the griffin seemed busy with the guards, ripping through their skin and feasting on their innards. If had eaten recently he would've puked, even if he saw worse at his loss in Riverton. If he had Valkyr he might actually fight off the beast, but he wasn't sure if he was even powerful enough.

As he reached the edge of the woods, silent, all the animals either sleeping or hiding, he turned his head and saw Potter. *I'm just going to leave him. Leave him to die. Alone.* He hesitated a moment too long. The griffin let out a sound that was between a roar and a squawk. Heavy legs pushed through the snow as the beast's wings began to flap. Raimund had to get to the trees and hope Potter would somehow make it.

Then a ball was in the air above the griffin's head and exploded. The beast cried as shards of ice got stuck in its face. Another ball and another explosion of ice. A woman emerged from the dark of the forest and held out a pale hand that reflected the ever-brightening moon. "Come with me."

Yvanne

Lord Aimora Dore rode into the winter town atop a black stallion. Both adorned in steel armor that reflected the sun more than the snow that covered Whitehall as of late. The chanfron on the horse's face befit with a horn making it so Lord Aimora was riding in on a unicorn. Behind him were dozens of men. They wore fur over their steel plates, wolf and bear and leopard. Two bannermen either side of the lord carried blue banners with a spotted leopard stalking his prey in the mountains, almost as white as the bear on her own lord father's banners.

Yvanne and Devro had been holding court. Hearing stories of peasants who crowded into the city as winter descended upon them, food harder to come by since the war started, being forced to sell their goods or bodies or raid their neighbor just to survive. Devro was passing judgment on a local rape committed by a cobbler when the men in the passes sounded their horns that echoed in the valley. "Lodean! Lodean! Lodean!" They shouted with every blow.

Now the peasants hid anywhere they could as everyone expected a fight. Lord Aimora only smiled as he took off his helm, his bald head with goosebumps. "*Aixo*," he said in his forbidden language. "My king, my queen." He bowed his head and his men followed, even some of the horses bowed with their riders. "I am sure our arrival caused much concern."

"My men are ready to kill you." Devro said in a low voice. *Trying to act a man and not afraid,* Yvanne thought as she took hold of his shaking hand. "Tell us why you are here."

The lord of Lodeanhold dropped off his black horse and went to one knee. "My men and I have discussed the state of this kingdom lately, and the horrors that the false king has inflicted on not just Greatbath but on all of the Lands. That has made our decision easy. We were going to stay neutral, but our hand has been forced. If you would, my king, please accept my undying loyalty to your cause."

Devro's eyes flicked to Yvanne but she said nothing. It wasn't her decision to make even if her husband wished it were. "Very well. Come here, my lord." Lord Aimora came and knelt in the snow closer. The knights and men of Whitehall, the ones who had killed Lodean for as long as they've carried a sword, furrowed their brow after Devro spoke. *I hope you haven't chosen wrong,* Yvanne thought. "I will allow the strength of Lodeanhold to fight with us, and I will make sure my men treat you as their own."

"Thank you, Your Grace, you will not regret it. Viguran has rarely seen the strength of the Lodean but I intend to change that."

"We've certainly seen it." A wheezing old man said from behind them. Yvanne's father, the duke of the Lands of Asara, David, was shivering under his black fur cloak. "My king, I strongly advise you seek counsel before agreeing to any terms with the Lodean."

Yvanne grabbed her father's arm. "I'm sure His Grace knows what he's doing. You need some sleep." Dera, the daken from Midvalley, held cloths in hand for David's fever.

"I strongly urge counsel," her father almost shouted, his voice straining from his sickness. "A Lodean is not to be trusted."

The Lodean looked at her father with disgust. Lord Aimora stood, "I know my people have had our differences with you in the past but we wish to fight for your king and daughter. Stop the madness that has plagued these mountains for centuries and join forces."

"Never … join … with you." The duke said through coughs.

"Enough, father. You're embarrassing yourself in front of your subjects."

David wrestled his arm from Yvanne and found Dera. "Take me to bed. Give me … some medicine," he wheezed and shivered in the cold.

Yvanne gripped her black cloak to give the appearance of warming herself, even though she was always warm as the stone in her necklace faintly shone and she pulled on all the strands of power that flowed every which way around her. "Please forgive my father, Lord Aimora. This winter has been especially hard on him, sometimes his mind wanders and he forgets himself."

"I understand. The past is hard to forget."

"But we will make a new future." Devro said with a beaming smile. "I look forward to seeing your men in action and I offer you a seat on my council. The Four know I need all the help I can get." Quiet groans and gasps escaped from the Whitehall men. If Devro heard it he didn't react.

"I am even more honored." The Lodean lord bowed before finding his horse and his men.

As Devro and Yvanne made their way back to the mountainside keep, he asked, "did I do the right thing? You've seen what the Lodean can do."

"I guess we'll find out, but I would rather have them on our side than Ultiir's. The Lodean can traverse the mountains like no other man, know all its secrets. Supposedly descended from dwarves. That's why some of them are still so short." The guards opened the door and the warmth of the fires in the keep washed over them. Yvanne could see the energy flowing all around the great hall and up to the ceiling, pulling just enough inward to keep herself from shivering like the rest. "At least I don't have to tell father. Him and the Lodean have fought numerous times. Revolt after revolt."

"Lord Aimora said the Lodean have never shown their strength, yet they always lose to the duke's forces." Devro said with a puzzled look. "Maybe I was wrong."

"I'm sure all will be fine," Yvanne said. "Maybe you can instruct them to watch over the Swallow Pass for now, in case the Terropians figure out how to tunnel through snow." That was their great worry as of late. Not of the hunger or the lowlands aflame or even Ultiir marching up the King's Pass. If King Anvrin decided to join Ultiir the Lands of Asara wouldn't stand a chance. The war would be over within a week. Luckily snow had stopped all from entering the valley where Whitehall resided.

"Any word from Tundavik and Mar?" Devro asked.

"Tiro received the message and gave it to me last night, but he doesn't know how long ago it was written. It takes weeks to get anything through the snow. They're in Ruwy, Mar's home, hoping to leave within the week. Who knows if they're already in Storyah."

"And Raimund?"

Still holding out hope his knight isn't dead. "Nothing. That doesn't mean anything happened to him, just busy is all."

Devro gave a shallow nod. "I'll go lie down."

"What about court? We still have a few hearings."

Her young husband, the king, waved a hand and disappeared into the abyss of corridors carved from stone. Yvanne sighed as she looked to the peasants standing in line. "Tomorrow. Enjoy the town for tonight."

Sir Groel ushered them out and the hall was empty. The cold, stone chair in the center. Where her father sat for decades and now her husband ruled from. But it wasn't *the* throne. That was in Vigur where Ultiir cast judgment atop it.

"Your husband knows how to keep the people happy," a voice full of sarcasm whispered to her. Lord Urses de'Marisco stood by the fire warming his hands. "I'm sorry. *His Grace.*"

"Have you ever held court, my lord? Not an easy thing. A lot of pressure to make sure all is right and no more problems arise." Yvanne smirked at the lord. He was older than looks were to be believed. He was cunning and smart and a long time councilor for the old, dead king. But Yvanne needed him. Urses de'Marisco knew too much to be kept in a prison or cast out into the cold.

"You both are young, but if the pressure of a few farmers arguing over a sliver of land is too much, how do you think he'll fare in Vigur? The problems are more dire. The consequences of one's decision felt tenfold. I support our king, but he needs to know that rulers rarely sleep."

"He mourns for Sir Raimund, Lord Geary, worries for Tundavik and Mar."

"And the lowlands are at war. The Eastlands descend on your people. The Flewthlands could join the fight if Tundavik and the drunken knight are successful. There are many problems. Thousands already fleeing their homes or dead. His Grace must act like a king to gain support, not a child."

"I don't think he would appreciate you speaking about him in this way."

"But you think I'm right?" The lord's baby-face gave a smirk. "Perhaps I should counsel him some more."

"You know how the others feel about you being close to Devro." Yvanne said as she remembered the anger from her brother, Pollard; the swordmaster, Arold; and even her own father. No one trusted the man who brought Lord Geary's head in a sack, even if Lord de'Marisco claimed it was Ultiir who sent him to deliver the message or die as well.

"Will I ever gain their trust?"

Yvanne smiled at Sir Groel who watched them with a hand on his hilt. "Maybe once the war is won and you've shown us you're loyal. Anymore I can bring to the council about Ultiir and his plans or have you shared all you know?"

"I might be wrong about the rest. He wants to name a new duke for the Lands of Asara, wants him to lay waste to Whitehall, and to bring all of your heads so he can mount them above the holy city. Not very holy is it?" Urses chuckled. "The Flewthlands and Pyre Blume is our only option to match Ultiir's might."

"I have faith in Tundavik and Mar." Yvanne let the energy go to feel the actual warmth of the fire. The sunlight was fading away as gray, winter clouds rolled over the mountains. The windows letting in less light. The charred hole in the wall covered to stop the chill, but the breeze still filled the chamber. "The Eastlands will have two fronts and be taken by surprise."

"And if Anvrin joins the fray?"

"We have time to figure that out. Perhaps the Lords of the Peaks will ally with us." She had never even seen the Lords of the Peaks or the Peakmen, but she had heard stories of their strength. It took a strong people to survive the cold death of winter in these mountains.

"I think the Lords of the Peaks are more likely to descend on us raining fire and looting as much as they can while we focus our efforts elsewhere, but I've been wrong before." The lord scratched his scarred nose. "Have you given any thought into ascending the peaks and asking for help?"

"And risk the mountain folk attacking?" Those wild men made enough trouble for her father, she wondered how he was able to keep the Lands of Asara together with so many groups fighting and killing each other. "I know winter isn't harsh in Keeland, nor Vigur, but here the snows trap us and we pray for relief."

"The Lodean must've prayed harder." He smirked as he turned to the fire, poking it and making a mess of ashes.

Jacka came from behind saying, "Your Grace, it's much too cold," she slipped gloves onto Yvanne's hands. "We must make sure you and the babe stay warm."

Yvanne touched her belly, forgetting she was pregnant underneath the layers of wool and fur. That morning Jacka had brought two buckets for Yvanne's morning sickness. She was already ready for the baby to be out of her. An heir. The men outside fought for her because they knew she was with child, she couldn't let anything happen to it. "Thank you, Jacka."

The handmaid curtsied and said, "Helge is with your father and the daken. Saying a few prayers."

"Yes I should go to him. Have you seen my sister and her husband?"

"They have been seen in Berga's inn as of late. I don't think they like the keep."

"Cada never did." Her sister and her husband had arrived a few weeks earlier, after their father sent out a call for all his children to muster forces and report to Whitehall. Only a few answered with letters before the snow stopped all traffic into the mountains. Cada and Sidoro were lucky to arrive from the west before the Swallow Pass was blocked. They brought a few men with red snakes on their surcoats. Not enough to make Ultiir tremble, but all help was appreciated.

Sir Rye had taken post at David Rely's door. The amount of new people in Whitehall worried the knights so they stayed more vigilant than ever before. He bowed and let her inside. Her father lay in his bed wrapped in furs upon furs. The fire so hot she had to forcibly keep all the energy away from her to not catch a fever. Dera was dabbing his head with a cloth while Helge and Cada were whispering prayers.

When they were done Yvanne said, "Cada, I wasn't expecting to see you here. Where's Sidoro?"

"Where I left him." Her sister said as they hugged. She wore a fur cap over her short, black hair. Hair which showed they had different mothers. "The inn is our favorite place in town and he likes to sleep. Not that he could with all the ruckus outside. What happened? Father came in here ready to lop someone's head off."

"Lodean," she whispered to not anger her father. "Not an attack, don't worry, they wish to be allies."

Cada huffed. "I see why father was upset. How did your husband handle it?"

"He did well."

"Good. If only I had known who he was when he passed through Sea Snake, I would've married him on the spot for a chance to be queen." She laughed. "Don't look at me like that, Sidoro would've been perfectly fine with it. And I have no machinations to take the crown from you, sweet sister." Yvanne laughed along with her sister. "Well, we're just asking Meret to give him strength. Your doma is adamant that's the only thing left to do."

"What does that mean?" Yvanne looked at the old doma who was hunched over her father. "Helge."

"Dera is the daken and I am the doma. She treats him with herbs and poultices and I treat him with prayer." The old woman said. "Together your father will grow stronger than ever. This isn't the first winter he has struggled and it will not be his last."

"Can everyone leave? I will take the cloth." She dabbed her father's warm head as the others left the bedchamber. "You'll be alright, I know it. My baby will see you and know you and enjoy childhood with you. The winter is almost over I promise."

David opened his eyes and stared into Yvanne's. "I cannot wait to see you become a mother. I have … fathered many children … and every time I envy the mothers. Your … mother was so strong … gods I miss her." A fit of coughing took over, he spat phlegm into a handkerchief. "You as queen as well … sitting on the throne. It will be a sight."

"And you will see it all. Once we win the war I'll send word for you to come to Vigur to watch Devro and I be crowned.

I'll have wild Northerners carry you down the mountains if that's what it takes."

"Do you believe ... we can win?"

Yvanne stopped dabbing the cloth. Joining the war was her father's idea, she had no part other than marrying the bastard prince. *He questions it now? After we've revolted against the crown, the lowlands are at war, and Tundavik is pleading for Pyre's help.* Taking a calming breath, she said, "Yes. We can win as long as we continue to gain support. Think of all the lords who rallied behind us after Ultiir's destruction of Greatbath. More and more death will follow and more lords will join us until we win."

"Like the Lodean," he said with a scowl.

"Better they our allies. Lord Aimora might be able to convince the Lords of the Peaks as well."

"No." Her father sat up and grabbed his head. "Do not let the Lodean treat with the lords alone, they will betray you, sic them on Whitehall while our armies are in the Eastlands or the Kinglands. If you really want the Lords of the Peaks on our side then you must visit them. You must." The duke of the Lands of Asara melted into his bed, clutching his blankets and shivering.

Yvanne called for Dera and disappeared into the mountain, wandering the halls. *Only the Lodean can traverse the snow-covered passes. Only the Lodean have pull with the Lords of the Peaks.* She ran into little Tiro as he gathered some flour from the stores to make bread. "I need you to gather the council."

Tiro bowed his head, almost dropping the flour. "What for, Your Grace?" His squeaky voice asked.

"I'm going into the peaks, and the Lodean are going with me."

Bertin

M ountains rose from nothing. Great red rocks topped with white peaks sprung up from the sandy grassland of eastern Telemaw. Villages dotted the valleys of the mountains where small rivers ran.

Bertin was exhausted. He had walked barefoot through the desert and now through the tough shrubs. His heels left red prints. The elves on horseback had canteens and purposely drank in front of him, his mouth so dry it ached. Rubbing his cheek he remembered how it had busted into a million pieces a few weeks back. They had left Lisan Biresdea weeks ago. Bertin had been huddled in the corner of his cell ever since Ioelena's death. The elves who snatched him from the cell didn't care about his feelings. Ioelena was a traitor. She deserved to die. *So what awaits me in Anha Jorbstah?* He couldn't believe it when they told him where they were going, the dwarvish city now home to elves. Anha Jorbstah was on the far eastern side of Adedor, thousands of miles from the desert. And he had to walk it all.

They stayed clear of the trading routes, nothing good could come of it for the elves. Caravans of camels, bandit groups, and Telemese soldiers populated the sandstone roads. The days were cooler then when he first arrived in the desert, but it was still too hot to be walking all day, and the nights were no better. Bertin froze as the elves wrapped themselves to sleep.

He didn't remember what a wool blanket felt like on his body. The way he sunk into a feather bed and his head on a pillow. He wanted to eat like a prince again. Feasts every night of chicken, lamb, or salted pork; all served with bread and pies for dessert. Washing it down with wine from Baragio. His only meal in the desert was scorpions. Occasionally, Thatar would bring him water from an oasis or the River Alhya, luckily water was becoming more common the farther east they went.

But he was still captive.

For some reason the Four or some other gods, maybe even the Dragon, cursed him to be held with little food and water thousands of miles from his home. From his father and siblings. *What did I do that was so wrong? I always prayed with mother and father in the domaton. Yet the gods hate me.*

After they bathed in the Alhya, villages and farms became more common. The Alhya was the lifeblood of the empire back when the Delerous Empire existed, now it was the breadbasket of Telemaw. Boats made of reeds like in Lisan Biresdea choked the water. Animals from all over Adedor, and strange ones from Kruhesh, grazed along the riverbanks. Farmers and their large families watched from their homes and fields while they held their hoes and rakes as weapons. The elves wrapped their heads with cloth, but it was obvious they weren't humans. Their faces striped with war paint. And parading a captive through the desert wasn't a usual occurrence. If the people called for soldiers it was too late, they never stopped moving long enough to be captured.

Except Cluo loomed in front of them.

They rested in a shallow valley between two mounds of grass. Bertin rubbed his fingers and toes in the green grass, pretending everything was alright. That he was back in Rowan. But Kelltar barked orders and that brought him back. He was always angry, always making the singsong elvish words sound like curses. He was the one who killed Ioelena. Cut her and left her to bleed out alone in the middle of the desert. Vultures and robbers had probably already had their way with her before they got back to Lisan Biresdea. The other three who had attacked her stayed behind, preparing for a fight in Vaandet. Kelltar wanted to deliver Bertin to the king of the elves himself.

Thatar filled his canteen from a small stream and proceeded to quench Bertin's thirst. "Almost there." He pointed to the walls of Cluo to the east. The city was between the Kash Mountains and the Purvon Sea. The only road that connected Telemaw and Riorskè. If the elves wanted to make it to Anha Jorbstah they would have to make their way through the city. "If I were to be honest," Thatar said, "I didn't think I would see the city this soon after we pushed our way west, but Kuslu is smarter than I." Kuslu had led the elves to take over Lisan Biresdea. He was the one who kept Bertin in a cell, and the one who ordered Ioelena killed. But he was far away now.

Kelltar was splashing water on his face. His dagger dangling from the side of his leg. *I could run over there and grab it. Cut his back open like he did to Ioelena. They could leave me for dead here, Baldewin would become king eventually, but at least I would get my revenge.*

"Are you listening"? Thatar stepped into view. "Don't make this more difficult. Some of the elves here participated in the Pywaln Uprising; they've been fighting the humans for centuries. You don't stand a chance."

"Not yet anyway." Bertin's body felt cold from the water spreading inside him. The euphoria felt almost powerful. "But we have weeks before we reach Anha Jorbstah. Weeks for me to plan."

Thatar laughed and sat beside Bertin in the grass, twisting and pulling blades. "I am not sure what you think Blaenda is going to do to you, but my guess is he will demand payment from your father and if he doesn't get it send you to Mi'rallen. He won't kill you. Our elders do not behave like yours where they hang elven children above the city gates."

"And if Kelltar doesn't make it," Bertin said as he still imagined killing the elf, "what will he do?"

Thatar laughed again. "Blaenda doesn't need to worry about that."

"Thatar." Kelltar began to speak in elvish. He was skinning a rabbit, the sun reflecting off the dagger into Bertin's eyes, the rabbit's blood smearing it. *Eventually that will be Kelltar's blood. I'll make sure of it.*

"We will stay here for the night." Vhistela told Bertin. She was a much older elf than the rest, she had visibly aged. Wrinkles and gray hairs reminded him of elderly humans. Bertin hadn't asked how old, but probably a few hundred years. She was a master at the bow and could shoot an arrow between the eyes of a desert falcon day or night, no matter how high the bird soared.

A small cookfire was made and the elves sang beautiful songs while they cooked rabbit and small fish. The most popular song was about the Dragon coming from his domain and returning the land to the elves. Bertin even hummed along. He had heard it too many times. The horses whinnied and drank from the stream, tied to a stump. Thatar gave Bertin a liver and he slurped it down. At the palace the liver would go to the dogs, but now Bertin was glad to eat it.

"How far do you think you'll get with me?" Everyone looked surprised when Bertin's now raspy voice spoke up. "You think the Rainvealandians will let you get to Anha Jorbstah? Especially if they find out who I am?"

Kelltar chuckled. "Did they bother us when we traveled west last year? The elves and the *ramoryr* have regularly seen things the same. Both have been banished from this land to islands and both have returned to fight against their oppressors."

"Didn't you go to war with each other?"

"On occasion," Eyln said. He was a younger elf, he reminded Bertin of himself. "But they've left us alone in Anha Jorbstah and we are grateful for that. In return we limit our raids on their villages."

"And why would they care who you are?" Vhistela asked, her brow a mess of wrinkles.

"You don't think they'd want the son of the man who sacked Bardekan?"

"Bardekan means nothing this far south." Kelltar said. "So you only have to worry about us and our elders, not a Rainvealandian king."

They all settled in for the night except for Eyln, who stood guard. Thatar slept close to Bertin like he did every night, but everyone knew Bertin wouldn't run, no way his bloodied feet would get him far enough. Bertin made sure to sleep by a rock. It protruded just barely from the grass, and he rubbed his fingers on it. Jostling. As the fire began to die down and

Vhistela took over the watch, Bertin freed the rock from the ground. Kelltar tossed and turned on the other side of the fire. In his head he imagined what would happen next. Bertin would stand with rock in hand, his wrists still tied but not able to stop him, then beating the elf's head in with the rock, blood spurting into the fire and caking Bertin's face. Vhistela would nock an arrow and a second later Bertin would be dead. He smiled.

Kelltar turned on his side. His eyes were yellow and stared directly at Bertin as if he read his mind. The elf's muscles bulged. His dagger in arm's reach. Wolves howled in the distant mountains. *They want me to do it. I should listen.* Kelltar huffed and rolled over. Bertin went to sleep with a rock in his hands and dreamt of fairies flying around his father's throne.

***

The next morning Eyln kicked him awake, a groan escaping Bertin before a yawn. Bertin's body ached from sleeping on the ground. He thought he would be used to it but he almost missed the cell in Lisan Biresdea. Thatar invited him onto his bay colored mare, Erona, and cut the ropes that bound his wrists so it wouldn't be suspicious when they reached the city.

The wall of Cluo stretched from the mountains to the sea. Men in red and yellow armor, who looked to be on fire, patrolled atop it. "More than last time." Thatar said.

"Maybe that's why." Vhistela pointed. Dozens of knights in surcoats with scorpions stood at the bottom of the gate. Makeshift hanging posts were built and elves swung from nooses. "The Dragon does not wish to make this easy."

In front of the Telemese soldiers were hundreds of people trying to get into Cluo. Travelers, merchants, refugees, migrants, and workers all formed a perfect line as the Telemese inspected each person, paying particular attention to their ears, ripping off hoods and taking coin or food as payment. The Riorsken guards would open the gate little by little, letting one or two in at a time. They glowered from atop the wall.

Kelltar kicked his horse, Mahru, over to Thatar and Bertin. The muscular elf glared at the prince. "Do not show them who you are, or you won't make it passed the wall."

"You don't think they'll see your ears." Bertin knew what was about to happen if he kept going, but he did anyway. "I can cut the points off if you wish." Kelltar smacked Bertin across the cheek, shattering whatever had healed from his time in the desert. He toppled from Erona and landed on his shoulder in the grass. Thatar and Kelltar started arguing in elvish. Bertin poked at his cheek but it was too painful to touch. His shoulder screamed in pain, his body didn't know what to make of it, but he couldn't show the elves he was hurting, afraid. He was the Prince of Rowan. His father the Uniter. He would escape these elves and make it back home to the cheers of the palace. But first he had to kill Kelltar.

Vhistela rode over on her black stallion and stopped the loud elvish curses. "Get up," she said to Bertin. He stood, wiped his face of blood, and climbed onto Erona without Thatar's help, never taking his eyes off Kelltar.

The line was even longer as they sat atop their horses behind a seller of onions. The Telemese guards carefully examined everyone and everything they wished to take across the border. *How are we going to get through this? Maybe the guards will free me.* It was a hopeful thought, but he didn't know if they would see him a captive or a traitor. And the other issue is where he would go. The mountains loomed in the north and the expanse of the sea was to the south. Elves to the west and mites to the east. Maybe Jorbstah would be the best place for him, perhaps the Riorsken king would send him to Rowan with an escort and a ship, but Bertin didn't even know who the king was.

A small boy began to pet Erona, who allowed it. Kelltar grunted. Thatar smiled at the boy. "Ever seen a horse this large?"

"Never." The dark skinned boy said. *"Omi patro volentas a camel."* He said in a mix of the common language and Delerous with his Telemese accent.

"Sacrae al Re'as!" The boy's mother yelled and pulled the boy away, swatting him.

"And you think the guards won't notice?" Bertin whispered to Thatar. The elf tapped his sword attached to Erona in answer.

The guards finally reached the group of hooded elves and Bertin. *"Lanto."* A tall man said before switching to the common language when the elves turned their heads. "Off."

The elves hopped off their horses, Bertin's feet burning as they touched the ground. A guard grabbed Bertin's face and looked at the welts and shattered bones. "What happened?"

"He fell off his horse." Kelltar said. Vhistela sighed as she stepped toward her bow on her horse. The guards tilted their heads at Kelltar's voice. A deep, raspy melody as if he were singing. Humans didn't usually speak like that. Bertin couldn't help but smile at Kelltar's stupidity.

The guards took a few steps back and called for others. The

tall guard grabbed Eyln's hood but the elf snatched the man's wrist. "Just let us through. No one needs to be harmed."

The tall man backed away and unsheathed a curved blade. "All elves are to be hanged for the war they declared on our king. We do not want to fight. Come peacefully." The commoners began moving away from the commotion. The elves' horses neighed and pranced.

Kelltar reached for the dagger strapped to his waist. "If you didn't want to fight, then you should have let us through." The elf threw his dagger and it embedded in the guard's face. Kelltar moved like a monster as the other guards prepared themselves. In one motion Vhistela grabbed her bow, nocked an arrow, and shot at more Telemese soldiers. Never missing. Thatar calmed Erona and climbed aboard, finding his throwing knives and unleashing them as guards ran forward. Eyln had his sword in hand and was cutting people to pieces.

The commoners fled screaming. The Riorsken guards slammed the gate shut, leaving the people to bang and plead to be let into safety. Bertin was pushed to the ground and had to protect his face from trampling feet. In a thick layer of dirt he stood and began to run with the crowd. He limped as his feet cried out in pain, his shoulder burned, and the bones in his broken cheek moved and cut at his skin.

The red rocks of the Kash Mountains were close. If he could reach them he could disappear, maybe find a shepherd to look after him while the elves hunted. *But if they don't get tired then I'm putting more people in danger.* He thought back to the father in Lisan Biresdea who died protecting him. All of his household guards dead. Ioelena. He slowed as screams deafened him and bodies rushed past him before coming to a stop.

The Telemese guards stood no chance against four elves that had been training their whole lives to kill humans. Blood turned the green-brown grass red. Arms and legs and heads littered the road. Cries of death filled the air. Kelltar stole a Telemese blade and thrust it into one final guard. Others had begun running away.

The elf was covered in blood, his muscles bulging as he took in deep breaths. Thatar scooped Bertin up with Erona and they rode toward the wall and the city gate. The people had cleared the way as Vhistela yelled and aimed her bow at them.

Bertin whispered to Thatar. "After all this you expect the mites to let you in?" Thatar said nothing as Eyln crunched bones under his boots and Kelltar attached the sword to Mahru's saddle.

"The ramoryr hold a great deal of hostility toward the *oléman*." Thatar said.

"We didn't think anyone would be able to clean the border of this filth." A fiery guard said from atop the wall in the common language. "Look at them running," he laughed. The people were racing into the mountains or back to the Alhya. "We will allow you to pass through Cluo, but you know the rules, no elf shall stay in the city after dark and you will be escorted at all times."

The gate opened. The red rocks and bay of Cluo lit up the dark west. Thatar smiled. "Still think we can't make it?"

Sophie

Drying her eyes and brushing her pants, she stared at the River Montla while wrapped in a woolen coat. Winter air from the mountains was cold but it wasn't what chilled her. Goldfield was full of lords and ladies who had come from afar to pledge their oaths to the new de'Tro king. Ultiir would be getting ready. Dressing in the ancestral robes of his house. The town was shining from the high noon sun and the snowy peaks of the Asara in the distance were blinding to look at. *Where the rebellion is taking place. Destroying the mountains and everything around it.* The fields that surrounded her were full of winter wheat and tended by hundreds of slaves. The masters carried whips and watched them close. Sophie didn't have time for any of it.

She didn't want to believe her body. It was long past her time to bleed this month. By autumn she would be the mother to Ultiir's child, his seed not poisoned like his brother's. The Montla was the life source of man and it called for her. Not to bring life. Instead, her death. The leader of her household guard, Sir Achen, stood near her. She could feel him getting closer with every step she took toward the water, not wanting to fail her, seeing the tears welling up in her eyes.

"I should've told my parents no." Sophie said. The knight

said nothing but handed her a handkerchief. As she blotted her eyes she said, "What would they have done? Disowned me? Send me to become a daken? The only land I would own when they died is Aele anyhow. No chance of me becoming the queen. I should've said no."

"If I may, Your Grace," Achen said, "you had to have known this would happen eventually. The king is not his brother."

Sophie looked at a mass of clouds gathering as she dried her eyes. "Not so soon after our marriage. I wanted time. Needed it. Ultiir is so much like Hurvir that I hoped they shared another thing in common." Her boot touched the water and Sir Achen's gloved arm went around hers. "I won't do it you know," she kicked the water, "I can't let Hurvir win, nor Ultiir. My parents wished for me to have a son to unite the kingdoms and that's what I plan to do." *Maybe,* she thought, *but my parents don't always get what they want or deserve. I've no reason to listen to them. Not from this far away. And Ultiir might not even win the war. Then where would I be? Devro would execute me for bearing the child of his uncle and the child too to stop another succession crisis.*

Sophie gave the handkerchief back and started up the hill to Goldfield. The ancestral home of the de'Tro family grew atop the many bluffs on the north bank of the Montla, ancient domaton dug into the dirt could still be found along the river where the people would pray to the Four and the Many. The new domaton was built in the center of the city, gold adorned the corners, opulence was common for the de'Tros. The great de'Tro manor was down the cobbled road from the domaton. Currently occupied by the queen mother, almost as ancient as the domaton mounds. The roads into the city were all paved for miles. It was always a surprise for Sophie as even the roads outside Udello were dirt. The wheat in summer gave the city its name. Golden fields stretching into the hinterlands. The largest number of slaves outside of Vigur in the whole realm.

Goldfield was rarely talked about by her husbands unless it accompanied curses. She didn't know what their childhood was like and she never asked knowing they wouldn't talk about it. Sir Achen led her across the winding paths through the fields. Slaves eyed her. Her guard always worried they would kill her, but she was more worried about the people inside the manor. The queen mother was never nice, seeming to have come from the depths of Veltoora itself. And the lords and ladies pledging their oaths always schemed. Even Ultiir worried her. How a man could kill his own brother and go to war with his young nephew she never knew, but it seemed common in the history of the world.

The sounds of cracking whips made her wince every time. The screams of slaves, men and women and children, made it worse. The whipping post was atop a stone for all to see in the fields. Now there was a young man with more scars and blood than skin on his back, the master laughing with every hit, the slaves glaring from below. The slave screamed out and his face fell to the rock, the master calling for him to "Get up or you'll be fed to the dogs."

Achen shook his head no, but he couldn't control her. She was the queen. Sophie hopped off the path and pushed wheat to the side as she made her way to the rock. Sweating slaves, even in winter, followed her every movement with their eyes. She walked up the steps to the rock, the masters' guards obviously confused and she grabbed the whip. "What is the meaning of this?"

"You bitch I—" the master saw the queen and fell to his knees, his dry lips kissing her hand, "Forgive me, Your Grace, I didn't mean it."

"Your name? And answer the question." Sophie shoved him away.

"Master Ayter, my Queen." The master bowed, his golden robes blowing in the breeze. "And this slave was caught stealing bread from the kitchens. Bread meant for the queen mother."

"So you decided death by dogs was the best course of action?"

"Theft is punishable by death, Your Grace, but I was never going to feed him to the dogs, his meat would be toxic to them I'm sure. We usually just whip them. Would you like to try?"

The slave on the rock closed his eyes at the sight of the whip in Sophie's hand. "If anyone were to be whipped it would be you." Ayter's eyes darted. "Clean this mess up and fetch some daken for this poor boy."

Ayter chuckled. "No daken would help a slave."

"Are the dogs hungry?" Sophie asked and the master nodded. "Then you better convince them or you and the daken who refuse will be their dinner." The dogs barked in the distance. "Go on." She waved him away. Stumbling, the master left and went into town. Sophie knelt by the slave, blood staining her knees. "What's your name?"

"Clava … Your … Majesty." His body shook and he tried to bow his head, but could hardly move.

"It's alright Clava. Help is coming. How long have you been here?"

"Born … here."

Sophie dabbed her eyes. Sir Achen was calming the masters' guards below. The master and daken still not in sight. "Well you have a beautiful home. I hope you enjoy the view every once in a while. I grew up in Vallnioc in Terrop, near the mountains. Having a view of the Asara is a gift from the gods."

Clava gave a pained laugh. "It is … beautiful … isn't it?"

"In Vallnioc we do not own slaves. It's unfortunate you weren't born there. Maybe you should visit. I have old friends there who would see to your needs well."

The slave squinted. "I cannot … leave …" he motioned to the slaves in the field who were still watching. "And if I did … it would be for Nuqtia. That is my parents' place of … of birth."

"I'm sure it's beautiful too."

"Brave or stupid?" The old Lord Tedbalt Masson said from the steps. "Guess we'll find out when the queen mother hears about this."

Sophie patted the slave's head and stood. "I do not fear her," she lied. "And she has to remember her husband died decades ago, mine is still alive and the king." *Hopefully she hears none of this.*

Lord Masson held out his arm for Sophie to take. The old man had recently chopped his gray hair and now it sat only atop his head. He wore a gold cloak instead of his usual white one. No longer the chief daken. He was the king's chief consultant on all matters of state. Lord de'Marisco would surely be upset when he returned. "I know Terrop is different, but helping slaves isn't a good look in Viguran."

Aytar and a few daken were coming from town with bandages and water. Sophie smiled, "well maybe that should change."

"I own many slaves on my lands. Some of them just do not want to do the work and find joy in stealing. You can't help them all." Tedbalt shrugged.

"Did you need something?" Sophie said as they began their walk into town, Sir Achen always following. "If not then I would really like to lie down."

"Have you been crying? Your eyes are red." Lord Masson's liver spotted hand rested on hers. "You know you can tell me anything. Remember your wedding?"

Lord Masson had made it as clear as he could without it becoming treasonous that he was an ally of hers. Something she still had to get used to. "Forgive me if I have a lack of trust in someone who plotted for months with the council to have a very important person killed." She said quietly, and not wanting to say the word 'king.' She didn't need any spies of the queen mother to hear her.

"At least Ultiir doesn't beat you." He looked at her once swollen cheeks. "Perhaps he is a better husband."

Sophie took a deep breath and was ready to be in a wool bed with a warm drink in her hands as she watched a fire. Not wanting to talk with an old man. "Unfortunately you can not help me. It has to do with Meret's gift."

Tedbalt nodded knowingly. "I was chief daken for many years, and no I was not a daken, but running the school and taking care of the daken in Viguran has caused me to learn some things, especially issues that arise with women once a month." Lord Masson stopped walking near a stone wall that separated the fields from the town. "Allies, Your Grace, are important."

What's the worst that happens? He tells the council? Ultiir?

Everything can change within the year. "Well if you must know," she took a deep breath before lowering her voice, "I am with child."

"An heir." Tedbalt smirked. "I'm sure you're excited."

"Thrilled," she said through gritted teeth. They stopped talking as merchants carted goods nearby. Achen had to push them away after they tried selling to her. "My parents will also be glad. I do worry about the rebellion though."

"If the bastard were to win you mean? Well we can't see the future, but tradition does not favor you or your child's lives if that were to happen."

Sophie rubbed her eyes. "Devro and I always got along. For it to meet such a tragic end." She hadn't realized she was biting her cheek. *I survived Hurvir's abuse and the council's plan only to be killed by Devro of all people ...* "I hope I can count on your discretion. The king, the council, the queen mother; none can know."

"I swear it on the Four, Your Grace," he touched four fingers to his heart. "Speaking of the queen mother," Tedbalt looked to the de'Tro manor that dwarfed the other homes. "The reason I came to get you was for her. A page was going to do it but I decided to take charge. She wants a private meeting."

Sophie curtsied to the lord and said, "I guess I have no choice."

The manor loomed over her as she went through the wooden doors. Inside was the great hall, jewels along the pillars, feathers from far away lands on the walls. Rila de'Tro would hold court for no reason other than to pretend she had power. Goldfield was the king's property and given to the heir to lounge around. Rila held court because Ultiir was always in Vigur, but she could not technically administer justice. Now, the hall was empty. Ultiir had yet to name an heir. If anything were to happen to her new husband Rila de'Tro would rule as regent until a distant cousin was found, or Sophie had her baby.

Sir Achen led her down a narrow corridor to the back of the manor. Ultiir and Sophie slept on the top floor with a balcony overlooking the expanse of wheat, Rila de'Tro's bedchamber was on the ground floor to keep her from going up the stairs.

An old knight, not as old as the queen mother, stood in front of her door and bowed when Sophie stopped. "Welcome, Your Grace." He knocked and opened the door.

Rila de'Tro wore red from head to toe. Still dressed in mourning for Hurvir, and probably all her other dead children and her husband. She sat at a small table near a stained window showering her chamber in reds and yellows. Her veil was sheer showing her wrinkled skin and sunken eyes. "Leave us." She told the guards, waving gloved hands.

"My lady." Sophie bowed.

"I think I should be the one bowing," the queen mother shook her head, "but I can hardly stand anyway."

Sophie clasped her hands together and stood as straight as she could. She didn't need Rila de'Tro admonishing her for something so small. "No reason for it, I understand. You requested an audience?"

"No need to act so formal, girl." The queen mother waved her hand as annoyance washed over her face. "This isn't an interrogation and nothing you say leaves this room, not even to Ultiir."

"Yes, my lady." Sophie nodded with a meek smile. Wondering why today was the first time Rila had requested a meeting.

They had been in Goldfield a little over a week. *Nothing good can come of this.*

"So which is better?" The queen mother said, the wrinkles on her brow moving with every word. "Hurvir or Ultiir? The last time I saw you the welts on your face had just healed so I'd wager to guess you like my miracle child a bit more."

"Ultiir is kind, but I do miss my late husband very much."

Rila de'Tro waved a shaky hand. "Don't lie to me girl, you're not good at it." Her voice was stern. "I'm sure any tears shed over my son were tears of joy. Finally rid of that monster. When his body arrived in Goldfield I didn't even cry, just another member of my family I have outlived. Shame you couldn't give him a babe and now we're stuck in this mess with that bastard."

"Devro was a sweet child the few times I saw him. I'm sure it's hard to see your son and grandson fighting."

"That bastard," she spat, "is no grandson of mine. An evil spawn from Veltoora wreaking havoc across our realm. The worst thing Hurvir did was fuck that whore in Maertan. My father would be ashamed," she shook her head and her face twisted with disgust. "I was the last de'Tro until my husband took my name and we bore children, and what does Hurvir do but sully it. Ultiir is no better. He's only getting older and just now married. Hopefully you fuck him right so he can have an heir and the bastard can be dealt with and my family name can continue in perpetuity. Don't make that face girl. I'm old. No reason to mince words."

Sophie felt like a child again getting reprimanded by her mother or nurses. "I will do my best to make sure I deliver an heir," she squeaked.

The old lady stood, her skin tight around her face. "Do

not pass up this opportunity. I did not think any of my heirs would have my name. I was going to bring shame onto this kingdom and most importantly my father and his grandfather all the way back to Marson de'Tro, but a banished prince found me." Sophie had heard the stories a hundred times of Prince Ferrick being banished from Rowan and finding his way in Viguran. She had to force her eyes to stop from rolling. "Your parents already have two sons to carry on the Margia name. So don't disappoint me. Let the second empire rise again like your parents and I have spoken about."

Sophie touched her belly, hoping the queen mother didn't notice. "You speak to my parents? I hardly get them to answer my letters."

"We've written back and forth quite extensively since you married Hurvir, and they begged for Ultiir to take your hand in marriage which I relayed to him. There are much bigger plans for our two families than you realize."

"I gathered as much when I spoke to them, my lady. Is this why you called me here? To talk about my husbands?"

Rila's wobbly steps took her to her bed. "I just wanted to make sure you had my son's interest at heart. He is my last child and I don't want you to hurt him. You would not only upset me but also your parents and all of your subjects."

"Analere is still out there."

The queen mother laughed as she carefully placed herself onto her wool blankets. "She forsake me and her vows when she became a daken. Always an unruly child. My favorite daughter was Philla but she had to go get herself killed by some mite. Did you know we threw him to the slaves for a good raping before he died?" Rila held her chest from bursts of laughter. "The mites deserve far worse than that, but Hurvir did send a few floating down the Jorbstah so I can't complain." Her beady eyes scanned Sophie and settled on her face. The queen mother's stare was that of hundreds of years of tradition. "Do not hurt my child, Sophie. The consequences of you not delivering an heir or taking the side of that bastard will be far worse than the mite got, and most of the slaves would love nothing more than to rape the wife of their enslaver."

"Of course, my lady." Sophie bowed again, not finding the door fast enough. She didn't wait for Achen before walking down the hall, her fast steps echoing. "How much longer are we in this fucking city?"

Tundavik

Celebrations for the new year were enjoyed by all this far north in Viguran. Every town, village, and hamlet they passed through had music and singing and dancing and feasting. Leftovers from Meret's feast. The Flewthlands was abuzz with excitement. If only he could get people this excited for a war. *I wonder how many people down south are celebrating? More likely crying over the death.*

Tundavik and Mar had to slip on their bear cloaks they received from Whitehall the farther north they went. Storyah was always warm in the summer, but winter brought the coldest air outside the Asara in Viguran. The cold winds from the Drewogh Sea slapped their faces as they rode.

They entered Storyah from the west near the King's Harbor. Ships flying flags from far away lands in Eotros clogged the harbor. Masts with peacocks, striped cats, and other large beasts brought onlookers to gawk and buy exotic goods that looked to be less expensive than the goods out of Viguran. The war had risen all the prices.

The domaton rose above the city, the four points of its star showing the cardinal directions. The temple of Dal, a small hut next to it where no one was allowed to worship, was just to the side. They rode along a large cobbled street in the center of the city, connecting the gates to the castle. Waves crashed against the snow-laden beach and rocks. The cold water sprayed their faces as they looked into the harbor. Ships with carved monsters on the helm and sails of yellow and red inlaid with winged horses and dragons unloaded their cargo. Storyah was Viguran's main port and the Eotrosi loved trading their foreign wares.

Great stone walls and towers covered them in shadow. A wooden gatehouse was full of men wearing yellow and gold armor. As Tundavik and Mar approached a guard held up his gauntleted hand and others crossed their spears. "Why do you come so close?"

"We have an audience with the duke." Tundavik dropped from Bera and handed a letter from Lord Rely. The guard read it and sent a page to fetch Lord Blume.

"Come all this way just to get us to join a war?" The guard said. "I guess I can say thanks," but the words were dripping with sarcasm.

The gatehouse doors opened and the drawbridge beyond the first wall lowered, the portcullis on the other side rising. "The lord duke will see you." The page bowed. "Follow me."

"Leave your horses. We'll have the groomsmen lead them to the stables." The guard said.

Tundavik and Mar walked across the bridge and under the portcullis into the outer bailey. Planters lined the walls and evergreen trees shaded the path. Tundavik imagined how the colorful flowers must give life to the keep in the summer. Ritaeum was dark year round. "We're being watched." Mar said pointing to the many towers that dotted both the inner and outer walls.

Tundavik saw archers staring back at him through the

embrasures. Wooden houses and shops contrasted against the great wall of stone bricks with people looking out the windows. "Lord Blume is a friend."

"At least he was two decades ago."

The page led them under another portcullis where the castle came into view. Once the seat of the kings of Plajul, the castle now housed the duke of the Flewthlands, but it was still as magnificent as before. Two grand staircases of marble, slick from snow, led them to the stone plaza where gatherings were held. A fountain made of stone showing Mother Meret feeding her children from her breasts was between the staircases. The Flewthmen had a knack for scandal, and loved hearing complaints from the High Doma in Vigur. A large gilded, metal door was surrounded by stone arches and stained windows.

But the page didn't take them into the castle. Instead they walked around the large mass of stone and down some steps into the lawn on the other side. No one could see them back there except from the towers. Servants clasped their hands together as Tundavik and Mar strolled by. The page motioned to a man with an axe. "The Duke of the Flewthlands, Pyre Blume."

Lord Blume grabbed a log from a servant and went to chopping it for firewood. It was as if he hadn't aged a day in the fifteen years Tundavik was gone, last seeing each other when the young Lord Blume sailed to recapture Ealna. Pyre Blume had very few wrinkles, his shoulders broad and chest wide with muscle, his graying hair was the only sign he was older. Tundavik rubbed his forehead of wrinkles.

"When they told me the Duke Tundavik Vandes was wishing to treat with me," Pyre swung his axe and cracked a log in two, "I almost choked on my chicken. 'Lord Vandes disappeared a decade ago, presumed dead. It must be an impostor,' I said." Pyre grabbed Tundavik's arm and embraced him. "Did the death of a certain king bring you back in celebration?"

"I wish." Tundavik smiled.

"I bet the whole of the Flewthlands lit up in bonfires when the death was announced." Mar said.

"You're right about that." Pyre said and Mar introduced himself. "Finding yourself on the side of the rebels?" Pyre asked Tundavik. "Did my father's spirit possess you?"

"Some say Ultiir is the rebel."

"And who wears the crown and sits the throne? I don't think the bastard is making laws in Vigur is he?" Pyre gripped a log with his large hand and threw it in a basket.

"Hopefully soon." Tundavik said.

"I don't truly care." Pyre kicked dead grass. "I may owe my duchy to Hurvir, but when he died I went to my father's crypt and toasted with him. 'I pray the dead warrior king never has a peaceful day in the afterlife.' I said. 'May you haunt him for all eternity with Dal.' My father never followed the Four, don't tell anyone. So," Pyre motioned for his servants to clean the mess of wood, "do you want a tour of my home?"

"We were hoping for a meeting." Mar said. "It's very important."

"Tundavik's never been up this way. The Woodlands aren't home to anything this magnificent." Pyre motioned to the castle walls.

"I like my trees." Tundavik said. *What am I saying? They're not my trees anymore.* "A tour would be good. You can tell us how the Flewthlands are doing."

Pyre wiped sweat from his brow and wiped his dirty hands clean. They entered the castle from a backdoor instead of the grand door in the front. Stone walls with torches kept the inside cozy, and the many corridors made it feel like a maze. Red and yellow carpets and rugs cushioned their steps. Paintings of the old kings of Plajul hung on the walls, followed by paintings of the dukes. Lord Blume's was last.

"What do you want to know about the Flewthlands?" Pyre asked after showing them some earthenware from a place called Xishi in the far interior of Eotros. "Wish to know if my men are ready for war? If my women can sow them pants and fix their shoes before it's time to leave?"

"I just wanted to know how being a duke was treating you." Tundavik said.

"Have this," Pyre gave Mar some liquor from Nowexert. "Tell me it's not the worst thing you've tasted."

Sir Mar drank and almost spit it out but drank some more. "I can't complain," he coughed but continued.

Pyre laughed. "The Flewthlands seems much better than the other duchies these days. Who would want to lead the Eastlands right now? And I'm sure Lord Rely isn't faring well with the Lands of Asara."

"He does what he can."

"When I heard news that David Rely was the one leading the rebellion I said, 'that old coot? What could he possibly gain from going against the crown? That man hardly lifted a finger when we were at war with the mites and now he wants to fight?' I was aghast. People are full of surprises." Pyre scratched his square beard of frost. "So what did you offer him?"

"His daughter is Devro's queen." Mar said. "They already

married."

"Marriage. That makes sense. Too bad my daughter is already married or I'd've offered her up. Queen is better than being the lady of Woodrun," he laughed. "Come." He walked them down a narrow hall to a small door, but beyond the door was the great hall.

The room reminded him nothing of Whitehall, but more like Vigur. The ceiling towered above supported by pillars of redwood. A yellow and red flamed rug covered the length of the stone floor beneath their feet. Arches rose and fell around the windows that lit the place a thousand colors like a rainbow. The high chair of the lord, or throne depending on who was asked, rose from a checkered floor of tile on the far end of the room. A long ornate metal table ran horizontally to the throne, it was covered in red and decorated with fine dining ware imported from far off lands. Armor worn by past knights poked out from the arches. Gray, blue, red, white, yellow, purple, even pink armor stood out. Great swords hung on the walls, Tundavik remembered one was named the Renegade and another Mother's Blessings, Pyre had told him all about the swords decades ago, though he couldn't say which was which.

"So if I can't have marriage, what is it you offer me?" Lord Blume sat on his high seat, a yellow cushion beneath him.

"Whatever you want. Devro sent us to negotiate, but I know you won't be unreasonable." Tundavik stood with his hands behind his back. The room made it seem like he was talking to a king instead of duke, a once equal.

Pyre Blume laughed. "Ever since Ferrick took us from Plajul and kicked the king out there is only one thing my people want, and I'm not sure your Devro wants to give it to us. I'm not even sure if my people want another rebellion. After my father's death I sued for peace because of all the fighting and death. We've had two revolts against the crown. What makes you think a third will be successful?"

"The Flewthlands won't be alone." Tundavik said. "Devro knew you would ask for independence, and he'd be willing to give it if you fought for him, and I swear, as an old friend, that I will make sure he doesn't break that promise."

"Forgive me for my hesitation." Pyre rubbed his brow. "I've heard grave news out of the Lands. Do you have anything to say to that?"

Tundavik wanted to tell him that not everything was bad, but that would be a lie. They couldn't take Riverton, Greatbath was destroyed, the lowlands were now soaked in blood, and the presence of the Terropians to the west loomed. Raimund was probably dead. Mar and Devro both could barely function at the thought. Lord Rely grew sick as winter went on. But surrender meant they would all die. At least if they fought they could still win.

"Ultiir is already going to admonish you for meeting with us. Have you heard of Redington? He took it and installed Henk Zazí as lord. Who do you think he'll choose to take over your duchy? Not your daughter. Your son-by-law? Someone else?"

Pyre reached into his pocket and pulled out a parchment. "I received this from Hurvir when he was alive, stamped with the heir's seal. *Remember Ritaeum.*" Tundavik felt like he was slapped in the face. He could feel Mar and Pyre's eyes burning him.

"I don't know what to say," Tundavik stammered. *If only I could've been the one to murder Hurvir. I should have done it all those years ago instead of running away to the West like a coward.* "You know what happened to my home. To my family. My people. I swear on the Four and the Many and every other god prayed to on this earth that I will not let that happen to you. We must stop Ultiir before he follows in his brother's footsteps. I can stop Devro. But war is the only way to stop Ultiir."

"I appreciate it." Pyre said, throwing the letter in a lit brazier near his throne. "I will allow you both to stay in the castle. Trust me, we have more than enough room."

"How long do we have to be here?" Mar asked. "We have to send word to Whitehall and ready the men."

"It will be a while," Pyre waved a hand. "I cannot just bring my people into war if they do not want it. I must call a council of lords where we will discuss and vote on the matter. But if it were solely up to me we would join. I hope you can make a convincing case."

Raimund

Raimund had taken the woman's cold hand and she escorted him through the twisting trees of the forested mountainside. Eventually they had reached a small meadow where a house was lit with candles and fire. That's when he had collapsed.

By the time he woke a steaming bath had been drawn for him, he had bandages on different parts of his body, a large one wrapped around his ribs. As he stood his body screamed for sleep. When he lay back down on the bed, the best thing to happen to him since Raior, the woman emerged from a doorway. Her head was covered by a black hood that had turned white from snow. She was carrying firewood. "Up, up," she motioned to him as she spoke the common language. "You need to wash or your wounds could get infested with maggots. We don't want that. I did my best with what I had, but I ran out of alcohol many moons ago. I put some herbs in the water to help you heal."

Raimund did as he was told, he was in no position to argue or fight if she was actually trying to kill him. *But she saved me from the griffin.* After he stripped off his pants and dropped into the warm water, he realized it smelled like dinner. Like a cook had just seasoned a chicken. "You're not a witch are you? Trying to butter me up to make sure I taste good."

"Witches only eat children, don't you know that." The woman's smile could just barely be seen from the candlelight. She dropped the wood into a hearth and went about making the fire. "Oh, this one's wet," she said and put her hand over the log. As Raimund rubbed a cloth over his sore body, the woman's hand became moist from nothing. She wasn't sweating. Then she threw the log into the hearth and continued to make a fire. *So you actually are a witch. Guess we have something in common.*

"Why did you save me? Did you save anyone else?"

The hearth began to burn bright and the woman left before coming back with a pot of stew. Raimund could see garlic popping up and down. "I wanted to save the others," she said as she stirred with a wooden ladle, "but you were closest to me. I can't hold back *bajagryf* for long without killing them, and I had no desire to kill that grieving mother."

"Grieving mother?" The herbs began to burn Raimund's cuts and bruises. *Please be working,* he thought.

"The bajagryf was from high in the mountains. They usually don't come this far down, but a few weeks ago I found a clutch of eggs that had been destroyed. Teeth marks it looked like. And recently I've noticed less and less goats and sheep. I've heard talk from travelers that even farmers in the region are losing their cows. Bajagryfs only eat humans if they don't have anything else to hunt. They're intelligent. They know who has killed most of their kin and it wasn't the cows."

"So the griffin was starving and angry her babies were taken? Did you talk to her or something?"

The woman pulled down her hood to unveil red hair that

matched the cookfire. Her face was pale and freckled. Her eyes looked like summer leaves. She reminded him too much of Yvanne which got him thinking about his friends. How he failed them. "I've read countless books about them." She motioned to a stack of books and parchments and letters on the other side of the room. Candle wax had dried over a few pages. "When you're up here you have nothing but time."

Raimund stood, his legs needing to stretch, and let the water drip off his body. The woman handed him a linen towel and he patted himself dry. "When did you come here?" He asked and her face lit with surprise. "I'm not just some criminal, and your accent could use some work. I'm guessing you learned Heller by reading. It's not *bajagryf*, it's *baiagryf*. You have an accent that reminds me of the Veck'kop."

"Perceptive," the woman laughed. "Was that a prison transport I happened upon? Now, I'm worried you're going to be the one to eat me."

"Has the North gotten that bad since I left that people are cannibals?"

"Merely a joke," she said as she put out her arm for him to take. "I'm Sile by the way."

"Raimund."

She went back to stirring the stew, blowing off the steam, and tasting it. The wooden home in the middle of nowhere began to smell like heaven to him. Even with all the feasts he's enjoyed since going to Viguran, nothing was ever has good as a Northern stew. He pictured his mother being the one to cook.

"What brings you back?" Sile asked, interrupting his thoughts. "I have a hard time believing you would travel to the North just to commit a crime and be captured."

"Pirates have gotten bolder since the war started. They captured and sold me. I'm sure there are stories in your stack of books where that happens."

"War?" Sile ignored everything else Raimund had said. "The war with the Rainvealandians has already ended has it not?"

"Different war. We seem to have a lot of those down south. Two people want to be king of Viguran. Tale as old as the kingdom itself."

"Are they fighting each other?" Sile asked and continued after Raimund's face puzzled. "Are they wielding the swords and dueling? Or do they have others doing that for them? I saw the devastation caused by the war with the mites, then when I came here I saw the toll that the Nowexerti wars had on the people. Just wanted to know how the commoners are finding it."

"I never asked." Raimund said before slipping his trousers on. They stank of blood and had stains of death of them, but it was all he had. Sile gave him a fur cloak, not that he needed it with the hearth burning. "Have you gone back to where the griffin attacked?"

"Why would I? As we were leaving I heard more shouts coming from the pass. Probably the local prison sending out men to fight the poor girl."

So Potter might be dead or he might be in prison. Raimund didn't know which would be better. He wanted the big, young man to live, but if he was alive in some Northern prison as winter grew even colder and darker, than Raimund might have to do something about that. "What's the prison like?"

"Trying to learn how you'd've fared?" Sile disappeared again and came back with two bowls and ladled some stew into them. Raimund let the steam wash over his face and the smell of garlic rest in his nose. "It's a giant crater. Some beast a thousand years ago or so drove a hole into the ground. Now it's used to mine ore for the Vidalis."

"So we're in Vidale. Not too far from Viguran. What are the odds they have a ship?"

"They're in a hole. No water for hundreds of miles."

"No riverboats even?" Raimund asked and the woman shook her head. "How am I supposed to get out of here?"

"No idea. Why do you think I haven't left?" She giggled. "You'll come to like it as I'm sure you know since you're from the North. Just need to grow accustomed to the winters again."

"I can't stay here and let my friends die." It wasn't something he liked to think about. What reckless things might they do if they think him dead? What would Mar do? "Do you know if the fat man lived?"

Sile shrugged, "well, he would've been a good meal for the *baiagryf*," she corrected her pronunciation, "but with the armed men coming who knows."

"So we need to look in the prison for the fat man then find a way to get south. If we travel east we'll hit the Drewogh Sea. There has to be some ship we can find. Maybe even pirates."

"And you think I'll help? I only saved you from the baiagryf because I was passing through and heard the screams. I have no desire to leave and fight prison guards and pirates and a war."

Raimund thought back to the ice shards that exploded from a ball, to the wet log that was dried. "If I had my stone I wouldn't've needed your help. Where's yours?" Sile didn't look up from her stew as she ate a carrot. "It's a moonstone isn't it?"

Sile reached under her cloak and pulled off a necklace inset with a stone that looked almost like a pearl. She brushed her thumb over it. "It is," she said as she stared longingly at the stone, like she was thinking about something sad. "And where is your stone?"

"In Viguran." Raimund sighed and put the bowl down. Valkyr had been Raimund's sword almost his entire life. It was like losing an old friend. He had fallen into that cave as a child and the steel reflected the sun into his eyes. He was drawn to it. It was if it the sword called for him. Even when he lost it to Drołaj the sword had found its way back to him. He didn't have faith that Valkyr and the sunstone would ever come back. "How is it being an éithrio up here?"

"No one pays me any mind." Sile put her stone away and wiped her eyes like tears had been forming. "What about you? When I was down there the Terropian king was rounding up any mages he could find."

"I tried to stay out of Terrop, don't worry." Raimund eyed some of the books in the corners, he could only make out a few with the light of the cookfire. The night was moonless. *Lessons in Monsters* was one, another the *History of the Kingdom of Vidale (not complete)*, and the *Lands Around the Asara.* "I was in Viguran than Rowan. The Gorthair in Gereduss keep to themselves more than others. Then I traveled to the Asara Mountains with the boy who named himself king." Sile blinked a few times. "Are you from the mountains?"

"No, but I lived there for some time," she said as she poked the fire with a rod. "The Noest are colder, more dangerous I think."

"Well I didn't see any griffins in the Asara so I would agree."

"You went to Whitehall?" Sile's eyes reflected the reds and yellows of the fire, they looked shiny again, like she might cry.

"Yes," Raimund nodded slowly. "I met Lord David Rely and his children. The boy was a knight. Lord Rely looked close to death. The girl was …" Raimund didn't know if it was his right to tell Yvanne's secret, that she too was an éithrio, but he was a thousand miles away. "The girl's an éithrio. She uses a sunstone like me."

Sile shivered like she were cold. She rubbed her hands together as the flames lit one side of her face. "I'll help you get back."

Yvanne

I still don't think you should be riding with my heir inside your belly." Devro said again. He had made sure to tell her how much he disagreed with their trip into the mountains. At first it was about leaving Whitehall without a king, then about her father needing her, now all about the baby.

"If he's as strong as you are then it will all be fine."

"That's a woman who knows how to calm her man." Lord Aimora Dore shouted to his Lodean and they all laughed. "Lodean women are much more argumentative. They never like to see us calm."

"Makes us better lovers." One man shouted to agreements.

Yvanne knew her brother so well that she could feel his eyes rolling even beneath his visor. "You wouldn't know, would you?" she teased Pollard.

"If anything the women are scared to anger their husbands. The Lodean are vicious. Cruel." Pollard said with a snarl.

"Do they look cruel to you?" Yvanne pointed to the men telling jokes and racing in the snow and singing songs in their harsh language. "So far they remind me of the march to Greatbath."

"Just wait until you see them in battle. You thought what

Ultiir did to Greatbath was bad? Some of the villages they've destroyed were never rebuilt. You can't find them on any map and can't find any of the people who called it home. All looted. All raped. All dead."

"And we're trusting them to keep us alive." Devro said.

"If you both didn't want to come then you could've stayed in Whitehall." Yvanne huffed. "I for one trust them. If they wanted to be rid of us or rape us or murder us they'd've already done it. We're far enough away from home. No one would hear us scream."

Pollard's surcoat puffed up as he took a large breath. Devro gripped his cloak tighter. Yvanne made sure to keep her cloak wrapped tight around her body as well, though she didn't feel the cold like the others, but her babe might need to be warmer, and no reason to raise suspicion.

Yvanne was more confident in their return to Whitehall because Helge read the future and said, "You will not die on this trip. Your father will see you again." The old woman had always complained of Yvanne trusting the visions too much, but so far they've never led her astray. "One day you will trust the future too much and be hurt by it," Helge had said. "The future is always changing. My readings are just interpretations. Sometimes I'm wrong."

"But usually you're right." Yvanne had said as she was packing her bags. "Why don't you trust your visions as much as I do? What harm can come?"

"You're being silly." Helge wagged a finger. "You know why I do not share my gift with others, and why I so sparingly tell you things. People will change how they live to adhere to my visions. Now that I said you'll come back from the peaks unharmed, what are you going to do? Be careless? Stupid?

Feel invincible? You are not. You can still be harmed, your life taken from you. Perhaps my vision means your body will return, have you thought of that? It could be alive or dead. In a box or on a horse. You must be careful."

"I will." Yvanne said before leaving with the Lodean. They traveled as far into the Swallow Pass as they could before the snows became too deep. The horses were upset, but the Lodean had them climb rocks. A few times Yvanne thought Snowfall, her mare, was going to tumble down the mountain, but she was a strong girl.

Now, the Lodean were looking for a meadow near a rock face. Of course the meadow would be covered by snow at the moment, so Yvanne didn't know how they were going to find it, but the Lodean seemed to know what they were doing.

"What is it we're looking for?" Pollard asked once they had finished setting up camp for the night. "All I see is white every which way."

"You will know once we find it." Lord Aimora said while drinking warm ale. "The mountains were once mined by dwarves. They left many secrets."

"A dwarven tunnel?" Pollard laughed. "Will we have to leave our horses and crawl the whole time?"

"Are you sure we can make it to the peaks?" Devro said in a quiet voice. "I want to make sure we can actually get there before putting our lives in more danger."

"Don't be afraid, little king," Besta said, a Lodean who was good at making everyone laugh. "Our weapons are to protect you."

"I'm not afraid." Devro crossed his arms.

The winter winds whipped through the valley they camped

in. Snow had been falling all day and into the night. The moon was full but could barely be seen through the winds. Lendia, the goddess of the moon, fighting with Anebra, the goddess of the cold.

"That is Ariga." Aimora had followed Yvanne's gaze to the moon. They sat opposite each other by the fire. The ripples of energy flowing into the night sky.

"I'm sure you know our name for her." Yvanne said.

"Lendia, yes. Legend says Ariga and Lendia are one and the same, just different names. Like how you call my people Lodean but we call ourselves *Lendiko.* Have you been around many Lodean in your life?"

"I've only heard stories."

Pollard decided to chime in, his red curls falling in his face. "Horrible stories."

Aimora and a few others laughed. "Yes, we are monsters. That is what your people say. We say the same about you." They laughed again leaving an echo. "I hope this journey forges a new relationship. We are both people of the mountains, even if some of your ancestors came from the rivers, your fiery hair tells a different story."

"It comes from our mother." Pollard ripped the skin from a cooked quail. "You probably saw her when you raided Whitehall many years ago."

"Possibly." Aimora said before waving a Lodean over who had red hair. "This is Orra. You have much in common. Both heads of flame. Perhaps your mother is descended from our people. Perhaps we share blood."

"No," said Pollard. "It is forbidden for a Veck'kop to mate with a Lodean."

"You wouldn't know." Besta said. "The number of women

who travel to Lodeanhold to feel the embrace of a real man is in the dozens every year. I suspect the Veck'kop don't know how to pleasure women." The Lodean laughed while Pollard scowled.

"I am a knight," Pollard said, "I definitely wouldn't know."

"Such strange customs." Besta added. "What people wouldn't want their warriors to have children? Small wonder your towns are so easy to raid."

Pollard stood and grabbed his sheathed sword. "Should we test that?"

Aimora raised a hand to stop Besta. "No need to fight. We share a fire and drink. We are allies at this time."

"Pollard, sit." Yvanne said through gritted teeth. "You should tell us more about your gods. The more we know about you the better we can serve you, right Devro?" Devro nodded as he shivered.

"Only one goddess." Aimora pointed to the dim moonlight. "Ariga is our mother, our protector, our creator. She birthed us into this world and she takes us out. A Lodean's soul stays in his body until night falls when she comes down from the heavens to lead us to our ancestors. Ariga once reigned supreme, but even a goddess needs rest. She created the sun to light our path while she sleeps, before waking to guide us in the night."

Pollard gave a sigh of annoyance. Yvanne said, "Lovely. No evil forces?"

"Merely men and their desires." Besta said. "Women are pure, men are not. We have no Veltoora if that's what you ask."

"So no matter how awful in life you still get to dine with your ancestors?" Devro asked.

The Lodean nodded. "Explains the amount of killings." Pollard grumbled.

"War causes us to do things we're not proud of." Lord Aimora said. "We've been at war with the Veck'kop since they took Viguran. Once our war is done we will go back to the peaceful ways of our ancestors."

"In all my studies I have never heard of peaceful Lodean," Pollard said. "I have heard of a lying Lodean. How do I know you're not lying now? That even if we didn't fight you that you'd be peaceful? I have a feeling you would descend on our towns and murder us all while your precious Ariga watches."

Yvanne put her hand on Pollard's knee to get him to stop before things got ugly. Aimora nodded amusingly. "Since you never stop attacking our people, you'll never know."

The camp was quiet except for the crackling of the fire. Eventually Devro's teeth began to chatter. "You should get some sleep, Yvanne," Pollard said while looking at Devro. *Not wanting to embarrass his king,* she thought with a giggle.

"I agree." Devro stood and held out his hand for Yvanne.

"If you both want to sleep that's fine, but I'll stay up with the Lodean if they'll have me." Yvanne said.

Lord Aimora nodded with a smile. Pollard rolled his eyes but found his way to the tent with Devro. "Have you traveled in the dwarven tunnels much?" Yvanne asked after taking a sip of some thick, warm drink the Lodean had made from mare's milk.

"There are only a few tunnels left." Aimora said. "Mostly in the high mountains. It is said that the elves destroyed most of the tunnels in the Asara once they conquered the land around the Ters-Veck. But those are stories."

"We'll be sure to ask for the truth." Besta said.

Yvanne was puzzled. "Ask who?"

"I see it!" A Lodean shouted while he pointed to a blue outline made visible by a stream of moonlight. It seemed to make a door in the rock face.

"Remember that for the morrow. We'll need some sleep first." Aimora said. "We'll reveal all our secrets in the morn, my queen. Lodean are said to be descended from dwarves, so we know quite a bit about the mountains." Yvanne had never thought about the Lodean hiding secrets of the mountains. They were always described as a backward people. *Guess father is wrong after all.*

Aimora cleared his throat and said, "May I sing you a song before we sleep? It's called *Kena Ristura*. It holds a special meaning in our hearts, the last song sung by King Thimoy Dehul before the Veck'kop descended on him."

Yvanne nodded, took in energy from the fire to keep warm, and let her body drift to the song. Aimora's voice was low. The other Lodean joining in every now and again. Pollard huffing in the tent behind her. Eventually, Yvanne slipped off the log and went to sleep on the ground, a hand on her belly.

***

The next morning, after sharing some hard bread and warm mead, the dozens of Lodean climbed up the rocks, helping the horses behind them. Besta had held Yvanne's hand, much to Pollard's chagrin, as she ascended the mountain. The blue outline of a door was even less visible in the sunlight than it was in the moonlight. Orra traced the shape with his finger. "Ready?" he asked his lord who gave a nod. *"Kifti lema'och."*

80

"The dwarven language of *dwanki.*" Aimora whispered.

After Orra's words were spoken the rocks shook, the horses whinnied, and the stone slid open. Air rushed in. Yvanne's hair became a tangled mess in her face. Devro's jaw had dropped.

Orra grabbed a torch lit by their fire and entered the darkness of the tunnel before the other Lodean followed. Pollard kept his hand on his sword. "I don't like this."

"You don't like anything." Yvanne said as she followed Lord Aimora. Orra let the torchlight find more wood and charcoal to light. A charcoal burner was lit and a stream of fire spread across the inside of the tunnel, lighting the many paths as far as her eyes could see. The entire mountain seemed hollowed out.

"You must know the words to get into a dwarven mine," Aimora said, "but they are in more places than you think."

"It's incredible." Yvanne said as she looked over the edge, finding out they were standing on a bridge, and far below a floor of many colored stone formed a pattern. "Dwarves did this?"

"Damn right you are." A new voice called out from across the bridge. The firelight showed a short man with long beard and hair walking their way.

"Stop." Pollard said but Aimora raised a hand.

"How do you do Achi?"

"Confused on why you want to travel the mines but other than that fine." The dwarf's accent was heavy and it was unlike anything Yvanne had heard. "Stop staring will ya? I don't gawk at humans and I'd rather they didn't gawk at me."

"That is the queen you're speaking to." Pollard said.

"Is she my queen?" Achi laughed, causing it to echo in the

mines. "I do not bow to humans, no dwarf does. Now, tell me whatcha want?"

Aimora said, "we wish to pass through is all. We need to speak to the Lords of the Peaks and this is the quickest way in winter."

"Is it winter out there?" Achi peered around them and nodded when he saw the snow. "I've been in *ilik terar* for months now. Mining away at some gems."

"Hoping to make some coin?" Besta asked.

The dwarf laughed again. "Humans love gems, what can I say? Easy to sell, especially south of the *t'ru nochi*." Achi rubbed his giant brown beard. "But I guess I'll let you pass. Wouldn't want the boy here to cut me down," he pointed to Pollard and laughed with the Lodean. "You shouldn't come across anyone else. The mine's been empty of late, most seemed to have gone south to Anha Jorbstah. They'd rather live with the elves than their own kind." Achi said as he shook his head.

"Anha Jorbstah was built by dwarves." Yvanne said. "Don't you want to see it?"

"Know your histories, ey? The elves slaughtered us and once you humans did the same to them they want to be allies. They can fight their own war." Achi's face was twisted. "Now, you better be going. Wouldn't want the lords to wait for their queen," he gave a laugh before disappearing down some steps.

"Half of my people will stay here, we decided last night," Aimora told Devro. "That way they can get back to Whitehall if things go poorly for us."

"Are you expecting them to?" Devro asked as he climbed atop his horse.

"You never know with the Lords of the Peaks."

Lord Aimora led them over the stone bridges and platforms. The horses didn't like being in the mountain as much as being outside. Snowfall kept huffing and Fariage had to be calmed by Devro. The clip clop of the horses echoed in the mines making it sound like an army marched over the stone instead of half a dozen people.

"You use these mines regularly?" Yvanne asked.

"If you mean during our raids then no." Aimora said. "They criss-cross throughout the Asara, even the Kash, but many of them have been empty for hundreds of years, some completely collapsed, and you have to know the words to get in. But they are quicker than going around the mountains if you can find one."

"And where will this one open?"

"Near Meadowton. The Lords of the Peaks go there in the winter to protect themselves from the weather. You did know that didn't you?" Aimora asked Yvanne who shrugged. "Do you at least know their names?"

"Of course. Lord Cul of Mount Meret, Lord Plantan of Mount Swallow, Lord Emni of Mount Samosay, and Lord Lise of Mount Doma."

"Lord Aute of Mount Doma." Aimora corrected. "Lord Lise died a few years ago and his second son inherited the peak."

"Good thing you're here to help, right Devro."

"Of course." Devro said as his eyes followed the flames that lit their path.

Yvanne sighed before turning back to Aimora. "How many other mines do you know of?"

"Only a few." Aimora waved his hands.

"There's one near Lodeanhold," Besta said, "and another near the Swallow Pass. We've heard stories from other Lodean that there is one connecting the Maera Steppe to Terrop. Very long that one." Yvanne didn't know if that were true. Dwarves were known for being greedy, and a shortcut through the Asara would bring them untold riches.

"One by the Swallow Pass?" Yvanne tapped a finger on her pants as she swayed atop her horse.

"Wanting to see the snow?" Aimora asked.

"Well we are very worried about King Anvrin sending troops to support his daughter once spring comes, aren't we Devro?"

"Yes, very worried," he turned his head to all eyes on him, "worried of what?"

"The Terropians."

"Yes."

Yvanne gave him a calming smile, hoping to bring his nerves down, to have his mind on important matters instead of wherever it was. "If the mines could be used to stop them from advancing on Whitehall then we might be able to win this war."

"Terropians hunt Lodean for sport." Pollard said. "They know how to take care of them."

"Hunting our people makes us angrier." Aimora smirked. "We'll look more into it when we get the lords on our side and we're back in Whitehall. I'm sure your father will have something to say about that."

"If he's still around." Yvanne placed her hand over her mouth. *I cannot believe I would say something so foolish in front of them.* But no one said a word. They rode to the end of the tunnel in silence.

Ultiir

You'll need to name an heir soon, Your Grace," Lord Tedbalt Masson said, "if you do not then we'll have to search far and wide if, may the Four watch over you, something tragic were to happen during this war. The most obvious person to take over will be the king of Rowan, your cousin. And having a Bruthaki on the throne would be a scandal."

Ultiir's eyes had glazed over from all the talking of his council, but Lord Masson always knew how to bring him back. "My father was Bruthaki and he reigned, don't you remember? Unless you have something against them? Against me?"

Tedbalt cleared his throat and shifted in his chair. The old man had gray hairs growing everywhere and his wrinkles had gotten worse. *Before long I'll have to name another chief consultant. Either from Tedbalt falling over from age or because he annoyed me one too many times.*

"I could never forget your father," the old lord said slowly. "King Ferrick was a wise and gracious king, but it was still a scandal at court when your family chose him to carry on the name."

"I also worry that Bartel has yet to answer our calls for an alliance against the bastard." The chief commander, Lord Alan Hirons said. "That man gave him protection for almost a decade, allowed him to build support, and spits in our faces when we need him."

"I do not want Bartel to be king anymore than you do." Ultiir said. "Once the lords have paid homage to me I will name a new lord of Goldfield. Hopefully Sophie will start giving me children and I won't have to worry about it anymore."

"Should we turn our attention to Redington, Your Grace?" Lord Dovi Lyons, the chief collector asked. Ultiir waved a hand for him to start. "As you know Lord Zazí," the banished lord of Redington who annoyed Ultiir even more than Tedbalt, "was welcomed in the city by large possessions and many greetings, but the rumors were true about the city's vaults being emptied. The governors lost the power of taxation and the city fell to ruin after the mites sacked it. Holding the city may be a waste of money."

"Once the ships come and cargo flows through the ports we'll make even more coin than before." Lord Serle Verrier said. The chief ambassador rubbed his hair from his eyes. "I've heard from many lords who have traveled here who are ecstatic about bringing new slaves, some ships have already disembarked and are on their way to Nuqtia as we speak."

Dovi nodded but said, "I just don't want us to spend all our resources on a dilapidated city when we have much more pressing matters just a few dozen miles to the north."

The chief commander looked through some reports. "The lowlands are aflame, yes, but so far every one of our commanders is reporting success. What happened at Greatbath did not inspire much confidence in lords to join the bastard's side."

"That was the plan," Ultiir said wondering which village he would have to order destroyed next. "Burn the village and make them fear us. But we should still worry. Goldfield is far too close to the Lands of Asara and I worry for my mother, and if I know her she will not come to Vigur even if that city was a step outside. She's a stubborn, ill-tempered hag of a woman, but I don't want her last few years in this life cut short by my nephew."

"I have sent word to many lords along the Ters-Veck to send whoever they can to this city," Alan said. "The mites are of no worry at this time."

"How can you be sure?" Tedbalt asked. "When Hurvir let his guard down the Çesdiri invaded Awaran and started a war. You know not to trust a mite."

"I would rather focus on this war than some imaginative one. And may the Four guide him." Alan said, bowing his head.

"What?" Ultiir asked.

"Your brother, His Grace, may the Four guide him in the afterlife."

Ultiir had forgotten Lord Lyons still had no idea what transpired at Hurvir's feast. How almost the whole council was in on the plan to assassinate him. Even his brother. "Yes, of course." Ultiir sat back in his chair and let the lords discuss Redington and the lowlands. Hurvir's blue covered mouth filled his mind. The way his body went limp as he choked on the poison. The crown falling off his head. It littered his nightmares too. And Ultiir didn't stop there. The High Doma still awaited trial for witchcraft and Lord Gofrei Geary's head was cut off and sent to the bastard in Whitehall. *Who else will*

I have to kill to keep control while war rages?

Ultiir stood and the lords followed. "Write to Lord de'Viere and ask how Vigur is doing in my absence." Ultiir said. Lord Edel de'Viere was the newest member of the King's Council, tasked with watching Vigur while the king was away. Tedbalt had convinced Ultiir of that. "I need to see my mother. I'm sure she'll have something to say about my avoidance of her." The lords bowed as Ultiir left the small chamber that was being used as their council room.

He never liked Goldfield. The town was so far removed from court, instead surrounded by slaves and fields. No one ever visited. The expansive Vigur was what he considered home, where all the lords and ladies came to play, where he was treated like the royalty he was, where it was easier to see the people and hear their struggles. Vigur was nothing like Rowan where the commoners scorned their king. In Vigur they embraced their rulers. Lavished them with flowers and love and smiles. It wasn't until Hurvir fucked everything up by going to war with the mites and causing widespread hunger and disease across the realm that the people began to be less trustful of the king. But Ultiir planned to change that.

His mother's quarters weren't far. Her and his father used to share a bedchamber on the top floor of the manor, but his mother was so frail that a wrong breeze from the east could break her body.

Rila de'Tro was staring out her window when he arrived. Watching the winter wheat blow in the wind. The leader of her household guard, old Sir Gid was speaking with her in whispers.

"Mother."

"How long have you been here? A week? And you have

yet to see me?" His mother said without turning from the window, shooing her guard away, and not letting Ultiir answer. "Was I such an awful mother that none of my children ever wanted to visit their home? Especially you. Lord of Goldfield and you barely set foot in this place." His mother turned and she took a sip of water. She was so old compared to before, and Ultiir had only known his mother as old, but now she could hardly move without shaking. The fat on her body gone. Shorter by a foot. "Analere didn't even see your brother's body. That's the second sibling she had missed being put in the crypt. What a wretched woman."

Ultiir already felt the headache coming on. He rubbed his temples and found a wooden chair. "I'm sure she was devastated by the news, but Pleat Isle is far away and even with Anebro's strongest winds she couldn't have made it in time."

"Always defending her," his mother sounded like she wanted to shout at him. "Wish you cared about me as much as you do protecting your sister."

"She is the last sibling I have," Ultiir said, choosing his words carefully to not upset her. "I know she has always been a disappointment to you, but maybe this time she was actually busy."

Rila de'Tro glared at her son. "My child who was a gift from the Four doesn't even care for his mother. I'm sure Vigura is laughing right now."

He took a deep breath to calm his anger, but he could still feel it bubbling deep inside. "I do care for you. I have men coming from all across the realm to protect you because you're a stubborn ass who won't let someone carry you to the safety of Vigur."

His mother shook her head and *tsked.* "None of your brothers would ever dare talk to me like that. They knew I would leave them in Goldfield to let my servants deal with them."

"Don't forget you did the same to me and my sisters too." Now the anger was boiling up, more of hearing his mother talk and it would spillover until he said something he regretted. Or didn't regret. Depended on how long his mother would live after a fight.

"The girls were always trouble, and I think they liked being with the servants. Some of them were awfully cute." She picked at her nails. "And you boys were the future of Viguran. If you weren't made tougher then the mites would've laid waste to this land. Sometimes a mother makes hard decisions."

Ultiir clenched his fists at his side remembering why he was avoiding his mother. Wanting to scream and cry at her. Wanting to push her out a window on behalf of his sisters. "Maybe Philla, Analere, and Analla were just happy to be away from you for sometime. Though the happiness vanished as the weeks went on," he tried to suppress the memories of their cries. "Goldfield was awful when you and father were away and you know it. Yet you still let the servants do whatever because you pretended to be too busy to raise us."

"A queen has duties."

"Father had duties, yours stopped once an heir was made."

Rila de'Tro looked like she had been slapped her mouth was so wide. "We ruled this kingdom jointly. I was in every council meeting, privy to all communications, helped him and his father reconnect and reforge the alliance with Rowan. You have only been king for a few months. I ruled for decades." She pointed at herself with a feeble hand and a loud voice. "Do not lecture me about duties considering your wife has yet to conceive. Do I need to show you how that works? A man who has had over forty feasts and has never taken a wife or had a child. You were always an embarrassment. Even Wyclef and Olmar look down on you in pity, and you can add Hurvir to that list too."

Ultiir knew his brothers would take his side against their mother, or at least he told himself they would. He stood while shaking his head. "I came here to convince you to leave for Vigur and to tell you, since I knew you wouldn't, that we are upping the number of men for your protection. Not to argue."

"Every time you come here there is an argument." Rila stood slowly, Ultiir grabbed her arm to help, and she embraced him. "I love you my son. I want you to be strong and the best of the de'Tro kings. That's why I am hard on you. Hurvir was such a good king. I want you to be better." She stepped back and smoothed her skirts. "You think I need protection but I do not. I am going to send Sir Gid with you when you go back to the sacred city."

"Sir Gid is as old as Hurvir was."

"Yet no knight can beat him even after all these years. There's a reason he has been my guard for decades."

"Sir Lovis has done a perfectly fine job."

"But with all those guards your brother still was killed. Sir Gid would've been able to save him but he was tucked away in Goldfield with me. There is no argument to be had. He will be going with you." Rila wiped away a tear from her dark eyes, she laughed when she saw it. "I haven't cried in so long. I miss your siblings and father everyday, I don't want you to

end up like Hurvir. If I ever found out who killed my son ..."
she trailed off when she looked out the window.

Ultiir felt all the air go out of him like he was punched. His
mother. Crying. Crying over all her dead children and he
had been responsible for one of their deaths. "I'll talk with
you later, mother." He left before she could see the tears in
his eyes.

The king stalked up the stairs, wishing they were the grand
steps in the elven-built palace in Vigur, where he wouldn't
have to think about his brother. *How dare she make me feel
bad about killing him,* he thought as he wiped his eyes, *he was a
monster to his people. Mother would never understand anyhow as
she was a monster to her children.* Sir Lovis stood by the door
to the bedchamber like instructed even though he protested.
"There are hundreds of slaves and lords that would see you
dead." He had said, but Ultiir made him watch the room and
call if Sophie came back so they could try for a child once
more. Now, he didn't want to think about an heir.

"Let no one in, not even the queen." Ultiir told Sir Lovis
who shut the door. The fire warmed the bedchamber even
though the doors to the balcony were left open. When he
went to shut them he saw the fields below. Not so golden
in the winter. In the summer the ground would resemble
the sun. Him and Analere used to play with the slaves in the
wheat. Hiding and scaring them. Some even got extra food
if they found the children quick enough.

He shut the doors.

On the wooden desk opposite the bed was a quill and ink.
He began to write to his last remaining sibling. He apologized
for killing Hurvir. He apologized for not helping her more
with mother. For not being there when the mites attacked.

For disapproving of her choice to become a daken.

He threw the parchment in the fire and began anew. This time telling her to come to Vigur by orders of her king and brother but he added a 'please' to make it sound nicer. *I don't blame her for not wanting to see Hurvir's corpse. The bloated mess. The lifeless eyes.* Ultiir began to tear up just like his mother. *She already had to deal with our sisters' death, and now all we have is each other.*

Ultiir threw the ink pot across the room causing a stream of black to ooze down the wall. He ripped off a tapestry of an owl with wheat and thought about throwing it in the fire, burning down the whole manor, instead he crumpled it up and tossed it into a dusty corner. Then he ripped at the bed. Wool sheets and down pillows causing a storm of white. Throwing goblets, gold jewelry, and candlesticks he broke the glass of the windows and doors. He screamed as tears rolled down his cheeks and scratched at a portrait of his grandfather above the mantle. His nails making claw marks across King Guret's face.

The king of Viguran fell to the floor and cradled his knees. Sobbing for his dead brother. The brother he killed. "What have I done?" He shouted to the gods. "Why did you let me do such an evil thing?" He lay on the floor in a puddle of feathers, ripped cloth, and tears.

Outside the door was arguing. A woman's voice directing her frustration at Sir Lovis. "Let her in." Ultiir said from the wooden floor.

Sophie walked in and her jaw dropped as her eyes darted across the room. "What happened?" Ultiir began crying again and his wife sat beside him. She rubbed his hands. "Is it the war? Your mother?"

"Hurvir. How can the gods ever forgive me for what I did?" He said through sniffles. "I'll be cursed to Veltoora, away from my family. I'll never see my sisters again or meet my older brothers. Father and mother will be so disappointed. We always disappoint them."

Sophie grabbed Ultiir's cheeks and stared into his eyes. For a moment Ultiir was lost. He was fine. Her beautiful eyes filled him with hope for the future. "You are the king of Viguran, the gods' chosen to lead the world of man. They will understand why you did what you did. The only person at your family's feast you'll have to explain yourself to is Hurvir." Ultiir started sobbing again, spit falling down his chin. "You know Hurvir will laugh about it. You know him. 'Dead by poison?' he'll say, 'you should've used a sword.' He was the Warrior, and that caused many problems for Viguran. This is a holy kingdom. The gods know you are the one who will restore its glory."

"Hurvir probably would laugh." Ultiir laughed himself. "You really think I can make this place better?"

"Once you end the war with Devro," Sophie brushed his blond hair from his eyes, "you will make this the envy of all the world, not just Adedor."

Ultiir kissed her smooth lips and his tears dried. He would make Viguran better than it was, but he had to deal with his nephew.

Aveline

Aveline held the tears back, but her father was dead. She was now an orphan.

King Bartel Thomas lay in a stone box ready for the crypt, a mask of gold shaped like his face covering his dead eyes and cold lips. He was wrapped in blue silk, the color of the River Bruthak. His head adorned by a fake crown and a ceremonial sword, just recently smithed and bearing his name, wrapped in his hands.

The lords and ladies of the court gathered in front of the palace. Lords Darry and Rean arguing which side to stand as they made the procession to the domaton. Royal Chancellors were mixed in as well, at least the ones who bothered to come. The High Chancellor, Hecher, looked bored, but he was always a close ally of her father after they rebuilt the kingdom. Emmett, the High Doma, was wearing the same blue as her dead father, a long cape dragging the dirt from the cobblestones.

Baldewin and Blis had returned from their fishing in Decaro when they received the news. Her youngest brother dressed in a deep violet tunic to match Aveline's long dress.

Both with small crowns atop their heads. Bertin didn't come back. He didn't even write. *Only because Telemaw is so far away,* she told herself, there's no way he knows. *He still lives in a world where he isn't an orphan.* What worried her was that Bertin hadn't written at all. Only one letter from King

Hasíb of Telemaw and never again. The one thing she hated was the oppressive heat south of the Ters-Veck, she couldn't

imagine a desert even if it were winter. Not that she liked the cold in Rowan. A light drizzle fell on them from the gray overcast that mourned with her.

Drums began to sound. Chants led by the High Doma filled the air. An old version of their tongue used to invoke the gods' blessings, Aveline never bothered to learn it, so she hummed as Emmett called to the heavens. Baldewin wiped away tears as Blis lay a comforting hand on his shoulder. The palace gates opened. The domaton stared back at them. They just had to make the short walk down the Royal Road.

Once outside the gates, Aveline could see how crowded it was. The lords and ladies stayed close together for fear of a peasant touching them or grabbing their clothes. The High Doma chanted while his guards moved onlookers from the street. Aveline and Baldewin were surrounded by their household guards and her father by his. Nothing bad can happen, she thought.

In other kingdoms this many people would be welcomed. Cheers and celebrations over the life of a monarch and all he accomplished, but in Rowan, and especially the capital, the crowd had little love for the king. The ones who did cheer or cry were silenced by the others. It was as if vipers stalked them. She wondered if this was how her grandmother felt on the way to her trial. There were still missing bricks and cracked stone on the shops along the Royal Road, the owner not quick to fix the damage from the Bruthaki Flames in fear of another outbreak of violence. *Will today be that day?*

As the four corners of the domaton grew larger like a mountain, the crowd grew rowdier. Yelling, cursing, laughing. Insults aimed at her father and her dead aunt; jokes about her mother and the jagged rocks she flung herself on; talk of more dead monarchs and stopping her brother's ascension to the throne. "Whore." "Bitch." Muncher." "May you rot in Veltoora." "Go back to the mites." Were all thrown at Aveline. Nothing she hadn't heard before, so she kept her head up and eyes on the domaton, but the words still hurt. The crowd was moving like a wave at the celebration of the dead king. The laughter drowning out the chanting of Emmett. Ivlin and Dern the Third huddled closer to Aveline as men called out their threats of violence and rape at her.

She heard some spitting, others began to throw scraps of food. The High Doma quickened his pace.

When they reached the steps of the domaton, Aveline and Baldewin were ushered to the door, though they had to wait for Emmett to address the crowd before they could go inside.

Thousands stood below her. The palace seemed a million miles away as the crowd cut them off from home. Chants and cheers about the "dead oppressor," and "Arvon's revenge," filled the air.

Aveline chose to focus on Emmett's eulogy instead. "The great King Bartel Thomas the Uniter has been called to feast with the Four and the Many." Cheering. "We must pray that Vigura has judged him well. Judged him for bringing a broken people back together, for restoring a divine monarch, for stopping violence in the streets." Booing. "King Bartel was a just ruler. One who saved us from the mites to the south and from one another. I pray he is at peace, and that

his successor will carry on his tradition." More booing as the
High Doma motioned for those closest to the dead king to
go inside.

They entered the domaton under the statue of Samosay. He
looked to the west, holding a pan flute in his right hand and
a letter in the other. Inside, the domaton was vast. Footsteps
echoed under the domed ceiling. She had visited the domaton
in Caiag Rock and Vigur, this one was different. Where
those had the images of history, offices for doma, and always
worshipers to call for aid; the domaton in Rowan was an
empty chasm of gray stone. Candles bringing the only light;
the small, circular opening in the dome letting rain fall onto
the cold floor. The lack of decoration and ornamentation
was to keep the worshiper focused on the Four. To Aveline,
the emptiness only made her skin crawl. It was nothing like
the temples in Rainvealand. The hundreds of colorful statues
showing the Ancient One's many forms, creating rainbows
along the walls.

Aveline squeezed Baldewin's shoulder as they surrounded
her father who lay under the one ray of sun, his gold mask
reflecting the light into their eyes. Sparkling. It hadn't hit
her that she would never see his eyes again, never see his face,
or hear his voice. It still wasn't real. This would end and she
would find her father on the throne or in his bedchamber.

They would joke and he would hug Baldewin and ask about
the fish.

The High Doma was saying some words, but Aveline only
looked at the lesser doma in black robes. They would take
her father to the crypt below. He would lay next to his father
for the rest of time. Aveline thought about the rest of the day,
what she was going to do. Maybe visit Brissa's Point, the site

of the old prison, named for her aunt. Maybe sleep for a few days. Find Mari and sob. She was an orphan now, but she wasn't ready to be.

***

The mite district was the worst of Rowan. Garbage and shit piled high in the roads; stray cats and dogs rummaging for food, attacking any who came near; men who flashed their daggers when they smiled to show they could hurt you. Aveline's guards hated it, but she had grown fond.

Underneath the criminals and trash were a people that had to stick together. Families never apart. The neighborhood ready to come together if a Bruthaki got too violent or vulgar with them. Her father always complained of the district, of the filth and the decay, but never once thought about helping.

Never questioned how the Bruthaki view of supremacy hurt these people just as much as it hurt the Gorthair.

She entered a tavern near the temple. Worshipers praying outside. *"Al ahi da,"* they chanted. Some days they would be whipped and driven from the street for going against the

Four, but the guards were busy near the domaton. Outside the temple two Rainvealandians were hanged. Lifeless bodies blowing in the breeze. Crows and flies all around, picking at their rotting flesh, the stench so bad Aveline could cry. They were hanged as robbers. Whether they did it or not didn't matter. How the Rainvealandians put up with it, how they didn't look back to their relative peace when the river was aflame with civil war and demand change she didn't know.

Inside the tavern a man was humming in the ancient tongue and fingering a stringed instrument. The vibrations echoing off the wooden walls. People, drunk and sober, watching and clapping with the rhythm.

Aveline sat at the bar and ordered a milky drink much too strong for her and a salad made from eggplant. Dern the Third ordered a wine from Baragio like he always did.

"I don't know why you insist on coming here. The drinks aren't even enough to get a child drunk."

"Ehir liçi eri meku." The barkeep said and Aveline laughed at the insult. The barkeep raised a brow. "You speak the ancient tongue?" He said in his language.

Aveline responded in the same tongue. "My father wanted to throw me from the window when I told him." Dern ignored the interaction. The surprise or disgust he felt when she spoke to the Rainvealandians in their own language vanished many years ago.

"Well then there's no reason for you to pay." He slid her coins back.

"It's alright," Aveline set down a golden coin stamped with a horse, "I can afford it." Dern shook his head, but his eye caught some serving girl with the smoothest skin she'd ever seen, and he made his move trying to converse with a woman who didn't know his language and was certainly not into him.

Aveline finished her milky alcoholic beverage and picked at her salad. Never did I think I'd be an orphan this young. She had always imagined her father and mother old, gray hair and wrinkles all over their skin, fat from overabundance. Now, she imagined her mother's crushed bones and bloodied skin, small pieces of rocks embedded in her skin, and her father wearing a gold mask to cover his look of death.

"Ripàsert?" A familiar, jolly, voice said. Neşe, a middle-aged Rainvealandian, with a fat belly and no hair picked her up and held her in his big arms. "It's been so long."

Aveline giggled like she was a child and hugged the big man back. Dern watched from across the room, his hand on his sword. "Thought I'd come here to drink. They don't make them like this in my home." She made sure not to say palace.

Kari, Neşe's wife kissed Aveline's cheek and said, "didn't know if we'd ever see you again. I'm glad we get to. You've grown so much, and your accent is almost perfect."

Aveline found Celat behind Kari. Their child was younger than she was, but only by a year, born during the Changing of the Face, an honor. "How are you doing?" She asked Celat.

"Is your father treating you well or making you clean the latrines with him?"

"I've been learning horses," they said, "hoping one day to drive a whole team full. Maybe carry goods across all of Adedor."

"Celat wishes to give their mother a heart attack." Kari said while grabbing her child and giving them a tight hug, Celat rolling their eyes. "But we'll talk about it some other time."

"I'd be happy to get you in touch with the greatest horse riders in the kingdom. Maybe instead of a traveler you could become a knight."

Celat's brow furrowed. "A knight of Rowan? I don't think they accept people like me."

"Of anywhere you wish."

Neşe put his large hand on Aveline's shoulder. "We don't need your help, ripàsert, we are doing just fine on our own," he said in a soft voice to not offend.

"At least think about it," she said to Celat. "Shall we drink?"

They were given some of the best alcohol the barkeep could

find before sitting around a table telling stories of their time apart. Aveline in North Ferga and life at the palace, Neşe telling of his adventures haggling with bandits during a trip to Ter Seere, Kari and Celat cleaning the temple. Dern flirted with many women in the back. None gave into his advances.

They laughed that her guard would have better luck with the pox ridden whores in eastern Rowan, but of course he didn't know that. The tavern got busier as the day got later. With every new Rainvealandian who showed up came another in shock that Aveline knew their language so well.

"Why did you come down here?" Neşe asked. "I thought you grew out of wanting to see us mites." He said it with a smile, but there was a hard truth in there. A pain. The small girl he had taught so much — the language, the food, the religion — never visiting him.

Aveline pushed the empty glasses away. "My father died."

Saying it was odd. She had seen the body before he was dressed for burial, had written to and comforted Baldewin, but it wasn't real if she didn't say it. "I guess I wanted good company."

Kari rubbed Aveline's back. "We are not mad," she said in the soothing voice of a mother, and Aveline's eyes filled with tears. It had been half a decade since she lost her mother, lost her mother's compassion and empathy, and her mother's disappointment. She missed all of it. She still lay awake at night wondering why her mother did what she did. Were any of the rumors true? Kari hugged Aveline like a daughter, holding her close and brushing her hair. "We know how difficult it must be for you to come here. I see the way your guard watches us, I can't imagine what the lords and chancellors think."

"I should apologize," Neşe said, "when we heard your father died, we didn't mourn, at least not for him. We felt sad for you. It is always hard to lose a parent, and our poor little ripàsert has lost both. But we were also glad. Celebrated even."

Aveline took a swig to clear her throat and wiped her tears.

"You don't have to be sorry or explain yourselves or anything.

I know how my father was viewed by some. I saw it on the Royal Road." She huffed. "Not everyone can be popular."

"You would be." Celat said. "Have you ever thought of being queen?"

"It's not my decision."

"I thought the chancellery chose the monarch," they said.

"Only sometimes," Aveline said, "it goes to the eldest boy. Bertin. Even though I'm older I'll get passed over, so I don't think about being queen much."

"You would be popular." Kari said. "I'm sure your brother won't be disliked either, but if you were by his side."

"If he ever comes home." Thinking about Bertin made breathing difficult. Mother, father, Bertin. I can't lose him too.

He's alive. Only having the time of his life in Telemaw, too busy to write.

"We should be going back." Dern said, looking sad at the beautiful women he tried and failed to bed. "The lords will be wondering where you are, and best not to give them a scare after your father's death."

Aveline agreed and said her goodbyes with another tight hug from Neşe, paid for everyone's drink, and left with her hood pulled high over her head. The mite district was bathed in orange from the setting sun. The roads emptying as workers made their way home or to the nearby tavern or whorehouse. Some kids were playing in a puddle, splashing Aveline as she went by. "They should try that with another royal." Dern huffed.

"They're only kids." Aveline kicked water back at the laughing children.

The palace grounds were full of knights and guards. Commoners stood outside waiting for the next king to show his face. Do they know Bertin isn't here? Are they planning to exalt him or kill him? Dern and Aveline sneaked in near the stables and were swiftly whisked inside. "Is something wrong?" Aveline asked.

"Nothing dangerous, my Princess." Vante, an old page, said.

"But the councilors wish to see you and the prince. Your father's, may the Four guide him, last wishes are to be read."

A light rain began again once Aveline reached the throne room, water gliding down the windows. Red and blue tapestries hung from the columns, under them the councilors, the lords of the sunset and sunrise, Blis, and Baldewin. A few scribes were there as well as the High Doma and the High Chancellor.

"Welcome princess." Caxton bowed. He was the royal councilor, the one with the most esteem and influence.

"We've been looking everywhere for you. I hope you don't mind that we started without you."

Aveline swayed from the alcohol. "Not at all," she found a place by Baldewin's side, "please continue."

Jac, another councilor, continued reading. "It is with my power as King that I bestow the royal lands along the River Bow to the Royal Chancellery as a token of appreciation for the work we have done in these so many years." Hecher straightened his back and smirked. "Now to the matter of succession. Prince Bertin, my eldest son, is to be crowned King of Rowan upon my demise. If, may Vigura guide him, Prince Bertin is not fit to rule, then Prince Baldewin, my second son, will rule Rowan with a regent until his age of majority. If a regent must be named then I will do so, instead of the Royal Chancellery." Hecher popped his neck. Aveline squeezed Baldewin's hand, praying that Bertin would walk through the doors at any moment. "The regent shall be named …" Jac coughed, the words stuck in his throat, stammering.

"Out with it." Another councilor, Wycleaf said. "It's getting late."

Jac lowered her father's parchment. "Princess Aveline has been named regent."

The room erupted in a frenzy of talks. The sunrise and sunset lords quickly began to argue, Hecher and Emmett began discussing the legality of it, Caxton said something about Queen Amalia, Blis merely smiled, and Baldewin's hand turned red in his sister's grasp.

Sophie

The king of Viguran looked more like his brother all the time, and while the lords paid homage to him she couldn't help but see Hurvir. Ultiir was dressed like her dead husband was the day he died. Layers of robes and cloaks over silk tunics stitched with gold. His purple robe draped to the floor with flying owls all around. Ultiir held his head high, but she could see the strain the jeweled crown placed on his neck. Sophie stood a little to the right of her husband wearing a dress as green as an emerald that her handmaids, Amalla and Renna, spent all morning slipping on her. A few of the lords kissed her hand after they were done with Ultiir. Even less were paying their respects to the queen mother who sat in the front row of the great hall. Rila de'Tro did not look happy. But when did she ever?

The lord of Rushton had just swore his allegiance to Ultiir when he came over to her and bowed his head. "My queen. I also pledge my loyalty and all of Rushton to you. May your marriage last until the end of days."

His dry lips kissed her hand as she said, "thank you, my lord, and if I'm ever in Eiselton please come visit." The lord backed away and Sophie could feel Ultiir's eyes on her.

The herald called once the lord of Rushton was gone. "Here

all the way from Riverton in the stead of her brother, the Duke Adyn Gallient, comes the Lady Annue Gallient."

Lady Annue had graying hair but other than that she looked like Sophie had remembered, not that Annue wished to see her. She was wearing a green dress with wolf fur wrapped around her neck, her hands gloved to protect against the cold outside. She bowed like the rest of the men, her dress stretching awkwardly, lords leaning to get an intimate view of the once queen. "Your Grace, I, on behalf of my brother, pledge not only Riverton to you but the whole of the Eastlands. Most of the fighting has been happening in the foothills of my brother's duchy. I hope he is handsomely rewarded for the great lengths he has gone to protect the throne for you."

"Rise Lady Annue." Ultiir said. "The whole court knows this cannot be easy for you after what my brother did, but, may the Four guide him, he is gone and I am not my brother. I welcome your loyalty and that of your brother's. The Eastlands will greatly benefit from pledging and fighting for me, I can assure you."

Lady Annue kissed Ultiir's hand and moved over to Sophie. Her deep voice became a whisper. "My queen. I should give you my thanks, and all those years ago I thought it would be Rasmi who would take him out."

Sophie hadn't given much thought to Hurvir's other wives. Rasmi was the duchess of Cedawr in Terrop, just a short jot from Sophie's duchy. Hurvir had cast her aside as well when she didn't give him children. Annue kissed her hand as Sophie said, "I do not know what you mean."

"Of course not." The lady winked. "Our dear old husband just choked on pie." Annue went back into the crowd of lords and ladies, Rila de'Tro with a disgusted look at Hurvir's first wife. The herald called for the lord of Forecreak but Sophie stopped listening. *She thinks I killed Hurvir. Does the queen mother? Does the entire realm?* Her hands fidgeted as the Forecreak lord gave them a kiss. *What does he think?* She looked at a glaring Ultiir. *I bet he's spread it to push suspicion off of him and the council. But he loves me. Why would he?*

Sophie swallowed the lump in her throat and found the queen mother's glare turned to her. *She has to know.* Before she could worry anymore the herald called for the lord of Montlahead. Sophie thought she was looking at Lord Gofrei Geary, but his corpse was headless. It was his brother who walked down the aisle to the king, Gilfred. They both shared the same dark complexion but Gilfred's head was bald and he didn't look to be always drunk.

No one in the crowd, save for maybe Rila de'Tro, could see Ultiir's face change. It was the slightest hint of discomfort. His eyelids lowered just a bit to hide the twitch in his right eye. Gilfred bowed at Ultiir's feet. "Your Grace, I am here on behalf of not only my nephew, the young Gerold, lord of Montlahead, but also for my late brother, may the Four watch over him." Gilfred stared at his leather shoes, his gray cloak falling over his knee. The crowd was silent. No one in the hall could forget what happened to Gofrei, his head cut off by Ultiir and delivered to the bastard in Whitehall.

"Do you have more to say, Gilfred?" Ultiir's foot was tapping.

Gilfred stood and glared at the king. "You murdered my brother. You cut his head off and sent his body to his wife and son in Montlahead." The cloak flew back and Gilfred flashed a dagger. The people in the hall screamed and shouted as the knife raced toward Ultiir's heart, but Sir Lovis and Sir Gid were much too quick. Lovis knocked the dagger to the floor and Gid jumped from Rila's side and pulled Gilfred away. Sir Achen yanked Sophie back as Gofrei's brother was screaming obscenities and curses. About Ultiir culling his enemies and naming them mages to protect himself. Ultiir was frozen as Lovis made sure he was alright. Rila de'Tro stood and shouted for the ceremony to end for the day, continuing on the morrow, and the great hall cleared.

Sophie wrestled away from Achen and Gid helped Rila up the steps. Both of them checking on Ultiir. "Punishable by death." Rila screamed. "That treacherous man won't see the stars tonight. If I were younger I would swing the sword myself."

"Relax, mother." Ultiir placed a hand on her old shoulder. "I thought you said Sir Gid could smell danger?"

Sir Gid straightened his back, "I am sorry, Your Grace, I should have known from the cloak."

"And that family has always been trouble." The queen mother said. "If only you knew their father and what he did to the poor people of Montlahead you would never ask for their loyalty again. I think it's far past time to name a new lord of that wretched town."

"Yes, the first thing I will do when I get back to Vigur is usurp the claim of an infant lord." Ultiir rolled his eyes. "I think it's past time I retired to my chamber."

"And what was Lady Annue doing coming here?" Rila de'Tro ignored her son and spoke loud enough for the echo to carry her words outside. "That bitch knows not to show her face in Goldfield after what she did to my sweet Hurvir."

"What did she whisper to you?" Ultiir asked Sophie and all

eyes turned to her, none worse than the queen mother.

Sophie stammered. "She … the lady wished me well in my marriage."

Rila crossed her arms. "That *does* sound like her."

"We'll be in our bedroom if you need us." Ultiir grabbed Sophie's arm and she never felt more happy to be with him. The queen mother was shrewd and smart and Sophie hated being around her.

"Give me a grandchild." Rila de'Tro called out as they climbed the stairs and Sophie blushed.

She stopped as they reached a landing, their guards trailing just behind. "Are you sure you're alright?"

"The dagger didn't touch me. I'm more upset by all those disgusting pigs-for-lords putting their mouths on your hand. I would understand if you scrubbed the skin raw." Ultiir said with a chuckle, but his eyes weren't laughing, they were serious.

"It wasn't so bad, they were just pledging their loyalty to us."

"You know how many wanted to fuck you? I could feel their eyes on you, and what was that with the Rushton lord? Why would you want him to visit you in Eiselton?"

Sophie's cheeks grew red and she wanted to roll her eyes at the odd accusation, but she needed Ultiir to be happy so he didn't cast her aside. "I was just being courteous, my dear husband. I can't even remember his name."

"Good." Ultiir wrapped his arms around her waist, grabbing her backside. "You know they can't pleasure you the way I can." He kissed her on the lips. "And these lips stay mine."

Sophie wanted to push away, the happiness she felt gone.

But she kept kissing as there was no reason to make him angry. "And your's mine."

When they were finished Sophie said, "I think I am going to take a walk along the river."

Ultiir handed his heavy crown to Lovis. "You seem to enjoy the Montla here more than in Vigur. You know it's the same river right?"

"I find it more peaceful when you can't hear the city and it isn't clogged with riverboats."

"You're not meeting someone are you?" Ultiir had a playful tone, but again his eyes did not. "Remember when we saw each other along the Ritae? It was magical."

"Of course I remember, but the Montla is the river of life and I enjoy it a bit more. I also think some alone time for us both will do wonders." Sophie hugged her husband. "You need some sleep after everything that's happened."

"I will sleep when the war is won."

Ultiir didn't want to let go of her hand, but eventually they parted ways. Sir Achen escorted Sophie to the Montla so she could cry and curse the gods and figure out what to do.

Sophie bundled up under coats of fur. *Is the city cold or is Rila de'Tro still around?* Sir Achen stayed even closer to her, bumping into her back a few times, always accompanied by a "Sorry, Your Majesty."

"Thank you for being so quick earlier." Sophie told her guard as they reached the steps to the wheatfields. "I'm not sure if Gilfred would've attacked me but just know I do appreciate you."

"It is my duty, my Queen. I couldn't live with myself if something happened to you."

"Would you let me go to the river alone?"

Sir Achen took a step back. "The king was nearly assassinated, Your Grace. Letting you go alone would be a dereliction of my duties. And the slaves."

She put her hand on her belly. "Let me go alone. It will be the last time I ask. Do not make me command you."

He straightened his back and raised his head like a good knight. "Yes, Your Grace, but please do not go out of my sight."

Sophie said nothing as she turned and followed the path through the fields, passed whispering slaves and joyous masters. The Montla roared like never before. Rain or snow was giving the river more life than the heat of summer. She wanted to jump in and let the current take her to Vigur. She didn't have to fear killings in the protection of the palace. Nor Rila de'Tro. She wouldn't complain if the current took her past Vigur and instead dropped her off at Udello or even the Seler Bay. *If only father and mother would let me. Why did I listen to them? Why did I stay? I should be a widow back in Vallnioc not dodging daggers and hurtful words from my mother-by-law.* "An heir. That is what's needed. You marry this new king and produce heirs for him." Her father had said to her by the Ritae, and she was a dutiful daughter who did what she was told. But she didn't want to give Ultiir his heirs. Any power she would get would go away the moment a son was born.

She closed her eyes and took in the winter air. The freshness of the air turned sour quickly. The smell of smoke overwhelmed her. The river's roars not drowning out the sound of shouting and running. Behind her the fields were aflame. Her face hot like it was noon on a summer's day.

Against her better judgment she went toward the fire, that

was the way into town of course. She stopped as her boot found blood. Master Ayter's head was split open, a mess of gray and red congealing around his dead body. Women screamed from the town, soldiers rushing to protect the lords and ladies and most importantly the king. Sir Achen, who was right at the steps, was gone. *Dead,* she thought as her mind raced. *One more piece of home gone.*

Sophie stayed on the path. Either the smoke or the thought of a dead Sir Achen made it hard to breathe. The sounds of dying men and women filled her ears, but she had to focus. The de'Tro manor was the safest place in the city and she wasn't close. If Devro was attacking she would be the perfect hostage. As she prayed for safety an arrow flew by her ear. Behind her a slave with a hatchet dropped dead. A guard in the city was waving, "my Queen. Come to me." His face was impaled by a spear before he could stop yelling.

She didn't know that guard, but the thought of Achen meeting the same fate drove her to tears. The smoke from the out-of-control fire and her tears blinded her as she ran. Before she knew what was happening she crashed to the ground. Shouts growing around her. Wiping away her tears she saw half a dozen slaves encircling her. Ready to rape or kill her. *This is what I get for being so ungrateful. I have a life inside me and I wish to jump in the Montla. Now the gods punish me.*

The queen closed her eyes at the shouts of "get her" and "rip her dress". The shouts turned away from her and into begging and pleading before there was no sound but the fire and her weeping. "Sir Achen?" She asked the man kneeling in front of her, but it wasn't her guard, it was a slave she knew. Clava.

"I wouldn't let those monsters get you." He held out his hand and Sophie recoiled. "We need to get you to safety. The town? Is that where you want to go?" Sophie nodded her head, coughing from the smoke. "I will take you." She took his hand and they ran toward the stone steps.

"What's happened? Is it the bastard?" Sophie asked as they dodged more fleeing slaves.

"Who? No, some of the others were upset like we always are, but my lashing was the last straw for them. We planned an escape. Now we're doing just that."

"A slave revolt? In Goldfield?" She had heard the reports of slaves revolting in the Eastlands, but this was the first in the Kinglands in years. They reached the steps and ran faster, hiding behind buildings and jumping away from soldiers and commoners. The de'Tro manor towered above the rest. Clava pulled Sophie forward.

As they neared the manor the number of soldiers grew. Clava hid behind a bakery, smoke from the fields darkening the city. "You can make it from here."

Sophie wiped her brow of sweat. "Why don't you come? I can tell them you saved me. You won't have to run forever."

"I do not wish to be a slave any longer."

"Just a servant, no slave." Sophie was gasping for air. "I am the queen, they will not question me. You can serve me in the palace."

"That is a slave by another name." Clava pushed Sophie into the street. "Goodbye."

The soldiers saw Sophie and started racing and calling for her. "Good luck, Clava." The slave - or freedman - disappeared into the town, following the trail of smoke.

Bertin

Humans were never happy to see elves. Elves meant destruction and violence. His father hanged any elf caught in the city, his ancestors led raids in the marches to route elves from their hiding places. But mites were strange. They welcomed the elves. People clapped and cheered for them as they rode through the streets of Cluo. Never had he seen such a spectacle. The people of Rowan didn't even cheer when their prince rode in on horseback, they wouldn't cheer if he got back to the city alive as much as he hoped they would.

He never knew why Aveline liked the mites so much. They were a queer people with queer customs and ways of living that went against everything they were taught growing up. Bertin liked the rebellious side of Aveline. The vein that would take over their father's brow when she made him mad. But Rainvealand? She even learned the language. The High Doma tried to curse Aveline for forsaking the Four and the Many for the Ancient One. It always made him chuckle. His sister wouldn't have it, did everything in her power to get their father angry with the High Doma, and eventually he was replaced.

"Why don't they care about the Pywaln Uprising?" Bertin

had asked Thatar as they were eating spicy noodles, his cheek throbbing but his stomach more hungry. "Anha Jorbstah?"

"No human is still alive to remember that. Vhistela will tell you how the ramoryr reacted all those decades ago. War and bloodshed followed. Mi'rallen was overrun." Thatar slurped his noodles, leaving a greasy mess on his chin. "But the humans north of the *Efryn* and the ramoryr don't get along do they? They were glad when we took part in stopping the *ropfryn* from controlling their lands and have been kind to us ever since."

"So if my cousin never attacked you'd still be warring and I wouldn't be here?" Bertin cursed Hurvir under his breath. "What a terrible father Devro has."

They had continued through the city, stopping by the ocean and taking a proper bath. Even Bertin was allowed to partake. The salt burned his cheek, but the rest of his body was relieved. While he was sitting on the beach overlooking the Purvon he scratched at his missing finger. It was somewhere in the heavens with the Dragon, the elves made sure of it. How mangled would his body be by the time he got back home? What else would be broken? Missing? *Father will hardly recognize me.* Kelltar didn't allow them to rest long, he wanted them in Anha Jorbstah before the next new moon and the Rainvealandian festivities.

Now, they rode beneath the Kash. The sides of the hills and mountains terraced as far as the eye could see and flooded to grow rice. Slaves being beaten for not working fast enough, straw hats popping out of the fields as the elves went by. They had been riding for a few days. The city of Agtera was deep in the mountains so they didn't see it, but the road to the rich ore deposits was busier than the border with Telemaw.

Perfect place to get lost, Bertin thought. *Kelltar can follow me into the city and I can surprise him with a chunk of iron.* But he didn't go. He couldn't risk another massacre like in Telemaw. *Even if they are just mites.*

"What's happening to me?" He asked himself.

"What was that?" Thatar turned. Bertin shook his head. "Don't worry you're not becoming an elf just because you share meals with us. Your people have nothing to worry about."

Bertin chuckled. "Ever had a human try to become an elf?"

"A few." Thatar said as Erona dodged a tree stump. "Humans who come live with us in Mi'rallen, learn our ways, customs, language. It's hard to trust them at first, but we've never had a problem. Even a few halflings running around."

Bertin couldn't believe why any human would throw their life away to live on an island with elves. After all the stories he was told growing up. The elves were monsters. "You have a family?" Bertin asked as he thought of Ioelena and her murdered brothers.

"Of course. I'm not very old though, born right before all of *Mi'tor* was at war with the northern empire, but Ariad is her name. She hopes to have many children when I return to continue our lineage."

"And the rest of them?" Bertin motioned to the elves on horseback in front. The high sun causing beads of sweat to fall off their necks. He missed the rains of winter. "I'm assuming all but Kelltar have someone out there."

Thatar laughed. "Even Kelltar has someone. A beautiful creature he is."

Bertin couldn't imagine anyone wanting to be with the violent Kelltar. "What's his name?"

"Chaill. I believe he is the same age as Kelltar even. Rare for us elves. Ariad is a century older than me." Thatar giggled. "She didn't want me to go to Oléma, but the Dragon willed it and I do not question the Dragon. Vhistela's family also worried for her. Her. The elf who can take down a dozen men with one arrow and disappear into the trees before any can find her."

"Wonder what my family's doing."

"Pillaging?" Thatar said with a smirk then dropped his eyes. "I'm sure they miss you too. Worried. What family wouldn't be?" He shrugged. Kelltar shouted in elvish and Thatar translated. "We'll stop behind that ridge," he pointed to a small, rocky hill.

"Surprised you haven't tried to run." Eyln said as they unpacked the horses and prepared a fire. "All this open land and you choose to stay with elves."

"Nowhere to go." Bertin helped Thatar with Erona's saddle. *Aveline would laugh in my face if she saw me this close to a horse. Laugh of how I was never a great rider. Tell me to join the groomsmen in the stables,* he smiled as he missed his sister joking at him.

"Kelltar thought we would have killed you by now." Eyln stoked the flame. "He thought you would try to run near the Alhya. Maybe you actually like us."

Bertin glared at Kelltar. The large elf was cleaning birds shot by Vhistela. His Telemese sword by his feet. "Maybe some of you." *They are elves,* he told himself, *there's nothing to like. You spit on the memories of your ancestors and all those who were killed.* But he looked at Thatar who brushed his mare and kissed her neck. The nicest of them all. And Eyln made conversation at least, Vhistela gave him food. Kelltar was the only one he truly hated. The elf who killed Ioelena. The one who needed to die the most. "I had never met elves before the desert."

"Were we everything you hoped for?" Eyln asked.

Bertin scratched his chin. "Destroying cities and sacrificing humans? I'd say the stories were true."

Vhistela emerged from a small river where she had bathed. "We are preparing for Nhamcaryn. The more land we take back the easier it will be for the Dragon to return and find us. Save us."

Bertin had heard of Nhamcaryn when he was almost burned alive, instead losing his finger. *Maybe the Dragon liked a human finger.* "No one ever tells me what this Nhamcaryn is," he said.

"The end of everything." Vhistela dried her naked body. "At least for you. The Dragon will bring about peace to our world, our kind. Elves will once more rule this land and humans will go back to serving us." *Won't be much different for me than.* She stood there naked, Bertin averted his eyes like he always did. "Did you not see her body?"

He knew Vhistela was talking about Ioelena. "What type of relationship do you think we had? All she did was release me. Nothing more."

The elf shrugged her clothes back on. "She was with you for weeks watching over you. How are we to know what happened?"

"No halflings were going to be born if that's what you were worried about." *Especially not with her back opened and bleeding.* "Where were you in Lisan Biresdea? I never saw you until it was time for us to leave."

"I patrolled the walls." She said as she found her green and brown clothes to blend in with the trees and dirt. "My aim stopped any Olemán from getting too close."

"What about when I escaped?"

"Patrolling the far western wall." Vhistela smirked. "You would have never made it into the desert if I were there."

"I had help." He said remembering Wilclef and how he sacrificed himself so Ioelena and Bertin could get away. *Just another one I killed.*

Thatar began to cook some of Kelltar's birds. The angry elf glaring at the world. "Why did you leave Rowan?" Thatar asked.

"*Atha Bàn.*" Kelltar huffed, the light from the fire casting shadows on his face. It made him look evil. Like something from Veltoora. The doma would've preached to run away from him as they tried to cast him away.

Thatar nodded, "Yes, Atha Bàn. Why did you leave it?"

Bertin had never heard the elvish name for Rowan before. What they called the city when they founded it long before humans arrived and took it over. "My father wanted me to see more of the world. He didn't know that the Oléman king …" he used an elvish word then cleared his throat. "He didn't know the Telemese king was an idiot who would get me nearly killed."

Thatar gave a cooked breast of the small bird to Bertin. All for him. The prince devoured it without a second thought, the juices poured down his chin. "We only heard bad things about the king. That's why Blaenda and the elders wished to attack him."

"Too afraid of meeting the Rowai horses in an open field?"

"Afraid or smart?" Vhistela said. "We know our weaknesses. Why do you think we've kept to Mi'rallen all these centuries?

I might be able to take down a hundred men with my bow but sooner rather than later a human will stop me."

"And we know how vicious humans are with captured elves." Kelltar said, speaking the common language for the first time in days. "The little ones hanged outside city walls. Others with hundreds of stab wounds, pieces of their body missing, crows pecking out their eyes. Your lot rape and torture us and expect us to stay hidden on our island and in the mountains. No more. Maybe that's the way our ancestors did it in the past, but our numbers have grown, our mages have gotten more powerful, and Nhamcaryn is coming. This might be the last chance we have to take back our home."

"I was taught the histories when elves controlled the land." Bertin played with the dirt by his feet. "The dwarven and human slaves. The way my ancestors were treated. You taught us all we know."

"Yet we didn't push the humans from this land. Our ancestors shared it as best they could. Since the humans have taken control they have never called for peace." Kelltar towered over the prince, his shadow looming with the setting sun. "How long have we cried for war to end? How many times have your people denied us? This was our home first. Some elves think we can live side by side, but every time we try we end up slaughtered. The humans don't want to share."

"So you want us all dead? At least my suffering would be over."

Kelltar moved quick as a lightning bolt. He slammed Bertin back into the dirt and held the dagger to his throat. "Should I do it? End your suffering right here and leave you for the ramoryr to find your rotting body?"

"Enough Kelltar." Eyln said. "This isn't what the elders

want." Kelltar shouted back to him in elvish, probably a curse.

Vhistela said, "You don't want to be tried for going against our elders' wishes. This isn't you Kelltar. I have known you since you were a baby. Killing someone who is beaten and starved? Weaponless? Let him go."

The elf clenched his jaw and growled like a wild animal. "What do you say?"

Bertin stared at Kelltar and his shaking eyes. "Not yet," he said before spitting in the elf's face. Kelltar pushed off of Bertin's body with all his weight, bruising some of his ribs. Kelltar cursed again in elvish while Thatar yanked Bertin to his feet. "I can't die yet. Not until I kill you." The elves stopped. Kelltar's nostrils flared but he found his horse and kicked until he was galloping under the rice fields.

Yvanne

When they emerged from the dwarven tunnels the sunlight blinded her as it reflected off the snow. Eventually a storm blew over and they hunkered down behind some rocks. Snow filled every nook and cranny of the mountains, all the passes, all the dens, and all the evergreen trees were a mess of white powder.

"How far to the lords again?" Devro asked as he brushed his clothes off and shivered.

"Meadowton is near," Lord Aimora said, "we just have to find it."

"And why do the lords and their people descend the mountains every winter?" Pollard asked. "We always heard they were strong for surviving the peaks, turns out they're liars too."

"Should we bring you to the peaks during winter and see how long you survive?" Aimora and the Lodean chuckled. "It is far too cold. Plus their people get to marry from the other peaks, keeps everyone from fucking their sister." Aimora laughed. "Shall we go? We don't need another storm to hit and I'm ready to see the lords."

As if on cue spear points emerged out of nothing and a dozen bearded men and long haired women with fur hats and long robes descended on them. Pollard whipped out his sword and readied for a fight until Lord Aimora said, "sheath your weapon unless you want us all to die."

"You do not command me." Pollard raged but Yvanne nodded in agreement with Aimora.

"Now is not the time Pollard," she said to her brother. "I trust Lord Aimora, and I also think we've found who we are looking for." Pollard chewed his lip but put his sword away, his face red but not from the cold.

"*Aris ra?*" One of the bearded men said in his language. Besta walked forward with his hands in the air and began to converse with the man. Spears and eyes followed him. The mountains surrounded them like a prison, and Yvanne prayed the Lords of the Peaks would be welcoming.

"Alright," Besta said after a short talk. "They will escort us to Meadowton and the lords will meet us there. So far they are surprised a king and queen of Viguran would travel all this way. They've never met one. Suspicious even."

The fighters with spears walked all around the Lodean. Their faces were angry. Their beards and hair white with snow. Some rode on horses much shorter than Yvanne's and stockier too. They seemed to be made of muscle. *Where in the peaks do these horses ride?* she thought as she imagined the peaks nothing but jagged rocks.

Lord Aimora pointed toward the mountains above. "Can you see the towers?" Yvanne looked and could barely make out what he was talking about. They looked like twigs hanging from a tree branch, but she could see them. Stone towers extending from the mountains, hanging over the edge of cliffs. "You can see the whole world from up there."

"Wouldn't you just see more mountains?" Pollard quipped.

"Do you see, my king?" Yvanne asked Devro.

"Oh yes," Devro never looked up. He kept his eyes trained on his horse's mane. "How do you think these lords will react?"

"I think we've nothing to worry about." Yvanne said. "It is an honor that you are the first king they will ever set eyes on, they will want nothing more than to help."

"I just don't want to go all this way to die in the mountains."

"Nonsense, Your Grace," Yvanne said before eyeing Aimora who chuckled at the young king. "We've a long and glorious rein ahead of us. We can't die here."

"I don't know …" Devro said and Yvanne was going to respond but he was looking to the other side, not talking to her. She didn't know who he was talking to, but she had more important things to worry about.

The fighters stopped as the mountains opened to a meadow, somehow the grass was still green, the flowers still blooming, the water still flowing, the people not wearing furs. The Lodean hollered as they stripped off their winter clothes and embraced the warmth. The meadow was teeming with people. There were houses and shops, cobblers and bakers, gardeners and shepherds. The bleating of sheep echoed off the rock faces on every side of them. Women and men and children enjoyed bathing in pools of water with steam rising off them. Fighters were on the other side of the village, swinging swords and stabbing with spears, running in armor and jumping over streams. Their grunts echoed with the sheeps.

"How is any of this possible?" Pollard said as he dismounted and helped Yvanne off Snowfall. "It must be magic."

"Magic or steam," Orra said, "what does it matter? This is

the best I've felt since winter started."

Devro even cracked a smile as he grazed the top of a stream with his fingers and drank. "Pure," he said before dunking his head into the water.

Some of the Lodean wanted to flirt with the naked men and women in the pools but the men of the peaks weren't letting them through. "Lord Aimora," Yvanne said, "remind your men we are here on business."

"Men! Put your cocks away!" Aimora shuffled over to them as he too took off his furs.

Four men from a wooden cottage emerged, all wearing green robes that dragged across the meadow. "You are here for us," one of them said. A tall man only a few years older than Yvanne.

"Lord Aute," she said and prayed she guessed right. The smile that crept over the man showed that she did. "It is a pleasure to meet you and the other Lords of the Peaks. We have heard many good things about you."

Lord Aute bowed his head. "And we've heard nothing of you."

"This is a letter with Duke David Rely's seal," Devro said. He handed the letter to an older lord. His beard white from age instead of snow. The seal was merely a bear.

"Is this what the Rely's chose as their seal?" The old man grunted. "Tell me the last time this David Rely fought a bear."

My lord —" Yvanne started before the old man interrupted her.

"— Lord Cul. At least pretend to know our names."

"I know you all," Yvanne giggled. "I can see the faces of the gods upon your robes." Their robes all had images of peaks embroidered, but the faces above the peaks were different.

Lord Cul's was of Meret. Lord Emni, another older man but not yet graying, of Sam the Sayer. Lord Plantan, who seemed made of muscle just like the horses, of Swallow. The young Lord Aute had a four-pointed star above his peak. Mount Vigura was in the Kinglands, the de'Tro's not wanting the holy peak to be given to the Relys centuries ago.

Lord Plantan laughed in Lord Cul's face. "I guess that does give it away. Katsi told us you are the king and queen of Viguran. If I may, you both seem young."

"You haven't heard about the war?" Devro asked.

Lord Emni rubbed his knee and winced. "Some rumblings from merchants before the snow came down, but a full on war, no. You coming to us means you're winning, I presume."

Devro stared at the flowers and said, "or losing."

Yvanne nodded but wished Devro would speak to the lords with more respect. The war could only be won with them on his side. "I hope you take no offense, but us losing is precisely the reason we're here. We don't want to involve your people in a war, but the Lands of Asara is in open revolt and you live in the duchy, so we hoped you would come to our aid."

Lord Cul furrowed his brows. "Come to your aid? What has any Rely ever done for us? We are a mountain people and have no reason to travel to the lower lands and fight and die. We've stayed out of every war you people have fought in."

"If I may," Aimora said, "we lords know each other. We have traveled the mountains, enjoyed each other's company, and even trained our warriors together. We share Lodean blood. I have decided, along with my people, that Lodeanhold will fight with Devro and Yvanne. The man who calls himself king is no friend to you, and, even worse, his wife is the princess of Terrop. If the Terropian king gets involved then the mountain passes will not be safe for anyone. I know your fighters are strong, but the Terropians have the numbers. It will be a slaughter."

"Predicting the future now?" Lord Enmi asked as he sat on a stump. "We do not know what will come, and our warriors will best everyone on any day. That's the reason you came to us right? For our warriors."

"Never meeting with any Lords of the Peaks until you need our strength." Lord Cul said. "Why are we supposed to care who sits the throne of Viguran?"

"It is my birthright." Devro said.

Lord Aute nodded in understanding but said, "sometimes we do not get what we want. Sometimes it's best to give up your dreams and find a new calling in life."

"No," Devro clenched his fists. "I am the king of everyone in Viguran and that includes you just as it includes the Lodean and the Del and the Ritae and the Veck'kop. I came here in person because my council said you would be stubborn and not care to fight for me, but I am not asking you, I am telling you."

Lord Aimora sighed and Yvanne closed her eyes as she took a breath. *All this way for nothing. All this way to be turned down and now the war is over.*

Lord Emni looked at the other lords before saying, "Perhaps we should discuss this in private?"

"Tell us about the one who sits the throne," Lord Plantan said. "We must hear your reasons for going against him if we are to decide."

"Ultiir?" Devro said. "He killed my father, his own brother, the king. That goes against all our laws in this land."

Lord Cul said, "again, why should we care? People kill each other all the time but it leads to war when it's your family. When we have a murder in the peaks we do not go to war. We speak about the best way to move forward, unlike you." Lord Cul shook his head in disgust. "How different will you be from this Ultiir anyhow?"

Devro shuffled his feet and stared at the ground so Yvanne said, "Ultiir's forces destroyed an entire village. Everyone, man, woman, and child was dead. It was the worst thing I'd ever seen and I've lived through famines and hard winters. Devro has never, would never, do such a thing. He values everyone's life."

"Except our fighters." Lord Cul said as he watched the people train.

"Terrop is an entire kingdom," Lord Plantan said, "we'll be cleaning bodies in the passes for weeks. All why you gallivant around Whitehall in your safety."

"No," Yvanne continued, "there are dwarven tunnels in these mountains, do you know them? Your warriors can use them to attack the Terropians in secret and vanish back into the rocks. While you do that we will be marching on Vigur. We will all be fighting. You in the mountains and us in the fields. It won't be pretty, but with your help we can win."

"I think we should do it." Lord Aute said almost as a whisper.

Lord Cul's face twisted and Lord Emni shook his head before saying, "maybe."

Lord Plantan smiled. "What's that necklace?" He was looking at Yvanne's locket. Her sunstone.

"It is the four-pointed star of my religion." *And the stone that gives me power,* she thought. She had seen the bands of warmth radiating off the hot pools, but no one took any in. If Lord Plantan was an éithrio he hid it well.

"I say we should join," Plantan said with a smirk. "We'll get to test our strength."

"You want my people to die?" Lord Cul fumed. "What have the kings of Viguran ever given us? Our ancestors used to live in the lowlands as well before they were all pushed to the mountains by the kings. Scores of people were killed. Now we're supposed to protect them?"

"What is it you want Lord Cul?" Yvanne asked as Devro twiddled his thumbs. "His Grace is ready to give you anything. Coin? Or is it freedom you want? Freedom for Mount Meret from Viguran? Freedom for all the peaks? You will get it if you join with us."

The Lords of the Peaks were salivating. Devro's eyes lit in shock but he said nothing. "Freedom?" Lord Cul rubbed his long beard. "How can we be sure you're telling the truth?"

"Trust." Yvanne said as she straightened her back to stand taller than the old man.

"Trust a Veck'kop?" Lord Cul laughed. "Trust a king and queen of Viguran?" He looked to the other lords but they didn't make eye contact, Lord Cul was alone.

Never trust a Lodean, is what her father said to her. But she trusted Lord Aimora enough to lead them to Meadowton. Now, she prayed Cul would trust her enough to join the war.

"If you go to Vigur and take all your men with you, who will be defending Whitehall from attack?" Lord Cul asked and Yvanne knew he would join, he wouldn't be asking if he wasn't planning it. "The other three lords can guard the passes, stop any Terropian intrusion, I want me and my people to defend Whitehall. You can't let your home fall while you're away."

"You're joining?" Lord Enmi asked. He rubbed his knees and stood. "Then so be it, all of us will join. The Lords of the Peaks will fight with King Devro."

And Queen Yvanne, she wanted to say but didn't. Devro's smile didn't reach his eyes.

"Then we should get to planning." Lord Aimora Dore laughed and the Lodean behind them shouted in agreement.

As Meadowton became livelier, Devro kept his head down. "You mustn't show them that you're troubled." Yvanne said. "It could demoralize them."

"But I am troubled." Devro pouted. "Even if we took Vigur, what's the point? Rule when I know Raimund is dead. Rule at the palace my father was murdered, where my uncle will probably die. And that's if Mar and Tundavik get Lord Blume to join our side."

"Just because you're king doesn't mean you need to be worried so much about the war. There are others fighting it in your name. Tundavik and Mar will convince Lord Blume, I'm sure of it, and now we have the Lords of the Peaks to stop any attack by King Anvrin. We're winning this war much more than we were a month ago. We just need you to give the fighters some confidence. We won't be here long, then we can plan our attack in Whitehall." Yvanne grabbed his hand and rested it on her belly. "You also need to think about the good. I will give you an heir within the year. That's something." Devro smiled as he rubbed her belly. "Let's go watch them train."

Flora

It was small and hot and cramped. Not that she would complain now that winter gripped the Flewthlands. The winds sweeping across the Maera Steppe and jumping over the Flit River to bring them snow. Her corset tightened around her torso with every bump in the road. Large jewelry swayed and clinked as the carriage kept on. She hated carriage rides, had since she was a child. Her father and mother would drag her along to the many lords of the Flewthlands, making her back ache and little legs sore from sitting.

Those seats were at least cushions of wool, these were bare wood. Lord Barnet Lovell, her husband, forbade her from walking beside the wagon. "We'll be there in short." He told her when the light first tore through the darkness of night. Now, it was midday.

As the carriage rose and fell over the snowy hills, so too did her view of the city, but she was lucky enough to take in glimpses. The houses made of timber, some clay, others stone. Saltwater pierced her nose and drove her wild. Reminding her of her childhood running around the castle and playing in the sea. The only good thing that would come out of this trip to Storyah was that she could see her father again.

She hadn't seen Lord Blume in almost a decade. When her grandfather decided to start his rebellion against the crown she was sent away to Woodrun for safety. That's where she fell in love with Barnet. Her father gave his blessing for the marriage, but didn't bother to come, and didn't visit when Little Flora was born either. *Always wanting a male to be his heir.*

As they rode near Northflat, a small village just north of Storyah, she looked at her husband and daughter. Lord Barnet didn't look back. He wore gray and had a blue coat, the colors of Woodrun, and his dark trousers and shoes matched the forest that surrounded their home. He always loved nature and could spend days looking out the window of a carriage ride. Ever since they received word from her father though he had been even more quiet. She didn't know why a lord's council could get him to be so upset. Florance, only seven, dangled her little legs off the bench. She wore a dress with a rainbow of flowers stitched throughout the fabric. Her blonde hair atop her head in a tower of golden rope with yellow ribbons holding it in place. Flora smiled as her daughter sang to herself.

"Getting closer." Tedbalt Ver, her plump driver, yelled out. The city beyond kept getting bigger and bigger. The walls would eventually dwarf the carriage.

"Mother?" Little Flora said while looking at her with her candy blue eyes, so sweet.

"Yes, my darling?" Flora rubbed her hand on her daughter's shoulder.

"Have I been here before? It doesn't look the same."

No, because your father hates this place and your grandfather never wanted to see you, she thought but she said, "No. But

I was born here just like your grandparents. Remember grandmother Rue?" Her daughter nodded. "She visited Woodrun from here many times before she died. I'll show you her dresses." Florance clapped.

"Dresses?" Barnet said but still looked out the window with a clenched jaw. "We're here to discuss war. Not play dress up."

"War?" Florance asked.

"You don't agree with the duke's call?" Flora asked, shushing their daughter.

"I will not send my men to fight for some bastard prince who thinks he's owed all in this world. We don't need another war. Your grandfather's rebellion wasn't that long ago, neither was the war with the mites. Don't you remember?"

"Like it was yesterday." In truth she didn't remember much. The fighting happened to the south of the Flewthlands, and Barnet was barely a man when he went to fight the mites.

"The Flewthlands lost thousands of men because of Hurvir's war. I lost five brothers and my father. Horrid things took place beyond the Ters-Veck. I don't want Florance growing up in a world like that."

Flora looked at the bronze statue of Meret on the outside corner of the carriage. Each corner had the face of a god. She regularly talked to them hoping for a response, knowing they were watching her from the eyes. "We are already in danger. War is already happening in the Eastlands and the Lands of Asara. What if Lord Rely decided it was time to invade? Woodrun isn't that far from the border."

"Do you mean to scare the child?" Barnet finally looked away from the window and placed a hand on Little Flora's knee, his hazel eyes comforting her. "We have knights to protect us, and Lord Rely is too old and decrepit to plan an invasion." He looked back at Flora. "Did you hear what happened in Riverton? Lord Gallient was able to stop them and he hasn't even been duke for that long.

"Then why not just send your reasonings to my father and be done with it?"

"Because your father is vindictive, so we must make an appearance. I will listen to the deliberations, counter with my own argument, then vote no. I also thought it was time you saw your father and Florance her grandfather."

That last part was a lie. Barnet would rather battle the forces of Veltoora than see Pyre Blume. No, his reasons were different, but he wanted to keep them a secret. Her husband went back to watching the rolling hills, Florance hummed a delicate tune, and Flora sat in silence.

The line to enter Samosay's Gate in the north of the city was long and horrendous. Packs of people shivered together. Frostbitten bodies were being thrown into a mass grave on the roadside. Carriages with lords and ladies sat in ruts waiting to enter. People from the Eastlands had been trekking into the Flewthlands since the beginnings of the war. They were searching for protection behind the large walls and archer towers and wooden barricades.

It was twilight when they finally entered the city and the gate closed behind them. Screams and cries for warmth went up as the portcullis went down. They showed their papers to the guards who ushered them through and told them to steer clear of the main roads due to overcrowding. Tedbalt found some alleyways that were just big enough for the horses and carriage. Curses and insults being thrown at them as they went. Flora had prayed to the large statue of Samosay that was built atop the gatehouse, praying that the war would be over soon. Praying that the Flewthlands wouldn't have to fight for years on end.

Storyah was definitely more crowded then Flora remembered. Vagrants wandered the town asking for coin, half naked whores offered their services, children slept on the steps of manses before guards kicked them out, gaunt people fought the rats for trash. As they passed the city square Flora remembered seeing the fountain of Vigura in the center as a child. He towered over her, pouring water from his jug. Now, he looked to be about her height, and the water had stopped for winter.

A lighthouse above the harbor punched through the dark of the night. A fire burning bright for all to see. Waves crashed below. Tedbalt opened the door to help them to the ground. White flecks of snow landed in their hair and melted on their clothes. The gates were already opened and the drawbridge over the moat lowered for their arrival. In the spring the flowers and trees would make a wonderful sight. Guards and servants bowed as they walked into the inner bailey. *I don't even know these faces,* she thought. They followed the paved path, Flora holding her daughter's hand while Barnet was stiff, until they entered the even darker halls of the castle.

The halls cut through the castle like a maze, some say Pyre the Maker designed the halls for his enemies to get lost. That didn't stop the Veck'kop from invading and ruling over the Flewthlands. They passed the elegant dining room, some servant chambers, and the kitchen smelling of cooked ham and buttered bread, before reaching the great hall. The arches jumping before crashing into the wall behind the throne.

Her father sat in the high seat alone, shadows dancing on

his face from the candles and torches. "Daughter, son." His teeth seemed to light up the room. "And who is this?"

"I'm Florance." The little girl said with a small hop of excitement. Barnet cleared his throat and shook his head at Little Flora. She bowed her head at her grandfather.

"I've read a lot about you. Your mother writes letters and tells me all about your fun in Woodrun. Will you come closer?" Flora nodded to her daughter who stepped forward, Pyre met her halfway and bent on a knee. "You have your grandmother's eyes. She would write to me as well when she lived in Woodrun with you all. She always said 'come visit this wonderful child.' Well, I'm glad to finally meet you." He clasped her hand before going back to his seat. "So, how are the goings-ons in Woodrun?"

Flora wanted to speak, but Barnet always spoke for Woodrun. He was lord after all. "Some people fleeing from the Lands of Asara have taken up refuge in Woodrun, and we're hoping Lord Rely doesn't decide to attack us like he attacked Riverton, but other than that Woodrun is doing fine."

"I'm sure Woodrun will stay quiet, not much happens there. And how is my daughter liking the village?"

Flora bowed her head. "I would sing its praises to the ends of the world. Woodrun is the perfect place to raise Florance. Much quieter. Especially with what's happening beyond the gates of Storyah, it's so cold out there and the stream of people seemed never ending."

"War brings refugees. Not to mention the migrants from Plajul looking for work they can't find in that kingdom. Usually we find a ship to take them. Who knows where they end up."

"Father," Flora said with eyes lowered to keep from seeing Barnet, "will you tell us about the council? Is it possible we could go to war?"

Her father picked his teeth and nodded before saying, "The bastard sent emissaries and I heard them out, but I cannot choose for my people when the lords are the ones who know them better. So whatever the majority says. Maybe war. Maybe not."

"The bastard didn't come himself?" Barnet's voice was like a growl.

"He sent a knight and a lord. No protection for them during a war which was odd, but somehow they managed to reach the city. I'm sure the bastard wants my ships."

"Is Lord Rely here?" Flora asked.

"No, Lord Vandes, he was the duke of the Woodlands some time ago."

"Not a duke anymore." Barnet said under his breath before saying, "How many lords have arrived? If it pleases my lord, I would like to get this vote underway and back to Woodrun as quickly as possible."

"Always so eager," the duke chuckled. "Woodrun is the farthest away so most have been in the city for a few days. A couple more and we'll be ready. I will let the lord and knight make their arguments and let whoever opposes them make theirs. I hope for a quick vote as well."

Barnet nodded. "Do you mind if we retire to our bedchamber? The ride was long and we are sore." Lord Blume nodded. Barnet didn't need to look at Flora and their daughter to know they were following him. Flora always did as she was told.

"I don't want you speaking with Lord Vandes," Barnet

sneered as they got comfortable in their bedchamber. "That man is trouble."

"You know the old duke?" Flora brushed Florance's braids out atop a rose colored bed. "I've never heard of him."

"I know him from the war. He led the fighting in Panscar and Suktir." Barnet was undressing from his gray and brown clothes to a nightgown, warming himself by the lit hearth on the other side of the room. The dark stone walls sweating. "He's not to be trusted."

"My father seems to trust him."

"Your father has always been a fool. Suing for peace when the Flewthlands had the upper hand during his father's rebellion, now trying to drag us into war. He's never known what's best for his people. That's why he called for a council to vote so we would bear the burden depending on the outcome."

Flora sent her daughter to a small bed next to theirs. The snowfall had worsened out the windows, filling them with white powder. "You've always doubted him."

"And I've yet to be proven wrong."

Then they all went to sleep. Barnet seemed always angry especially around bed and when they talked of her father. Flora always went to bed hoping for something different.

***

The morning was cold and fresh snow covered the footprints and dirt from the days before. Florance was playing with Lord Umid's children. Throwing snow in the air and building forts. Even though she hadn't been in the castle walls in so long, Flora felt safe. Long before her grandfather's rebellion she would run along the parapets, dodge guards trying to grab her, leap over cows and hay, jump into her parents' arms. In Woodrun she sat in the manor and watched the trees change in the fall. They were dead now. Not to be reborn until Swallow's Feast.

Flora jumped as a voice came from behind. "I've never been to Woodrun." She turned and saw an older man with peppered hair and beard wearing a red tunic and the ugliest yellow trousers. "Tundavik Vandes," he bowed.

"Pleasure," Flora returned the favor, looking for Barnet as she did, but never finding him. "I'm not sure if it's customary for a duke to bow to a lady though."

"Yes, but I'm no duke. I guess that means you've heard of me."

"My husband, Lord Barnet Lovell, has told me about you. Both of you fought together during the Bezir campaign."

Tundavik scratched his graying beard. "Not a name I remember. Maybe if I saw him."

"Perhaps." Flora said as she thought, *he doesn't seem untrustworthy, but Barnet will be furious if I disobey him.* Then she got lost in his sad, brown eyes. Weary. "And I doubt Woodrun would be to your liking. There isn't much to see but wood," she giggled.

"My home was Ritaeum. I think I'd be fine." Tundavik watched as Little Flora threw snow on a dog who barked and played with her. Flora had heard of awful things befalling Ritaeum, but she never listened close enough to remember. "I hope you know I don't wish to drag you into war."

"Not me, just thousands of men and their lords."

Tundavik giggled and gave a quick nod. "With the Flewth-lands on our side the war will be over much quicker. I can promise you that."

"The only way the war ends is if one of the claimants dies. My husband has told me about your efforts in Riverton, and if the bastard's forces can't even take that city then I don't see you taking Vigur and killing Ultiir."

"Your people are strong. If we are to lay siege to Vigur we will need them."

"You are actually trying to take the capital?" Flora asked, looking into his sad eyes to find a hint of jest.

"If all goes to plan then the war will be won by summer. We'll be feasting to Vigura in the castle with Devro as king, and I think the only way for that to happen is if these lords vote to join us."

Flora smiled but inside she wasn't sure. *Does he already know about Barnet's vote? Is he speaking with me to get my husband to change his mind? Who could've told him?* "I'm sure the deliberations will be exciting. I need to go clean my daughter," she curtsied.

Tundavik said, "and I need to go find my knight."

As Flora was leading Florance back inside, wiping snow from her hair, she saw Barnet atop the wall. His eyes bore into her with disgust.

Ultiir

Sir Achen lay on the table with a purple bruise across his face and coughed as the daken poked and prodded him. Rila de'Tro stood over him. Sophie, whom he was sworn to protect, was upstairs. She wanted to be alone. *She didn't even want me there.*

"So much for a royal guard," his mother said, "letting the queen go off on her own, letting a bunch of dark-skinned slaves knock him down and almost kill her. This is why Sir Gid is going with you to Vigur. If he were in charge of Sophie's protection she wouldn't've even been by the water when the revolt occurred." Rila de'Tro held her head and Ultiir watched his mother hobble over to a chair. *Never did I think stress would be what kills my mother,* he thought.

"It all worked out. Sophie and Sir Achen are both alright."

"And who does that woman think she is?"

Ultiir took a deep breath. "The queen."

Rila chuckled. "No queen would ever put herself in that situation, and did you hear what she did to poor Ayter? Now he's dead too. I knew that man for decades and the slaves had the audacity to kill him and run off like cowards. What kind of kingdom are you running to let this happen? A bastard gaining support for the throne in the Lands, slaves revolting in the Eastlands and now the Kinglands. This is all a mess. It's like Veltoora has been unleashed on us."

"Slaves revolt all the time, mother. The last time I came was to stop a revolt."

"But not like this. Usually they kill a few and our soldiers can take care of this. Who's going to grow the crop? How are we going to be fed? This is all a disaster. Say goodbye to our home. To our kingdom."

"You're being dramatic." Ultiir said. The daken stopped what she was doing for a moment and glanced at the queen mother before going back to rubbing oils on Achen's face.

"Dramatic?" Rila stood, looking fifty years younger as the blood rushed to her face. "Never have I seen Viguran in such disarray. You know the histories as well as I. The bastard war? The princely states? What about the betrayer? At least the kingdom came back from those, sometimes even stronger than before. But I don't see it happening this time. The kingdom that I love, that I ruled with my husband, about to be washed away like a storm and it's all my fault. I wasn't hard enough on you or Hurvir as children and look what's happening. We should've made you stronger men. Stronger rulers. But we were weak minded. We let you get away with too much and now you show leniency to the bastards and the slaves and those who go against you.

"Where are the Margia's? Why have you and your queen not demanded Terropian help? That was the agreement when we convinced Sophie to marry you and they have gone back on their word. Of course, Margias always go back on their word, so who's surprised? Why haven't you demanded the help of the Rowai? Bartel is your cousin and you let him slight you. We protected both Terrop and Rowan from the mites' aggression and this is how they repay us? And you are too weak to do anything about it. I am ashamed to call myself your mother."

The room was silent except for Achen's moans. Rila and Ultiir stared into each other's souls. "Are you done?" Ultiir asked.

"If you understand my point."

"I don't." Ultiir said. "What I do understand is that we are going back to Vigur tonight, and I am done worrying about you. Fix Goldfield yourself," he waved an angry hand as he sneered. "Protect the city from the bastard and his forces alone. I hope you do not die, I really do, but the child who hid in the cupboards with a bruised face worse than Achen prays you do." Rila sat back down, her legs shaking. "I am going to collect my queen and we will be out of the manor by tonight."

"Don't forget," his mother said as he was leaving the chamber, "the only reason she married you was because of me. Without my letters to her parents she would be gallivanting around Terrop fucking anyone who laid eyes on her like the whore she is."

Ultiir slammed the door and Gid jumped. "Still coming?"

The knight nodded. "Protecting the king is the highest honor."

"Then pack." *Such a good protector he gets frightened by a door,* he rolled his eyes with the thought. *Maybe mother wants me to die.*

He scratched his head as he and Sir Lovis climbed the stairs to his bedchamber. The slaves, before the revolt, had cleaned it enough to make his outburst seem unnoticeable save for the broken glass on the doors. Sir Velle, a young member of

Sophie's guard, was in front of the door. "I take it that means the queen is still in here?"

"Yes, Your Grace." Sir Velle said in his accent that reminded him the knight came from Terrop. "I am sure she will be glad to see you."

"Always." The door creaked open and Sophie was sitting on the bed, her hair a matted mess and her eyes red.

"My mother just said the most outlandish thing to me, my darling." He grabbed Sophie's hands and kissed her fingers. She blushed. "She told me that your parents convinced you to marry me." He laughed while Sophie stared out the window. "She's convinced that she runs this whole kingdom, that she can get anyone to bend to her will." He bent down and began to kiss her knees but she pulled away. "What's the matter? The slaves didn't hurt you did they? Why won't you talk to anyone?"

"They scared me is all."

"I'm your husband and your king. You should be able to tell me everything. And if not then I can find the doma."

Sophie pushed him away and warmed herself by the fire. "I don't want to talk to a doma. Any words I have with Meret will be for her alone." She held out her hands and the flames licked her palms. "This is how close I was to dying. To burning. Being left for dead in the wheatfields of one of the most awful places in this world. Your mother would've had a fit."

"You can't let her get to you. She says whatever to make you upset. Like what she said to me." Ultiir touched her shoulder but this time she went to the balcony. "What she said about you and your parents isn't true is it?"

"And what if it was?" She said without turning. "What if

I only married you out of duty to my parents? Would that make you love me any less?"

He coughed from surprise. Her voice was cold, shrewd, manipulative like his mother's. "I would feel hurt, but I know it isn't true. I know you love me."

She crossed her arms and shivered as the breeze came through the balcony. She stared straight out, not looking at Ultiir. "Am I the reason you killed Hurvir?"

Ultiir rushed to her and closed the doors to the balcony. "Keep your mouth quiet. Do you want all of Viguran to know?"

"Did you kill him for me? Were you jealous?"

"I told you the reason. He destroyed this kingdom. You were just a prize."

"Prize." Sophie sat on the bed. "Merely a prize. Your mother helped run this kingdom and all I'm good for is being shared between brothers. Both with cocks that wither away and don't give me a child."

"What?"

"All I'm good for is fucking. That's why you went to bed with me before we were even married, isn't that right? The moment you saw me you wanted one thing and marriage wasn't it. Well you got what you wanted, and committed fratricide in order to get it. Now what?"

Ultiir's face was red. He didn't know from embarrassment or anger. "Why are you talking like this? Why are you pretending I don't love you? That you don't love me? Did some runaway slaves scare you that badly?"

"Tell me one time I said I loved you."

Ultiir took his turn looking out the glass doors. His mother had found a bench and was chatting with Sir Gid while yelling at some men who were cleaning the debris from the revolt. "So what she said is true. You only married me because your parents and my mother made some pact." He huffed. "To think, I talked Urses out of his plan to kill you too."

"Kill me?"

"And I married you for what?" Ultiir began to chuckle. He had to laugh to stop himself from destroying the room again. "You never gave Hurvir a child. Why would you give me one? Everyone always said he had a poisoned seed, but what if his wives were all just barren?" Sophie shifted in bed when Ultiir turned to her. "I find it fitting that I find all this out now. Not only do I have to deal with my mother but now my wife. All husbands must feel the way I feel." He made his way to the door. "We'll be leaving soon. You can follow me or not, but you will not rule the kingdom like my mother did. You do not deserve it."

Sirs Lovis and Velle were speaking with Lord Masson as Ultiir shut the door. "Come to see the queen?"

"Umm," Tedbalt stammered. "No. To see you, Your Grace."

"Good. If Sophie is too young for me then she is far too young for you." Ultiir put his arm around Tedbalt's shoulder and ushered him down the stairs as Sir Lovis followed. The young Sir Velle took up his position against the door to keep the queen safe.

Tedbalt shifted Ultiir's arm off as they made their way down the stairs. The old lord was trying to hide how difficult it was for him, but Ultiir could see it. He held the wall. Watched his feet. Wobbled a few times. "There have been reports of slaves." Tedbalt said. "Some of them have been captured and killed, but most have gotten away. Somewhere in the Eastlands they're going. I fear for Goldfield without the slaves to harvest the wheat. Even Vigur will suffer."

"Tedbalt," Ultiir said, "I do not care what happens to Goldfield." He pointed out a window to his mother still barking orders on the bench. "My mother is a vile old woman who should've treated her people and the slaves nicer. There's a reason we do not have problems in Vigur. It's because I actually care."

Tedbalt said, "of course," and they found their way outside. Ash still littered the cobbled streets and the air smelled of smoke. The fields outside were blackened husks of the winter wheat all dead. Unless his mother was too proud, they would have to import food from the Woodlands or Eastlands, at least the parts not ravaged by conflict.

Ultiir sighed, wishing it was over. "What of the war?"

Tedbalt gulped. "The bastard has sent an envoy to Storyah to treat with the duke."

Ultiir glared at the world. "Pyre isn't an idiot. He will not choose the losing side. Just ask his father."

"I'll still worry. Pyre Blume has never hidden his quest for independence even if he didn't support his father's revolt. If the bastard makes a generous offer it could continue the war for many years."

"He's already married David Rely's daughter. What else is there?"

"The same thing he can offer the runaway slaves." Lord Masson's face wrinkled. "Freedom."

Ultiir took a deep breath, he kept curling and uncurling his fist into a ball. It seemed like everything was going against him now. If Devro could get the Flewthlands and the vicious slaves on his side than the bastard had a chance at winning. "Drogue de'Vil. I want him named as the new duke of the

Lands of Asara.

Tedbalt huffed. "And what has the lord of Blackrock done to deserve such an honor?"

"The de'Vils held back the mites for months when they crossed the Asara-Luft. I pray Drogue has his father's might and can swiftly deliver the traitors in Whitehall to me."

"A lot of faith in a man who didn't even come to Goldfield or Vigur to pay homage."

"Any more news from Duke Gallient?" Ultiir asked, ignoring Tedbalt.

"More of the same. He wrote to his sister, who is still in the city surprisingly enough, saying that the lowlands are aflame and that he is winning. Do you have as much faith in him as Drogue? Do you think he can hold back not only the Asaramen but also the Del?"

"The Flewthlands will not join Devro's side. I will be sure of it."

"Your Grace." Lord Dovi Lyons came up from behind, his face red and breathing rough. "Lord de'Viere received our letters and sent back his own. Grave news out of Vigur."

"Worse than a slave revolt in my home?" Ultiir asked.

"The peasants rioted in the Rat's Nest and ships were looted in the North Docks. Some are calling for your head, my King"

"Riots." Tedbalt's brows rose. "Seems our people are becoming more and more like the Rowai every year."

Ultiir's fist was clenched, his mother was watching him from across the lawn. "The difference being that I am not a Rowai king, and the people of Vigur will have much to answer for if they think I will listen to this violence. I already couldn't stop a slave revolt. Vigur will be different."

Aveline

They think I'll be like my grandmother." Aveline told Mari as they sat in bed together. "Don't they know it wasn't her fault the kingdom broke into flames?"

"I think they teach it differently when you don't have a royal tutor." Mari played with Aveline's mahogany hair. "The good thing is they're wrong."

"Well I wouldn't say that." Aveline walked across the room and opened the door to her balcony, a cool breeze causing the red curtains to dance with her feet. "Father never taught me to take over. Blis taught the boys differently. They learned the laws and military strategy and how to compromise or enforce your will with the Royal Chancellery. I learned how to ride ponies and the best dress to wear depending on the season."

Mari came from behind and gave Aveline's neck soft kisses. "You needn't worry. I'm sure your brother will be back soon and he will deal with it. Then we can sail away for some adventure."

"And where are we going?"

"Anywhere you want. Being a princess takes a toll, and you have all the coin to hire ships." Mari chuckled. "Nuqtia is supposedly beautiful. We could hunt for the empire's

150

treasures down there."

"Getting sand everywhere does not sound like my kind of fun."

Mari disappeared into Aveline's wardrobe, ruffling through dresses and shoes. "You didn't say that when we spent the night on the beaches near Estia." Mari pulled out a dress the color of a dark rose that would cover Aveline from head to toe. "How about this one?"

"Anything will do. We'll need to find Aida for help though."

After Mari found Aida they fought with the dress to get onto Aveline's body. She was scrubbed clean and her hair tied in a small bun atop her head. The dress had long sleeves and flowed past her shoes. The headdress was sheer so her hair and earrings could still be seen. She made sure to wear not only rings from her mother, but from her grandmother as well. The ones her father had smuggled from the city when the palace was overrun. *Let them think I'll be like Queen Amalia.*

Tomas was standing outside her door today. He wore a smile like always, nothing able to sadden him. "You look lovely, my Princess. Ready to push back on some councilors?"

"It will be a sparring match." They started down the hall, leaving Mari and Aida to tidy Aveline's room. "Has Baldewin chosen a household guard?"

"Delmar will stay in place, even though the knight feels like he failed."

"I didn't know sickness could be bested by a sword."

Tomas chuckled as he led his princess down the stairs to the main corridor lined with paintings of the past. The morning sun peeking in through the gray clouds that made Rowan a dreary place during winter. "I heard William was fuming after your last meeting, of course he couldn't speak his mind, but Wycleaf made sure to translate. What made them so angry?"

"They wanted Baldewin to take a tour of Rowan, something that hasn't been done since my grandfather was crowned, and even he only stayed along the Bruthak. It's like they want him to be killed."

"I'm sure Hecher is foaming at the thought." Tomas said. The office of High Chancellor was powerful in the beginning of the flames before being snuffed out by the People's Chamber. No doubt Hecher wanted to return it to its heyday.

"My Princess," a servant, Atite, said, "your brother," she thought for a moment, "His Grace, is in the sunrise courtyard with Nico."

The sunrise courtyard was on the eastern half of the palace. Despite its name one could not see the sun until it got closer to noon. Baldewin stood on a stone bench by a marble fountain, the centerpiece being a naked elf pouring water from a jug. "Perfect for a royal portrait." Aveline said to her brother with a roll of her eyes. Blis and Sir Delmar stood in the shadow of the palace. The knight still wore a look of sadness, his eyelids hanging. No one blamed Delmar for her father's death except Delmar.

Baldewin was dressed in velvet with a red cloak draped over his arm, a fake sword at his side, and a small golden crown on his brown hair. "Nico isn't going to paint the elf in the picture. He's going to make her into a human."

"His Majesty insisted on the fountain being in his portrait." Nico said with a brush in his hand.

"I wonder why?" Tomas whispered with a sly smile.

"You know the sunrise courtyard is my favorite place," Baldewin whined, "it was mother's favorite spot too," but she could see a hint of blush growing on his cheeks.

Aveline said, "I know, my little king, it reminded her of Ashtree." Rowan trees had been replanted following the flames, some of them the same age as Aveline. "I believe the councilors are wanting to meet."

"But I'm king, so they can wait."

Blis leaned over, giving Aveline a perfect view into his nostrils full of hair. "I called for Punki to come down to stand in for a while. Now, we're just waiting for that baker father of his to release him for the day."

"Punki will make a wonderful king." Aveline said. Nico hadn't gotten very far, but Baldewin's face was nearly finished, the most important part, and the rest had been sketched. Punki would make a perfect stand in.

"What do the councilors want today?" Baldewin asked.

"Who knows?" Aveline said. "Wycleaf will probably want you to meet with Hecher to discuss taxation."

"Boring." Baldewin yawned. "When do we get to the fun stuff?"

"You mean battles, Your Grace?" Blis asked.

"You've told me all the stories of father retaking the kingdom, how much glory he got, the way he dealt with the traitors. I want to do things like that."

Aveline shook her head. "When father was your age he was riding horses and begging his mother to not upend hundreds of years of traditions so the Royal Chancellery wouldn't turn on them. Not fighting off the Gorthair."

"And battle isn't all that fun for the men you send to fight." Blis said. Aveline had forgotten he had sailed the Seler

Bay fending off Rainvealandian attacks. "Taxation might be boring, but remember what happened to your grandfather after the Nowexerti Wars. His tax policy helped cause Rowan to burn."

Baldewin yawned again. "You've told me that a lot, Blis."

"Because it's important."

"Because you know it puts me to sleep." Baldewin laughed. "I promise to not raise taxes and cause a war. Is that good?"

"Convince Hecher, my little king," Aveline said. "He's the one who brings the vote to the Chancellery."

A small brown headed boy with flour dusting his face popped out behind a bush, laughing as his escorts caught up to him. "Finally." Nico said. "Your Grace, feel free to go enjoy your day."

Baldewin gave his ornamental clothes to Punki and changed into a small black tunic, he kept the crown on his head and Punki wore a brass replica. Nico went to work cleaning the boy's face of flour.

Blis, Aveline, and Baldewin walked the corridors of the palace, Delmar and Tomas behind them. She had heard stories of the jewels from around the world decorating the palace. A human touch on an elvish building. Now, the halls were bare with holes where the inlaid jewels once were found. Sometimes she wondered if the peasants who stole them were wealthy and living a better life or just threw them into the river to float out to sea.

"I want you to remember, my little king," Aveline said, "to be cautious around our councilors, around the chancellors, around anyone who isn't us."

"I know, I know." Baldewin picked at his thumb. "They want to steal the crown from my head or something like that.

Wait til they see me with a sword." He mimed swinging a sword.

"Your sister speaks wisely, Your Grace." Blis huffed. "Remember the flames and all that occurred. Talland stealing power from your grandmother. The Bedlam Assembly and the chaos that followed. It was a dreadful time."

"Hecher's too stupid to figure out how to take power."

Aveline bit her tongue. *Just a child. At his age I was still playing with dolls, and here he is governing a kingdom.* "With any luck Bertin will arrive and you won't have to deal with Hecher or Caxton or anyone else."

The door to the throne room towered in front of them. For some reason no page or guard was standing at the door, waiting to open it and announce their arrival. Delmar used his might instead.

A table was placed near the throne. Scrolls and maps and parchments covered the dark wood. The seats creaked as Lord Darry and Lord Rean whispered to one another. Hecher was studying a map. The royal councilors were huddled too close to the throne, the marble shadowed by them. Blis cleared his throat.

Caxton was reading from a parchment, the tongueless William over his shoulder. Taken by the mites when he was off fighting fifteen years ago. Aveline always felt glad to have her tongue when he was around.

"Your Grace," Jac said, "my Princess Regent." The others finally noticed them and bowed, the lords of the sunset and sunrise standing. "We were expecting you a quite a while ago."

"The king is never late." Aveline smiled before adjusting her grandmother's necklace. "What's in your hand?" She asked Caxton.

Caxton, flipping his black mop of hair from his eyes, laid the parchment on the table. "Unfortunately, we've received news about Bertin."

Aveline's breath caught in her throat, the tears arrived before she could stop them. *Not the regent crying in front of these men.* She took a deep breath and thought of Mari. Her handmaid would comfort her later, now was business. Her eyes dried. "Let us sit."

Baldewin trembled as he climbed the throne to the purple cushion, his legs dangling above the floor. Blis stood in the corner with the two guards and Aveline sat at the head of the table. "It's not a very fun day for news." Hecher let an ominous note hang.

"Let's not scare them." Councilor Wycleaf said.

William smirked as Caxton began to speak. "Letters from Lisan Biresdea in Telemaw have arrived. Your father thought Prince Bertin was to study in Vaandet, but the king of Telemaw had a different plan. It appears your brother's been captured by elves," Aveline formed fists to stop her hands from shaking, "but we can tell you he is still alive. Another letter dated just a few weeks ago from the same elven prick, pardon my language, said that he is being taken to Anha Jorbstah."

"Where?" Baldewin asked.

"Why?" Aveline asked, which was the more important question. She knew the ancient city of Anha Jorbstah was located in the Pywaln. "Why is a prince of Rowan being smuggled across Rainvealand by elves?"

William shrugged and Wycleaf said. "We don't know, and we don't know how we're going to find him."

"Send an army to scour Rainvealand." Baldewin said with a roar in his voice, or maybe a squeak. "A mite has surely seen him."

Hecher straightened his back. "We're not sure that's a good idea. If you haven't noticed, Viguran is falling apart. Your cousins are at war."

"Why should I care?" Baldewin asked.

"The histories of our two kingdoms are long and at some points tenuous," Hecher explained, "but that is our sister kingdom. Your blood sits on the throne. A Viguran in chaos gives our enemies," he looked at Aveline, "the mites, a greater advantage if we were to war again."

"The *mites*," she hated that word, "couldn't even beat our father when he was piecing our kingdom back together, yet somehow they're going to overrun us now?" Aveline said, Tomas trying not to chuckle.

"You never know with them." Lord Darry said as he rubbed his eyes. "Just go to the mite district and see how sporadic they behave."

Caxton raised his hands. "Our regent enjoys her time in the mite district." He let that hang for a moment too long. "But the council has agreed Viguran is a larger priority at the moment. Ultiir has retaken Redington, a city that has been independent since Valor the Betrayer was overthrown. We cannot let that stand."

"You decided this with the regent and king absent?" Aveline's face was burning. "Do you want to command the troops like Talland?" She asked Hecher who only stared into her eyes. She knew he wanted her to apologize. It was a serious accusation. Talland had been tried and killed for treason. But Aveline's eyes didn't waver. "This is not the People's

Chamber, we are not in the flames anymore. Our father was the Uniter, who brought back our home from destruction. He did not allow the High Chancellor to keep his power. He restored the monarchy. So it is not your decision to make without the king present, nor me. We will listen to your advice and come up with a plan, but we will not take orders from you."

Her voice echoed throughout the throne room, she hadn't realized how loud she was speaking. The councilors looked at each other, William with a smirk. Caxton's black hair had fallen in his face. "What my sister said." Baldewin added.

Wycleaf leaned forward. "What do you think?" He asked the little king.

"Like I said before, I don't care about Viguran."

Aveline added, "Hurvir didn't help Rowan when it was destroying itself, and he's been nothing but cruel to Devro. I feel for our cousin against his uncle, but we cannot pick sides. And we know where Bertin is going. It is imperative we find him."

"Forgive, my Princess Regent," Wycleaf said, "but I don't think the mites will tolerate Rowai troops in their land, especially after our sack of Bardekan all those years ago."

"You all would leave our brother with elves? Do you think they're going to let him go?"

"If we paid." Lord Rean whispered.

"They will kill him," her jaw ached from clenching it. "With or without coin."

"But Redington has fallen." Caxton said. "How do you think the rulers of Viguran would react if we took Edincassone? There would be war, retribution. We cannot sit idly by and not punish Ultiir."

"War?" Baldewin hiccuped. "You think we should side with Devro?"

Caxton said. "We should free Redington. We can send a small scouting party to look for Prince Bertin."

"Redington is our gateway to Eotros." Hecher rested his elbows on the table. "We mustn't let this trading partner be taken away."

"You think this will bring me glory like father?" Baldewin was trying not to act excited, but Aveline knew her brother too well.

"Immense." Was all Hecher said, the other councilors nodding.

Aveline trained her eyes on Baldewin. His legs were shaking, his breathing growing faster. *Please don't do it. Save Bertin. Put this mess behind us. What happened to Hecher and taxes?*

"Then we will free Redington." King Baldewin said.

Aveline pushed her chair back until it fell and marched out of the throne room.

Tundavik

And where are you going?" Tundavik stood by the lowered drawbridge in the outer bailey wearing his awful red and yellow that Pyre thought would look so good on him. Mar was also in red and yellow, though his resembled flames. The knight was laughing with other men-at-arms who had come from their homes to Storyah with their lords.

"Wait for me near the sea." He called out to the men. "Worried about me?" he asked Tundavik and put his hands on his side, but not in a serious manner, Mar was rarely serious.

"Just don't want you to miss the council meeting later." It was finally the time for the lords to meet and discuss the Flewthlands joining the war. Tundavik could hardly sleep. The fear of him failing keeping him awake. "I know what happens when you go into town, not a whore will be safe."

"Nor a tankard." Mar stepped out of the way of a horse pulled wagon full of fresh rolls made from winter wheat. Tundavik loved the smell, but the cold air kept him from enjoying it. He would rather be inside. "If I promise to be back before the meeting will that make you feel better?"

"I'm not your father." Tundavik rolled his eyes with a laugh. "Fuck some people, drink a tavern's full, bet on some cards.

I'll just need help later and would rather not do all the talking."

"Afraid they'll vote no? You heard Lord Blume, he wants to go with us so why wouldn't his men?" Mar shrugged his shoulder. "Even if they do vote no I've never met a duke who actually listens to his people."

"I doubt Pyre wants a revolt on his hands."

"No, I guess not. The last time that happened he sued for peace and a hundred freedom fighters were executed by Hurvir. Still," Mar moved a slick piece of hair from his brow, "no way they go against us. We promise freedom. Ultiir promises nothing. Even if the Flewthlands go to war and we lose, what will Ultiir do to them? Kill Pyre? He isn't his brother, at least not yet. I doubt he does what Hurvir did in Ritaeum."

Tundavik looked at the servants and workers and guards. Some clearing snow, others repairing small holes in the walls, the guards patrolling. *If Ultiir is like Hurvir all of these people will be dead soon, and it will be my fault,* he thought as he shuddered at the possibility of a blood soaked ground.

His head began to hurt.

The woman from his dreams had barely spoken to him as he went north to Storyah, the occasional dream telling him she was still there, waiting, but nothing like in the Lands of Asara or when they were traveling across the Eastlands. His headaches had mostly subsided. *Either the woman has stopped haunting me or is dead. Maybe she was able to stop Nhamcaryn herself. Whatever that is.*

"Tundavik?" Mar snapped his fingers with a worried glance. "Get lost looking at the snow. I'm sorry, I shouldn't bring up ... your home. If I don't like thinking about Ruwy then I can't imagine what you feel like."

"Have you heard of Nhamcaryn?" Tundavik asked even though he didn't want to, but having the dreams and the thoughts alone made him feel worse, he needed help.

"What?"

Tundavik stepped back into the cold, stone wall, not believing he let bad dreams affect him. "Sorry. Daydreaming. I don't know why I said that."

"You need sleep, old man." Mar patted Tundavik's back with a laugh. "Nhamcaryn? You're going to be speaking full on Archel next."

Archel was the language of the elves that used to live in Rowan. *Maybe it would've helped if I made more attention to my teachings on Rowan as a child.* "It's an elvish word?"

"What's it sound like? Definitely not a human word. I'm sure you can find some book that will tell you about it. Maybe even an elf," the knight motioned to the city. "They used to run this land, surely there are still some around. Now, can I go or are you going to daydream again?"

"Go, but be back soon and be sober."

"Whatever you say, commander." Mar gave a mocking salute and disappeared out the castle walls.

Tundavik rubbed his temples as his boots crunched the snow-covered ground. The baileys and interior of the castle were abuzz today as the council was to take place. Almost every lord from the Flewthlands had arrived or sent word of their decision. He wondered how everyone would fit in the same meeting chamber, but realized this was a castle not the keep in Whitehall nor in Ritaeum. This was a seat of power. And Devro desperately needed them to showcase it to the rest of Viguran.

As he walked inside the mess hall, a long room full of linear tables, he found the lady of Woodrun eating eggs and toast with her daughter who slathered more butter than needed on her bread. Tundavik walked over to the table where they sat. Lord Toware and Lord Ed sitting farther down. They were the lords of Riverend and the Seeded Field respectively. They had come with hosts dozens of men strong and seemed eager to go to war. *Hopefully they will be my allies in the council.*

Tundavik motioned to sit across from Flora who nodded. "Have you ate?" She asked as he sat.

"Just some bread earlier today. I think I need to take some of this food to the Lands of Asara when we're finished. They're probably rationing tack as we gorge." He wondered how those in Whitehall were doing with the thick layers of snow. He and Mar had left just before the worst of the blizzards set in, and even then they were running low on food. The fields and stores in the lowlands were being destroyed. Not one merchant wanted to make the journey.

"Is this gorging?" Flora gave a sweet smile as she pointed to her eggs. "Half a helping. The other half went to Lord Peter. And the bread used for toast had to be cleaned of mold. The war may not be in the Flewthlands but we're eating like it is."

Tundavik chuckled at the thought of eating eggs on the front, and at Little Flora dropping a dollop of butter to be cleaned by the hounds. "During the campaign along the Bezir you wouldn't believe what some of the men ate. Things not suitable for your daughter to hear. But Panscar barely had any trade flowing in when we looted the city, and the road to Suktir not any better. I wonder how the Eastlands are faring at the moment."

"If the hordes of people traveling north are any indication than not good." Flora sipped her morning mead. "Should we continue this talk atop the wall? It's beautiful seeing the city and sea up there, and I know the guards will let us up."

Once Florance was sent to play with Lady Lueva's children, Tundavik and Flora walked up the steps onto the stone wall. A layer of frost had covered the city in the night. Slick streets and shiny roofs reflected the morning sun as it climbed in the east.

Flora gripped the ermine neckline of her coat and said, "I would come out here with my mother and we would watch the people go about their day. Bakers loading bread. Cobblers mending shoes. Drunks finally leaving the taverns. Children running and playing. Do you have children, my lord duke?"

I'm not a duke anymore, Hurvir made sure of that, was what he wanted to say. Instead he said, "yes. Ertha and Guis. The loves of my life." Tundavik felt his wrinkled forehead, the thought of not seeing them growing up and having children of their own and ruling their lands made his eye twitch. "They're gone now."

"I'm sorry, my lord." Flora placed her hands on the stone parapet overlooking a bakery down below. Smells of cooking bread and smoke from the fire filled Tundavik's nose as his stomach growled. "How do you like Storyah? I'm sure it's nothing like the West with their mountains and cool waters and vineyards lining their hills. What city did you live in again? I'm not sure my father said."

"Baragio. Beautiful city it was indeed but there was a lack of mountains. Before coming back and ending up in Whitehall I rarely ventured into the western rocks. Too dry for me."

"And the snow? Did you miss it and all the cold it brings? My husband sometimes wishes we lived in Somertin for the heat."

Flora's skin was bright as the sun reflected off the slick surfaces back at her. "I did miss it. Your husband is Lord Barnet, right? I still haven't seen him."

"I doubt you will."

Tundavik leaned on the parapet, his body getting closer to the heat radiating off of Flora. "And why is that?"

"My husband isn't fond of you and would be furious if he saw us talking. That's why I wished to speak here." Flora's cheeks went red. "I've now realized what a bad wife I'm being by disobeying my husband. Not a very good role model for Florance," she trailed off.

"You aren't allowed to speak to whomever you like?" Tundavik chuckled. "Is this a thing in the Flewthlands? I could never control my wife in the Woodlands, and if I had she would've fought back. She taught our children how to be stubborn."

Flora picked at the snow on the stone, clouds of another winter storm gathering behind her. "I've heard of the awful stories that befell your family. Everyone speaks of them. They see you walking down the corridors and whisper rumors and treat the word 'Ritaeum' as a curse."

"People like to talk."

"Will you tell me?" Flora shook her head after speaking. "That was wrong of me to ask. You owe me nothing."

Tundavik looked into her blue eyes. It was like looking at a clear sky in summer. Calming. "Why don't you tell me some of the rumors and I'll correct you or not."

It took a moment for Flora to finally say, "okay. They talk about the Rainvealandians sacking your home. How King Hurvir, may the Four watch over him, brought his might as not to lose a duchy capital, but getting confused in the chaos and killing your family and subjects. Terrible."

"That sounds about right," Tundavik lied, not wanting to tell her that Hurvir massacred his family for the fun of it, "but for me I hope Vigura sent Hurvir to Veltoora to dance with demons." Flora held her chest in surprise and giggled. "I plan to see Ritaeum after the war is won. I want to see what's changed."

"I hope you get to, and I hope the war goes your way. I worry," the lady of Woodrun paused, chewing her lip. "My husband, as I said before, isn't too fond of you, and I worry he will campaign against you and your war effort. He wishes to keep the Flewthlands neutral."

I need to find out who this man is, Tundavik thought. "Go to the meeting. If the duke's daughter is on my side then I can't lose."

"Barnet says I'm to go nowhere near that meeting. I have to watch our daughter and tend to our accounts."

Tundavik bowed his head, his shoes sinking into the snow. "Then I will see you later."

"Good luck, my lord duke." Flora curtsied and fluttered her lashes.

As the day continued and the sun was hidden by clouds of snow blanketing the castle grounds in white, Tundavik followed a page to the council chamber. It was up a few flights of stairs. Down long hallways of stone. And atop the castle. Tundavik waited alone save for a few servants getting everything ready.

The room was open-aired and round. In all directions he could see the world moving on without him. Somewhere to the west was the Asara, to the east was the Nokys. Beyond the thatched roofs of the city to the north was Ceal in Plajul and to the south was Ritaeum. They were all watching him. Hoping the war didn't spill beyond the borders of the Eastlands and the Kinglands and the Lands of Asara, but Tundavik was determined.

On the large stone pillars that held the ceiling were maps and tapestries. Maps of Viguran and the surrounding kingdoms; maps of the Rainvealandian states; maps of the islands in the Nokys. The tapestries were made of ornate colors sewn with images of kings and queens cloaked in gold. Tundavik rested his palms on the stone table in the center, not even able to throw a pebble to the other side if he tried.

As dogs below howled at the rising moon, the dark wooden seats began to fill. One chair to the north was slightly raised and covered in velvet. Lord Blume sat there. Lord Barnet had servants bring his own chair too, the only other person who wasn't on a bench. His seat was etched with blossoming trees. Lords squeezed either side of Tundavik as hundreds of men filled the room, bringing warmth with their bodies and coldness with their eyes.

Mar never showed.

"Welcome, my many lords." Pyre Blume said to the roundtable as he stood. Surcoats of white and red and blue and gray dotted the room. The insignias were a mix of lions, bears, birds, trees, rivers, waves, rocks, and castles. There had to be more than one hundred people piled into the chamber. "I have received an urgent message from Duke David Rely of the Lands of Asara. He sent envoys in an attempt to sway the Flewthlands to his side of the war, supporting the bastard in his quest for the throne against his uncle. As lord I cannot, in good conscience, commit my men to war. For that reason

I have called a council of lords to determine what our land is to do. We may stay neutral. We may fight for Hurvir's son. We may even fight for the one who already rules in Vigur. It is up to you." Lord Blume sat on his velvet and relaxed his shoulders. "We will begin with Lord Tundavik Vandes' plea."

"If I may, my lord duke," Lord Arnate of Grassridge said with a puzzled look, "when we rose up against Hurvir with your father, Lord David Rely did not support us, so why are you asking us to support him in his revolt?"

"This is about more than just one duchy," Pyre said, "this is about the whole of Viguran. Lord Vandes will share with you the reasons if you let him." Lord Arnate held up his hands in surrender.

"Lord Arnate raises a good point," Tundavik said, "and his lord duke gives a great answer. Onto Blume's rebellion was about the Flewthlands gaining freedom from Viguran, Devro wishes to see Onto's dream become a reality. He is willing to give you all your independence, to do whatever you like. You need only fight against Ultiir. That man is not only a regicide but a fratricide as well, something the gods look down upon."

"And we're supposed to care about Hurvir being murdered?" The young Lord Olette said, a violet flower on his surcoat. "That man brought only destruction. He dragged us into not one but two wars with the mites, and sicced his armies on the Flewthlands, again, not once but twice. The whole duchy celebrated when we heard the news. So we either choose Hurvir's brother or his son, not a very good choice for us."

Tundavik scratched his graying beard and said, "As some of you might know, I once ruled in the Woodlands. I know what it means to be a good leader and how to take care of your people, Lord Blume does it well. I have overseen that Devro gets the best teachings and is surrounded by men who will guide him to become a just ruler." Lord Barnet chuckled silently across from Tundavik, and Tundavik still had trouble placing him. *Sometime long ago ...* was all he thought.

"Why wouldn't we just declare independence by ourselves?" Lord Ed asked. "There's no need to pick a side. While they war we can harden our defenses and crown our own king." There were murmurs of agreement, something Tundavik couldn't have.

"My lords, if you do not join with Devro and Lord Rely then the war will be lost. Ultiir has taken to massacring whole villages to secure his power. What do you think he will do to you when he's done with the Lands of Asara? He already sent a letter to your duke with threats akin to Ritaeum," that got the lords talking too. Pyre had a page bring the note and it was passed around to angry faces. "Ultiir took the throne from his brother because Hurvir had just legitimized Devro as his son and heir. Ultiir couldn't have that so the King's Council took it upon themselves to crown him. If a man can kill his only surviving brother with no remorse, what do you think he'll do to you?"

"We cannot let this threat go unpunished." Lord Rickart, called the Crazed, bellowed. "Any man who threatens the Flewthlands does not know of our strength. He can try as he might to massacre our people and destroy our land and villages but we will send that regicide to Veltoora where he will scream for all eternity."

"Sit down, Lord Rickart," Lord Barnet said. "If I may, I agree this threat shouldn't be allowed, and we can discuss what to do with Ultiir next, but agreeing to side with Tundavik will only bring that death and destruction you fear to us sooner. Right now we know peace. We're supposed to throw that away over the word of a bastard? Bastards are not to be trusted, this is known, but Tundavik would have us march on the Eastlands and kill people we just recently saw as allies, friends, family. It's easier for him to go to war since he's been in the West all these years. He doesn't understand how Viguran has changed without him here.

"The Book of the Four tells us that men make wars, violent, terrible men. Our gods wish for peace, none more than Mother Meret. Why should we send our young men to fight in a war, experience the decay and violence? How is that right? Just? I have heard rumors that the bastard started marching to Whitehall from his banishment before his father was even killed. Bastards always plot and scheme. His father was a warmonger and it seems as if Devro is as well.

"My lords, I will have a hard time voting to join Lord Rely in his revolt. My men in Woodrun answer to me, not the duke of the Lands of Asara or his manservant," Barnet said as he sneered at Tundavik. "I think neutrality is the only way to help the Flewthlands and our own lands prosper."

The hundreds of lords argued into the night, some agreeing with Barnet and others agreeing with Tundavik. No vote coming. Pyre wiped bags from under his eyes as the moon and stars rose into the night sky. Tundavik's fingers made music on the table. Barnet spoke about the horrors of the Bezir campaign all those years ago, and Tundavik, with wide eyes, finally remembered how he knew the lord of Woodrun.

Raimund

Frost crunched below his torn boots as Raimund and Sile made their way over the red streaks in the snow. Wolves or some other creature must've come and taken whatever the griffin left over from the men she killed. A layer of new snow had fallen, but the heat of the sun had already melted some of it, leaving the dark stains of blood and guts. One streak was near the forest. Liznar. Another deep pool of red was where the two guards fought and died. Where the griffin was hit with ice spikes.

"How did you do it?" Raimund asked as he motioned toward the spot where the ice ball exploded. "It was like nothing I've ever seen before."

"When you've been alone for years like I have you learn some things. Teach yourself how to survive and fight in case anything happens. This part of the world is always worried about monsters. About humans." Sile stood over the bloodstains of the guards. "In my experience humans are worse. The baiagryf killed because she was hungry. We kill each other for fun," she shrugged. "Wonder how many we'll kill if we break your friend out of the hole."

"Hopefully not much." Raimund said as he thought about all those who died in Riverton under his command. How many would die as the war continued and more and more lords and knights chose sides? How many peasants and farmers? As he looked around the bloody scene he wondered if he made the right choice following Devro to Viguran. He could've stayed behind. Gereduss wasn't much but he had grown to not hate it. *Now, I'm back North expecting to never see Devro again.* "Do you know which way they went?" He asked Sile as she went over to where wagon debris lay. "I'm sure they took Potter."

"We can't be sure of anything until we see him," Sile sighed, "but I agree." She looked at the mountains that surrounded them, large and small gaps between the peaks were filled with gray clouds. That's where the passes would be. Only Sile would be able to lead Raimund to the prison where Potter might be. "They came from that way," she pointed to a forest with a clean cut through it. "That's the pass they used. Hopefully the hole isn't too far away."

"You've never seen the prison?" Raimund asked as they moved through the snow and ice, leaving a path for anyone to follow, but mostly a path to help them get back.

"I don't explore much outside of hunting and foraging."

"You lived here for years and haven't explored the region? How did you even find this place?"

"I came north on a ship from the Flewth-Vet then took a smaller boat from the Glybelm to the mountains. Walked a few days and thought it was a nice place to spend the rest of my days in solitude." Sile brush her hand over a tree trunk, wiping leftover snow to the ground.

"Sounds like a good way to die from the unknown," he said. Raimund shivered as they went deeper into the forest. He wished he could warm himself. It had been years since he had to brave a freezing winter without the help of his sunstone. *I don't know how people do it year after year,* he thought as he pulled the cloak from Sile tighter. His face was kept warm from his new beard that had been growing in since he was taken, and his black hair had almost grown to his shoulders. He would need to find scissors once winter was over and chop it off. But he was thankful for it now.

A moan pierced the air. Winter birds took off from their trees and snow fell over Raimund and Sile. Then another moan. It sounded like agony. Sile cocked her head and listened to the small cries, whimpers. She set off into the forest, pushing evergreen leaves from her face. Raimund had no choice but to follow her. "You don't even know what it is," he panted as he ran up behind her. "Could be a trap."

"If it was the sound of a *myzlić* I would know."

Raimund hadn't believed the prisoners when they spoke of some beast, the potvoryn, in the mountains, and he never believed in myzlićs, shapeshifting monsters that lured you to them then killed and drank your blood. He had more important things to worry about for most of his life. Real things.

Sile pushed through a thicket and the griffin was lying on her side. The shaft of a spear pointing out of her chest. Blood was leaking down the side of her, congealing on the ground. A black stain. The griffin moaned and cried as she breathed slow. Her eyes were glassy from water.

"Oh dear," Sile said. The griffin didn't like that and thrashed. She tried to walk, but the injury was too much and she fell in a heap. "We need to help her."

Raimund grabbed Sile's arm to keep her from walking. "You saw what she did the other day. She'll eat you without a second thought."

Sile yanked away, her brow furrowing, "No. She is intelligent. She'll know we mean her no harm. Now, go pet her by the beak and I'll get the spear out."

By the beak ... but Raimund didn't have time to argue. Sile wasn't backing down and she trudged through the snow to the spear. The griffin rustled. Wings flapping ever so slightly. The griffin let out a squeak, a slight caw, a grumble of a roar as Raimund went near her face. Her eyes were large, dark disks as they watched him approach. The colors of her feathers and fur made her look like she was alight with fire. Red and yellow. Like the setting of the sun when she first attacked. Raimund put his hand near her beak and she snapped. Fangs gleamed from within. But Sile motioned for him to try again. He slowly moved his hand near her nostrils, where she took a large sniff. She had started breathing rapidly as they got near, but her breath slowed as she allowed Raimund to put his fingers on her beak. The large, yellow jaw was mostly smooth, but there were also ridges. Red stains lined the opening. Raimund felt like the beast was staring into his soul. Reading him. Seeing his whole life story.

"Baiagryfs are a good judge of character," Sile said as she gripped the spear shaft and positioned herself to start pulling and the griffin puffed out her chest more as if to help. "See? Intelligent." Sile took a deep breath and pulled with all her might. The griffin's eyes were even wider now, and her glassy eyes made it look like she was crying from the pain.

Raimund kept his hand on her beak, even putting the other on her fur above her eyes, she felt like a cat who lived in alleyways. Her fur matted and greasy. But she didn't kill Raimund or turn to bite Sile. Instead, she let out a groan of relief as Sile got the entire spear out of her chest.

Sile dropped to her knees and gathered snow to rub it on the bleeding wound. "I can't do much to heal her," she said, "but if you had a sunstone you'd be able to close the wound. Stop her from bleeding to death."

Raimund looked into the griffin's eyes. The large disks of nothingness looked sad, like she cried out for help. They reminded him of all the men who died while he led the attack on Riverton. When he failed.

"I can try anyway," Raimund said as he dragged his hand over the griffin's body so she knew he was still there. He placed his fingers near the wound. In the summer it would be infested with maggots and flies, but only ravens called out from the trees this time of year. Waiting for their meal. He closed his eyes.

Thinking of Valkyr and the sunstone was his first idea. Remembering the flames that he could shot from his fingertips. His red-glowing nails. The energy that pulsed through his body. But nothing. He turned to thinking about fire. Just fire. The flames that burned Riverton's walls. The flames that consumed his childhood home and his parents' life, the guilt he felt from it. The possibility that it was his fault his parents died.

Nothing.

Raimund took in a deep breath of cold, harsh winter hair. His lungs pierced with ice. He needed to warm himself, but he was running out of ideas. Then he decided to think about Gereduss. The girl he saved in the alley. Devro. Mar. If they were hurting like this griffin was he would do everything he could to help them. Mar was his best friend. They had traveled for years together. Devro was … he was his son. He had raised the boy. Raimund was more a father than the king ever was.

The griffin called out in pain but didn't flee as a small stream of fire and heat shot from Raimund's fingers. He kept them near the wound. His fingers looked like candle. The small flame heating the wound and killing any infection. He knew he was done when the griffin stirred. She pushed herself up with her mighty paws and looked back at him. Her eyes bright. Then she walked off, flapping her wings just a bit, looking like it still hurt.

But Raimund beamed as the griffin made her way through the branches, trees cracking as she pushed them, large tracks being left in the snow. He had helped her. She wasn't hurting as bad anymore. He had done it right. Sile smiled at him. "Let's go find that prison."

***

Sile crouched behind a snow-covered, jagged rock. Raimund followed her lead. The prison was a hole just like it was described, but it was the largest hole he had ever seen. He was expecting maybe a ten foot drop, just enough to keep people from climbing out. Instead, it was certainly over a hundred feet deep. The prisoners below would hardly be able to be seen if it weren't for their grays and blacks against the white backdrop of winter. The walls of the prison also weren't rock like he was expecting. They were sheer plates of black metal with no holds and looked slick to the touch.

"Somehow we're going to have to bring Potter up that," Raimund said as he pointed to a staircase that went all the way down, hundreds if not thousands of steps.

176

"Well he had to've made it down."

"Not with every guard with a crossbow and a spear ready to aim at him." The guards were atop the walls, looking down, watching everyone. They wore fur over their leather or steel armor. Some shivered. Others looked as comfortable as if it were a warm summer's day. Raimund and Sile, even with her moonstone, could never hope to go against dozens of guards. All armed.

"First we need to find him," Sile said, "then make our plan."

"Well, for one, he looks like he feasted everyday before he came here. Other prisoners are surely starving. Let's hope they didn't eat him," he giggled but Sile wasn't laughing. "See anyone like that?"

"I see specks, some smaller or larger than others. Maybe he went to hunt the beast."

Raimund took his eyes off the prison and wrinkled his face. "You mean the griffin? Don't tell me you believe in the potvoryn as well." Sile pursed her lips. "What's with this place and superstition?"

"You can make fire from your hands, have a magical stone on your sword, save a griffin, and still not be superstitious?" Sile shook her head. "I told you something was pushing the griffin farther down the mountain. What else if not the fabled potvoryn?"

"Why would the prison allow their captives to leave and hunt a monster?"

"It's tradition," she shrugged, "if you come back with the beast's head you get your freedom, no matter how awful your crime. Of course, no one has successfully completed it. They either come back empty handed or die."

"Or run away."

Sile dug her hand into the snow, flakes sticking to her glove. "It's possible, but could you survive out here alone? No magic? They die sooner or later."

He looked to the prison again. The guards walking the perimeter, joking with each other, distracted. A wooden house was off to the side. Large enough to be barracks. Smoke bellowing from chimneys. Below the specks moved like ants, but one was certainly larger than the other, and when Potter looked into the sky Raimund could see the chubby man's cheeks. *I'll get you out of here, I promise.* "That's him," he said and Sile nodded after she followed his finger. "So we need to somehow get him to agree to hunt the beast and we'll be free to go. Sounds simple enough."

"How do you plan to do that? He might as well be a million miles away." Sile scratched her chin. "We'll have to go down there and bring him up. Not sure how."

The wooden barracks called out to Raimund, and he looked at his hand, the hand that had glowed red for the first time in weeks. "I have a plan."

Yvanne

A little higher, a little higher." Lord Aimora Dore slightly lifted the bow she was holding until a deer in the distance was in her sights. "Pull back and release."

Yvanne pulled on the bowstring and imagined the arrow piercing through the air, a trail of smoke behind it, finding itself in the deer's eye. Instead, when she released the bowstring, the arrow flew maybe ten feet and landed in the snow. "Next time," Aimora said before nodding to Besta who drew back his arrow and skewered the deer in the throat.

"You should train with my men," Lord Aimora said as they made their way back through the snow to camp, "then you'll be able to shoot an arrow."

"Why would a queen train with her warriors?" Pollard asked as he rolled his eyes.

"Just look at the fighters who follow Lord Cul. Men and women alike. Adds more numbers on your side if you have women fight for you too."

"And a better chance of being defeated," Besta laughed as he dragged the deer carcass behind him.

When they found the camp, some Lodean went to cleaning and cutting the deer. Yvanne found Devro who was talking with Lord Cul about the war, telling him about the fighting in the Eastlands and the lowlands and the little they had heard once the mountain passes had been covered with snow. *Hopefully everything's alright down there,* she thought as she remembered the charred remains of Greatbath.

Once the deer was eaten most went to sleep. Wolves howled in the distance keeping them on guard. Yvanne could hear people shivering outside her tent, but she kept herself warm. Warm enough to drift asleep and dream of fairies dancing around her father.

When they woke the camp was to be torn down for their journey to finish. They had gone through the dwarven tunnel just yesterday and found the rest of the Lodean huddling for warmth as a blizzard blew over the area. Aimora promised them they could be the first to loot the palace in Vigur. "Do that and taste my blade," Pollard had said to sound threatening. He blushed when the Lodean had laughed at him.

The valley where Whitehall sat was getting closer, the evergreen trees and rocks began to look familiar, she was ready for the comforts of the keep. "Lord Cul, when was the last time you descended the peaks?" Yvanne asked from atop Snowfall, a foot or more taller than the old lord on his stout horse.

"One of my daughters, Palla is her name, decided to marry a lowlander," Cul said with a twisted face. "All my other children married those of the peaks, but Palla was stubborn and had descended the mountain once before to see a tourney in Riverton. She met a man, the son of the lord of Lowton. My wife wanted me to support Palla so I went and got a hefty dowry, so all worth it in the end," the old man laughed. "This was long ago, I believe your father had just become duke. Even he was at the wedding."

"And where is Palla now? Still in Lowton?" Yvanne asked.

"Dead like most of my family." Cul said without explaining any further. "But I'll be happy to see your father, even if the Duke David Rely forgets us. We can talk of what will happen when we win this war."

Yvanne had rarely thought of how her father or the councilors would feel when she offered independence to the Peakmen. *I've already heard enough from Pollard to last a lifetime. I don't need to hear father's complaints.*

The Swallow Pass wasn't nearly as full of snow anymore, puddles pooled around their feet as they sloshed their way under the noon sun. "The king!" Sir Loc shouted from a ridge above. "The king and queen return!" Eventually the pass echoed with the call to Whitehall that their ruler had returned.

As they entered the valley where the village lay, dozens of guards and villagers greeted them with low stares and sad eyes. Yvanne found Cada in the crowd and went to her sister, praying the whole time that the war hadn't taken an even worse turn. *Please don't be about Tundavik or Mar or the Flewthlands. Please tell me Ultiir is not marching on us right now.* It was worse than she thought. Tears filled her eyes after Cada said, "Father is dead."

Devro looked like he had been punched, any semblance of a smile on his face after getting the Lords of the Peaks to his side gone. Murmurs came from behind as the Lodean reacted to the news. Yvanne clenched her fists. Helge was near the door of the keep with her head lowered. "Take me to him." Yvanne told her sister.

Pollard followed close behind, but he didn't shed a tear, Yvanne wouldn't let hers drop. *The queen will not be seen crying,* she thought over internal sobs. As she walked her anger melted the snow below, but she didn't care if anyone saw the stone on her necklace glowing or whispered of her being a mage, her father was gone. Cada led them down a staircase in the far back of the mountain. Yvanne pulled for energy, but none came from below them. The crypt was only full of death, not life.

The stone walls had holes dug for bodies to lay, most were already full. Yvanne would have to commission more if more members of her family were to die. "We already buried him." Cada swallowed. "We didn't know when you two were coming back. I'm sorry."

"It's fine." Yvanne played with her sleeve as she stared at the words that read *Duke David Rely.* The hole where his body rest was covered. Around him were his many wives, none of them Yvanne and Pollard's mother.

"What happened?" Pollard asked.

"Dera, the daken, said he was old. Nothing she could've done."

Pollard shook his head of the tears forming in his eyes. "I don't believe it. Have the daken interrogated to find out if this was some Ultiir plot."

"No." Yvanne put her hand up. "Do not sully his memory with a witch hunt. Dera is a kind woman and father was older than some elves. It was his time."

Pollard rubbed his hands over the words, "I didn't think when we left we'd never see him again."

Me neither, Yvanne thought, *and I was worried he would complain about the Peakmen. Stupid.*

"He only grew more tired and more sick," Cada said, "you didn't want to see him."

"Did Helge at least pray with him?" Pollard asked.

"They prayed to Mother Meret to allow him to feast with all who died before him. The whole town prayed as well for his safe passage in the afterlife. It was a sad affair."

There were boots echoing in the halls behind them. "My queen," Sir Loc bowed as he entered, "I am deeply saddened by the loss of your father, our duke, but the councilors have requested an urgent meeting. I'm to escort you."

"I'll escort her," Pollard said and Loc nodded. "They didn't even have the decency to wait. To allow us to mourn."

"The war is important." Yvanne told Pollard as they and Cada made their way to the front of the mountain keep where the councilors would be waiting.

Lord Aimora was off to the corner, the others not getting close to a Lodean. The old, grumpy Lord Cul was breathing heavily in his chair. Arold, the swordmaster, was looking through maps of the Lands of Asara. Before winter had set in, Sirs Raimund and Mar and Lord Vandes and her father all gathered around the table. She felt lonely now. Happy Pollard and Cada were at her side. Her sister went to her husband who was playing with candle wax. Pollard sat in a chair instead of joining the guards in their white armor by the door. Devro sat at the head of the table. The place her father would normally sit.

Yvanne choked back tears as she sat near her husband. Lord de'Marisco opened the door and bowed with a, "sorry I'm late, Your Grace."

"We were just starting," Devro said as he picked at his nails.

"My king, queen, lords," Arold bowed. "I am happy to report that training of the new recruits has gone exceptionally well. The Lodean and the men are getting along perfectly fine. I am excited to begin training the warriors of the peak."

"My fighters need no training." Lord Cul swatted away the notion. "And I find it odd that you leave out half of your people from fighting while you are at war, but I digress."

"Women are too weak to fight, my lord," Arold laughed. "Not all of them were born to the roughness of your mountain peaks."

"Why did you call this meeting?" Yvanne said before Cul could argue back. "I know you all have been able to mourn my father but I have not. So get on with it." She just wanted to sleep. To dream of her father and mother and simpler times, not this war.

"Apologies, my queen," Arold said.

"The snow has begun to melt in the passes," Sidoro said. "My sea snakes are itching for battle and we have received a few runners of late."

Lord Aimora approached the table with the letters. "Lord Osbern Lot has been able to keep the Crossing secure from Lord David Viero's assault from Winterlake. Lord Tedbalt of the Yellow Tower has fallen to forces from the Brownfork."

"There's also news from Lords Emallen and Amil." Arold said as he passed the letter to Devro. "They report the northern passes are safe, nothing to worry about."

"And the King's Pass?" Pollard asked. "That's where trouble will come from."

"Nothing yet, sir." Arold scanned a map. "With Lord Cul's presence I assume the Swallow Pass is secure?"

"The Lords of the Peaks will guard it from any Terropian attack." Devro said. "If we can trust them."

"We can," Yvanne jumped in just as Cul's mouth was beginning to open. She didn't need Devro to cause the relationship to sour. "The Lords of the Peak have shown to be our allies. Lord Cul is here to help defend Whitehall."

"Any news from Albert?" Cada asked. Lord Albert Rely was the lord of Canniage and heir to the duchy. He was their eldest brother. Yvanne didn't even know which of his father's wives was his mother.

"We sent word to him just as we did you and all of the other children of Lord Rely," Arold said, "but winter has made it difficult."

"Even if the snow melts tomorrow, it could be weeks before we see him or any others." Pollard said. "So right now we are in the middle of a war without a duke for the Lands of Asara and no lord of Whitehall. Morale will drop."

"I am king," Devro said. "I am still here. They weren't fighting in the name of your father but for me."

"Having a leader would help," Lord de'Marisco whispered from his chair. "The king can't rule the duchy, what will Lord Blume think? Lord Valles? If joining our side means losing their lands and titles they will think twice about it."

"There are no sons other than Pollard in Whitehall to take over," Arold said.

"There are two daughters," Urses said, "and one of them has never left Whitehall."

"A duchess?" Arold laughed. "There has never been a duchess of the Lands. I say we wait for Lord Albert to reply."

"And I say we don't have time." Urses said. "The men rallied around Her Grace after Greatbath and when she announced her pregnancy. Make her duchess and invigorate the men even more."

"Would you take it?" Cada asked Yvanne. It hadn't even occurred to her that Urses was talking about her, but she was in Greatbath, and she was the one pregnant, and all the men did rally behind her.

Follow in father's footsteps, she thought. *The Duchess of the Lands of Asara does sound nice. Father would be so proud.* "If you all agree it's for the best." She said as she kept herself from crying. Crying from either joy or sadness she couldn't tell. "Until Albert comes back to take his rightful place."

She heard Aimora say, "it's a splendid idea," and Lord Cul say, "take it," and Sidoro say, "it will boost morale," and Urses whisper, "it's yours."

Arold, the swordmaster who probably never dreamed he would be a senior member of the king's council, nodded slowly and said, "go ahead," before looking to Devro. "What does the king say? It's your responsibility to grant her the duchy."

"I don't think it matters," Devro rolled his eyes, "but since you all say it does I will give the Lands of Asara to my wife as is my right."

Yvanne was happy her father was able to make her queen, but even with all the privileges it wasn't what she truly wanted. She smiled and thanked everyone. That night she cursed the gods for taking her father and thanked them for what had happened. She went to sleep as the Lady of Whitehall, Duchess of the Lands of Asara, successor to her father.

Bertin

Water steamed over him. Bertin hadn't felt clean in far too long, he couldn't even remember he last time. Even the waters of Lisan Biresdea felt sandy. But the hot springs on the northern side of the Kash Mountains were clearer than the sky, and he could feel the dirt and grime slipping off him.

"I told you this would be nice," Thatar said as he sunk farther into the water, only his head showing. "Any place you'd rather be right now?"

Bertin shook his head with disbelief. "Of course. I'd rather be in Rowan."

"The palace wasn't as grand as the humans made me believe," Eyln said as he stripped and dropped into the pool. "I've seen much better elvish palaces. The one in Dà Sruthros touches the sky, reaches for the Dragon. It's magnificent." Bertin was incensed that he knew Eyln was talking about Vigur, but using the elvish word. He never thought he would know anything the elves said.

"When did you last see the palace in Rowan?" Bertin asked. "My father told me it was better before the commoners ransacked it."

"Last century sometime," Eyln waved his hand, "it didn't

leave an impression."

Vhistela stalked over from the horses who were munching on any green grass they could find. The lack of sea winds made the north half of Riorskè more arid. Bertin liked the lack of people though. Kelltar and Vhistela had been talking for what seemed like hours. "He wants to leave soon," she said, dipping her toes into the water. "Kelltar doesn't like how close we are to Jorbstah."

Glares became more common the farther east they went instead of the parade they received in Cluo. "The closer we get to Anha Jorbstah," Vhistela had told him, "the more people remember an ancestor who died when we took the city. Here, north of the *Keàs Ora,* even elf hunters make their home." The old elf shuddered. She had never looked scared. "They like to traverse the mountains and steal anyone they can from us. We don't know what happens to them."

A few days ago, while Thatar kept watch while the others slept, he had told Bertin, "Vhistela's second daughter was taken by hunters. The whole of Anha Jorbstah scoured the mountains for months but it was no use. Her daughter was gone."

"What do you think they did to her?" Bertin remembered what had happened to Ioelena's brothers. The horrid things the humans did to their bodies.

"I don't even want to think about it." Thatar said, both watched Vhistela's chest rise and fall as she slept. "But the ramoryr feel differently over here, so it happens more than we wish."

Luckily for them, the capital of Riorskè had only one major wall they had to get through, the one north of the city that stretched along the pass separating the Pywaln branch from the Kash Mountains. It had defended the city from Veck'kop attacks for hundreds of years, even his cousin couldn't break through the wall, instead he dumped the bodies of thousands of Rainvealandians into the small tributaries and let them float down the river.

They had been able to pass through the gate unnoticed since the Ancient One was changing faces that night. The whole of Rainvealand lit bonfires and prayed. The elves and Bertin hid in the northern foothills, walking under the snowy peaks of the Kash until they found the hot springs. Now, they had been resting for a day or more. Kelltar's face was always red and bulging.

"What does he think is going to happen?" Thatar asked Vhistela. "Hunters haven't been spotted in months."

"We haven't been *here* in months," she said. "Who knows what the scouts have seen. The elders were worried when we left." Thatar and Vhistela started conversing in their language. Bertin didn't know enough to figure it out, so he went to rubbing the hot water on his face and behind his ears. He touched his cheek too hard and it throbbed. It had been broken in Telemaw and hadn't healed well. He wondered what it looked like under his skin. All the bones shattered and trying to fuse. His missing finger also reminded him of the desert. All that he endured.

The back of Kelltar's bald head faced Bertin. He was sitting on a ledge by the horses, taking in the view of the rugged foothills and grasslands that stretched for hundreds of miles. *If I could get him in here maybe I could drown him. Ioelena would want to see him drown.* But Bertin was too worried he'd never get away. He'd surely get lost in the wilderness unless he could find Jorbstah, but he never learned the language of the mites like his sister. He would be lost there too.

"Who are these elders you keep mentioning?" Bertin interrupted the elf's conversation. "Isn't this Blaenda your king?"

Eyln chuckled as he rubbed a soft rock on his skin. "Human leaders find it easier to talk with one ruler than many. Blaenda is merely a figurehead. The elders make the decisions together, and Blaenda tells the world."

Kelltar turned to them, grabbed Eyln's clothes before throwing them to him, and said something in elvish. "Time to go," Thatar said. "Not much use in arguing with him." He pointed to a vein that was popping out of Kelltar's head. "He's trying not to yell."

Bertin stood first, much to Kelltar's surprise by his widening eyes. He found his clothes. Brown and dark from all the dust and grass and mud he's had to deal with, not even the pools could wash it all. It was nice not standing or walking. His feet hadn't been able to rest since leaving Rowan. Sometimes they got so bad they started to bleed again. Vhistela had thrown him a white cloth to wrap around them, and he was glad she did.

The other elves followed suit slipping into their trousers and tunics. Bertin ran his fingers through his brown hair and for the first time didn't get a handful of dust and dirt, he was happy.

Then he heard the words, *"Sin kemsi?"* A young girl was standing on the path that led to the hot springs. She was wrapped in long cloth, only her black face and hair could be seen. *"Mekus zak, uyer le inksel."*

"It's alright," Bertin said before Kelltar stepped forward. The girl didn't like the large, muscly elf moving toward her.

She stepped away but tripped on a rock landing on her back. "Kelltar," Bertin said but Thatar flashed a look that said "keep quiet."

Kelltar kept stepping forward. *"Umak,"* she said on the ground, her teeth chattering from fear. Kelltar pounced like a lion. Bertin didn't know why the other elves were letting him attack. *This is why we hate them, because they do things like this.* Kelltar reached the girl and … and offered a hand. She took it, though Bertin could see her hand shaking and her eyes grow when she saw Kelltar's pointed ears.

"Adaş?" a man called as he came around the corner and saw the girl and the large elf holding hands as Kelltar helped her to her feet. "Adaş! *Edus zak! Ehliki!*" The girl snatched her hand away and ran toward the older mite. She looked back once more before the man dragged her away.

"What was that?" Bertin said after silence had filled the air.

"Just some ramoryr," Eyln said, "coming to enjoy the springs I reckon."

Vhistela said, "Now we really need to leave. Who knows who that man was. He could come back here with an army if he chooses." This time there was no arguing. The elves all packed up before the hour was over and continued east.

***

A lion roared from somewhere in the jagged mountains as the horses made their way along the foothills. Bertin imagined the beast attacking Kelltar. It wasn't a nice thought. The elf had killed Ioelena and countless Telemese, wanted to wage a war on all humans. *Yet he helped a mite girl.* Bertin's face twisted in disgust at Kelltar doing something nice.

191

Bertin was on the back of Thatar's horse. Erona gracefully climbed the hills and took careful steps over rocks and outcrops. "How far away are we?" Bertin asked. He wanted to be done with traveling, and wanted to see what his fate would be in Anha Jorbstah.

"We'll go around that mountain," Thatar pointed to a tall peak covered in white snow in the far distance, "until we reach the Pywaln Pass. Then a couple more days journey if we go at this speed."

"Great," he rolled his eyes.

Then there was a shout from behind and they all turned. A dozen or so horses were racing toward them. "What is this?" Thatar asked as he stared at the riders.

"*Ritheg!*" Kelltar shouted and kicked his horse to a gallop.

Bertin didn't know who was following them but he held onto Thatar as hard as he could as Erona flew over the shrubs and kicked up dirt. His head was swinging as Thatar glided his horse over the hills and small valleys. Bertin quickly looked and the riders were still following them. One of them was even standing atop the horse and loosing an arrow.

The arrow pierced Eyln's horse in the head and the two went crashing down.

Vhistela reared her mount around and nocked three arrows before loosing them as she jumped from her horse and hit the ground. Three mites were hit. Their horses racing away from the commotion. One of the bodies being dragged as his foot was caught in the stirrup.

"Guess we're fighting," Thatar said. He brought Erona to a stop and jumped off. Bertin didn't want to go, but the elf grabbed his arms and pulled. "*Aronar,*" Thatar whispered to his horse who galloped toward the hills. He pulled out his sword, the thin blade reflecting the sunlight, as the mites came upon them on their horses.

"Probably should've kept your horse," Bertin said as he clung to Thatar like glue.

"No need," the elf smiled and jumped as a mite ran towards him. Thatar did some flip and his sword cut the mite's head clean off.

Kelltar threw his knives and sent his steed away. Vhistela was nocking and loosing arrows. Eyln was standing, shaking off the dust, and mourning his horse. He found his sword and faced the mites. Bertin stood helpless. He would rather be hiding with the horses than with Thatar, choking on the dust cloud made by the mites' steeds.

Eyln charged with sword in hand. He aimed for the horses' legs, dodging kicks and hits from the mites atop. His blade cut through a horse leg like it was butter. The horse screamed as blood spurted and it came tumbling down. The rider falling in a huff. Eyln pushing the sword into the rider's chest. He smiled as the others gathered around. *At least this will be over quickly,* Bertin thought, *why these few mites would attack some elves doesn't make sense.*

Then he saw it in the distance. More riders. The dust cloud looking like a storm behind them. "How many hunters are there?" He asked to no one. Thatar's eyes got big and he shouted in elvish. Vhistela and Kelltar quickly saw and began to race towards their horses. Eyln was still in the midst of the mites. They whacked at him with long blades. Eyln snarled like an animal and lunged a few times. The final lunge was too much, he stumbled back, and a mite took the opportunity to swing a sword toward his face. Before Bertin could turn away he saw the elf's cheeks and nose split in two, the bottom half of his face hanging by loose skin and muscles.

Vhistela shouted, "Over here!" as she loosed arrows at the mites who killed Eyln. She was with the horses by the hills, a steep wall of rock was protruding from the shrubs. Thatar pulled Bertin as the elves ran to her. Kelltar threw some more of his knives as he reached Vhistela. *"Kiftellan,"* she said to no one.

The rocks started to shake, and Bertin checked to make sure it wasn't from more elf hunters. Then the rock face shifted, like a sliding door was being pulled opened. "Quickly," Thatar pushed him.

"What is this?" Bertin asked as they were swallowed by the darkness of the cave.

"Safety," Kelltar grunted.

Flora

Her father's study was a small room just off his bedchamber. During her childhood she would run into the study at daybreak and sit with Pyre Blume while he went over reports and spoke to his courtiers. It was smaller than she remembered. The desk sat near the hearth, which was roaring with fire as snow and ice fell outside; gray light hit the stained windows and turned blue and yellow; her father sat with his eyes closed, resting them.

Flora drank her warm mead from across the fire. The warmth of both making her sweat. *Better than freezing outside,* she thought as she remembered the hordes of people at the city gates. "Tired of all the lords and their households taking up space in the castle?" She asked her father.

His eyes were tired. He was only getting older, even chopping wood or sparring with his guards or swimming in the sea couldn't stop that. "Maybe I should've just told Tundavik that the Flewthlands were going to join him then send word to everyone. Would that've been so bad?"

"It wouldn't've made you popular." Flora said as she twisted a strand of fabric on her chair. "Do you ever wish Hurvir wouldn't have allowed you to take over as duke? Grandfather could have been the end of your line and we could have lived a peaceful life, say, in Plajul. I've always found Ceal to be beautiful with the elven homes."

"We're in a castle here. In Plajul we'd be nothing but farmers wondering why our king has abandoned us."

"King Leddo is a fine man from what I've been told."

"That man is a fool and if the Vigurites hadn't've conquered us after the Nowexerts were done with us *we* would rule in Plajul. I'd be a much better king than Leddo. Maybe I can sway a few of the lords if I promise to conquer north of the Flit." Pyre rubbed his liver-spotted hands together. "How does your husband feel? Still doesn't want to fight?"

"His memories of warring with the mites are not pleasant."

"Rubbish." Her father rolled his eyes and shook his head. "I allowed that man to marry you because Woodrun is second only to Storyah and he tucks his tail at the first sign of trouble. His father would be ashamed, he said to me once 'my son is a strong one, fiercely loyal, a great commander.' I think Bertam Lovell lied. *That* was a loyal man, he knew how to fight, hated those in Vigur. His son is a cheap imitation."

Flora's eyes were wide as she took a sip. *Is that how he's always felt about Barnet? He would've loved it if I never married the man.* She shook away the thought of never marrying Barnet as that would mean Little Flora wouldn't be here. "He was never supposed to be lord, you know that. He wasn't raised the same way as Beomont was or any of his other brothers."

"Have you tried to change his mind?"

"Why do you want us to go to war so bad? You don't seem the slightest bit worried that we could lose. That men will die. And if Lord Gallent's forces attack us here then the women and children can die too. Woodrun would be one of the first to fall. I do not want my home to be destroyed and everyone I know killed."

"Woodrun is not your home," her father muttered.

"It's been more of a home than Storyah this last decade. You rarely wrote and never wished to see us, not even Florance, and then you invite us to Storyah but it's just because of the council vote. What happened? We were so close once."

"This is about the war and the future of the Flewthlands. I want to accomplish what Sir Garth and my father tried to do but failed. I think this is the best way."

Flora stood and faced the fire, the flames causing her eyes to water from the heat. Or maybe those were tears. "I can try my best to talk to Barnet. He also wants freedom, but I'm not sure if I can get through to him. He's so stubborn. It got worse once he found out Lord Vandes was here. I don't know what happened between them, but as long as Tundavik is here then I don't see Barnet voting for war."

"You must convince him. I don't know anyone else who can."

"No matter which way he votes I will leave Storyah after the matter is closed. This isn't my home anymore, and it certainly isn't Florance's home. Even if Barnet marches south we will go west. Pray that Woodrun isn't attacked."

"I did miss you," her father said as he watched the ice form on the window. "I was so busy. I had to take back control and gain respect for stopping the rebellion. Many believed I betrayed the very ideals of our people. Leaving Storyah might've caused some other lord to challenge me. I received too many letters that said 'you are a traitor.' I had to show them I would listen and not run away and hide."

"Is that why mother came to Woodrun? You were too busy

for her?"

"You know she was sick. The daken said the streams in the woods might help her. I didn't want her to leave, but she made up her mind. I'm just happy she got to spend her last few years with you and Florance."

Without thinking her arms wrapped around her father and her tears spilled out. She had missed the way he smelled of salt from the ocean, the way his arms felt when he hugged her, the scent of mint he chewed on. "Thank you for saying that." She began to wipe her tears away. "I will see what I can do about Barnet."

There was a quiet knock on the door before it opened. "I'm sorry, my lord duke," Nama, a maid, said as she bowed her head low. "But she insisted."

Little Flora came clacking in her boots, holding the maid's hand. "Mama, isn't it time to pray? I've been waiting. What's wrong?" Her little voice asked as Flora wiped her tears and nose with her sleeve.

"Nothing, my sweet. Yes, let's go pray."

As Flora guided her daughter down the hall to their quarters she asked, "and who are we praying to today?"

"Samosay?"

"Are you sure?"

Little Flora chewed her lip just like her mother would. "I'm sure." Flora nodded. "I wish to pray for the soldiers. I want to pray for Samosay to make their journey peaceful and to bring warm air from the west."

"Sounds good. What have you been up to today? Did Nama take good care of you?"

"Oh yes. We played in the snow, but not the yellow bits," she scrunched her face. "Then we drank some water with honey in it. I wanted fruit but Nama said we were running low. Why?"

"The war."

"Are they fighting the fruit trees?"

Flora giggled as she opened the door to their chambers, the fire already burning in the stone hearth which meant her husband was near. "No, my silly child, but it's winter and the war messed up the harvest. Hopefully later this year we can get some nice lemons."

They knelt in front of the fire, placing four fingers on their hearts, then bowing on the dusty floor. Florance had been practicing of late, she didn't even need help. "Dear Samosay," her daughter squeaked, "we ask that you keep the animals safe from harm during the war. We ask that you keep the soldiers safe on the roads. We ask …" Little Flora eyed her mother, hair falling in her face.

"We ask that you deliver us some good news from the war. News that people are alive and well." Flora said. "We thank you Samosay."

"We thank you." Florance finished and her mother went to fixing her hair once they were done bowing. "Did I do good? Do you think Samosay heard?"

"He always hears."

"I thought it wonderful." Barnet came from the privy chamber. "I could see you becoming the doma of Woodrun when you're older."

Florance giggled. "Then I could stay with you both and not have to go to a different home like mama."

Barnet glared at Flora for a short moment as he fixed his black sleeves. "Yes, well, if you do have to go somewhere we'll be sure to visit."

"Florance," her mother said, "why don't you go make your bed. I noticed it wasn't well put together." Little Flora went to fix her wool sheets and feather pillows in the bed by Flora and Barnet's. "May we talk?" she asked her husband.

"You've come from a meeting with your father so I assume this is about the vote. It's getting ever closer and he's worried I mean what I say?"

"I just think it's the best time for the Flewthlands to push for independence."

"Been talking to Tundavik as well? Did he eat breakfast with you again? Did you show him around the castle and where you used to play as a young girl?"

"I haven't spoken to him in days."

"You were to never speak to him." Barnet's nostrils flared as he warmed himself by the hearth. His dark tunic was embossed with a thousand trees that became yellow from the flames. "I have other lords telling me they see you together. Atop the walls. In the dining hall. You're making a fool of yourself and of our marriage."

"Nothing is happening."

"All done." Florance said and Barnet slipped back into being a father.

"Good job, little one. Can you bring me my chain from the chest? The one with the four pointed star?" Then it was back to being just a husband, almost a stranger. "I merely wish to keep you safe. Tundavik is not an innocent old man. The things he did along the Bezir were horrific."

"He sacked Panscar and you sacked Suktir, didn't you? You know better than most that a leader cannot always control their soldiers."

"I don't want to continue this conversation. If your father

wants me to change my vote then he can speak with me instead of sending you to do it. Or better yet, why not have Tundavik do it? I would like to see if he can stomach looking into my eyes." Barnet opened the door and called for Florance to follow once she found the chain.

Flora was left alone with the fire as a snowstorm blew in from the west.

***

The man she most didn't want to see, well maybe except for Barnet, watched out a stained window with her in the hall. "Where were you off to?" Tundavik asked after he stopped to be by her. They were very close. The old lord smelled like a forest, like the place he grew up.

Flora was aware of every servant and page and maid who passed by. Of all the stories they would tell their lords and friends. *Is the next one going to be about a kiss we shared by the window? Under the light of a four pointed star?* "I was off to the kitchens. I wish to eat my food in my chamber tonight."

"With your family?" He asked and Flora shook her head. "Well, a lady shouldn't have to eat alone. Is there a reason?"

"My husband and daughter are enjoying dinner with Lord Toware and Lady Lueva tonight. I declined. I'm sure he wishes Toware to join his side of the vote." Flora chewed her lip, always chewed her lip. "Barnet isn't comfortable with us speaking, so I should probably go on."

"I remember him." Tundavik said before she walked away. "He was so young then, but I remember fighting and taking the cities along the Bezir. He was there. A good soldier."

"That doesn't explain why he doesn't like you."

"Maybe seeing me reminds him of all the hard times. All the other men in his family died during the war, right? He should be happy he survived. But old wounds are hard to heal and imagining your family's deaths over and over can be excruciating."

"So nothing bad? He says you did horrid things along the river."

Tundavik's eyes lowered. "It was war. A lot of people died, but I assure you I did not carry out massacres like Hurvir did in Jorbstah if that's what worries you."

"No," she said. *What does worry me about him? He's right, it was war. Barnet probably did awful things too, as well as my father.* "Barnet said he would speak to you about his vote if you wish. I'm not sure he can be swayed, but it's a start."

"Thank you so much." Tundavik said. Flora blushed. She had almost never heard a thank you from her husband. Not even when she went through labor and birthed his daughter, so Flora did something she never thought possible, she let the rumors come true, and kissed Tundavik by the window. The four pointed star in the glass watching their every move.

"I'm sorry," Flora said as she watched the hall for onlookers. "That was inappropriate. Sinful. I need to go pray."

"Do you?" Tundavik asked. Flora kissed him again. His beard warming her chin. They stopped kissing for only a few moments as they made their way to Lord Vandes' bedchamber. He dropped his ugly red and yellow and pulled off Flora's blue coat. She had tears in her eyes. Not sadness. Happy tears. As Tundavik kissed down her neck and chest she became overwhelmed with the thought of Barnet. How he never gave her what she wanted. How he always mistreated her. How he wouldn't let her speak her mind. But

Tundavik was different.

"On the bed." Flora moaned in his ear. The old duke lay naked on the bed and Flora straddled him. She hadn't been with a man in so long. Not since her daughter was conceived. But the moment wasn't about Florance or Barnet. She forgot about them, about her father, about Woodrun, about the war while she rode atop Tundavik.

Sophie

It was dangerous to be so close to the Lands of Asara, but Ultiir insisted they take riverboats instead of horses to Vigur so he could get there quickly and put down the riots. Sophie felt naked in her boat. It was small with a cover to block the sun and rain, but the sides were open for arrows to pierce her. Lucky for her the north bank seemed empty, everyone fleeing or fighting.

Sir Velle never left her side. His armor ready to stop any attacks. Sir Achen was still bruised but he too stayed close to her. Tedbalt decided it was best for him to ride with Sophie instead of taking his own boat which she hated, but at least the old lord seemed honest. Now more than ever she needed allies by her side and Tedbalt was the only one she had. Ultiir was in the lead boat. He had stopped speaking to Sophie after their argument. When she didn't stop him from believing she was only marrying him because her parents ordered it. *He doesn't realize I can think for myself.*

"How bad did Lord de'Viere say the rioting was?" Sophie asked Lord Masson who watched the swimming fish below.

"He only mentioned some burned storehouses and watch-towers. Nothing we can't handle, and the palace is swarming with guards, perfectly safe for any in the Noble Lands. Your ladies in waiting are sure to be fine."

"Lady Volles would certainly be able to protect the Queen's Council with just her words. No one would dare challenge her."

"Like getting a wooden spoon from your mother, that one." Tedbalt laughed and sat beside Sophie on a wood slab meant for a fisherman. "I'm sure they are dying to hear every detail of your trip. How will you tell them?"

"Tell them what? The slave revolt, Ultiir's argument, the queen mother?"

"Perhaps your babe."

Sir Velle tensed as he looked over the water, Sir Achen picking at his fingers like he didn't know. "Perhaps this discussion should be had at another time. You know how voices carry over the water."

"Still haven't told His Grace? That might bring your marriage back together."

"I'm fine with the way our marriage is now. Hopefully I won't have to, excuse my language, fuck him anymore. I will gladly spend my nights alone."

"His Grace, forgive my characterization," Tedbalt gave a knowing smirk, "will never let you out of his head. He will most definitely knock on your door at night with a smile and no clothes."

"He won't be smiling." Sophie touched her belly, hoping she didn't look pregnant yet. She still needed time to figure out her best course of action. "Looks like we'll need to find him a distraction. My dead husband spent many nights in the King's Brothel. I don't see why Ultiir can't do the same."

"He'll have more important things to worry about once we reach the palace."

"Smoke." Sir Velle muttered.

The city walls loomed over the fields in the distance, beyond them smoke towers painted the sky black. Riverboats clogged the Montla. "Probably merchants escaping with what they can." Tedbalt said. "I see Lord de'Viere's city guards aren't maintaining order very well."

"Maybe my husband was wrong to kill Gofrei."

"Treason to say something like that. Lord Geary was spying on everything we did. Good thing I'm on your side."

"What is *my side*?" Sophie asked with a roll of her eyes. "I am the queen. I hold no power like every queen before me. If Ultiir dies I cease to exist in this realm. What man would want to marry a woman whose last two husbands were killed? So far I have no children so any line my parents wish for me to strengthen won't go on, and if I have a girl she'll be excluded from the monarchy anyhow. You think the Margias will extend a hand to you? Once I stop being queen my parents will forget about Viguran and any who might've helped me. I have few guards so I can't fight. My lands aren't the most profitable. So what exactly are you hoping to gain from joining *my side*?"

The old lord gave a slight nod as he thought through his answer. "As chief daken under your first husband I was never taken seriously enough. I warned Hurvir of the awful things befalling our kingdom, how some of his councilors were upset with him. He brushed me off as an old loon. Now, Ultiir has made me his chief consultant, but holds me far. You can see the distrust on his face. I was rewarded with helping but, as you know, we lords always desire more. The queen of Viguran has been a powerless position for far too long. I think it's time to change that."

Sophie was rocking with the boat. She chewed her cheek as she wondered if Tedbalt was this serious. He would gain nothing from siding with her. "What if I don't believe you have good intentions? Will you scurry back to Ultiir and tell all?"

"You still question whether you can trust me. Vallnioc raised you well I see." His fingers pattered on the wooden boat. "I guess you'll just have to find out." Tedbalt went over to Sir Achen and held out his hand. "May I see your dagger? Yes, sheath too." The knight handed them over and the old lord in turn handed them to Sophie. "I know it doesn't befit a queen, but if Ultiir tries anything you can use this."

Sophie took the dagger. The leather sheath slick in her hands. She had never fought anyone before, but a dagger might've came in handy during the slave revolt, and who knew what Ultiir was planning next. "What happened to your wife, my lord? You didn't have any daughters either. Why so kind?"

"Everyone deserves kindness, don't they? Especially a queen."

But not your slaves, she thought as she noted the lord didn't give a very clear answer.

"Look at the docks." Tedbalt said as the boats passed the walls and the city came into view, the guards switched from facing the north bank to the south.

Storehouses, markets, crates, riverboats all sat aflame in the North Docks. Chanting carried over the water. Mobs of peasants shouted and looted and grabbed weapons and torched buildings. Some threw rocks at the king's entourage. "Vigura help us." Sir Velle said as he gripped the hilt of his sword.

"Think they'll call this the Montla Flames?" Lord Masson asked with a smirk.

"My husband says this will not be like Rowan. I'm not sure what he intends to do."

"Make it worse I fear." Tedbalt scratched his beard. "Queen Amalia also wanted to make an example of the people protesting against her, she fanned the flames and destroyed her kingdom"

Sophie had learned enough about the Brutahki Flames from her parents, making sure she would never repeat the same mistakes as the Rowai queen. Amalia had killed the protesters and not only rioting took place, but the complete abolishment of the monarchy for nearly fifteen years until Bartel united the realm. "Maybe Ultiir is more like King Bartel than Amalia."

"Ultiir is just like his brother. What did Hurvir do when riots broke out? Used all of his power to crush them. Banned mites from the city, took children of rioters and pawned them off, created resentment. I pray to the gods Ultiir chooses a different path, but I know he won't."

Sophie coughed as the smoke blew to the water, cloaking them in black. Eventually they made it to a peaceful part of Vigur, the Noble Lands, where all the lords and ladies of the court lived. She couldn't imagine it ever burning. The nobles loved their homes much more than the peasants who disregarded their neighborhoods and burned them once a decade.

They made it passed the palace walls and the small dock crawling with palace guards welcomed them. One by one, at the slowest pace Sophie knew, the riverboats emptied. Lady Ficca, with her dark hair braided into a tower, quickly found her and wrapped their arms together. "My queen, you must tell me everything that happened in Goldfield and I can tell you all the news from Vigur."

"I haven't been away that long," Sophie told her lady in waiting, "what could've happened here besides the riots?"

"Oh we don't care for the rioting. Many scandals unfolding in court."

Sophie rolled her eyes. *Not even in the palace and gossip finds me.* "Well I'm excited to meet with my ladies. Won't you gather them?"

Lady Ficca bowed and ran toward the looming palace. Dark clouds formed in the sky, swirling near the tallest tower in the palace that engulfed them. The first time she saw the palace in Vigur she felt so small, and all these years later she felt the same. No one could conquer the majesty of the palace. But she could try.

Renna and Amalla disembarked their boat and rushed over to Sophie, fixing her dress and wiping dirt from the sleeves. "My queen, how was the journey?" Amalla asked.

Renna said, "Oh how I wish we would've been able to sail with you, but Lord Masson had to be close to you."

"It's alright Renna. Lord Masson was a fine companion and the journey was swift. Much better than riding the horses over the same ground I've tread dozens of times." Guards parted as they made their way along the cobbled path to the palace. Muddy footprints making a trail on the stone. "My ladies in waiting would like to meet, so you two can prepare my chamber for later."

"Would you like to change first?" Amalla asked. "The Queen's Council likes when you wear yellow."

"I'll stick to my red gown."

"But red could mean mourning." Amalla continued. "You don't want them and the other nobles to think someone close to you has died again, think of all the explaining you'll have to do."

I am in mourning, she thought as Ultiir was surrounded by his council and talk of the riots fell over the land. "It will be quite all right. And I'm sure you two would like some privacy after sharing your quarters with the servants in Goldfield."

Renna and Amalla both blushed. "Whatever you say, my queen." Renna bowed.

"Shall I escort you to your meeting?" A familiar voice said. Sufar, Ultiir's household slave, gave a low bow when she spied him. "My queen, His Grace has instructed me to stay close to you, usher you about the palace, of course with your guards in tow." Achen and Velle were merely a step behind. "After the slave revolts in the kingdom he is worried for your safety."

"Is he expecting a slave revolt on the palace grounds?"

"His Grace is not ruling anything out. We live in difficult times."

"And you're supposed to protect me, how? My guards carry swords and wear armor. You wear silk and carry letters."

Sufar laughed, his teeth whiter than most slaves from years of attending Ultiir. "I can speak the slave's language. Know their hearts. If any of them wish you harm I will quickly tell your household guards and stop the threat."

"Sentence your own kind to death?" Achen said as he winced.

"Difficult times, my good sir." Sufar said. "May I escort you?" He held out his arm for Sophie to take and they were off. Ultiir eyeing them while Lord de'Viere explained when the rioting started.

"You missed all the excitement in Goldfield. The slaves revolted and ran." Guards opened the large doors of the marble palace and Sufar hurried inside. "Would you've joined?" Sophie asked.

"His Grace has given me a good life, much better than the others. I do not wear chains, I can go almost anywhere I wish, he taught me my letters and numbers. I would not run away even if staying meant certain death."

Loyal. I see why Ultiir wanted him to watch me. "It was a violent ordeal anyhow. Revolts don't seem like much fun, and why bother when the king's forces will surely capture them all in a few weeks time?"

"My thoughts exactly, Your Grace."

They didn't bother going toward the throne room, the court was surely in session and the arguments would be flying. Sufar led them down a short corridor to where the Queen's Council discussed 'business'. "You are too kind." She said to the slave. "Sir Achen go find the daken and see to getting something for the pain. Sufar and Sir Velle can protect me from the vile rumors inside this room."

Inside sat Baroness Mara sipping some wine with Ladies Ficca and Rila browsing the old books on the shelves. "My queen." Mara said, her lips red. "Do tell us about Goldfield."

"Goldfield wasn't all that exciting," she wanted to move on already, not relive that nightmare, but the ladies would ask for it again and again if she said nothing. "That was a jest." The three women laughed as Countess Filra came in wearing a black dress. "The queen mother was as much a tyrant as she's ever been. On top of that the slaves decided to run away and burn the crop in the process. Lady Ficca told me there was news here?"

"Is that all you'll say about Goldfield, my lady?" Ficca said. "You were away for weeks."

"I want to know what's been happening here." Sophie pursed her lips. "And where is Abre and Lady Betal?"

The baroness gulped. "They have left the capital, Your Grace. Lady Betal was recalled by her husband, the lord of Ghostfield. Apparently he supports the bastard."

"Whom he says is now legitimate." Lady Ficca said. "Even though our king says his brother never wished for that."

"The forged letter from Lord Geary has spread around like a fire." Rila said. "Even in his death he still causes problems for our home."

"As for our Lady Abre Volles." Filra piped up. "Her husband died of the pox."

"With no heirs." Ficca added.

Countess Filra continued, "Abre went to Oceantree in hopes she'll be given the lands and titles."

"A woman cannot inherit such a thing." Sophie said as she imagined herself wielding the power after Hurvir was killed.

"She wanted our support but we couldn't give it." Rila said. "It's scandalous what she's doing. I've never seen her more determined. She claimed she'd rebel against Ritaeum if necessary."

"That's suicide." Sophie said. "What makes her think Lord Valles would even agree?"

Mara took another sip of wine. "Haven't you heard? The duke of the Lands of Asara is dead. His daughter, the rebel queen, is now the leader. Not only are they waging war on us they wage war on our customs."

"Little Yvanne is a duchess?" Sophie asked. The last time

she saw that child was during a bad harvest. Her and Devro delivered food to Whitehall. They were both babes at the time. "The whole kingdom's a mess at the moment." *But if Yvanne had her way she would be queen even if Devro died. And if I have a daughter what will she get in my world?* She touched her stomach, pretending to pull at a string on her dress. "Do you think Abre would go against us?"

"For Oceantree," Mara said, "I could see it. Any woman who thinks they'll gain more under the rebels might go against us."

"So we need to change that."

Raimund

As he wiped snow off the log, he thought of Valkyr. Raimund missed his sword too much. Any other knight would get over it and move on, even a family heirloom could be replaced as long as it was done with dignity. But Valkyr was apart of him. Valkyr reminded him of his parents, of Mar, of Devro. Simpler times when he would polish his sword from training instead of killing men.

But he didn't need Valkyr now. He didn't need any stone to help the griffin's wound close. He didn't need it to light the log on fire.

He concentrated his thoughts on Viguran. How Ultiir's forces could be spilling into Whitehall at any minute and killing everyone he knew. Mar would die protecting Devro, but the bastard boy would still be murdered by his uncle. The usurper. Yvanne would be next. Raimund's breathing quickened as he felt a tinge of heat on his palm. He didn't know if it was fate or a coincidence that bought him and Sile together. But the girl in Whitehall looked her spitting image, and he wanted to unite mother and daughter again.

Wood cracked and he opened his eyes to see a small flame dancing on the log. No one was around. He pulled his cloak tighter as night settled in. There wasn't a snowstorm yet, but clouds were moving in fast from the east, so Raimund and Sile would have to orchestrate this plan quickly and seamlessly. He had little fate in Potter.

Sile was somewhere in the darkness, hiding behind rocks. There wasn't much around where the great hole was that held the prison. The forests cut down for the wooden barracks of the guards. And now Raimund had to set it alight. Sile was against it at first, but Raimund promised no one would die. He didn't know if that were true. *Am I really going to kill for Potter? I barely know him.* But he imagined it was Devro being held in some cold northern prison and his qualms went away.

So he threw the burning log through an open window in the barracks and hoped it would be enough.

There were shouts and guards along the perimeter came to investigate the wooden building. It was up to Sile now. Raimund didn't have a sword. He couldn't fight guard after guard. But they were falling for the distraction. Smoke started to rise from the window and the perimeter of the prison was empty for the most part.

Red hair flashed and Sile was moving from a outcrop. She reached the front of the barracks as Raimund went around the side, readying himself to go find Potter. Sile's stone shone bright as she held out her hands and a sheet of ice grew from the ground to cover the door. The guards were fighting the fire but Raimund heard them question the ice, asking a god, Kuja, what was happening.

Now was his chance. Raimund raced to where the long, metal stairs started. A guard who hadn't gone to the fire was by the steps and reached for his sword with a look of shock, but Raimund pushed him over the edge of the wide crater. Then grabbed the guard by the tunic and yanked him back up. *Damn Sile,* he thought as he saved the guard, *making this harder than it has to be.* Raimund took the man's sword and gave him a few punches to the head for him to stay down.

Then he started down the steps. They seemed never ending, but far below he could see looks of confusion as smoke trailed through the air. Guards from below took to the stairs and started to climb. Raimund would have to fight them off as well. He gripped his newfound sword, promised he wouldn't kill, and started running as fast as he could without tripping. He jumped two, three, four steps at a time. Each flight having to turn, and there seemed to be a hundred flights. He slipped over some ice at one point, but caught himself on the cold, metal wall. His fingers leaving red marks.

Looking up to make sure Sile wasn't calling for help, he saw the smoke start to mix with snow, and knew they only had a few minutes before a blizzard engulfed them. He turned his attention down once more, the prisoners faces came into view. Scruffy, long beards, moth eaten coats and trousers, frostbitten noses all looked back at him. A half dozen guards were ascending the steps straight to him, but a large drift of snow caught his attention. It was a huge pile of powdery mess, probably deep enough to catch him, but it was a stupid idea. Then he saw the fat man. Potter was looking up in disbelief at the smoke, not turning his head to the stairs.

"I will not die like this," Raimund said as guards started to unsheathe their weapons as they neared. "Potter!" He shouted and jumped.

There was a puff of white and darkness swallowed him. He didn't know where he was. If he were alive or dead. If the snow was full of ice or rock or if it wasn't as deep as he thought. His mouth was full. His eyes covered. He thought of dying in snow, if he wanted that to happen he would've died with his parents long ago. Raimund felt warmth. The smell of burning wood filled his nose.

He wiped his eyes clean and saw that his body had made enough heat to melt the snow around him, he started to push forward and claw his way out of the snow drift as light peeked through. Then he saw Potter and dozens of other prisoners all staring back at him. The guards above split in two. One group continued climbing and the other started back down.

"What're ya doing?" Potter asked, his mouth was agape. "I figured you was dead."

Raimund took a deep breath, his lungs wheezing for air, and he placed a hand on Potter's shoulder. "I didn't give up on you," he panted. "Now, will you follow me out of here?"

"I don't know, the smoke," he pointed out of the whole as snowflakes mix with soot started to fall on them. "Something wrong is going on."

"It was me," Raimund started to push Potter toward the stairs. The other prisoners had figured it out without Raimund needing to explain it to them. They were now running up the unguarded stairs, the guards above shouting at them, but no one listening. The metal stairs were overrun with men all wanting to be free. "Now let's go."

He didn't give a chance for Potter to turn around, he pushed him to the first step and the young man decided to continue. They were the last up the stairs as everyone else was already running. *Means I won't have to fight off the guards.* And he didn't. The first few escapees were cut down and injured by the guards swinging their shortswords or daggers, but they became overwhelmed eventually, and the prisoners didn't promise Sile that no one would be killed. The three men who were protecting the stairs all screamed as they were hurtled over the rails. Red and gray innards covered the snow in a splash.

"I think I'm going to be sick," Potter grabbed his mouth.

"No you aren't." Raimund pointed to the rim to distract Potter from the dead below. "We're almost there. I have a nice place for us to stay before we set out to head home. You want to see your family again, right?"

"Of course," Potter muttered.

The fat man tripped over a few steps, but steadied himself, and they were off again. More snow started to drift into the hole. Raimund's black hair became speckled with white. Outside of the prison the smoke could barely be seen through the rapid winds of snow and ice that darkened the sky.

"Are … we …" Potter was panting as they climbed step after step. "… going to … fight?"

"We'll see what happens." Raimund said. The prisoners above reached the edge and started running in all directions. The guards that had gone to investigate were attacked and their weapons stolen. Raimund and Potter crested the last step and was hit with snow. The burning barracks could hardly be seen, but there was a fate light. "This way," he shouted over the snowstorm that beat at them.

If they stayed close enough to the edge of the hole then they could see where not to walk. But the wind was pushing hard. And men were running all around, not able to see. One prisoner ran straight over the edge. His screamed was lost in the wind until a splat echoed. "Keep going," Raimund said. He kept his hand on Potter's back. He didn't come all this way and brave a snowstorm and guards to lose the fat boy to a fall. "We'll get out of this storm, I promise."

"Can't … see …" Potter was still panting, Raimund wasn't much better. But the light was getting brighter. As Raimund moved toward it he fell and Potter tumbled with him.

The winds had died. The snow had stopped falling. All was calm. As Raimund cleaned his face he saw Sile standing over them. "This must be Potter," she said, her necklace glowing a bright blue. "Stay close to me and we'll get out of here."

"How?" Potter said as he looked around. It was as if they were in a bubble. A dome. The snow and wind beat at the barrier but nothing got through.

"I'll explain later," Raimund said as he stood and helped Potter to his feet. "Let's get you out of here."

Aveline

A nd there was nothing you could do?" Mari asked.

"The laws passed after the flames limit my power as regent." Aveline watched her hair being brushed in the mirror. *Always getting ready.* "If a majority of the councilors and the chancellors pass a motion then the regent cannot change it." She tugged at her grandmother's necklace, and hummed along with some lute player in the gardens below. The instrument serenading them through the open balcony, blowing in with the wind. "We have Amalia to thank for that."

"I'll never understand why you put up with them. All these lords and chancellors and even the peasants." Mari brushed Aveline's brownish hair, making eye contact through the mirror. "Maybe if there were two queens the men would listen."

Aveline laughed but Mari's face was serious. Her eyes narrow. "A royal cannot marry a woman," Aveline said, "even a peasant would be looked down on for not being able to further her line. I have to gain an alliance for my fa—" she caught herself, "for the good of the realm. Further the Thomas dynasty in case anything happens to my brothers. And no matter how hard we try, you can't give me a baby."

"Then stop being a royal." Mari put the brush down, leaning over Aveline and caressing her cheek. Aveline laughed at first but soon realized that her handmaid wasn't joking. Mari's face was still rigid. "What's there to like?"

"Besides wealth and power?"

Her handmaid huffed. "The people hate you. Despise you. They killed your grandmother, probably killed your aunt, tried to kill your father. They cheer at the steps of the domaton for the king's death while you weep in the palace halls. Grab some gold vases and diamond jewelry and run away. With me." Mari knelt beside the princess, inches from her mouth. "Live a life away from danger and deceit."

Aveline wanted to kiss Mari, instead she stood and brushed her own hair. The person she saw in the mirror was tired. Always tired, and even more now that she was regent, always having to listen to lords who think themselves better than her brother and her. She had to show them who was better. *I am the princess. They are nothing,* she thought. "You know I can't do that."

"It's not like you'll be queen anyway. I'm sorry to say it, but what if Prince Bertin doesn't come back? Your young brother is already on the throne, and you'll only be regent for a few years. If, may the Four have mercy, Baldewin were to die then the Chancellery will elect a new dynasty as they have before. They will pass you over."

"We'll see." Aveline looked at the bed trying to will Mari to it. Her handmaid shook her head. "Don't tell me you're going to leave me? Should I hide my jewelry?"

"I know all your hiding spots, and don't think I could ever leave you." Mari grabbed Aveline's hand and they began to dance. The distant sound of the instrument strummed into the bedchamber. They swayed together, resting their heads on one another, trying not to step on the other's bare feet.

There was a knock and Aveline shot back. "Another death?" She said half-jokingly.

When she opened it a short, bowing page was at her door. "My Regent, your suitors have arrived."

"Suitors?" Mari laughed from behind.

Aveline didn't want to stop dancing with Mari, but the lords and chancellors wished for her to find a husband already and hopefully stop any sort of succession crisis. "Let me get ready." Aveline thanked the page.

***

Aveline stood in front of the marble throne, a dozen or so lords or their sons or their best men were staring back at her. Some were shaking. Some were solid. She had already seen a few and none offered were what she wanted except for Mari off to the side.

"My Princess," bowed a lord older than her father, "I know what you might think. 'How could this old man give you what you wanted?' Let me tell you that the lands of Queen's Valley are even more fertile than my loins." Mari chuckled and Aveline clenched her jaw at her handmaid wishing for her to keep quiet. She didn't need the lords to feel slighted, and she certainly didn't need more rumors swirling. "I have fathered some fifty children in my lifetime, some of them great lords and ladies of Adedor. Not only would you enjoy the fruits of Queen's Valley but also alliances for your brother's throne across the continent." Lord Eile bowed with the help of some servants and clutched his cane with deep breaths when it was over.

"Thank you, Lord Eile, for that wondrous offer, I have to listen to some others before my decision can be final." She said with no emotion, even though she tried to sound enticed.

"Of course, My Princess."

A young lord, with far too little clothing to attend an audience with the princess, stepped up. His veins bulged from his muscles, long golden hair tucked behind his ears. "The lord of Bridger, Your Princess Regent." The herald called out. "Lord Seau."

"My Princess," the lord began and went on about his endowment, the lands of Bridger, and the future of the monarchy. Aveline heard very little. After Mari's laugh, Sir Delmar had decided to speak to her, and her handmaid looked only at the ground. All the princess could do was wonder what he was saying. *He saw us when he told me about my father. Wonder if he told anyone? Told Baldewin?* "… that is why I have come to ask for your hand in marriage. I know your father—"

"One minute my lord." Aveline interrupted. The lord's eyes grew wide and his cheeks red. "Sir Delmar. How is my brother?"

The knight's back straightened as stiff as the pillars that held the ceiling above the throne room. "His Grace asked me to see to your protection today. He is asleep in his bedchamber."

"You are distracting me from these great lords by conversing with a handmaid. I believe the doma would have words about you flirting considering your vows."

"My Princess Regent, I would never." The court murmured and chuckled. Lords and ladies who had come to watch

Aveline choose a suitor didn't know how to keep a secret. If Delmar wasn't careful the whole of Rowan's nobility would know in a few hours. "My vows were taken under the Four and the Many. I would never forsake them." He bowed.

"Then do your duty and guard me. Not that I need it from these gracious gentlemen, but you never know what could come flying in from the window." Aveline saw Lord Seau's red face and smiled at him. "Lord Seau hearing of Bridger and … of other things …" the lord smirked "… give me much to think about. Unfortunately, I am running late for a very important meeting with the counselors. Since Sir Delmar decided to interrupt this gathering, I figure we can finish tomorrow. As regent I have more duties than I know how to deal with. If you excuse me," Delmar helped Aveline to not trip, her heels cramping her feet and click-clacking down the steps.

The court whispered, some ladies giggling and fluttering their eyes at Lord Seau. Once Aveline was in the corridor with Mari she told Delmar, "forgive me for my outburst, sir. You are a good knight and protector. But I wanted to hear more about Lord Seau's large cock." Aveline's words dripped with sarcasm and the girls laughed, but Delmar didn't have an ounce of humor in his steel body. "May I speak to my handmaid alone? I will punish her."

"Of course, my Princess." The knight turned to watch the palace grounds from a window.

"Punish me?" Mari whispered. "I don't want to hear it."

Aveline waved a hand and asked, "What did he say to you?"

"Just that I should not be giggling at renowned lords."

"Because Lord Seau is such a renowned lord. He seems to think dressing like a whore will gain him favor," Aveline giggled as the throne room began to empty, Lord Eile needed help to walk over the slick floor. "But no one thought anything of it. Only that you were a stupid serving girl laughing at the wind."

"Stupid?" Mari laughed before her smile faded and her eyes turned low. "He's right though. I shouldn't draw any more attention to us."

"Which means you'll drop this ridiculous notion that you're coming with me and the fleet to Redington." Her handmaid wouldn't take no for an answer. Baldewin and the councilors were to sail to the City of Reds later today, Aveline decided it would be best if her little brother wasn't left alone with the warmongers. Mari thought it best she come too.

"No." Mari brushed her hair back. "I'm still coming. What princess travels without a handmaid?"

"You're stubborn."

"So are you."

"I don't want you to get hurt." Aveline wanted to grab Mari's hand, but the throne room was still emptying, her suitors eyeing her with lust for power. "There will most likely be fighting in Redington and I've never known you to carry a sword."

"And you think they'll let you fight?" Mari gave her a beautiful smile. "Zoell will be the only woman who carries a sword that day. I will stay in safety with you. I promise not to die."

Aveline sighed. "I guess this means we should be going to see the captain."

***

The port of Rowan was much smaller than it used to be, at least according to the stories and ancient maps that Blis would show off sometimes. A few ships were docked just upstream from the city walls. The majority of the Rowai fleet would be found in Bruthaki Fields or along the western coast. A letter had already been sent for a few ships to depart for Vaandet to search for Bertin. *I pray they find him.*

Sir Delmar and a horde of other knights and guards walked with the king, Aveline rode on a litter, Mari walked to her side, even the fat Blis walked the Northern Road. The road had become dirt once they passed under the city gate. Commoners and farmers watched from their small homes on the outskirts of the city, probably drooling that the king was leaving, the palace open for the taking if they tried hard enough.

"How did this morning go?" Blis asked from the ground.

Aveline hated riding in a litter, but she didn't have a choice with her safety in mind. Her head shook and bounced with every step. "It was fine. A dozen or so men came to ask for my hand in marriage. I have many options."

Blis pulled on his belt and said, "the realm has many to choose from," she followed his gaze to Mari, just ahead of him. "I'm sure you'll make the right choice."

"Perhaps we should discuss this when we're on the ship?" Aveline didn't need the guards spreading rumors.

"Just know that I support you in any decision you make, and I'm absolutely positive your parents would as well."

She scratched at her eyes as tears formed, not wanting the world to see her cry. "Thank you. Hopefully the lords know the dowry required will be quite large." Aveline and Blis laughed together. "How are you feeling about Redington?"

She asked as the ship's shadow cooled her even more than the morning rains of winter.

"I always support the king's decision." Blis said as the horde of people stopped moving. He helped Aveline off the litter and kept her close as they walked the short path to the river dock. The great wooden giant of a ship cast a shadow as dockworkers, servants, guards, and sailors all readied it for departure. A hundred oarsmen were ready to travel downstream. "But we both know this is more the council's decision," he whispered. "Which is quite unfortunate. I just hope everyone returns back in one piece."

"You think we can actually take Redington?" Aveline asked. She had never been, and would actually be happy to see the old city, but she knew nothing of its defenses, of its port. She hoped Caxton at least knew what he was doing.

"It will depend on how much Ultiir wishes to hold onto it," Blis held out his arm for Aveline to take as a section of path had turned to mud. "The last time Rowan and Viguran went to war, we won. Let us hope we can do it again."

She looked at Baldewin, he stomped in the dirt and mud, his leather shoes dirtying. "The most powerful kingdom in Adedor ruled by a boy. Do you think if the old laws were in place that father would still make me regent? I would hold considerably more power. I'm not sure he would trust me with that."

"What's it matter?" Blis laughed, his belly moving with the rhythm. "He made you regent now. You're the closest person to Baldewin and you know you can influence him."

"Not well enough, we're off to war."

"It's a long journey." Blis said with a smile as the ship loomed overhead.

Tundavik

The red towers that touched the clouds overlooked thousands who descended on the city. Tundavik led the knights on the attack. The mites were clad in armor as black as the charred bodies of their dead brethren. A tree with hundreds of branches and roots and a thousand leaves plastered his breastplate. It was freshly painted in blood. He didn't see much of what happened in the city streets, only hearing the brawls and screams. Tundavik was focused on the Peak of the Ancient. The castle built on the northern slope. His men had to reach the great red fortress before nightfall to end the fighting and conquer Panscar.

Knights from the many regions and duchies of Viguran surrounded him as they fought through the streets. They ascended the Hill of the Ancient, fighting off any mites who dare attack. Tundavik and his men spat on every holy book they found, how the Rainvealandians could still stick to the beliefs of their ancestors and their god with an ever-changing face was beyond him.

The path to the mountain was steep. Behind him smoke bellowed from red bricks. Everything wooden charred and collapsed, tall columns of red stone toppled and crashed into homes and shops. Thousands burned. The sky was covered in gray ash that spread like a plague. Cobblestones flooded with blood. The castle was the heart of the city, and it would stop beating permanently.

Rainvealandians in their black armor pushed back. Bands of red wrapped around their gauntlets, boots, and chausses. Red falcons on the cuirasses. Their helms flat-topped, with slits for eyes, and small holes to breathe. They stood tall in the castle bailey. Battleaxes, warhammers, spears, swords, and shields readied for their defense. Tundavik and the man who followed cut through the mites like fruit trees. Red juices poured on the green grass.

Pushing through the courtyard and crashing into the wooden door of the castle, Tundavik led the fighting in the halls and soaked the tile in pools of blood.

The city fell within hours of the castle being taken. Tundavik had invaded across the river from Keeland, some had taken boats to block escapes, others sacrificed themselves at the Iron Gate. The mites never stood a chance. Celebration lit up the night sky, men standing near the fires to laugh and drink and fuck anyone passing by. The castle cellar was looted. Tundavik and his men drank until the next morning when Lord Barnet Lovell found them.

***

He rubbed his temples to forget the memory.

As he waited downstairs he had too many women and men come up to him. Breasts dangled in his face and their looks turned sour when he turned them down. It wasn't the nicest brothel he had seen, though he wondered how nice a whorehouse could be. Mar was somewhere upstairs.

Fetching him was Madam Atrona. Tundavik had walked into more brothels than ever before, all along the city's main square, the brothel square. Mar was nowhere to be found until Madam Atrona remembered the knight had walked in drunk with a sword at his hip and a pouch full of coin. *Where did he even get that much? If I had known we would've ate real food and not just hardtack,* he thought as he crossed his arms.

"Sure you don't want to come upstairs with me?" A woman with goosebumps up and down her half dressed body asked, she was trying to keep her teeth from chattering, but the fire from the hearth wasn't giving enough heat. "Even if you lack a lot of coin I can still make it fun."

"I'm just here for a friend. He'll be down any moment."

"We can all three have fun." The woman said before Madam Atrona slapped her bare back.

"Leave the gentleman alone, he does not wish for your service." Atrona's face was red but the slap mark was redder as the whore disappeared with her head lowered, and tears in her eyes. "I am terribly sorry about that. I try to run a nice establishment but the whores aren't quite up to par with some of the brothels I saw in the South."

"It's fine, no reason to be harsh to your girls," Tundavik said as he stood. "Where is Sir Mar?"

"The sir would not budge. I think it's best you leave him here to get sober. He's been fucking and drinking for days. A little alone time might be best."

Tundavik started for the limestone stairs. "You just want his money."

The corridor wasn't long, but it had many doors and small rooms where moans escaped from. Guards walked the length of the corridor. Occasionally they would peek into the rooms and enjoy a show. Tundavik had only one thing in mind. Get Mar. The lousy knight had been gone from the castle for days as he made a name for himself across the city. Drinking in every tavern. Fucking in every brothel. The only reason it took so long to find him was for the amount of sinful behavior that blossomed in the city. Anything to separate them from the Veck'kop to the south.

Under an image that showed a woman doing a handstand while playing with a man's cock was where Mar supposedly had his fun. Tundavik didn't knock on the wooden door, rot at the bottom. Instead, he pushed it open and was attacked by the scent of sweat and sex and alcohol. He stepped over clothes and inside was a large round bed where Mar slept with a man and woman.

Another man was standing naked swinging Attana, Mar's sword. He jumped when he saw Tundavik and the sword clanged to the ground. "Are we adding one more?" He said with a Southern accent.

"Get out."

Grabbing his clothes, the naked man ran out the door. Tundavik sheathed Mar's sword, stepping over empty bottles, some broken and some not. He found a bottle of wine that was nearly full and dumped it on the trio in bed. The woman and man hopped out. Shivering when their naked bodies hit the cold hair. Mar stretched himself awake. "I thought we were done with that?"

"Get up, Mar," Tundavik said as he motioned the other two to leave. "Where have you been?"

"I don't know why you're asking that when you're standing over me. Obviously I've been in the whorehouse. Do you know how much wartime has risen the prices? It's outrageous."

Tundavik threw a pair of black trousers at the naked knight. "Get dressed and let's go. We need to be back in the castle before another blizzard comes through."

"A blizzard?" Mar looked outside, letting the city see his cock. "And these aren't my pants, their Fasha's." The knight found his garments and slipped into them. "All better? Now you can look me in the eye."

"I would rather talk outside so I don't have to deal with this stench."

"And I'd rather talk in here so I don't lose my pecker." Mar laughed. "You'll get used to it after a while." The knight sat on the bed and motioned for Tundavik to sit next to him, which he received a 'no' to. "Why did you come looking for me? Don't trust I can make it back to the castle by myself? It's toward the sound of waves."

"You disappeared on me. You said you would be in the council meeting with me and help sway the lords to our side. You didn't show."

Mar took a swig from a bottle of ale and used the blankets to wipe off the remaining wine stains on his face. "Sorry. I was busy as you can see."

"You don't want the Flewthlands to help with the war? You think Lord Rely's men can fend off the Kinglands and the Eastlands by themselves? We're doomed without them."

"What's the point?"

"You don't care if Devro dies?" Tundavik asked as he towered over Mar. "You helped raise that boy."

"Of course I care about him," Mar said with slightly slurred speech. "But if this war has shown me anything it's that anyone I care about will die. Raimund was only the first."

"We don't know if he's dead."

Mar drank more ale. "You know as well as I do that if he was found in Redington he would be hanged, drawn, and quartered. The knight who led the attack on Riverton. Even if he did escape he wouldn't've made it to Whitehall."

"He could be wandering around the Eastlands for all we know." Tundavik said and Mar just shook his head. "Why is this war any different than the last? You're the savior of Vikry. You went into that city and killed so many mites they lost track. Freed those people of their occupation. You were surrounded by death."

"I didn't have Raimund and Devro then. Reran didn't have a wife and son. I was trying to prove myself to a king who couldn't give a shit about me and chose some coward fucking knight to take my place as a member of his guard. I have nothing to prove anymore. I just want to keep my people safe."

Tundavik put his hands on Mar's shoulders. The knight's gray eyes were cloudy. "What do you think will happen to us if Ultiir wins? He won't let the rebels live. You agreed to the war as much as I when we climbed the Swallow Pass instead of turning around for Gereduss. The only way to keep everyone safe is to win. We need the Flewthlands to do that."

"I'd rather drink myself to death than die in battle. One seems more violent," Mar chuckled but his eyes were low. "You know, I thought this would be easy. Ultiir was never a strategist, he only looked smarter because of his brother, but I guess I was wrong. We picked Lord Rely instead of a stronger duke." He laughed again. "Should've asked the Rowai king to help. We wouldn't even be here."

"King Bartel helps us and we've caused the whole of Adedor to be at war again. I say we did the right thing."

Mar twiddled his thumbs with a hunched back, his eyes on the messy floor. "How'd you do at the meeting? Surely you have enough votes and the lords are just being secretive."

"I was doing fine, but a certain Lord Barnet hates me," Tundavik sighed. "Many of the lords seemed to agree with what he was saying. Pyre and I have been speaking to a few but I'm not sure, and the vote is only getting closer."

"Who's Lord Barnet?"

"We fought together against the mites. He didn't like some of my tactics."

Mar went to drink the wine but stopped himself, setting the bottle on the ground instead. "Have you talked to him? Threatened him? Done anything to get him on your side? Maybe with him he can convince the others to join you."

"I fucked his wife." Tundavik laughed and Mar, surprise on his face, joined in. "I didn't do it to make him angry. It was nice though."

"Whatever you say." The knight stood and patted Tundavik's back. "I didn't know you had it in you my old lord duke."

Tundavik rolled his eyes. "Are you with me?"

Mar watched the people outside shiver from the cold. "Once this is over we go to Redington to find Raimund, and we keep Devro safe the whole time. I already don't like being away from him for this long."

"Deal." Tundavik said and the knight, who stunk of alcohol, embraced him.

Sophie

Sophie watched the city from atop a balcony. Beyond the palace walls, beyond the Noble Lands and the Gods' Gift lay the Rats Nest. Undesirables lived there. It was full of vagrants and shady merchants, lined with whorehouses and taverns where only the Four knew what was in the drinks. The streets were always lined with trash and shit dumped from the windows above. It stank of spoiled food. Flooded with piss.

Now, it was on fire.

Even as the sun was setting behind her the flames made it look like sunrise. The docks were set alight on both the Montla and Ritae, mostly by the poor vagrants who wanted nothing more than the city to starve. Ultiir decided it would be best to punish the rats. Dozens of knights and city guardsmen, armed with spears and lances and swords and shields, mobilized in droves to drive the rioters away from the docks and into the Rats Nest. Something must've gone wrong because that whole part of town was burning. *Or it was Ultiir's plan. A great way to rid the city of the rioters and clean the nest.* But she wouldn't believe it. The kingdom of Rowan shattered into a million pieces when Queen Amalia sicced her guards on Gorthair protesters, eventually she lost her life and was thrown in the Bruthak. *What will happen to us? At least my body will flow to Udello so my parents can give me a proper burial.*

"How do you think this will end?" Sophie asked Baroness Mara who stood next to her wrapped in a spotted coat. "Can these walls hold back the peasantry if they decide to descend on us?"

"You don't agree with your husband, His Grace?" Mara said. "Don't let the slave hear you." Sufar stood just a few paces inside. Always watching. Listening.

"I hope he does and relays the information back to Ultiir. The city gates are already full of refugees from the Eastlands and the Lands of Asara. Most went to the nest because it's cheap with loads of work needing done. Now where will they go?"

"As queen isn't that your decision? Most queens help the poor and needy, build homes and hand out food."

"So I have to clean up after Ultiir?"

"When my husband and I go home to Sheplan, I'm always cleaning his messes. Worn clothes on the floor, holes in the walls, the occasional whore who turns up with a bastard. Small things compared to you. But that is a wife's duty, is it not?" Baroness Mara gave a smirk. The Queen's Council had done nothing for days except talk about supporting Abre in her quest and changing inheritance laws. An impossible thing. But, after some convincing, the ladies in waiting all agreed to help Sophie and the possible daughter she might bear.

"I don't want to have clean Ultiir's mess. I will gladly feed him to the people if it meant I would be able to flee." Sophie heard Sufar clear his throat. *I know you can hear me,* she thought.

"I should get going," Mara said. "It's been a treat watching the city burn but I need to find my husband and talk with him about the inheritance, isn't that right?"

Sophie and the countess embraced before she descended the steps of the wall. Sir Velle clasped his hands together. "Should we go as well, Your Grace? I doubt the fire will grow any bigger."

She rested her head in her hands and leaned on the wall. The elven marble homes beneath her, pristine. "What if the fire reached the Noble Lands? Some dead lords would do the kingdom some good." Velle swayed on his feet. "You don't have to say anything. Most of those lords see me as nothing more than a whore. I married two kings. My first husband is dead. My second is waging war not only on the bastard but also his people. I'm sure they're scared shitless that he'll come for them next. Tearing apart the realm is all he can do. If I were the ruler none of this would be happening. I would've invited Devro to feast with me, I would've answered the demands of Duke Pyre Blume, I would've saved this holy city. Now, I can only watch it burn. The de'Tros have done nothing but ruined this kingdom while my family line built Terrop." Sophie sighed as she stepped away from the outside wall, firelight keeping the sky from going dark with night. "Tell him I said all that," she told Sufar who only gave a smile.

Since returning from Goldfield Sophie had Amalla and Renna lock the door to the queen's quarters. Both Sir Velle and Achen as well as her other household guards stood as three in front of her door instead of just one single man. She didn't want to risk Ultiir taking his anger out on her. She couldn't forget the slaves almost raping her. Clava saving her. *Where are you now?* she frequently thought about the now freedman.

The fires swept over her bedchamber in her dreams. Fires from Goldfield, fires from the Rats Nest. Smoke blackening her lungs. Amalla and Renna barely fleeing. Ultiir dead in the throne room, his body burning, his screams causing Sophie's ears to bleed. She wanted it to stop. Wanted her parents. But she was alone. Not even Lord Masson was there to protect her as he hanged from a tree like a common peasant, his eyes stuck watching her every move as the world burned around her.

"Wake up, Your Grace." The old man said as she opened her eyes. Tedbalt quickly jumped off her bed and averted his eyes to her nightgown. "Your handmaids and knights couldn't wake you so they called for me."

"Remind me to have a talk with them." She said as she glared at Sir Velle and a few other guards at the foot of her bed. "All of you out. Lord Masson, I will see you outside the palace."

Renna and Amalla got to work. They had already drawn and heated the bath causing Sophie to melt into it, but the heat reminded her of her dream. "You couldn't wake me?"

Renna spoke soft, but quietly, like she was being watched. "I saw a spirit possess a friend of mine once in Masa Naq, even the elders couldn't wake her. Perhaps a stronger spirit resides in the palace. The spirits of kings and queens."

"Spirits?" Amalla laughed while using a cloth to wash Sophie's arms. "It must've been a terrible dream you had."

Sophie caressed Amalla's cheek. Whatever life she had before had left a few bumps along her face. "It was horrid. I'm glad to be awake though. The guards were to let no one in and I don't appreciate them disobeying me."

"Sir Achen was stricken with fear. You should've seen his sweats." Renna said. "It was very sweet."

"That man is my most trusted knight." Sophie grimaced at the tone of Renna's words, as if she wanted the knight to flirt with the queen. "I would rather jump from the windows than bed him."

"I could do it instead." Amalla laughed again while Renna flicked water onto her dress. "Shall we dress you? Lord Masson said you were meeting."

Sophie was put into a gray, wool dress with a fur neckline and cuffs. She kept her hood up as she glided across the palace grounds passed the slaves still working in the winter and the masters shouting at them. Sufar was behind her. Velle and Achen had tried to evade him but the slave was like a watchdog.

Lord Masson stood by the palace gate and men armed with spears. The smell of smoke clung to the air. "Greetings, Your Grace, I assume your morning has been fine."

"Splendid. I had some cheese and crackers while I dressed." She motioned for the knights to stay back, Sufar along with them, while she stood by Tedbalt's ear. "I am being watched and I do not appreciate it." The old lord glanced at the slave. "How are we supposed to do our business?"

"I will take care of it." Lord Masson called out for Sufar. "My good man, I know the king ordered you to stay with the queen, but I fear, as a slave, you cannot go beyond the palace walls. With all the revolts you understand." The guardsmen's brows narrowed at the sight of Sufar and his green robes.

"Of course, my good lord." Sufar said. "I will await your return."

As they walked under the gatehouse Sophie said, "that was easier than I expected."

"I'll make sure he never bothers you again." Tedbalt said before they walked onto the cobbled streets.

***

"Welcome to the King's Brothel." Lord Masson said as he pushed a curtain to the side and sunlight flooded in. It was no different than any other homes in the Noble Lands. Elven mined, elven built. Marble columns with etchings showcasing the many positions the whores have mastered which made Sophie appreciate their flexibility. Marble ceilings where golden chandeliers hung. It didn't look gilded either, real gold just above her head. Marble floors with rugs, thick and thin, dyed in an array of colors but mostly purple to show off the brothel's royal visitors.

Moans escaped from upstairs, but other than that it was peaceful. Oblivious to what was going on to the east even with the faint smell of ash in the sky. A woman tall enough to pass as a giant curtsied as low as she could without her velvet hennin falling. "Welcome to my humble home, or as you know it, the King's Brothel. I am Madam Taire."

Sophie gave a nod, Sirs Achen and Velle both wore red cheeks as men and women finished upstairs. "Thank you for allowing me to visit. Surely the queen isn't the most popular figure to your ladies."

"Nonsense. I know many who would gladly take you to bed, show you a different way than your husband, not to say His Grace isn't exceptional in bed," the madam put her hands up to show she meant no offense. "We have had many queens come through you though. Some looking for men and others for women. One time I even handed over a mite to a queen. It would've been a scandal if it got out. Our secret." Madam Taire giggled.

"How long have you owned the brothel?" Sophie asked while she admired paintings of love making on the wall.

"I have seen a few kings and queens in my day." The madam's wrinkled face smiled. "Lord Masson is a repeat customer and has told me you are looking for a courtesan to make the king happy."

"Repeat customer?" Sophie eyed the old lord who was busy conversing with a wealthy patron and his two whores. "But what he said is true. All of this war and rioting and slave revolts have caused my husband a great deal of stress. I would do more to help him but I'm just as busy."

"A queen is always busy." Madam Taire smirked. "The amount of coin you are gifting me is enough to buy the whole brothel, so I have chosen the best girls for you to observe. They know who pays them and they love to gossip."

Lord Masson must've told you more than he said, she thought as the madam waved a cryptic hand for her to follow. Achen came behind while Velle stayed with Tedbalt. "Promise not to faint on me?" She asked her knight.

Sir Achen, who had healed fine save for a scar on his neck and torso, puffed his chest. "A knight fainting at the sight of tits? I've seen hundreds of dead men, killed a few myself. Naked whores are nothing."

"Then you haven't seen my girls." The madam said when she opened a dark door into a chamber lit only by candles. Three girls wearing sheer blouses stood near a large, oval bed fitted with red silk. "I give you the temptresses. Atrice," the small dark-skinned woman bowed her head. "Utain," the red headed girl with curls curtsied as if she wore a gown. "And Vierana."

Vierana, strikingly pale with black hair, flourished her hands and bowed at her waist like a man. "My queen, my good sir."

Sophie needn't look at Achen to know how he was feeling. She could hear his deep breathing as he eyed the almost-nude women. "I trust Madam Taire takes good care of you?" Sophie asked.

The three women nodded and Utain said, "would you like a demonstration? I've never been with a queen before and would love to try." The whore whimpered as a small whip from the madam hit her on the backside. "Forgive me, Your Grace, that was inappropriate."

"It's quite alright Madam Taire." Sophie beckoned the whoremonger over. "No reason to bruise the girls before they see Ultiir."

"Of course, my queen." The old woman's smile didn't reach her eyes. "Do you see one you like? These are the girls who earn me the most coin and the men their trust."

"Ultiir would drop his breeches for any of them," she laughed, trying to see if any of the girls were put off by her comments about their king. Vierana's brow had lifted. "I would like to see Utain and Atrice only."

Madam Taire shooed the pale woman away who left with red cheeks. Sir Achen had to have his eyes pulled away from her bare ass by Sophie's hand. "I thought tits didn't tempt you."

Achen cleared his throat and whispered, "You didn't say they would look like this."

"They look like girls. Younger than me and I'm already younger than Ultiir." She forced a smile on her face as she turned her attention back to the girls. Utain's hard nipples made Sophie uncomfortable. "Utain, do you know much about His Grace?"

She cleared her throat. "I know he is lovely. I have seen him walk and he is as graceful as any before him."

Sophie didn't need a whore to see Ultiir as wonderful. "Just Atrice," she said and Utain followed Vierana out. "Tell me about yourself. I want to make sure the king is getting what he deserves."

Atrice brushed dark hair from her face. "I come from the South, but I'm no mite. I am descended from the Lanlar. Madam Taire found me in a back alley in Hazari, knee deep in pig shit and fighting off the people who groped at me, but a girl has to do whatever it takes to survive in this world." She had a hint of an accent, and Sophie worried Ultiir would be upset at the thought of bedding a Southerner. But Atrice had to work. "I've been here almost five years. I saw His Grace, the dead king, many times, never bedded him though. Madam Taire thought I was better suited for the nobles who grew tired of their wives."

"Any bastards? We're already fighting one war, we don't need to damn our children to one as well."

"A war? Haven't heard much news about that, except for Lord Monluc's excitement. Men love to talk about war as they fuck." Atrice smiled at Sir Achen, the man's face redder than the candlelight. "And bastards? None. Rainvealandians have ways of making sure that doesn't happen if we don't want it."

"So you love to gossip?"

"Very much. The other girls all gather 'round the fires during the day when men are pretending to care for their wives and tell each other stories. Sometimes these stories get passed around like a … well like a whore."

"I enjoy gossip as well, and I have much better stories than the other girls." Sophie smiled at the whore than at the old woman. "Madam, I think I found the one."

Aveline

"Sailing is boring," Aveline heard Baldewin say to Blis near the entrance to the king's quarters. "But Caxton said we need to play nice with the leaders of the House of Awaran. Try to get their coin or something."

They had been sailing for weeks though it felt like years, so she understood why her little brother would think it was boring. After the majority of the fleet had joined them in Bruthaki Fields, they docked in smaller towns along the western coast of Rowan. Baldewin was a new king and people wanted to see him. People outside of the Gorthair Marches that is. Coastburg and Dunniage held large celebrations even though the king was only going to be in town for maybe a day. They didn't mind. And Baldewin didn't seem to mind the attention either.

But now they were sailing the Ters-Veck, trying not to crash into merchant ships or small fishing boats or colorful carracks from the east. She had heard from a few sailors of the Eotrosi ships being able to glide over the vast expanse of steppeland, Aveline had just shook her head and smiled at the tall tale. "I haven't seen you training with a sword," Blis said as he and her little brother disappeared into the room.

The monarch's ship in the past would've had goldwork and

jewels and banners of the richest purples and blues, but after the flames and the destruction of the kingdom, her father rebuilt the navy with less ornamentation. Other than the large quarters for the captain, and an even larger one for the king, the ship looked like any other in the fleet. It was good to not stand out. *We'll need all the help in Redington we can get.*

The deck was being scrubbed by sailors, others pulled splinters from their fingers or toes. Captain Pitor laughed with Caxton and Jac and Wycleaf. William had stayed in Rowan with the High Chancellor to oversee things while Baldewin was gone. *Trying to gain even more power,* Aveline thought, but remembered that Blis had told her it was best not to worry. She should've walked over to them and learned what was so funny, but she saw her guards and Mari standing over the railing, watching the water, and her fears about the councilors plan for her little kingly brother vanished.

Mari had looked beautiful the longer they sailed. Aveline wasn't sure if it was the salt and sun or because they hadn't had a chance to be alone together since Rowan. She missed holding her close, but sailors are nothing if not gossips.

"... that's why I left Moon Bay," Zoell was telling Mari a story she had told the other guards and Aveline a million times. "But I was welcomed back with open arms when I put down some Gorthair rebels that threatened the village. Now there's talk of a statue of me being built. But I told them —"

"— no one but the Four deserve statues," Aveline interrupted. "You haven't been boring poor Mari with your stories have you?" She laughed so the knight of Moon Bay would know it was only a joke.

"I like her stories," Mari said.

"See?" Zoell laughed with the men, "I told you I would find

someone who likes to hear me talk."

Dern the Third itched his nose and said, "then you can keep her. Bore her instead of us of tales of Moon Bay."

"Are you going to tell her about your fight with the Greenriders, Dern?" Tomas asked. "I'm sure Mari would especially love to hear about the pissing your pants part."

"Like I've said," Dern's bald head was red from the sun but growing redder with embarrassment, "I was a young squire and afraid of horses at the time. It was really Sir Ceval's fault for thinking I could handle it."

"While I'm sure Mari would love to hear about all of your adventures, I would like to speak with her alone for a minute. Need to discuss dresses for Awaran."

"No need to lie," Ivlin said, "let's try to find some food that isn't fish."

"They don't bore me and I actually do like hearing of their journeys," Mari said with crossed arms after the guards had left.

"Of course," Aveline rested her elbows on the wood railing, someone was shouting "Row," below deck and the oarsmen were moving with great speed. "If they were boring I wouldn't keep them around. I actually needed to talk to you about what's to happen after Awaran."

"We're going to sail to Redington and I'll hide below deck just like you asked." Mari rolled her eyes. "Though, between you and me, I think a handmaid can wield a sword better than your brother."

"I don't doubt that," Aveline said. She wondered how Mari would react when Aveline shared the news of her actual plan. "I spoke with my guards, they agreed with me on what to do next." She caressed Mari's finger on the railing, out of view, but, for just a moment, she didn't care if anyone noticed. "I need to find Bertin. Dead or alive he is my brother. If the elven letter is to be believed then they are taking him to Anha Jorbstah."

Mari pulled her finger away and straightened her back. "Leaving me. Can humans even get to Anha Jorbstah? All we hear about is how cut off from the world it is."

"It's worth a try," Aveline said as a large city started to grow up from the bluffs and fields along the Ters-Veck. They had passed Udello early in the morning, which meant they were about to pass Tharet. "Rainvealand is big. Maybe Bertin escaped the elves and is wandering around."

"And you think you'll find him?" Mari scoffed. "You're not a tracker."

"I trust my team to find him. He's somewhere down there," she motioned to the south bank of the river, oars thrashing the water below. "I can't let him die out there. I don't want to lose him like my mother and father." Aveline heard some sailors laughing and pointing at Tharet, the walls within walls separating those who lived in the city. It all made her want to cry. "I also don't want to lose Baldewin. I trust no one on this ship to guide him or protect him other than Blis, and what's that you said, you think you can wield a sword? I need you to sail with him to Redington. Stay close to him."

"And why would he listen to a handmaid?" Mari's eyes were red. Either from sadness or anger, Aveline wanted to run away with her and not worry about anything else, but she was the regent, and her brothers were in trouble.

"Blis has agreed to keep you close. You'll be by Baldewin all the time."

Mari sighed and whipped her hair back as her eyes settled

on Tharet.

The city was easy to see from the river, its port growing larger with construction, workers getting water, some getting whipped. Rainvealandians getting whipped. Small riverboats arriving carrying those from north of the Ters-Veck to move into the city. Aveline had never gone to Tharet. She had no plans to visit as long as the Terropians held the city, but she still wanted to see the pain caused to the Rainvealandians. Men onboard continued to shout and cheer as they sailed by. Enjoying the horror that had fallen upon the Rainvealandians in the city. Aveline tapped her foot. Mari put her hand on Aveline's twitching fingers. "I'll stay," she said. "I'll protect Baldewin with my life."

Aveline cracked a smile, "I don't want you to die though."

"I told you I don't plan on it. I plan on seeing you and Bertin waltzing back into Rowan and for us to finally run away to a better place." Mari smiled. Aveline knew that Mari understood how Tharet made her feel. How the cheers from her own people made her feel. "Nothing you can do."

"My brother is king." Aveline huffed. "If I can't do anything then who can?"

Large banners with white mountains had been unfurled on the newly constructed walls. Hundreds of soldiers carried swords and spears. They poked and prodded the Rainvealandians around the city. She had heard that the Rainvealandians made sure they were in their homes before nightfall or gangs of Veck'kop would descend on them. Worse of all was that the walls kept the Rainvealandians from leaving even if they wanted to. The king of Terrop wanted to show the world that the Veck'kop were superior in every way. She wondered if this is how the Gorthair felt back in

Rowan.

"Maybe when you're done with Bertin you can help." Mari said.

"I have a feeling the Anvrin Margia won't listen. He doesn't listen to the House of Awaran nor the Rainvealandian states. Why me?"

"You're the regent of the most powerful kingdom in Adedor, are you not?"

"Tell the chancellery to support the Rainvealandians and get laughed out of the hall. The only thing we can do is watch from our ship."

And they did. Never taking their eyes off the city until it disappeared into the horizon, Aveline wondering how the world could be such a cruel place.

***

Vikry rose on the confluence of the Ters-Veck and Montla-Ritae rivers. The House of Awaran kept it's large government buildings in the center of the city. Aveline and Baldewin walked together through the narrow streets, a mass of guards with horses on their surcoats around them. The Awaran guards had surcoats with two meeting rivers and a four pointed star in the center. Vikry was human built, much of what the elves had built was gone. The lack of elvish-mined marble surprised her. She expected the city to look like Vigur, but instead it looked like a city in Rainvealand. Bricks and clay.

Statues of Vigura were all around the city, the most she had ever seen. Most of the statues had the god holding a great sword in varying positions. Sometimes Aveline felt like

Vigura was going to strike her down.

"The city was named for Vigura," a representative from the Grand House was saying, she thought his name was Caral. "Though in the old tongue he was called *Vikra.*"

"Fascinating," Blis said, but Aveline rolled her eyes because Blis most certainly knew that already. He was the king's tutor. He knew almost everything.

"I'm tired of walking," Baldewin whispered to her as they rounded a corner and the large domes of the upper and lower houses became visible over the stacked homes and shops.

"Complaining about sailing and complaining about walking. I think, my little king, you just like to complain."

"Well, I thought the grand dukes were going to come to our ship. I wasn't expecting this. It can't be safe to walk through the streets with the all the people. I'd at least like a wagon." Baldewin took off his small crown and fixed his hair that had blown sideways in the wind. The Asara Mountains sent down a chill from the east. Snow-capped peaks watching over them just like the statues of Vigura.

"Awaran is nothing like Rowan. They don't even have a king to hate, so it's perfectly safe," she told her bother, but it did feel weird. Everywhere she went in Rowan, other than the mite district, she would feel hateful eyes on her, eyes ready to topple the monarchy again. No one in Vikry seemed to pay them any mind. She liked it. The people didn't gawk in envy or cower in fear or sneer with hate. She was just a person. *Maybe Mari and I can run away here. She would love the mountains being so close.* Mari had stayed on the ship with a dozen of sailors and workers and guards. She didn't protest. She was over protesting.

Caxton, pushing his dark hair from his eyes, looked to

Caral, and said, "So how are the grand dukes doing? We don't hear much about them in Rowan other than their continued argument with the king of Terrop."

Caral cleared his throat and glanced at Baldewin before saying to Caxton, "The grand dukes are doing all they can to make the House of Awaran strong. They are worthy successors to our last grand dukes."

"I've heard," Jac piped up, "that the grand dukes are infatuated with the mites."

"Is now the best time?" Aveline rolled her eyes as she stepped over a rock and heard a dog barking in the distance. "We're here about Viguran, not Tharet."

"Well," Jac smirked, "Terrop is one of our closest allies, and Awaran is going against them. What makes you think the grand dukes will agree to help?"

"Why don't we wait and see what they do." Aveline said as the rows of homes and shops parted and the two grand palaces —or— houses grew up from perfectly manicured gardens. Pointed trees lined the walkways, sunflowers bright and yellow, peonies making a pink trail. The upper house was made of stone, strips of gold held the glass that created the dome which let the light of day in. The lower house was brick, right across from the upper house, it's dome of leaded glass. A fountain of Vigura between them, water shooting from his sword that he held high in the air.

Two people, a man a woman, stood near the fountain. Both wore velvet robes of blue and had white ermine coats. Caral motioned to the man and woman and said, "I give you the Grand Duke Peliz Fonds and the Grand Duchess Lue Sant."

"How do you do?" Peliz Fonds said with a deep voice, but he said it to Caxton. *That man doesn't even look like royalty,*

Aveline thought of the councilor dressed in grays and browns.

"We're fine," she said before Caxton or Jac or anyone else could get a word in, and the grand dukes looked to her and Baldewin with slightly widened eyes.

"I hope your journey was pleasant," the duchess said. "We hear stories from sailors of the rough seas in the Seler Bay."

"All went well, even as winter started blowing from the north." Caxton said with a smirk. "Hopefully we aren't interrupting any important sessions. We wanted —"

"— His Grace wanted —" Aveline said pushing Baldewin a step forward. "His Grace wished to speak with you both about the problem of Viguran." Baldewin said nothing. He seemed frozen, so Aveline rested a hand on his shoulder. "Go on, my little king," she whispered. Jac cleared his throat as if he were annoyed.

"We … wanted … uhh …" Baldewin trailed off. Aveline didn't want to speak for the boy anymore, but if she didn't than the councilors would. She didn't need this stupid expedition to bring more people into war.

"As regent," Aveline started when she noticed Caxton's mouth about to open, "I can speak for His Grace. We have sailed the long journey here, and wished to meet you, because we wanted to know of any pressure you can apply on Ultiir. This new king has taken Redington. I'm sure they are an important trading partner with you." The dukes nodded. "We were hoping you could apply pressure to the Montla-Ritae. With force if necessary. Possibly engage in fighting as our allies." Vikry was quiet in the gardens outside the upper and lower houses, but Aveline made sure to get her voice heard. She wanted the whole town to hear her if possible. "We know how powerful Rowai forces are, but—"

"You wish for our men to die in their place?" Lue said. "Not a very compelling argument."

"The councilors," Wycleaf stepped forward, "have advised the king and regent that we merely want you to block the river. If Vigurite ships attack then you can stop. *We* don't want your men to die."

"It's only until he take Redington," Aveline swallowed. "It won't be long. You saw how many ships line the docks. It will be over in a matter of days." Aveline was still resting her hand on her brother until he whispered, "ow," and she realized she had been clenching his shoulder. Her hands were red and she could feel her face getting hot. She didn't want this war at all, but the councilors seemed to be doing everything in their power to turn Central Adedor into a wasteland.

Caxton relaxed his arms. "The king, the regent, and us councilors want the same. Awaran ships to block the river, and a few armed men to make the threat more real. I don't think that's too much to ask for, and we should not be arguing when our goals are the same."

"I agree," Grand Duke Peliz said. "In fact I'm tired of hearing it already, I can't imagine what the shipmates must feel." He and the grand duchess whispered. Caral was beckoned over and he nodded along with them.

"We don't want any of our fighters to die," Lue said and Aveline thought, *neither do I.* "We can bring a measure up in the houses tomorrow and see if it passes. There might be some debate. Some will worry about bringing Awaran into a war when we try to stay as neutral as possible."

Caxton bowed his head and said, "We will wait in the ships. Our crews need some rest, and you can vote on the measure. I do hope you block the river. Make sure to tell the houses that we do *not* want your men to fight."

The grand dukes only nodded and smiled before heading back to their respective houses. Aveline shook her head. She didn't want the war to go on for long. She needed the Awarites to join in with men. It would be much simpler if Ultiir surrendered Redington and no fighting were to occur. But the councilors steamrolled her. Baldewin didn't help at all. And now she had to go find Bertin.

Ultiir

Sufar's neck was snapped. His legs and arms bent making him look like a spiral. Blood had pooled and dried. It was sticky underneath Ultiir's boots. "Who did you say did this?" His emotionless voice asked Master Vachen.

"Three other slaves whom we have detained in the guardhouse. They claim this maggot was getting too close to the slavers. Too close to you."

"They're still alive?"

"Barely. We beat them near to death before we received your orders. I can have a caged wagon ready by tomorrow for the public hangings alongside the old doma."

Ultiir wouldn't let a tear fall. Not for a slave. But Sufar had been with him ever since he became the lord of Goldfield and heir to the throne. Over a decade. A decade gone overnight. "I want them hanged in Meret's Square." He whipped around with his red cloak and marched across the palace grounds, slaves peering at him from behind bushels of wheat.

"Your Grace," Lord de'Viere said, coming up from behind, "I caution against the public executions. Meret's Square is so far from the palace. The Rats Nest has been burned, anger continues to grow, and you are doing the unprecedented by hanging Albon. The air is ripe with unrest."

"Are you telling me your men cannot stop a few peasants and vagrants from crippling this city? I don't know why I'm even asking." Ultiir went up the steps of the walls forgetting Sir Gid, the old knight, was behind him. By the time they reached the top the old man was clearly struggling to breathe right. Beyond the walls was a sea of roofs. Tiled, thatched, flat. *Hundreds of thousands of people all looking to me to bring order and Lord de'Viere is fucking up every which way*, he thought as the younger lord reached the top. "What do you see?"

Edel de'Viere stammered before saying, "I see the holy city."

"Good for you. I see a people afraid. Afraid of the war in the mountains reaching their homes. Afraid of their brethren burning their city to the ground. Afraid their king can do nothing to stop it. I will not abandon my people. I will send every soldier and knight and guard and fucking servant we have to clear the streets of disorder so I may hang traitors on a beautiful winter day. Vigura smiles upon me for being swift in my judgment. I know it."

"Your Grace, just for safety —"

"I will hear no more about *my safety*. I, and all of my men, will be perfectly safe in the streets because this is my city," his neck was straining and he could feel it getting red. "I don't want the commoners to forget it." The remnants of the fire could still be seen from this high up. Houses and shops and vagrant holes smoldered. Any underground crime extinguished. The rat holes were closed so the city may prosper. "If you'll excuse me I need to retreat to my chambers."

Sufar usually laid out Ultiir's robes and doublets and

trousers for the day. This time he had some servants do it. When he entered his room, Sir Gid staying behind to converse with Lovis, he found a woman trying to read a letter. "A gift from Lord Zazí for your work in taking Redington." Sir Lovis had told him.

"I do not wish for company right now." Ultiir told the girl who was obviously a whore based on the see through dress and lack of undergarments. *Lovis must've enjoyed bringing her here.*

She bowed her head and said, "Lord Zazí told me you would never appreciate me as a gift, but I told him I could get any man to like me. I guess I was mistaken, Your Grace."

"It's fine." He didn't have time for any nonsense from Henk Zazí. There was a reason he was all the way in Redington. "Reading my correspondence?"

Setting the letter aside she said, "I will have His Grace know that I cannot read nor write. I know of only two other whores who can. We do not need words to make our point, but I would love if you told me what the letter said. A king must get all sorts of letters"

Ultiir chuckled. "It's merely a letter from the Woodlands. Duke Valles still refuses to join me in the war. Prick that man is. He's been going on and on about people disappearing. As if that doesn't happen everywhere."

"The war must be so stressful for you. All those traitor lords and knights who fight for a bastard. I would rage."

"And you know so much about the war because?"

"Lord Zazí made sure I knew everything there was to know about you so I could make you as happy as possible. It's very important," she held her hand close to his shoulder waiting for approval which came in the form of a nod, "that I make my king very happy."

Her touch caused him to tense. "And if I tell you to go?"

She unclasped his cloak and let it drop to the floor before unbuttoning his tunic. "Then I will go. Would His Grace like for me to go or would he like for me to stay?"

He let his cock get the best of him when he said, "just this once," and the whore undressed him then herself before riding atop him, letting the day and the thoughts of Sufar slip away, but Sophie stayed on his mind. As he watched the whore do her job he imagined it was his queen. The queen who only married him out of duty to her parents and not love. But he had so loved her. Thought about her every waking moment. Now that love was gone, killed by his mother, buried in Goldfield. Now he let a whore fuck him.

***

The next day, Sir Lovis helped put him in armor, always heavy and sweaty. Atop his armor he wore a purple surcoat with an owl clutching golden wheat and his long, velvet red robe. The whore covered her naked body with blankets as Lovis cleared his throat more times than Ultiir could count.

"You never told me your name." Ultiir said as he slipped into his long boots.

"Atrice."

Ultiir kissed her hand, sunlight from the east keeping them in its glow. "Well, Atrice, why don't you stay here and I'll be back later. Don't want to lose you."

"His Grace will never lose me."

"It's a glorious day," Ultiir told Lovis and Gid as they left the king's quarters, "let's make the most of it. I will meet you both at the gatehouse. First, I wish to speak with our prisoner."

"Are you sure that's safe, my king?" Old Gid asked.

"See you at the gatehouse," was Ultiir's answer.

The dungeons below the palace were where the elves mined copper for their weapons and tools. Once the humans took over Vigur the mines were used to house rebel elves and traitor humans. It was dark and cramped, Ultiir brushed against the walls. His cloak snagging. The jailer, Olier, was whistling a song about two lovers finding each other in a cave when he saw the king enter.

"Your Grace." The bald-headed jailer bowed. "I wasn't expecting you. I thought Lord de'Viere was coming to get the High Doma."

Ultiir tapped is foot. "Prisoner, Olier. That man is not a doma."

The jailer stood more at attention. "Of course, Your Grace. Shall I unlock his cell?"

"Wait a bit. First I wish to talk with him."

Olier allowed Ultiir to pass through a metal door leading to the cells. He walked with a torch in hand to light his way. Albon would be seeing daylight for the first time in months, also the last time. Bones littered some of the cells. Long dead prisoners that other kings forgot about. One of the skulls was said to be that of Valor the Betrayer, but Ultiir couldn't be certain.

Albon groaned as the light cascaded over him. "Ultiir," he sneered. "Come to tell me news? The war? Your marriage? I'm sure you're having many problems lately."

"Nothing I can't handle.

The old doma was wearing tattered black robes. The skin

on his face was tight, his eyes sunken, and the bags under them large and dark. The stench of piss and shit caused Ultiir to repeatedly hide his nose in his sleeve. "Wearing armor today?" Albon asked. "Worried I'll fight my way to freedom? That my supporters will attack?"

"You lost your support when we paraded you through the streets as an éithrio."

"Charge your enemies with crimes of witchcraft and watch them fall, that's your plan right? Who's next? Lord de'Marisco or Lord Masson? How about your loving bride?" The once-doma's lip curled. "Did Maller perform the marriage ceremony well? Does that old coot even know what he's talking about half the time?"

"He listens to me and heeds my advice, that's more than I can say for you."

"The High Doma should not take advice from a king. We have the gods."

Ultiir bent over to make eye contact with the mage. The evil spawn. "Well the gods seemed to have abandoned you to this cell. Do you dream of something different? Do you imagine yourself following me and crowning me and not being arrested? Or do you dream of elves and dwarves mining your cell knowing one day it would be full of humans?"

"I dream of peace," his voice was smooth. "Enough of this talking. I welcome my death and for the embrace of the Four and the Many and all of my ancestors."

"But you are a spawn of Veltoora, are you not?" Ultiir grinned as Albon's eyes fell. "A force of evil. A force used to turn us away from the Four. You think you have support but they know what you are and I'm sure Meret's Square is full of people come to see you die." Ultiir called for Olier and Albon was pushed out of his cell and the dark, sweating dungeons where he was loaded into a caged wagon with the slaves who killed Sufar.

"Everything is ready, my king." Master Vachen said as the whips flew to keep the slaves back while the cage door was shut and locked. "I pray the rope takes its time today." Ultiir agreed and got into his iron carriage, gilded to look gold, with his knights.

The streets had gotten quiet after the riots and the cleansing of the Rats Nest, but word spread quickly that Albon was going to be hanged today. Near the palace wall were scores of nobles and their families and their servants, even babes still suckling their mother were in the crowd. The mood was somber at first, no one saying anything. Once the Noble Lands were behind them the mood changed. The peasantry were always savage. They screamed and cursed and threw rocks and food at Albon and the slaves.

City guards shoved people out of the road, knocking them into the cobbled streets or else they would be run over by dozens of armored men and horses and wagons. One man ran to the caged wagon to free Albon. A crossbow bolt found its way into his eye.

The crowd grew louder as they passed the domaton. Maller of Forecreak and the lesser doma all stood on the stone steps and prayed as Albon went by. Some of the people shouted support for Albon and denounced Maller. That was the last shout they gave. Most were crying "witchcraft," or "demon spawn" at Albon which gave Ultiir a laugh. *They hate him as much as I. This is victory Albon, something I'll taste again when the bastard is dealt with.*

One man threw a rock at Ultiir's carriage, so he watched

his men beat him to the ground with a smile. "Must be from the Rats Nest," he said to Lovis. The knight had a sweaty upper lip. "Nervous?"

"I don't like this. Too many people and not enough of us."

"The difference being we have steel and iron and they have rocks and day-old bread. We'll be fine, sir. I do not fear them."

Lovis looked at his hands, "I do."

Some young man was standing atop a crate, his head over the crowd as he shouted and tried to work them into a frenzy. "Do you see the way they mistreat us? Shove us aside? This is not acceptable, this is lunacy! Why do we put up with —" the man was taken by two guards. He shouted curses as he was being dragged away.

Ultiir's train of men turned down the shadow road which led to the Shadow Gate in the southern reaches of the city, avoiding the burned Rats Nest and the charred remains of those who dared to fight back. Soon they would reach Meret's Square and all of this nonsense with the doma would be behind him. *If only Sufar didn't have to die too.*

The slave had told him how Sophie wanted to change the laws of inheritance as if that was something she could do. How she disappeared from the palace grounds with Lord Tedbalt as if she were having an affair with the wrinkled prick. How she kept her quarters locked at all times in her paranoia. How she hated him. Well, now he hated her and nothing she did could change that. *She didn't even come today to watch Albon hang. The man who wouldn't marry us. Who wouldn't crown me.*

"Was she always like this?" He asked himself.

"What was that?" Old Gid asked and Ultiir paid him no

mind.

The last of the ash blew away as he descended the carriage steps. Meret's Square was much closer to the city walls than Ultiir liked. At any moment the bastard and his armies could flow over it and kill them all. How many of the commoners would rejoice? Vigura Gate was the largest entrance to the city, and it had been full of refugees fleeing from the foothills of the Asara, but the city could only handle so many. Meret's Square had been cleaned of the vagrants and refugees and all other trash. In the center of the square was a marble well. In trying times that water kept the city afloat and away from the sicknesses teeming in the Montla and Ritae. Next to the well was a raised wooden platform where a rope hung. Three more were being added for the slaves.

"Hear me!" shouted Lord Edel de'Viere. The crowd quieted save for a few murmurs as Albon and the slaves were led in chains to the platform, each given a rope. "These men have been charged as traitors to the crown. King Ultiir de'Tro has sentenced each one to death. The three slaves from Kruhesh have killed a …" the lord paused as he read from the parchment Ultiir had written and signed "… killed an adviser to the king in an attempt to break free from the palace. This man," he pointed to Albon, some shouts of support rising from the crowd, "has shown himself to be an ally to Veltoora and an enemy to the Four and the Many. This most holy city cannot allow vermin like this to live within its walls. His Most Holy, the High Doma, and the conclave of the domaton have issued a decree agreeing with King Ultiir in his quest to rid this world of demons. The accused may give the crowd their final words."

The slaves started shouting all at once about their innocence in killing Sufar while the peasants of the crowd laughed at them and waited for Albon to speak. The tattered man allowed the noose to be placed over his neck before glaring at Ultiir and saying, "The Four curse you to an early grave." The crowd enjoyed that too. Laughing and hooting and agreeing.

Ultiir's cheeks burned. Rou, the executioner, gripped the lever and pulled the wooden floor away. One of the slaves died instantly, the other three kicked and groaned as the nooses choked the life from them. Another slave dead. Then the last. Albon was the only one still alive. His face purple, eyes bulging, legs kicking as his hands gripped the rope for his last breath.

Then he stopped.

Some of the crowd cheered, some were quiet, even a few of his men looked hurt by Albon's death. But Ultiir was beaming. *How could anyone be upset at the loss of an éithrio? The man practiced dark magic. He went against me.*

"A perfect execution." Master Vachen said once he found the king. "You must be proud."

Ultiir didn't have a chance to answer as Sir Lovis said, "We should leave."

"The crowd is too large," Old Gid agreed, "they can overwhelm us."

"Don't you hear the cheering?" Ultiir wanted to spin around and bask in the glory, but he had to stay composed as king. "There's nothing to fear."

"Some of the people look rather displeased." Lovis pointed to a few angry faces and crying eyes. "Please, Your Grace, the palace is much safer." Ultiir rolled his eyes as he nodded. *They fear me now that I killed a High Doma. They would be stupid to try anything.*

His hope was to stay in the square for a while, enjoying the sight as they cut the ropes and loaded the bodies to be thrown beyond the wall in some mass grave. The perfect ending to Albon the traitor, instead he got in his carriage and was on his way before it was noon. His driver whipped the horses to move. Guardsmen used their spear points to part the crowd.

Ultiir slid the window closed as they reached the Gods' Gift once more. The doma were still saying prayers and people chanted below them wishing Maller was the one killed instead. The streets sounded angrier this time. Lovis and Gid both had faces of worry.

There was a crash and the carriage stopped. Shouts of "get him," and "kill him," and beat him" rang out from unfamiliar voices and accents. Screams pierced the quietness of the carriage and commands were given by the guards. Lovis gripped his dagger while Gid felt for his sword. The carriage started to rock like the earth was waking and shaking as if they were in the West, but it wasn't the earth, it was the peasants. Ultiir slid away from the door as it was tipped back and forth with laughter and yells.

Then the carriage flipped onto its side and Ultiir's world went black.

When he woke with dizziness Lovis was atop him, armor and all, his dagger inches from Ultiir's eyes. Gid had fallen across from them. "The king is mine!" a man shouted from above, standing on the fallen carriage. The door opened and he leered in. His eyes were wild and his mouth foamed. "Come here, *Your Grace*, I have something to show you." The skinny man held a butter knife in hand.

Lovis stood and pushed the man off the carriage with a

crash. The crowd stammered over and the knight ascended out and held his hand for Ultiir. As he grabbed Lovis' metal gauntlet, a burst of red stickiness covered the carriage and Ultiir's face.

He spit out the blood as Lovis fell limp into the carriage, his head split open by a rock. Ultiir's eyes filled with tears, but the commoners would not see him cry. Old Gid stood with a helm on and jumped out of the door like he was fifty years younger. Lovis' dead eyes stared at Ultiir. Blood trickled between them.

"Your Grace." Gid yanked Ultiir out of the carriage the best he could. "We must get to the palace." His sword was bloodsoaked and a dozen peasants lay dead with forks and rocks and stolen spears. "You must stay with me."

As they jumped from the carriage to the cobbles below the streets had descended into war. The guardsmen couldn't do much to keep the peasantry back as they threw themselves into the spears and beat the guards to death. Once they picked up the fallen weapons they went wild with rage, killing any guard or soldier they could find. The carriage driver and his horses were dead and were being ripped apart by the angry crowd, the whip being used to terrorize the men at arms. Master Vachen crying as the whip bloodied his back.

Gid cut a fat woman down and pulled on Ultiir's hand. "Hurry, Your Grace." They raced away from the bedlam behind them, cutting through side streets and small alleys. Ever so often coming into contact with someone who wished Ultiir harm, but Gid was as amazing as the queen mother said. No one could stand in his way. His sword was slicing through anyone as if they were just cooked pork. Their arms and heads falling into bloody heaps.

The Noble Lands were full of the richest of Vigur running for their lives. Running to the safety of the palace. It was like a wave of death behind them. Ultiir and Gid ran as fast as they could, Ultiir's legs screaming for him to stop, but the peasants behind weren't slowing, and they were killing and looting anything they came across. Lady Rila, one of Sophie's ladies in waiting was found by a fountain before being raped and murdered by the frenzy.

The gates of the palace welcomed them to peace, they just had to get there. Gid stopped to cut down a horde of monsters following them, blood flying as if the old knight were painting. Ultiir jumped under the gatehouse and crawled into the palace ground, knights surrounding him and keeping any peasant away.

Once Gid was inside, his face red with blood, Ultiir shouted, "Close the gates! Close the gates in the name of your king!"

As the portcullis started to fall, the nobles outside ran and screamed and pleaded for them to stay open. Lord Tyter crawled under the teeth but was too slow, the portcullis crushed his body as his family screamed, the wave of death behind hitting them, the peasants ripping at anyone who couldn't get to safety. Flooding the gatehouse with blood.

Sophie and her guards had run out of the palace along with dozens if not hundreds of lords and ladies who had already taken refuge. "What did you do?" The queen glared at Ultiir. He stood, gasping for breath, his legs crying in pain, and slapped Sophie so hard she fell to the ground before making his way inside the marble palace.

Flora

Please forgive me for my sinful ways, Mother. What I did goes against all your teachings and the holy book. I am so ashamed of what I've done but I humbly ask you to please not turn your back on me and my family. Little Flora needs you and I wish to not have her be tainted by my ways." Flora didn't want to get up from bowing on her knees. The stone of the domaton was even colder in the winter, but she kept her nose to the floor as punishment. *An adulterer. What have I done? I have condemned myself to Veltoora with all the demons and evil men of the world and left a mark on Florance that may never go away. And if Barnet finds out ...* she had to stop her thoughts before they overwhelmed her.

Tears had stained the stone below. Other parishioners walked the floors of the domaton, kicking up dust. No statues or paintings were allowed. This domaton was nothing like the one in Vigur that Flora had seen only once before. Bare feet came beside her and a man in a blue robe lifted her. Pain piercing through her soles like being stabbed a thousand times. "What is wrong?" The doma wiped her tears and dirt from her nose. "Why do you cry so much?"

Barnet was off to the side, wearing nothing but a brown robe, conversing with another doma. Flora had to keep quiet in fear of the echo reaching his ears. "I have committed a grave sin and fear my afterlife will be ruined for it."

"What did you do that was so bad? The gods are merciful, you know this."

"I am an … adulterer," she whispered and choked back tears. "I have been unfaithful to my husband and now an embarrassment to my family."

The doma guided her along the cold stone to the center of the domaton. Snow had fallen and ice had formed in the center where the opening in the dome was. Clouded skies were overhead. "We all commit sins, my dear, and you are not the first woman to be unfaithful. Sam the Sayer parlayed with a plethora of those who were unfaithful. Do you know what happened to them?"

"They were allowed to feast with the gods."

"Because they knew what they did was wrong and spent the rest of their mortal lives doing good and staying true to the Four and the Many." The doma put his bare feet in the snow. "For others this would hurt. The cold would burn. For me I feel nothing but warmth for I have the love of the Four on my side. Try it." Flora stepped on the snow, almost slipping, and clenched her jaw as her feet cried in pain. "Remember all your teachings. Remember the Four and the Many are here to help and guide you."

As she thought about the winter and Meret's feast, and the coming of Swallow's feast her feet stopped aching. As she thought of the warm winds sent by Anebro during Vigura's feast her chest filled with heat. It was as if the snow was melting beneath her toes. The pain gone. "How should I repent? Annulment?"

"Annulment is worse than adultery, I fear. You must

tell your husband the truth and be ready to face whatever consequences he bestows upon you."

A lump in her throat and tears in her eyes formed. "I will," she croaked.

Barnet seemed a million miles away as Flora slowly walked to him. He had just finished speaking with a doma when she bowed her head at him. "Shall we go?" She asked instead of telling the truth. *No reason to tell him now, not in this sacred place.*

Her husband examined her face. "Crying? Were you moved that much?" Flora nodded and led him to the arched doorway where they cleaned their feet of the dust in water from the sea, stripped off their brown robes, and dressed in their regular attire. Both wearing a mix of grays and blacks and thick coats. "Spring will be here soon." Barnet said as he helped Flora down the steps of the domaton to the street. The temple of Dal sitting empty across the way. *Maybe Dal can help me more,* she thought but stopped herself because that was also a sin.

As they climbed into their carriage, Tedbalt Ver helping them up, Flora rubbed the bronze statue of Samosay. She needed him to give her speech. "I have something to tell you." She said to her husband once the door was closed.

"First," Barnet interrupted, "Tundavik has reached out to me. He wishes to meet and I'm going to take him up on that offer."

Flora's words got stuck in her throat. "Very well," she said instead of confessing, "do you think he'll be able to convince you?"

Barnet laughed and scratched the stubble on his face. "That man will never be able to convince me of anything. I'm meeting with him because it's what your father would want and we want him happy, right?"

"Enough," Flora surprised herself by saying that. "Tell me why you do not like Lord Vandes. These secrets have gone on long enough and I'm tired of it."

"The Four gave you strength?" Barnet said with wide eyes. "Fine, but just know I didn't want to tell you." The carriage jerked and rolled over the cobble toward the castle. "I still think it stupid for Lord Rely, high in the mountains, to revolt against the king over a bastard, but if Tundavik were not here I might actually fight beside him. Woodrun has always wanted to be free from Viguran, but that man leading the armies south makes my blood chill.

"I was on the Bezir campaign as you know. Tundavik led thousands of us; Dels, Lodean, Veck'kop; all united against the mites. Devro has the bastard law on his side, and I support laws. Tundavik does not. I would gladly lead my men into the battle, but he came back from the West. Why did he have to come back?" Barnet frowned. "After Tundavik left the campaign to go to Ritaeum I led the march into Suktir. Me. I never get any credit even though he wasn't even there."

"So you're mad about that?"

"Do not interrupt." His nostrils flared. The carriage bounced over a rock as Barnet said, "This story should not be uttered in front of a woman, but you demand it. It was in Panscar. After the hell we endured in the fighting, I walked the streets. Celebrations galore. I was appalled at the mites being torn from their homes, raped or killed or both. Peasants. The armies were broken. Most of the soldiers died in battle or were injured or fleeing. The red roofs turned black from the fires that filled the air in smoke. All those men Tundavik led went about looting, not just food, but anything they could get their hands on. Auctions took place near the river to fuck any women they could. After the deed was done the girl would be drowned in the Bezir. I saw a child's head smashed into the cobblestones. A face that still haunts me. Guts filled the sewers. The knights of the Woodlands worse than anyone else, all with a huge tree painted on their breastplate. Any woman or girl was taken in the open."

"Barnet," she said as she actually placed a comforting hand on his knee just for it to be shrugged off, "this sounds like a usual war. It's awful but it happens. I'm sure Tundavik didn't know."

His eyes burned and his face was red. "I walked into the castle on the hill to report what I was seeing. Usually commanders would put a stop to the madness, but what I saw was Tundavik passing liquor and laughing with his men while the Princess Analla, Hurvir's sister, was being raped in the corner, he offered me a drink. She died the next day." Barnet wiped his eyes. "I will not let that man lecture us on honor and duty and freedom when he allowed his men to behave like animals."

"People can change," she said meekly. *Tundavik would not let such a horror happen on his watch. He's a nice man. He's a just man.* She felt like ripping her tongue out for saying those words.

Barnet's eyes changed from anger to hatred. Maybe sadness. "You still defend him. After everything I've said. After you forced me to tell you. There's a reason Ritaeum was destroyed and the people massacred, and it wasn't because Hurvir was having a bad day. He wanted revenge for his sister. That's why Tundavik left the campaign and Viguran and went West. But you won't believe me anyway. Why did the gods give you to me as a wife? What did I do to deserve you?"

The carriage ride was silent afterward, the sounds of Tedbalt driving his horses was the only thing she heard. *He's lying,* was what she kept repeating in her head. But why would Barnet lie? He was never one to mince words. Weeks after their marriage he had said, "I don't love you as much as I thought I would." Her heart had broken and continued to break everyday after that. It got worse when he yelled and cursed and went north after she gave birth to a girl. Barnet came to love Little Flora, but he never forgave Flora for not giving him an heir.

When they reached the castle Barnet leapt from the carriage and crossed the muddy baileys. Flora's boot sank into the earth, Tundavik helped her. "I've been searching for you."

Flora didn't look him in the eyes. "Barnet is looking forward to your meeting."

"Did you find anything out that could help me?" Tundavik followed her as she tried to walk along the dry parts of the path. "What's wrong? I promise I have not told anyone what occurred between us. I would never."

"I'm not upset about that, well, a bit, but Barent told me awful things." Flora stopped on a dry patch of grass. Spring would be here soon with rain that would leave nothing dry.

"What did he say? It couldn't have been that bad?"

"He told me about the fighting in Panscar. How the mites were beaten and on the run. Barnet remembered the things done in the city and castle during the celebration."

"He told you stories of war and not what he wanted?" Tundavik's face dropped. "I need his vote. Does he want land? Whores?" Flora flinched. "Knights? Gold? I can get him whatever he desires, did you tell him that?"

"He told me about the evil the Vigurite knights, especially those from the Woodlands, brought onto the innocent people of Panscar. The raping and pillaging. I was always told knights were honorable and fought fairly."

"Those were stories your father and mother sang so you would fall asleep. War is not honorable and certainly not fair. Nothing happened in the ancient city that did not occur anywhere else along the Bezir. And what do you think the mites did to us? To the people of Awaran? Nothing done in Panscar was any worse than what has happened in the endless wars men have fought."

"Barnet told me about Princess Analla." Flora stood tall with her arms crossed. "The rape."

Tundavik took a step back. "I did not rape anyone if that's what he's implying. My wife and children awaited me in Ritaeum. Your husband is a liar, I'm sorry to say. We were rummaging through the cellars for wine and ale and drinking our fill. The Princess Analla was already dead. We sent word to Vigur and began our march to Suktir within days."

Flora remembered how Tundavik didn't correct her when she asked about the Rainvealandians killing everyone in Ritaeum. *This is how I can tell who is being truthful.* "Then Hurvir destroyed your home? Is Analla's death the reason or did the Rainvealandians take over? Tell the truth."

"I don't know the mind of that sick man. He did whatever he wanted and killed my family." *There it is,* she thought even though in her heart she wished her husband was the one lying. "For that I never thought I would come back here, but something called me back. And now I'm on the side of the son of the man who murdered my family and friends. I want him to be better. That's why I need to win this war for him. Ultiir will be like his brother, but I have the power to change Devro. To understand that killing innocent people is wrong. I want to honor my family. To make Adile and Guis and little Ertha proud. I failed to protect them, but I will not fail to protect any more families."

"I'm not sure I can believe you," Flora kicked a pebble. "Maybe if you win we can speak again." She turned away from Tundavik and went to the castle. Barnet waited inside.

"I told you he is dangerous." Her husband said.

Bertin

As the dwarvish door opened, Bertin covered his eyes from the sun that bathed them all in light. Jagged peaks encircled them, clouds gathered overhead. There wasn't much winter in Rainvealand, but the highest mountains had snow on them that blinded him when he looked. There was one peak that was closest to them, and it was where the elves were going. Their horses carefully going down the mountainside. Kelltar hacked away at shrubs and trees and vines. Thatar smiled and pointed at the peak. "It rivals your cities."

Bertin only saw wooded ridges and jagged rocks. No city in sight. At least not until the ground vanished in front of them and a pool of water separated the place they were going from where they were. As Bertin looked past the trees he finally saw the peak up close, except it wasn't a peak at all, it was a mess of tall, pointed towers that looked to grow out of the ground below.

"I told you," Thatar said as Bertin's eyes were wide.

They had traveled for what seemed like days in the darkness of a tunnel mined by dwarves hundreds of years ago. Kelltar was the only one able to find and light a torch. It had been difficult trusting him, but there was no other way.

Vhistela and Thatar had both prayed for Eyln. "The Dragon wishes for elves to be burned, that way our spirit floats to his domain," Thatar had told him. "We will light a candle for him in Anha Jorbstah."

Kelltar shouted in his elvish jargon and they all followed him to a rope bridge. "Careful with the horses," Vhistela said as she dropped from her horse. Bertin could see tear stains on her cheeks, she had been crying as they made their way through the dwarven mines. Eyln always on her mind. Thatar would cry with her when they rested. Kelltar never cried, he only cursed the humans who did it.

The rope bridge swayed as eagles flew near it with the mountain breeze.

"Is this a good idea?" Bertin asked before Kelltar pushed him onto the bridge, his whole world shaking.

"You can test it out first." Kelltar laughed.

Vhistela rolled her eyes and Thatar dismounted from Erona. "This bridge has never collapsed and it won't now." Vhistela said as she led Efyl over the wooden beams. "Don't let Kelltar scare you."

Bertin stayed close to Vhistela and had Thatar behind him. He made sure to not walk with Kelltar and risk being thrown over into the water below. *Crystal clear so they'll see me struggle and drown,* he thought as he looked in the ravine.

Smoke rose from the tallest towers, something normal mountain peaks didn't do. "They see us and are sending word to the city below," Thatar explained. "Maybe a celebration will be had for us. Taking Lisan Biresdea and capturing the crown prince of Rowan will raise their spirits." Thatar slapped Bertin's back with a laugh.

"Derdo!" An elf shouted from the land as Vhistela reached

the other side of the bridge. They had a long conversation while Bertin's stomach lurched with the wind and the swaying bridge. Soon Vhistela waved them to follow.

"What was that?" Bertin asked, wondering where all the celebration was.

"They've been having problems." Vhistela said with a lowered brow. "Not humans."

"What else is there?" Thatar asked and Kelltar huffed.

"Archad is going to bring us to the elders so we can hand over Bertin, hopefully they'll explain all."

Archad, an elf with long, brown bangs covering his eyes, carried a black sword over his shoulder. His armor was leather and a scar ran down his forearm. Bertin asked what had happened but the elf merely stared at him. Thatar told him, "some of these elves have never seen a human so close, heard your speech. They only know the ones who hunt and kill. Best not to make conversation."

The paths they walked along were made of stone so smooth that Bertin could slide across it if he wanted. Walls protected them from the rocks and water below, intricate molds and etchings of dwarven history told a story that Bertin couldn't read. Dwarves were known for their lavishness, at least that's what the elves told him, and Anha Jorbstah didn't prove them wrong. The towers that rose above them were far too big for even humans. Spires piercing the clouds, rotundas casting shadows, stained windows with images of giants watching over them. The buildings and towers rose out of the rock like a fungus. The elves had planted thousands of trees to cover Anha Jorbstah in a green blanket and to make the city more elven than dwarvish. Small fairies of all different colors flew around Bertin's face and giggled. He felt like he had heard their laugh before, but all he wanted to do was swat them away like bugs.

As they climbed steps, the town at the bottom of the rock came into view. Hidden by the mess of leaves and branches were black and gray stone homes and shops. Elves gathered in the squares and along the paths and gawked at Bertin, he even saw some angry stares. *Just like Rowan,* he thought as he imagined the people who hated him. There were even elven children. Their pointed ears not yet big. Their hatred for him not so intense. They ran around his legs and laughed as he jumped back before their parents snatched them away.

A stone door rumbled open and they entered the rock, above them the many towers loomed. The rock was hollowed out and turned into a fortress. An armory, a bakery, slits in the rock for bows, boulders tied high above ready to come crashing down on intruders. Dwarves watched him with sour faces, whispering in their tongue. Gnomes, even smaller than dwarves, snickered as he passed by.

"What're they saying?" Bertin asked the elves.

"We don't speak their language," Vhistela said.

"Then how do you communicate?"

"The same as all you humans do," she said, "we taught them our language. *Arals* are stubborn though and hate using our words. Reminds them that their ancestors lost the wars all those centuries ago." Vhistela explained while looking at the dwarves before they ascended a staircase made of rocks and shiny pebbles. "Gnomes are nicer, at least to us."

"Don't upset them," Thatar added, "they don't take kindly to humans."

Bertin was sweating when they reached the top of the steps. They led him into a large room with columns of granite and a half dozen stone thrones on the other side. The elves bowed and Thatar pulled Bertin down with him. "Why —" Bertin began before Thatar put a hand up for him to be quiet.

Behind the thrones came six elves with graying hair and skin, tired eyes, and shaky bones. They sat and beckoned for them to stand. Kelltar began speaking. Vhistela and Thatar nodding along every so often. The old elf in the center was a male, and Kelltar seemed to be talking to him the most. *Blaenda,* Bertin thought as he clenched his fists.

"The elders are glad you came," Thatar turned to him and said. "Their plan is to send a message with a hawk to your father and demand arms and human coin in exchange for your safe return."

"Tell your king —"

Again Thatar put his hand up. "Remember, Elder Blaenda is no king and will not be addressed as such."

"Tell your *elders* that my father has never negotiated with elves and won't start now."

"You will die then." Thatar said with a sad voice.

"We will give you time to think," Blaenda said in a deep voice that echoed. "We will exchange you for weapons and gold or we will send your head to your father so the human kingdoms know the elves will punish those who harm us. You shall spend the night in the dungeon."

Dungeon ... again, he thought as the elves escorted him out of the chamber and back down the millions and millions of steps. "What were you all talking about?" He asked as they descended. The cold stone his prison.

Kelltar's face turned red but Thatar held a hand up. Bertin's body had already braced to get punch or slapped, so he breathed a sigh of relief. "Nothing important," Thatar glared at Kelltar. "We told them about the journey —"

"— about Eyln," Vhistela whispered.

"— and what Ryfor plans to do in *Oléma*."

"Sounded more serious than that," Bertin said as they passed the door they had used to come inside and went farther down. Deeper. Toward whatever dungeon awaited.

Thatar laughed. "Before you know it you'll learn our language my little *dyr*. The elders were whispering of the Dragon's return."

"Something we've been waiting a very long time for," Vhistela said.

Kelltar grunted as they reached the dungeon.The torches were the only light. It looked like normal cells, Bertin was at least happy about that. He had heard dwarves loved placing cells above pools of lava. This cell was normal. Except the bars were made of stone and it was freezing as if they were in the North for winter. Bertin didn't fight. There was no need to. He was in an elven city and anywhere he ran he would fall into the water below or die trying. Kelltar gave him a extra shove though into the cell before he closed the door. Across the room, in a different cell, were two dwarves. Their long beards being used as blankets, they looked groggy, like they were just waking up.

"They say Nhamcaryn is upon us." Thatar said and Kelltar rolled his eyes. Bertin's face must've looked confused because Thatar explained, "the coming of the Dragon. It is already happening. This is the year. The elders want us to get ready for another journey. We have to find the source."

"What source?" Bertin said.

Vhistela stepped forward. "Humans do not need to hear this. The Dragon will bathe the world in fire and it will be reborn as an elven homeland. We'll finally be able to return to our homes and lands."

Kelltar was tapping his foot so Thatar said, "we'll see you in a few days Bertin. The elders will write to Rowan and we will see what happens."

The three elves left Bertin alone with the dwarves who whispered to each other. Bertin sat on the hard ground. Not only did he have to survive Anha Jorbstah and the elves, but now he had to survive some dragon. He went to sleep dreaming of fire.

Yvanne

Yvanne saw little Tiro sitting in a dark corner, his back hunched with whimpers escaping. They were deep in the mountain keep. Only torches giving light. She bent down, placing a hand on his knee. "Is it Tito? Is your father alright?"

Tiro jumped like he had seen a goblin and stood at attention. "My lady … my queen. Forgive me … I …" he started to weep again before sitting down in a heap. "It's not … my father … it is … yours."

"Tiro, my father is dead. He's been dead for weeks."

The young boy wiped the tear stains from his cheeks. "I know. I failed you."

What is it with these boys and feeling like they can fight a sickness? "He was old and feeble and it was only a matter of time. You did nothing wrong. Have you prayed for him? Good. That means you have done something for him and have yet to fail me."

"I was watching the door when the daken came out and told me. I froze. Couldn't tell anyone so she had to run out instead. I saw his lordship with pale skin. His eyes never blinked."

"It's alright. Why don't you go find your father and bring

me some bread. We can share it together."

Tiro wiped his nose and tears and sniffled. "Father's been running out of his wheatstores. He's ready for the passes to be teeming again with life."

Maybe once the war is over, my little Tiro, she thought as she patted his knee.

Then a horn blew.

Yvanne and Tiro made their way outside, cold air hitting her like a rock before she pulled in the warmth from the fires around the village. The townsfolk gathered as knights in their white armor, glistening from the sun, rode in from the passes. Devro was with Lord de'Marisco oddly enough, but they too found the knights. "Your Grace," Sir Loc said as he jumped off his horse. "We've received word from a band of scouts led by Sir Rickart. They say an army is marching up the King's Pass heading for Whitehall. A black rock adorned their standards."

"Lord Drogue de'Vil, Your Grace," Urses told Devro. "Ultiir must've named him the new Duke of the Lands of Asara. Lord Drogue always hated Lord Rely, some quarrel over a creek or something," he waved his hand. "The lord of the Blackrock has always been ready for battle, usually with the mites, but this time the lord has different plans."

"How long do we have to prepare?" Devro asked.

"We can not say, Your Grace," Loc said. "The message just reached us but could've been sent days ago. The runner collapsed from exhaustion, so hopefully it has been merely a day or two."

Devro's eyes darted around, Yvanne wanted to go talk to him, but Urses whispered to him. "Yes," her husband responded, "that's what I was going to say. Have every man of fighting age prepare for battle. Any who can't fight will … will …" Urses whispered again. Yvanne was glad the lord was helping, but the smirk on his lip gave her pause. Devro continued, his voice growing louder but still getting drowned out by the crowd until Sir Loc shouted for them to quiet. "Any who can't fight has my permission to go deep into the mountain. It is the safest place to be."

***

The keep closed in with its dark walls all around her. She was pushed against a window in the front room. Pollard stood at the door with his sword at his hip and a halberd in his hand. Sidoro stood at his side with a warhammer. Lord Aimora and his men were somewhere among the rocks. Lord Cul and the Peakmen standing near the opening of the pass as the vanguard.

The entire town piled into her home. The women and children who were not fighting stayed in the back of the keep with Cada. The others joined the men with their poleaxes, spears and longswords. A small boy, the helm too big for his head, stood near Pollard. She wondered if that boy would come back. Yvanne would watch the battle through the window. Whitehall would not fall today. *I hope,* she thought as she rubbed her stomach. Devro stood next to her in armor. He looked like the other boy. The gauntlets a little too big, the boots far too wide, his helm falling over his eyes too many times. Lucky for him he wouldn't be needed for most of the fighting. Just to boost morale.

"You'll do great," Yvanne rested a gloved hand on his metaled shoulder.

"As long as I don't die," he audibly gulped. "I'm not my father. I'm not a warrior who can lead thousands into battle."

"How many wars did he win? You don't need to be your father."

Devro nodded as the sun was nearing its set and still no movement. The keep stood still with bated breath. Lord Drogue de'Vil would try to take the village out from under them. He would think it would be defenseless, easy to capture. He would be wrong, and he would suffer the consequences. Behind her, she heard the mumbling of prayers, she said a silent one, hoping it would help, but she knew the only thing needed for them to win was strength, and a little luck.

Armor as pitch black as a moonless night sky emerged through the pass. Mail and steel holding swords and shields filled the narrow gap. Those in front beat drums that rocked the keep and echoed menacing jolts throughout the Lands. Behind them the cavalry. They wore helms shaped in the gods' image, allowing only the mouth and eyes to be visible through small slits. Most wore the faces of judgment, of Vigura, but she saw a few nurturing faces, of Meret. That confused her. How they could think descending on a small village was nurturing she didn't know.

Lord Cul and his warriors were quick to defend as black-clad men beat at them with swords and spears. Those of the peak were to keep Lord Drogue's men in the pass as long as they could. Pollard would give a signal and Lord Aimora would rain down. So far everything was going as planned.

Her brother slipped on his white helm and found a bell. They didn't have a large bell tower like cities, so hopefully the jingle of this one would be heard over the death. Pollard stepped outside and called, "retreat!" as he rang the bell.

"Retreat!" It was a dishonorable move, but Cul thought it the perfect tactic. The people of the peaks began to run toward the keep. Lord Drogue's army confused for a second. Hesitating. It was just what they needed.

Pointed helms with blue ribbons emerged. She saw Lord Aimora drop his sword as Drogue's cavalry began to ride forward.

Boulders and rocks began to fall on the unsuspecting faces of Vigura. The men didn't notice until it was too late. Horses tried escaping the pass, but it was of no use. The jagged rocks gained speed and crushed any and all below. Yvanne wanted to look away, but she had to make sure this worked.

Horses bathed in blood as their bodies were smashed to the hard ground. Steel plated knights had no where to go as the pass filled with killing. Their helms in the face of Vigura did not help them as the rocks, big and small, broke their heads into small pieces. The inside of their bodies spilled out making a slippery mess. Knights in mail and steel and leather tumbled and scurried as they tried to leave the pass of death.

The rocks continued to fall on the mass of men and horses. The cavalry could not survive this.

The footmen ran from the pass, arrows flew up into the mountains. Yvanne could not see if one of the Lodean were hit, but she could see the arrows that filled the pass along with the rocks, Lodean now aiming at the attackers. The knights were not agile enough to dodge the rain of pointed steel. Arrows dug themselves into the mail of the knights, ripped the boiled leather to shreds, and some lucky ones slipped through the openings of steel plates.

Pollard swayed in anticipation, waiting for the moment to strike. His halberd moved with his body. The spike atop the axe was newly sharpened, ready to pierce. He dropped the visor on his helm and glanced at his sister. Yvanne locked eyes with her brother before the war. She could see the fear that exuded from them. His first battle.

Her brother turned and nodded to Sidoro. Her sister's husband screeched a war cry and the doors burst open with all the might of a hundred knights. The armored men ran and screamed as they crossed the center of town and into the invaders. Yvanne's ears picked up the squeaks let out by the young children who joined the fight.

The spears and poleaxes and other polearms were first. Pollard and all near him on the front line lowered their weapons and jabbed through anything in their way. The poleaxes and warhammers smashed into them. The dazed attackers who had just stumbled from the pass found themselves with weapons embedded in their armor.

Pollard began to beat against the elite knights wearing black painted plates of steel. Sidoro rammed his spiked hammer into any man he saw. Their bodies lurched and toppled once the steel head met mail and leather.

Lord Aimora and a few of his men climbed down the tumbling rocks until they were at the pass along with Pollard and Sidoro. Aimora took his longsword and attacked the men in leather. He swung at arms and legs that were unprotected, severing any limb he could find. The blood spurted and Lord Aimora Dore chanted in his mother tongue.

His Lodean soldiers followed with their own attacks. Swords, axes, spears; all went toward the enemy. Armor was dented, men were knocked over, blood spilled from gaps. She saw legs and arms fly into the air and men sobbing as they knew death was near.

Yvanne hadn't noticed that Devro, who was to run out with Pollard was still in the keep, swaying in his large metal boots, shaking.

"You must go outside," she told her husband. "The troops need to see their king is with them."

"I don't want to die," Devro said. The helm covered his face but Yvanne knew he was crying. "Gofrei tells me how dangerous this is. How I should just turn around and run back home."

"Gofrei isn't here right now, so you can't let his old whispers haunt you." She put her hand on his back, not wanting to push him, but feeling like she could, and they took a step outside. The cold air piercing her bare face. "Show these people that you are the rightful king and you deserve their love." She turned to Sir Loc, who was to stand guard and watch her. "Go with him."

"Your Grace, my duty is to protect you," the knight said.

"Please." She wouldn't take no for an answer and the knight forced a nod.

Devro sniffled than cleared his throat, "Okay," he whispered to no one. His boots left prints in the snow by the door, Sir Loc with his sword drawn following close behind. Eventually Devro was near some Lodean who called out that their "king was here!"

"Don't move." A voice said to her right. When she turned she saw a dark-skinned boy dressed in black without a helm. He was far too young to be fighting. *But we've some younger than him on the front lines,* she told herself. "Lord Drogue told me to kill the queen and king so we can get on with it." He held out a dagger. His face was bruised and a hint of blood was on his neck. "So I came to kill you and give my lord his duchy as was promised by the king."

Yvanne didn't think anyone else was watching her. Cada and those who couldn't fight were deep in the mountain, awaiting victory or defeat. And the fighting was still raging. She saw the energy all around her, felt the stone on her necklace heat her neck, and was prepared to burn the young boy to save her life. But Tiro had other plans.

Little Tiro had found a knife and buried it into the attackers skull. Drogue's young solider collapsed with his mouth agape and a smattering of blood and hair in the snow. "Get back inside," she told Tiro without thanking him. "Go, go." Tiro and Yvanne hobbled back into the keep and barred the door as per the instructions. Tiro's knife was still outside, fallen next to the dead boy, but he was standing like he was still holding it, ready to kill any attacker. His face was snarled. His jaw clenched. *I don't like that face,* she thought before he relaxed and went back to being just a boy. *Hopefully I never have to see it again.*

Tiro and Yvanne watched the battle out the window. Devro stood with the Lodean, flinching in his armor as arrows pierced the sky. Pollard and Aimora and Cul all fighting the men of Blackrock. She finally saw the lord that attacked them. Lord Drogue's armor was fine steel, his helm matched his men, but the slits were smaller. He rode through the pass on a war horse with black, shiny armor as nice as his. He dropped a lance and rammed it into men in his path. Their armor was of no use. The steel and chain broke, and blood gushed from the dead men. Drogue turned his stallion and faced back. Pollard stood in his way over a newly deceased man.

The lord kicked at his horse's side. The stallion reared and charged at Pollard. The lord's lance fell once more. The point aimed right at Pollard's white armored heart.

Yvanne wanted to cry for help, but there was no one to hear, and Tiro wouldn't be able to do anything. She stared closely out the window, through the dust and blood. Pollard fought off a man in leather, then struck a man in mail. He used a small dagger to stab through an eye slit in a helm of Vigura.

The lance was advancing. The horse kicked up stone and clouds of filth. She saw the back of the lord's armor. He was gaining speed with every jolt of his steed. Pollard turned at the last minute.

Her vision blurred and darkened. The worst thoughts she ever had ran through her mind. She imagined the blow to her brother's armor. The crushing of his chest and organs as the lance blew through him. She didn't want to think of that possibility. Maybe the wound would be easy to heal. Perhaps the doma or daken could help him. Or Pollard would die on the field of his first battle. Yvanne would lose her mother then her father then her brother then …. then …

When her eyes cleared, and the dust settled she saw what happened. A slough of blood spilled over the rubble. The armored horse lay dead with a fresh stump for a leg. The limb had fallen to the side. The old Lord Cul held his sword that had turned red with the horse's blood. Pollard held his sword and had took his helm off. His face was in a state of shock.

Lord Drogue found a sword near him and held it ready for battle. His men surrounded him after he let out a call. Pollard slipped his helm on and gripped his sword. Aimora joined his side with his bloodied longsword. Sidoro ran over with his warhammer.

Drogue led the charge. His men screamed with their weapons drawn. Pollard called for his men and they came as quickly as possible. Lord Aimora called for the Lodean. The battle grew larger and closer to the keep. The chambers rumbled with the sound of fighting.

Yvanne lost the sight of her people in the clashes that followed.

***

When the fighting stopped, and mountains cleared of dirt, she saw the aftermath. There was more blood this time. More men curling and calling for their gods. Yvanne carefully stepped out with Tiro as her guard. Her shoes sank in the blood as they made their way to the sprawl of bodies.

She kept her head up as they walked over the dead children who had decided to fight. She couldn't bear to look at them. She held her belly and thought of her child. The stench of death made her stomach churn. She wanted to vomit but kept her composure. The images of chopped limbs and broken bones burrowed into her mind.

Tiro helped Pollard to his feet. He threw his dinged helm to the ground and steadied himself on Sidoro. "We did it." Sidoro told her brother. Cada came running from the keep and jumped in her husband's arms.

Yvanne smiled at the sight of her brother. "You led a successful charge. I was worried for a moment."

Pollard returned the smile. "Worried about me?" he panted. "You should have … more faith."

Lord Aimora was talking with his Lodean, horses racing

into the pass to chase after the Blackrock men in retreat. "Your Grace," Aimora dropped to one knee. "We've a problem."

That's when she realized Devro was gone, and no one could find him.

Tundavik

"I heard he disappeared, no one ever saw him again until he showed his face here," a washerwoman said. Tundavik stood, shivering, outside a side door to the castle, the servants' quarters just inside, and they were talking about him. Rattling off rumors.

Another servant said, "Someone told me he murdered his family and ran off to Eotros."

"How awful." Tundavik could hear the sound of clothes being dunked in water and scrubbed, one of the other servants hung them on the line.

"I thought he would go to Ritaeum, but he showed up here of all places."

"He must really like warring," a young girl giggled.

"Ritaeum is stained in blood." One of the servants whispered, she was much older by the sound of her voice. Years of use had strained it. "He doesn't want to go back there and relive the horror."

"Surely they washed the floors."

"No," the old woman said, "the blood cannot be cleaned. Gilda told me the ghosts of women and children wander the halls of the keep and yell out in their deathly screams."

"That's why I would never go south. Too many cursed

places and people," the young one said in her higher pitched voice.

"In Ealna they don't sleep. A sorcerer told me he had cursed the city and everyone would die in a coming war. I guess he meant this war."

"Didn't all the sorcerers die?"

"They're still out there," an ominous tone filled the room beyond the door. Tundavik shivered from the cold breeze that still swept through Storyah, he wasn't afraid of warlocks and witches. "They're waiting to come back and take their revenge on those who wronged them."

"Perhaps Tundavik is one and he came to kill the lords."

When Tundavik heard Pyre Blume whistling some song about a man swimming across the Nokys he decided he was needed elsewhere. Not to listen to the rumors and stories washerwomen came up with to pass the time. He walked across the damp grass, his boots shiny from the wetness, and found Pyre starting up the stairs to the castle. The moonlight highlighted the duke's wrinkles. "My lord duke," Tundavik said as he reached Lord Blume.

"How are you, Tundavik? Do you feel the heat of spring coming?" Pyre opened his arms wide like he was basking in the sun instead of the cold winter night.

Tundavik only felt a chill in the air, but the castle doors opening let out the warmth from the dozens of hearths always with flames. "I'm worried about the war. If my meeting with Lord Barnet doesn't go well and the Flewthlands stay neutral then it is lost."

Pyre motioned for Tundavik to follow. They emerged from the mess of corridors into the empty great room. Pyre rubbed a scuff off his high seat. "Since the snows are melting we've received even more messengers telling us of the war day and night."

"Anything I should know?"

"Only a few stood out. Riots in Vigur and Goldfield. Lord Straiver of the Byway is burning the lowlands and pillaging the villages. Lord Oda lost the Whitefork and was taken prisoner, but a few of his knights have gone east to the Brownfork to help in their defense. Lord Moncy has declared for Devro and set fields and villages alight near Nopra's Tear, fighting intensely with Lord David Viero of Winterlake."

"Sounds like more of the same."

A shadow overcame Pyre's eyes. "One more thing. The Lands of Asara now has a young duchess. David Rely has died."

Tundavik cleared his throat with disbelief. *I didn't realize that old man was so sick. Now I'll never see him again because I had to come to Storyah. If Barnet doesn't go with me then David will have died in vain.* "So Yvanne is duchess," he said even though he couldn't believe it. "That has to be the first time a woman has taken over."

"Maybe Flora has a chance." Pyre laughed. "If Yvanne can take over then what's stopping her? It will prove her mother right and be sure to piss off many of my lords who want my seat after I'm gone."

"We can't afford to make any of your lords angry with us. We'll have to tell them Yvanne becoming duchess is only because of the war and once she is crowned queen in Vigur whichever one of her brothers is heir will be named duke." Tundavik hoped Pyre wouldn't push too hard for Flora to succeed him. He didn't need anymore complications.

"Have you spoken to Barnet yet?" Pyre asked as he sat.

"Many respect his opinion and he doesn't wish to talk to me. 'His lord is enjoying the sights of the city,' is usually what they tell me. Hogwash, but no matter. The other problem is that you're both stubborn asses."

"Later. He wishes to meet tomorrow night atop the walls. He might try to push me over or hope I freeze to death."

"As long as you convince him," Pyre laughed then straightened his face. He twiddled his thumbs as he said, "He's a good man. He'll come around."

***

Keeland was small and damp from the summer rains, the humidity causing Tundavik to sweat even more in his black armor. They would begin their march across the Ters-Veck into Panscar once the sun set. Red towers rose from the mist of the mountains on the other side of the river.

"Are you ready for the fighting?" Barnet Lovell asked. He had a patchy beard that would grow in once he got older, but now he was just a young man.

"That city will become even redder." Tundavik chuckled.

"I hope so. I fought in the Iron Gate, repelled a mite invasion, and many of my friends were cut down, not to mention my brothers and father before that." Barnet was lucky. The Iron Gate, the bridge held up by the gods in the mountains connecting Keeland to Panscar over the Ters-Veck, was a bloodbath. Tundavik lost too many men that day.

"They would be proud."

"That's what I hope." Barnet slid on his pointed helm. His surcoat covered in the dark trees of his wood. *I can make a quick friend of him,* he thought as he pictured the woods in Ritaeum. *A lifelong friend.*

***

"My wife has grown fond of you." Barnet's voice cut through Tundavik's memory as the moonlight cascaded over them. The waves crashing below the walls.

Tundavik shook his head of the old thoughts trying to creep in. "You're lucky to have her."

"I forbade her but she does what she wants. Always wanting to upset me that one." Barnet leaned on the wall, spat at the ground below. "Did you fuck her?"

Tundavik almost choked on his breath and felt like jumping over the castle walls. "Why would you ask that? We're to talk about the Flewthlands joining the war."

"Did you?" The lord of Woodrun's eyes were sad, half his face covered in shadow as he look at Tundavik.

Tundavik nodded and threw his hands in the air, "so now what? Challenge me to a duel?"

Barnet laughed and wiped sweat from his brow. "You may be old but I'd still lose, I was never much of a fighter, plus I still need an heir."

"Can Florance not be the heir to Woodrun?" Tundavik asked. *I need to see how many of these Flewthmen would support a woman. I can't lose them just because Yvanne is now a duchess.*

"Perhaps in another life, but the laws of Viguran forbid it, and not all of us are so quick to go against them." Barnet looked over the wall. "Florance will not be the first woman to rule Woodrun if I have any say."

He didn't know what came over him, maybe it was the

299

sadness in Flora's eyes or the glares Barnet would give her and their daughter, but he asked, "Do you hate Little Flora?"

Barnet faced him like he had been slapped. his eyes burning. "Never call her that. How dare you question the love I have for my child. I would go to Veltoora if it meant saving her."

"Others speak about your hatred for Lord Blume, Flora, and Florance."

"We shouldn't believe rumors." Barnet huffed but the burning seemed to die down. He sighed and said, "True, I don't care for Lord Blume all that much, but I love Flora and my daughter with all my being. How does Flora repay me? By laying with another man," he gave a sad laugh. "Oathbreakers are usually hanged in Viguran."

Tundavik watched Barnet's face scrunch with regret and flare with anger. With hatred. "What happened to you after I left Suktir? You've become so hateful."

"I was the only one of my family left. Bertam, Bene, Birenge, Bruge, Beomont, and my father all died years before Suktir yet their ghosts still haunt me. I was disgusted in Panscar by all the death. All I could think about was if my family was treated the same way before they died." The lord looked to the sky, stars twinkling overhead. "After Panscar, I led so many battles and sackings along the Bezir as we marched to Suktir, but who gets all the credit? The man who left because he raped the king's sister."

"Do not repeat that, you know it is a lie." Now he wanted to throw the lord of Woodrun over the walls and watch the waves beat his body against the shore.

"She was bloody and crying. The king's sister. You were hailed a hero. Do you ever picture all the men you killed? Hear their screams in your dreams? Now, you want us to go back to war and kill more people, our own people."

Tundavik tried not to think of the castle in Panscar, but Barnet was trying to bring back the memories. He wouldn't let the lord do that to him. "I want you and the Flewthlands to help put the rightful king on the throne."

"A boy. A bastard. You believe he's different from his father?"

"We'll find out when Ultiir is deposed." Dark clouds gathered in the west, bringing with them rain instead of snow, Tundavik rubbed his arms to keep warm. "We didn't have this meeting to exchange war stories. What will it take for you to support Devro?"

Barnet crossed his arms and said, "Something your ancestors would know very well. Something the Four and the Many could never give. All I need is a promise and I can convince those who follow me to vote with you."

"Just a promise? You'll trust me that much?"

"Many centuries ago, it was the Lovells who ruled in Storyah, their duchy extended farther north and west but we can't always get what we want. My ancestors were deposed by the Blumes. My family has always supported independence, and the closest we've gotten was during Onto's rebellion, but what does Pyre do? He makes peace with our enemy. There have been a lot of talks in the decade since, but just know I have support."

For a moment Tundavik was at a loss for words. He knew exactly what Barnet was going to ask and wished nothing more than to be wrong. "Treason, isn't it?"

"I wish to be the duke of the Flewthlands. I'll get everyone to support you. Once Vigur is taken my men will march back here with a proclamation from Devro naming me duke."

Tundavik rubbed his beard, it was a matted mess. "How long do I have?"

"How about tomorrow? I think that's more than enough time to think about it, and we'll be closer to the vote."

Once the meeting was over Tundavik paced on the cold ground in the bailey with a light mist before the storm hit. Flashes of light beckoned the coming of lightening. Everyone else who was enjoying the night sky had gone inside at the first hint of rain. He sat on a damp sandstone block. Thinking. *David is dead and I'm supposed to betray Pyre now? There will be no one left in this kingdom that I know.* He wanted to sleep. He wanted to never wake up. It was too much to betray an old friend, but without Barnet's support the lords might vote against Tundavik and the war would surely be lost.

Tundavik's red and yellow clothes marinated with the wetness of rain. Growing darker with every drop. Boots kicked mud and Mar stood over him. "Old man, shouldn't you be inside? Your bones are too brittle for the rain," he laughed.

Tundavik joined in but the laughter never reached his eyes. "Lord Barnet wants something impossible to join our side. I'm not sure I can give it to him."

"You gave David a queen for a daughter. How hard could it be?"

"He wants the whole of the Flewthlands." Tundavik said as he wiped rain from his face, hoping no one else heard. "He wishes to rule the duchy and depose Pyre. Probably kill him."

Mar bent down in the mud to face Tundavik. "So tell the other lords that Barnet is talking treason. No way they support that cunt then."

"He says he has support all over the duchy because of Pyre's willingness to parlay with Hurvir."

Mar moved his hair from his eyes. "Everyone knew Pyre ending the rebellion would haunt him later in life. Didn't think it would be so soon though."

"Pyre is an old friend and I'm supposed to betray him. Betray his daughter and granddaughter too. What would my family think?" Tundavik didn't know if he was wiping away rain or tears.

Mar, with a moment of hesitation, placed a hand on Tundavik's shoulder and looked into his eyes. The knight's gray eyes were kind. One of the few times they weren't glossy from drinking. "If someone wanted me to betray Raimund to save a million people. I don't think I could do it. But you're not me. When was the last time you saw Pyre? Did he come to your aid in Ritaeum?" Mar scratched his head. "It's your choice. But why does Barnet think he'll win anyhow? Take Vigur then march on Storyah to protect Lord Blume. We'll have the whole kingdom on our side and Barnet will be thrown into the sea."

"Usually I'm not this conflicted."

"Just think which is better, easier. The Flewthlands on our side or Pyre's life?"

"Betray a friend to win a war." Tundavik shook his head with a nervous chuckle. "That sounds crazy."

"War makes everything harder."

Tundavik finally stood, his legs numb, but he had made his decision. He needed the Flewthlands. He needed Devro to be on the throne and to be better than his father and uncle. He needed to keep the people in the Lands of Asara safe. Even if that meant Pyre's death.

Aveline

It was as if Viguran wasn't at war as Aveline watched the people of Ealna go about their business. The canals were clogged of small boats, full of trade and life. The roads bustling with markets and teams of horses. The port had ships from Kruhesh and Eotros and Okros and other parts of Adedor all unloading their goods to be shipped all over the region.

"They're charging a ship's worth down there," Ivlin said when he and Bert returned from the market. "Don't let the looks deceive you. The war is causing hurt here too."

Aveline polished an apple with her shirt and crunched it, it was softer than she would've liked. "Good thing we have a ship's worth of coin."

In a small boat in a canal below the massive ships of Rowan, was Caxton. The chief councilor was meeting with city leaders, trying to get them to cut off trade to the rest of Viguran. She hoped. The banners for the leaders weren't those of Viguran, no owls for miles, instead the banners showed the great rock growing out of the steppe that symbolized Maertan. The Maermen had control of Ealna ever since the war with the Rainvealandians, much to her cousin's chagrin. They were lucky the city was apart of a different kingdom. It gave them a safe place to rest that wouldn't pull them into war.

"The whores were charging double!" Dern the Third cried as he waltzed up the gangplank, though he also wore a smile. "Good thing I can get my fill right here," he eyed Mari who shook her head with laughter. Aveline, her guards, and Mari all stood on the upper deck of the ship, watching below. Baldewin was somewhere with Blis, probably in his room, waiting for Caxton to make more decisions.

"I hate feeling left out," she said. "I'm allegedly regent yet it seems like all the important tasks are given to the council, especially Caxton."

"Probably due to Awaran," Bert muttered before raising his hands. "I mean no offense. But everyone saw that Caxton had more of a say in Awaran. That means something." The Grand Duke and Duchess of Awaran had agreed to help, but with Caxton's version. Aveline still had to deal with the threat that hundreds of Rowai men could die.

Zoell whistled slowly. "Well, the princess regent and king haven't been in charge for very long. Caxton and the councilors have been around for a decade or more. They ruled very close with King Bartel, may the Four guide him."

Aveline sucked her teeth. "Perhaps Baldewin and I need to have a talk. We can't let Caxton make all the decisions. He and the others are going to drag the entire kingdom into war, more than they already have."

She walked over the damp deck toward the king's quarters at the stern. The captain was above it, shouting and laughing with sailors near the great wheel. *Baldewin will be all alone with these people, he'll only have Blis to guide him,* she thought before sadness took over, *and he'll have Mari.* She had wanted

Mari to follow her. To talk with her. Make her laugh. But Mari stood near the guards and laughed with them instead. It was their last day together until Aveline found Bertin, and she couldn't do what she wanted with Mari. *I will show her how much I love her after I return.*

Inside the king's quarters Baldewin lay on the cotton blankets of his bed. He toyed with a stray piece of wood, probably peeled from the deck before someone could smooth it down. He didn't even look up when his sister arrived. Aveline sat on a velvet chair. Through the leaded windows on the back she could see more of Ealna and the canals. Ships making their way to the port. "Didn't Blis want you to practice with swords?"

Baldewin waved the piece of wood like a sword. "There it is. Practice is done."

Aveline crossed her arms. Her brother's crown was on a table beside the bed. She forgot how young he was as they were sailing. Ever since her father died it was as if Baldewin had aged ten years in her eyes, but he was a child, her baby brother, and he still acted like it. She uncrossed her arms. "I know the men would like to see you more. You've spent so much time in your cabin since we left Awaran. You didn't even see the Iron Gate." The Iron Gate was the bridge between mountains that crossed the Ters-Veck. It connected Viguran and Attamek to the south. One side of the bridge was held up by a statue of Vigura, the other by the Ancient One and the ever-changing face.

"I didn't want to see it. I like my bed more." Baldewin sat up and threw the piece of wood across the room. His brown hair stood on end from laying down for so long. "Blis tells me the same thing. All anyone ever says to me is what I *should* be doing. I miss the way it was."

Me too, she thought. "You're king now. I wish father didn't die too, but that's the way it works."

"I wish it were different." Baldewin sulked. "It'd be better if we were born some cobblers' children."

Aveline giggled, "Go tell the cobblers' children that you want to change places." She motioned to the room, the golden etching along the wood, the polished floors, gleaming ceilings. "They would gladly switch." Aveline brought herself to Baldewin's bed and sat beside him. "You got us into this mess," she said with a laugh so the words wouldn't sting as much, no matter how true they were. "If you'd've listened to me and not agreed to sail to Redington we'd be in Rowan right now. Your portrait probably finished."

Baldewin nodded with a sigh. "Whoops." They laughed together. "Hopefully you find Bertin and I don't have to do this anymore. I liked fishing in Decaro."

"I'm sure, my little king," Aveline wrapped her arm around him and hugged him. "Don't worry. I'll come back with Bertin and he'll deal with Caxton and the other councilors. William won't be the only one without a tongue."

Baldewin winced but laughed again. "What are you going to do? It's your last night before you have to camp everywhere," he said with disgust.

"Maybe don't switch your life with a cobbler family." Aveline started laughing, slightly tickling her brother, who joined in. The joyful chorus filled the cabin.

***

Mari was ashore, fending off flirtation from docksmen when

Aveline found her. "Make way for the princess regent," Dern the Third said as he pushed the men away.

"Not my bloody princess," a dockworker spat. Dern stared at him with fiery eyes and the worker sulked away.

"I think they like you," Aveline said as she locked arms with Mari and they began to walk down the cobbled street, avoiding puddles caused by earlier canal flooding.

"Well I need someone to protect me maybe I can choose out of that lot," Mari giggled and pulled her arm away. "We don't need gossip."

Aveline put her hand on Mari's soft cheek and said, "Let them gossip," she kissed her, happy to finally me alone with her, until Dern cleared his throat. "Of course," Aveline said. Dern knew they shouldn't linger too long near the ship and the rest of the Rowai. Mari was of course right, they didn't need the gossip, but she didn't care, so Aveline took Mari's arm back and they began their walk into the city.

"What do you have planned for tonight?" Mari asked as they strolled past a bakery that was closed for the night. Leftover bread being devoured by stray cats and dogs. "A candlelit walk over the canals? Seeing a show?"

"This isn't Rowan, and the war has stopped Ealna from being so lively." Aveline said as two men in an ally flashed their daggers with smiles until Dern came into view with his plate and steel. "I've something better than all that. My guards were out all day trying to find the perfect sendoff."

"I heard what they were looking for," Mari chuckled, "I'm not too fond of whorehouses."

Aveline pulled a strand of hair from her brow. The white stone that made up the great buildings of Ealna reflected the moonlight back on them. The domaton was more ornate than any she'd ever seen. The statues of the Four almost lifelike; the windows arched and the glass made up of every color she could imagine; the roof gilded which probably reflected the sun back into the heavens. *I'm far from home,* she thought as images of the gray slab they call a domaton popped into her head. But the flogging of a Rainvealandian near a city well reminded her how similar Ealna and Rowan were.

"This way," she pulled Mari away from the person being beaten and found a small inn. It didn't have a name or even rooms, but Ivlin thought the place perfect. When they entered there was nothing but lit candles. Dern bowed and closed the door to stand guard outside. Aveline gestured to the candles and said, "not quite a canal."

"Did you do this?" Mari's eyes shifted. "You decided to light an empty inn with candles. I've never known you as a romantic."

Aveline grabbed Mari's hands and kissed her. "It's a thank you for agreeing to watch over Baldewin for me, and for understanding why our future looks dim."

Mari nodded and pulled away slightly, "So you're going to tell me this is our last night together, and when you return we'll pretend like we never knew one another and you'll find some wealthy lord or prince and marry them and bare their children and—"

"Stop," Aveline interrupted. "You'll drive yourself mad with those thoughts." Aveline pulled Mari into a hug and started swaying, their faces touching. "Let us enjoy this night and all the nights to come. Once I find Bertin and this whole Redington thing is over with, we'll run away just like you wanted. Even take a few jewels." She could feel Mari's smile on her cheek as they swayed. "You just have to promise to be safe out there in the Nokys."

Mari said, "Of course," and began to hum a tune. "You also have to come back. You've already said you would and I don't like it when you break your promises."

"Deal," she kissed Mari. As they danced the shadows did the same on the walls. They were bathed in reds and yellows as the candles burned.

"Am I supposed to get on the ground now?" Mari flirted.

Aveline shook her head and held Mari tight. "Not tonight. Let's just spend it like this." The two swayed and danced all night as the moon rose and fell. They danced together until it was time for Aveline to go south, her brother awaiting her.

Raimund

I don't know much about magic," Potter said as he wrapped himself in a wool blanket near Sile's hearth. The fire blazing. Warming them all. "And that both you have it," Potter shook his head, his jowls bouncing, "wish I'd've got it," he giggled.

Raimund was heating cider over the fire. Sile had found it buried beneath all her books and melted candles. The warmth reminded him of Viguran. Eventually it would be spring and summer down there. Devro would complain and Mar would roll his eyes. Raimund chuckled to himself before his eyes dropped. *If they stay alive,* he thought. As he passed the cider around to Potter and Sile he said, "if only I could show you what I really could do with my sword." If Raimund had Valkyr he probably could've cut down all the guards at the prison. Of course, Sile would be upset, but it would've been faster.

"Healing a baiagryf with yours fingers was impressive enough," Sile said.

Raimund nodded with a smile. "Surprised no one's ever broken out of the hole before."

Potter shrugged as he blew on his drink. "I could barely understand any of them anyhow, but I think a few did long ago. I saw a few walk up the steps with the guards. If only I went with them."

"They were hunting the beast," Sile said. "They're probably dead. Consider yourself lucky you didn't go." She shivered even though the room was blistering hot. "I fear for what is to come."

"Don't listen to her," Raimund said as he saw Potter's eyes grow with fear, "she's superstitious. Within the next few days we're going to go to the Drewogh and find a boat to take us to Viguran. I'm sure there will be a ship somewhere that will take you West. Might be a long journey though."

"In the prison we had to mine the ore, if we didn't do well, we was beat." Potter lifted his shirt to show off a purple bruise. "All I wants is to sit on a ship for weeks," he laughed. "What about you?" He asked Sile. "Very cozy house you got here. Gonna abandon it?"

"I might," she sipped on her drink, "depends on what I find in Viguran." She stood and peaked through a window. "Looks like the wind has stopped. I know we just got back, but I'm running low on food. Didn't think I'd have to feed three people."

"You want us to hunt?" Raimund said. "We can do that, maybe find a deer." Potter looked around the room with eyes of worry. "Just need a lookout," Raimund said.

Potter nodded so they draped a couple of fur cloaks over their shoulders, and slipped sheepskin gloves on their hands. Raimund took Sile's bow, and wandered into the snow-covered hills. "I've not hunted much," Potter said as they neared some trees a couple miles out from Sile's house. "My pa took me a few times, but he was faster without me."

"It won't be too hard," Raimund said. "I'll do the hunting

and you watch my back." He had taken a sword from the prison and had strapped it around his waist. "I'll do any fighting if we run into a wild boar or whatnot."

Potter peered into the forest. The dark trees cast a shadow over the sun, the snow wasn't as deep as other areas. "You think they are any ghosts in there? Monsters?"

"Ghosts aren't real," Raimund answered with a roll of his eyes. "And the only monster I've come across was the griffin. After she ate some of us it turned out she was nice," he chuckled. "Let's go."

They entered the forest and the blinding light of the sun reflecting off the snow subsided. Raimund could actually see without squinting. The bow was in hand, a few arrows at his side. *He* hadn't been hunting in years. Almost all of his food since Mar brought him to Viguran was bought with coin or served at a feast. He forgot what the rugged North was actually like. He hunted with his father many times. His mother sometimes accompanying them. They would dress and eat deer almost every week if they were lucky. Right now, Raimund was not lucky.

The forest was quiet. There were no footprints. No animal calls. Like it was dead.

Potter shuddered. "There was someone in the prison who I could speak to," he said as the wind whistled through the trees. "He called himself Fat Jack. He told me all these stories. He was 'fraid of the forest you see. He said that the first Hellers who came North would sacrifice people in the forest. People who went against the gods. They weren't buried properly. Fat Jack said that the undead walk the forest."

"You can't believe everything you're told," Raimund said, but the crack of a tree branch under Potter's boot made him jump. "I used to live in the mountains near some primeval forests, quite a ways from Irto. Never saw any undead walking around. You've nothing to fear."

"I believe you," Potter said even though his eyes were still big.

They walked for what seemed like a hundred miles until Raimund turned around and still saw the path between the trees they had entered through. "Are you afraid of the woods in the West?"

"In Verva?" Potter shook his head. "No monsters or undead live out there. The Western kings are good at keeping the trouble out. You think we're going to find any deer?"

The vast emptiness of the forest answered Potter's question. There was nothing. Raimund did his best to mimic how his father would hunt. He stayed low. He hid behind natural cover. He even tried making an animal call, which Potter only laughed out. They still had nothing when the sun was directly overhead and flakes of snow started falling.

"Camp time?" Potter asked. Raimund didn't answer. He wasn't sure if the boy was serious or not. "Can I at least piss?"

"I'll be here." Raimund stayed put and Potter waddled off to find privacy.

He decided to sit on the ground as he waited, lying the bow next to him. The snow soft on his trousers. He still shivered, but he could make a small flame with his fingers, which warmed his face. That's when he heard a scream. He jolted and flexed his sword.

At first he thought it was Potter. Until another scream ripped through the air. It wasn't a normal scream, not a scream for help, but a dreadful scream, and it came from farther in the forest.

Raimund stumbled over some fallen logs and saw footprints. They made a trail.

The trees were tall all around him. They looked to be hundreds of feet in the sky. Every branch was prickly and poked at him as he made his way through. The footprints were shallow and going quick. He used his sword to cut through the plants. Another scream pierced the air. He swung harder and faster. He had to see what it was. Another. And another. They grew louder with every step. He reached a small flowing brook.

It was there he saw it. Not a ghost or ghoul, but a beautiful lady with long red hair. She sat naked on a tree stump. Her body curved just right. Raimund couldn't help himself. He moved closer and closer. Every step throwing a piece of clothing off. First his boots then his gloves. He undid his buckle and pulled off his shirt. The cold felt like pins on his chest, but he did not care. He could feel none of the pain. He pulled his black pants off and threw them to the ground.

When he reached the beautiful naked woman, her face began to change. He had a slight hesitation but kept going. He went in for a kiss on the neck and he saw the claws reflect in the sunlight that peaked through the trees. He felt them sting across the back of his neck. He yelled out and fell. Scurrying, he found his sword and lifted it, but he could not use it. He didn't want to use it. Her nose caved in, her eyes fell dead, and her body turned decrepit. That made him want her even more.

As he tried for another kiss she pushed him to the ground. She was about to her on top of him when she hollered in pain. Potter had stabbed the beautiful creature in the back. Raimund stood, his bones chilled from the air, and watched as the monster convulsed until it didn't move anymore. "I … I … killed it." Potter stammered.

Raimund flew back and grabbed his clothes. As he was dressing his eyes were wide and jaw dropped. "I don't understand. What was that?"

"A monster seems to me." Potter said as he looked at the dead husk.

"She …" Raimund rubbed his neck, his hand came back with small amounts of blood. "She lured me here. Wanted to kill me. You killed her."

Potter was staring at his sword. "I did. Good thing you brought me with you huh," he smiled. "And you told me there was nothing to be 'fraid of."

"Let's get back to Sile, make sure no monsters decided to come out."

"But we don't have a deer."

Raimund winced at his neck throbbed. "I need some herbs or something."

They started the long trek back to Sile's cabin, or what seemed like a long trek. Raimund hadn't kept watch of the sun to tell how long it had been since they set out. But as they neared where they had entered the forest from he could tell it was sunset. They moved over the same small hills as earlier in the day. Jagged, black rocks of the mountains rose all around them.

A familiar smell hit Raimund's nose. Potter could smell it too as his nose wrinkled. They crested a hill and looked down in the small valley that Sile lived in. At first he thought the setting sun was illuminating the world in oranges and reds and yellows, but it wasn't. The fire was.

Sile's cabin burned, a roaring blaze bellowed into the sky,

the smoke dancing with the coming night sky. In front of the cabin was a woman. Raimund and Potter raced down the hill and found Sile's half charred body. Blisters and blood covered her. Her eyes were lifeless. "Oh my," Potter said as he bent down and looked closely at the dead woman. "Was it the prison guards? Revenge?"

Raimund heard a low rumble and his eyes followed his ears. In the distance, to the mountains just north, a black shadow flew away. The potvoryn.

Ultiir

Atrice tried as best she could but Ultiir could not bed her, she used her hands or mouth but he felt nothing. Even if he closed his eyes, all he saw was Lovis' smashed head. Lady Rila's dress being torn. Lord Tyter's impaled body. Blood soaked streets.

"How do you think the King's Brothel fared?" Ultiir asked the whore as he lay next to her, their naked bodies rubbing, him feeling nothing. "I pray to the Four that Madam Taire remains unharmed."

Atrice rubbed her smooth fingers over his lips. "Those girls could fight off the forces of Veltoora if needed. I wouldn't worry."

"Have you trained with a sword?"

"I know how to use a dagger and a whip," her lashes fluttered, "some of my clients appreciate my know-how."

Ultiir sat up to feel the warmth of the fire on his chest and face, Atrice rubbed her fingers on his stomach. "The bastard is near winning and he doesn't even know. He wastes away in the mountains with some young, fertile queen when he could be marching on this city right now. The people would welcome him. Hell, even some of the lords would welcome him. Sophie would gladly hand over my severed head if it meant her life was spared."

The whore sat behind him and wrapped her arms and legs around his body, warming his backside as well. "You are the king. You are strong. I have heard stories from many-a-man who talk of the histories. The city rioting doesn't seem all that bad in comparison."

"You're just a whore though, what do you know?"

"I know that Derga the Emperor held together the largest amount of land since the Redmarines. He kept the peace for nineteen years against a whole slew of people, even with revolts and riots. I see you lasting longer than nineteen years."

Ultiir licked his dry lips. "And his son, Valor, was killed by his own advisor. I could just as easily be him."

"They will call you Ultiir the Emperor." She rubbed her soft hands over his arms, feeling his muscles, and her feet on his legs. "And I can be by your side while they chant your name."

Ultiir's body was warm as her touch tingled him. "I'm sorry to say, but no whore has ever been queen, and I'm already married. Unless you think me my brother?"

"If he could get his marriages annulled, why couldn't you? Wasn't the High Doma handpicked by you?"

"You certainly know an awful lot for being a whore," he said as he kissed her arms. "How long were you in the King's Brothel?"

"A long time," she didn't elaborate as Ultiir's cock had gotten hard and she went to work. He imagined the people chanting his name, "Ultiir the Emperor!" while he fucked her.

***

319

After he dreamt of the commoners roasting Lovis' skin over the fire and waking up in a pool of sweat, Atrice helped him into his clothes for court, black and red were the colors of the day. "I've been in Madam Taire's employment for five years."

"You don't need to explain your past to me. I trust you." Ultiir didn't know if he meant that or if it was his cock talking.

"I want you to know, I want you to fully trust me. I might be some whore but I come to care about those I couple with. You're no exception." Atrice laced his boots as she continued, "Hazari is worse than you can imagine. It's no holy city. The people were awful, always grabbing at me, trying to rape me, none were as sweet as you." She got off her knees and kissed Ultiir, her lips even softer than Sophie's were. "Madam Taire saved me. Allowed me to become my own."

"What happened to your parents? Did the mites get them?"

"King Hurvir invaded. I was just a babe when they died and had to fend for myself in the ashes of war, survive the streets. I was selling my body before I even had my first blood. But it brought me here. I would never change a thing."

"I'm glad." Ultiir kissed her cheek. "Stay here while I go to court?"

"What's so special about court today?"

Ultiir found his small golden crown and placed it atop his head. "Well the riots and killings made quite a few lords angry. The city guards have cleaned up a bit but there are still reports of palace steel being used by the monsters. Lord Omma also told me he spoke with Lady Rila before she died. She was hoping the crown would support Lady Abre Volles in her stupid attempt to gain Oceantree. I have to tell all the lords that Abre will get no support from me and inheritance laws will not change."

"Does that mean I can't inherit the King's Brothel when Madam Taire dies?" The whore giggled.

"We'll have to see about that. Now, I must be on my way. I believe Sir Lovis …" he stopped himself. His longtime guard was dead. Killed by the peasants. And Ultiir couldn't do anything to save him. *Who's next? First Sufar then Lovis. Maybe my mother will finally die.* "Sorry, Sir Ard will be guarding the door."

As Ultiir left his quarters with Sir Gid, Atrice said, "don't spend all day."

***

The throne room was bursting at the seams with lords and ladies, their children and servants, other nobles who thought they were important enough to be heard. All complaining of the riots. The Noble Lands wasn't hurt as badly as other areas of the city, but still a few homes looted and burned. Lady Rila's husband, a wealthy shipping magnate named Vendo, was crying for the king's forces be turned loose on the vermin. For "the peasants to learn their place and once again bow to their superiors."

Lord Tyter's son, Tylar, vowed revenge as well. Claiming he would recall his banners from the fighting in the Eastlands and turn them on the people of Vigur. Count Ompter would not let that go. Wailing on about the new Lord Tylar's desire to seek the throne. All Ultiir did was roll his eyes and look to his council. Lord de'Viere promised the city was back in order. Lord Hirons explained many times that no army could be recalled as they were either fighting in the lowlands,

Whitehall, or on a ship to Storyah. Lord Lyons did his best to rid the notion of the crown money going to the victims' families. *As if I have all the coin in the world to just give away,* he thought while rolling his eyes at the gold-colored molding on the ceilings.

Lord Masson was the only member of the King's Council not at court. Ultiir made it his mission to keep Tedbalt put of the loop as much as possible. Sufar had told him that the old lord and Sophie stuck away together. Surely plotting. And when the old prick showed up in his white daken garb with a new gold belt to show his status and Queen Sophie in tow, it confirmed that man was no friend of his. *Next session I'll strip him of consultant and send him to deal with the plague in Pleat Isle instead of my sister.*

Sophie was wearing silk as Swallow's Feast drew closer and the cold winds started to die down. Her diadem sat firmly on her brown hair, sparkling in the light as if a star. "Started without me?" She asked as she took her seat beside her husband. "You know how much I enjoy court."

"I didn't want to disturb you. The ladies are surely aghast at your face."

His wife touched her cheek where Ultiir's hard slap had knocked her down. It was purple and bruised and the slight outline of his hand could be seen. *Makeup to make it look worse. What won't this woman do?*

"What have the lords spoken of?" She asked in a low voice as the lords of the court screamed over one another.

"The better question is why you and Lord Masson were together? Fuck the old man so hard last night you thought his heart stopped?"

Sophie giggled. "Believe whatever you want, but we just

so happened to meet in the corridor. Both confused why we weren't invited. You must've known how important today was after what you let happen? Lady Ficca has been beside herself since Rila's death. The servants nor Mara can get her to eat, and her husband is on some trading mission to Alqinzi. I've had to console the poor woman."

"Would you have handled the rioting better?" Ultiir said through his teeth over Lord de'Viere's pleas with Lady Yura that the Noble Lands were once again safe. "The Rat's Nest was destroyed and the troublemakers spread throughout the city. I couldn't've stopped that."

"You are so wrong." Sophie straightened her dark green gown, and leaned closer to him to take up his whole view. "The people hate you, Ultiir, in every corner of the city. Look around you," she gestured to the hundreds of people crammed between the pillars of the throne room, "even they despise you. You destroyed their peace. My father always spoke of the importance of keeping the people happy lest they rise up against you, and that was especially true of the wealthy ones. The peasants might hate you, but all they have is bread. The nobles have the power and coin purses to topple dynasties. Maybe your brother was a better ruler than you."

Ultiir stood and puffed his red cloak around him. Time to show Sophie that he knew what she was trying to do. To stop her before she even started going on about inheritance. "We must now speak on the matter of Lady Volles." The room quieted except for a few mummers of distaste. "This is an easy matter then we can get back to talking about the Noble Lands and how I intend to keep this city under control. With a few of the lords dead in the riots we have some lineages ended, except for the women in their family. Lady Volles has gone to Oceantree to press an illegal claim. I must announce that I, as king, will never support—"

"My husband," Sophie stood and smiled at the crowd, "do not make any rash decisions. There is a war going on and things change ever so quickly. Lord Tylar is the last male descendant of Lord Tyter, but he has a daughter. If you were to reject a women's claim to her father or husband's lands and titles does that mean Lord Tylar's lineage is to end if he were to meet an untimely death?" The young lord's face was full of shock. "Lord Tylar is descended from Lord Trouve Temps, one of Valor the Iron's closest friends and advisers. You would damn his memory like that?"

"What are you doing?" Ultiir said through gritted teeth.

"What Lady Volles is doing is foolish, yes, but her family have been dukes of the Woodlands in the past, and she only has daughters. The Volles name would die with them if you had your way. We do not need to send men and arms to Lady Volles, but this matter is surely not more important than this holy city being desecrated by the common people."

Mutters of agreement escaped the crowd. Ultiir took a deep breath as he clenched his fists to stop them from flying at his wife. "We could merely have a discussion on the matter."

"I think we have more important things to talk about," someone from below called out.

"Leave Lady Volles to do as she pleases," another said.

"Why shouldn't my daughters inherit something?" Lord Tylar was asking the few around him to nods.

She's beaten me. That damned Tedbalt and she made this whole plan to upstage me. "Then let us discuss this holy city and how I plan to save it," his jaw was so sore it hurt to talk.

After Lord de'Viere laid out his plan to have the Noble

Lands and Old Town guarded day and night, with sweeps done hourly by his city guards, the lords and ladies were happy. Some even claimed they would return to their homes with their retinue. Ultiir, Sophie, and the council stayed after the long wait for the throne room to empty. The sound of Ultiir's knuckles cracking shook the chamber.

"How did you know?" He asked Sophie once she was done speaking with Lord Verrier who had been in touch with her parents. "Why did you come today after missing so many court sessions before and right when I was to mention Lady Volles?"

"It was a coincidence, nothing more."

***

Nothing more, the thought echoed in his head the whole way up the steps and down the long corridors to his chambers. "She had to know."

Sir Gid merely nodded. "I've been in your mother's service for decades, Your Grace. Sometimes a woman just knows when something important is to come."

"But it isn't important. Viguran has stood for hundreds of years with no female inheritance. Why change now? Is Sophie pregnant with a girl? Is she planning to murder me and take the throne for herself and her parents? Whether Lady Volles succeeds in Oceantree or not doesn't matter to me and I doubt to most of the lords, but it matters to Sophie. Sufar had told me she was speaking to a few lords and her ladies in waiting were doing the same. She has a much bigger plan than I give her credit for."

"Your Grace," Sir Ard bowed as they reached the door of

the bedchamber. "I must tell you that the whore was missing for a few hours. Claims she was with Madam Taire per usual. I know you wanted me to keep an eye on her."

"Thank you, my good sir." Ultiir waved him away as his hands clenched the door handle. Then he let go. The whore had said multiple times she was meeting with her employer to find new dresses or talk about new positions to try with him, but she never was. The whore had been meeting with Sophie. Just like how he wanted Sufar to spy on her, she sent Atrice to spy on him.

"Clever."

Bertin

ertin's body ached as the cold, hard ground of a dungeon brought it's familiar grasp on him. He was lucky there was crack in the smooth wall so he could tell when it was day and night. *At least I can count the days as the months drag on,* he thought, even though he had only been in the cell for a couple days. The two dwarves whispered to each other in cells across from him. Always looking at him. Laughing. Bertin understood none of it.

"What do you want?" He sneered at them. The dwarves laughed some more. Bertin had a phantom itch where his small finger used to be. *Are they laughing at how mangled I am?* He touched his cheek. He touched his hand. The bruises on his ribs. The scars on his face and arms. He was a prince treated like a criminal. No matter how far he traveled with the elves they still saw him as the enemy. *They're my enemy too. Just wait until father saves me.*

The stone door to the dungeon opened, elvish guards came in and Thatar followed behind. He looked clean. His clothes were new. They looked to be made out of leaves.

"I wish to show you something if you don't mind." Thatar said. Bertin faced away from him. He wasn't going to be treated like a prisoner and as a friend. If Thatar really cared for him he wouldn't have let him sleep in a cell. "You won't have to walk around in chains if that's what you're worried about." Thatar came closer, leaning behind Bertin's back. "I have food for you."

Bertin's head didn't want to go, but his stomach did. It ached and growled for food, and the thought made him drool. He stood and nodded. The guards opened the cell and Bertin followed Thatar out. The dwarves in the back pleading he guessed.

"Where are we going?" Bertin asked once they were back in the town and dodging elves and dwarves and gnomes and all the other creatures. "Will the elders like this?"

"Something you should know is that I am a …" he thought for a moment, "… a rebel."

Bertin laughed as Thatar led him down some steps and through an even thicker wooded area. "If you get thrown in the dungeon at least ask for a cell near me. I'm tired of the dwarves."

"You can't let them get to you. Those two are mischievous," he said as he stepped over a tree root. "They've been banished more times than I can count but always come back. The elders threw them in the dungeons to figure out what to do." Thatar stopped at a house made of wood and tree bark. It seemed to be an extension of the forest around. Other than small cuts for windows, Bertin wouldn't even know it was a place to live. "My Ariad will be so excited to meet a human. She's only killed them. Not that she'll kill you."

Bertin chuckled. "I get to meet Ariad?"

"Of course," Thatar pushed on the wood and a door opened. "Just let me see her first."

After Thatar disappeared inside, Bertin went over to the

edge of the cliff. The water below blinded him as the sun hit it, and pebbles fell beneath him into the ravine. More stone paths went farther down, and a few fishing boats were docked. *Where does this water go? Maybe I can take a boat and sail toward the ocean. Even Thatar may help.*

"Bertin, come," Thatar waved for him from the house and Bertin kicked more rocks into the water below. "This is my Ariad." Thatar said once they were inside. A fire burnt in a stone pit dug into the rocks below, and a brown liquid was steaming. A slender elf spooned the drink into wooden cups and handed one to Bertin. He bowed his head at Ariad. She was taller than him, her hair trailing down her back, with deep eyes that looked him up and down, and had black skin that reflected the firelight.

"Soachin i edwech." She said before taking a sip.

"Soachin i edwech." Thatar repeated and took a sip. "Say it," he told Bertin before he took a drink.

"Soa ... soachin i ... soachin i edwech." Thatar and Ariad nodded their heads and Bertin took his sip of the brown drink. The drink was so hot it burned as it made its way down, but afterwards he felt like he had just woken up from a deep sleep. Like he could lift the whole mountain and throw it across the sea. "What is this?"

"Just a drink." Ariad said in a silky voice. "What's happened to you?" She asked as brushed her hands over Bertin's never-healing cheekbone, and his missing finger. "I'm assuming this is not a journey you wished to take."

"What gave it away?" Bertin laughed and the two laughed with him.

"Eat with us," Thatar said, "we only have until dark, don't want Kelltar angry."

"He's always angry." Bertin said.

Ariad had made a dish of mushrooms and long noodles that were easy to slurp and made them all giggle like children. It made Bertin realize how little he enjoyed his life over the past few months. Death and pain had followed him. *Yet I still want Kelltar dead. One more death on my conscience. At least I'll sleep happy afterward,* he thought with a smile as he took a bite of mushrooms, glad to be eating a full meal again, even if it was elvish and might be his last.

"So how is it like Atha Bàn?" Ariad asked as Thatar cleaned the wooden dishes of noodles.

"We call it Rowan," Bertin said, and his eyes held a stare for a moment. "I feel like I've forgotten it, I've been away for so long. But it's a great city, the people don't enjoy us as much but other than that I don't have much to complain about." Ariad nodded and Thatar sat next to his wife. "How long have you lived here? Thatar told me you are older than him."

"Yes," Ariad pushed her hair behind her pointed ears, one of them cut, a scab in its place. "I took part in the retaking of the Pywaln. I was born in Mi'rallen around the year," she thought for a moment, "around the human year 1150. Don't give me that look. Vhistela, who Thatar said you traveled with, is even older. One of the oldest. She could be elected elder if she wished, but she chooses to fight."

"She might not have long left," Thatar said. "I believe the oldest elf, according to our stories, was five hundred. Vhistela is almost there."

"I'm barely a man and I've been through enough to not want to live five hundred years," Bertin said. "I'll settle for a human lifespan."

"That's because you humans look at the negative far too

much," Ariad's smile looked like that of a parent to a child. "A long life is a blessing from the Dragon, and you can meet so many people and see so many things. One of the reasons I hope we are successful with humans. I want to walk the same grasslands that my ancestors did. I've been to Mi'rallen and Anha Jorbstah and some journeys into the mountains. I am almost two hundred years old and humans have kept me isolated from the world. But I'm happy we were able to meet. Maybe I can use lessons from our interactions to make peace with humans I encounter on our travels."

Bertin cocked his head. "Travels?"

"Ariad wants us to make our way north with the elders. They believe the source is there. Ariad wants to see the underground elvish cities along the Efryn which are supposed to be marvelous. She wants to give birth there."

"Well I hope you do."

As the night continued and the moon rose over the mountains they enjoyed dessert that Ariad had traded with some gnomes, a thick bread with saffron inside. The sweet smell was a wonder to Bertin who had smelled like horses and blood for months. No one had come to retrieve Bertin. Thatar didn't seem worried. Kelltar would be the only one upset, he assumed. Vhistela was probably seeing old friends.

"If you weren't a prisoner would you like it here?" Ariad asked.

"I think so," Bertin said but pictured the boats down below. "Where does this water flow? The ocean I'm assuming."

Thatar laughed. "Planning to row yourself to freedom? This water was discovered by gnomes thousands of years ago. It flows from under the rocks. You'll be lost in the darkness for the rest of your life."

"You wouldn't help me?"

"Go against all I've been taught?" Thatar looked at his wife and they stared into each other's eyes for a moment. "It's too dangerous for us. You saw what they did to Ioelena."

"What Kelltar did."

There was a series of booms outside, like a thunderstorm had rolled over the city. Thatar went to a small cut out in the wood and looked out. "Perhaps a party celebrating our return?"

Ariad went to the window. "No one told me, but surely that's all."

Bertin took another bite of the saffron-infused bread while the two conversed in their elvish tongue. *If they're celebrating it would be a perfect time for Thatar to help me escape. This time I won't let anyone get caught.*

Then there was a banging on the door. Ariad opened it to find a panting Kelltar who shouted. Bertin didn't like the veins bulging from his head and his red cheeks. Thatar hoisted Bertin to his feet. "Humans have come. Elf hunters. They're on a rampage. Kelltar seems to think they're here to rescue you."

"Mites rescuing me? They'd rather kill me along with all of you."

"That's what we said," Ariad said as she took her bow from the wall. "So we need to go fight. Do you have a weapon you prefer?"

"I can't fight," Bertin said before she put a sword in his hand.

"Help us protect our brothers and sisters." Ariad's eyes pleaded and Bertin nodded his head without thinking.

As they ran out of the tree-turned-home Bertin thought

of the last time he fought. The father in Lisan Biresdea who died, Wilclef's death, eventually Ioelena's death. That time he was fighting the elves, this time he was fighting humans.

Flora

Florance ran along the ocean, small footprints appearing behind her. Spring was getting closer. Swallow's feast would soon be upon them. It would be like no other feast Flora had experienced. The food would be minimal, the drink expensive, most of the men would be south fighting a war. Tundavik and Barnet had their meeting and now the lords voted to join the war on the side of the bastard. *Then we get our independence and father is crowned king,* she thought as she followed behind her daughter. *I wonder how different it is to be seen as a princess instead of a lord's wife.*

"Careful." Flora called out to Florance who climbed atop slippery rocks.

"Mama —" Little Flora called out but something on the horizon caught Flora's eyes. Large sails emerged from the distant fog, wooden bows crashed through the sea. With every passing moment more and more ships appeared. Before the cold waves had returned to wash over Flora's feet the number of ships doubled. Florance was dancing in the waves oblivious to the world around her. As the sun hit the sails she could see they were adorned with an owl holding a golden bushel of wheat in its talons.

Flora dropped the blue fringe she was holding, splashing the water at her feet. She raced over to Florance and gripped her hand so hard it became red. "Mama, what's wrong?"

"We must get inside and warn the others." Flora said as they raced to the castle.

There were only a few guardsmen at the gatehouse, the others inside to protect any lords should the voting get tense. They were playing cards when Flora found them. "You fools! Ring the bell! Ultiir has come with ships."

"I don't see anything." A bald guard said without looking up from his cards.

"You are fools." Flora grabbed the rung to the ladder and began to climb to the guards and Florance's surprise. *I just need to ring the bell then Florance and I can hide inside. Or should we start running? Surely Ultiir wouldn't follow us to Uphain,* she thought as she found the silver bell. As long as someone was manning the larger bell on the other side of the castle then her pleas would be heard. If not then it would take longer to get the men outside. *I don't even know how they're going to battle ships.* It didn't matter though, she had to warn them.

She swung the hammer with all her strength and the bell roared over the walls. Then she waited. And waited. And waited.

Finally the other bell sounded. It shook the very foundations of the castle. Other bells around the city started to ring as well. The city turned into a chorus of instruments.

***

The great hall was as full as it could be as lords and ladies and knights and men-at-arms and servants all huddled to figure out a plan to stop the invading ships. "What if they only loose arrows at us?" "How are we to fight back with no fleet?" "We're doomed!" Flora held her daughter close as everyone clamored to get a word out.

"I'm scared," is what Florance said and Flora gripped her tighter.

Lord Blume held up his hand to quiet the room, with the help of Rickart the Crazed's booming voice. "We don't know what Ultiir's plans are. The ships might not even attack, so it is hard to plan, but we will defend the walls and the beach. If the attackers think we will fall easily then they are wrong. Lord Barnet will lead the men on the beach with Lord Rickart while Lord Vandes shows us what he's learned in the West by protecting the main gate to the castle with me. More orders will follow once we're outside and in position."

"The false king thinks he can scare us until we piss our britches and head home!" Rickart the Crazed shouted over everyone's heads. "He is so very wrong. The people of the Flewthlands would never and have never run from a fight. Let's go kill the bastards!" Cheers erupted and the hall emptied as everyone made their way to either safety or the frontline.

In the bailey the men were in a frenzy of barking and following orders. Archers lined the walls overlooking the beach. Men in mail grabbed their swords, spears, axes, or warhammers and lined the roads outside the gate and the beach below.

Flora found Barnet showing Florance a smooth rock. "My husband, I hope you make it back."

Barnet mussed Florance's hair and stood. "Don't worry, I will. I won't let these men hurt you or Florance. Some of the women are going into the cellars. I think you should follow."

"We will stay in the bedchamber and watch out the windows. If it looks dire then we will, though hopefully we can sneak out the postern and find protection in the city."

"I don't like it," he said with a breathy voice, "but very well." Barnet hugged their daughter who had tears in her eyes before saying to Flora, "keep her safe."

"With my life."

Her husband went to find his armor and Flora saw Tundavik slipping gauntlets over his hands. "Good luck, my lord duke. Hopefully you can show everyone that the Flewthlands didn't pick the wrong side in this war."

"I plan to." Tundavik said before disappearing under his helm.

As the ships got ever closer, the drawbridge was raised and all the women, children, old men, sick, and dying found hiding spots in the castle.

***

Flora and Florance got comfortable in their bedchamber. She snuck a butter knife away from the dining hall and gripped it tight, not that it'd be much use against swords. Little Flora played with her hair and looked out the window. The inner bailey was silent.

"Where do you think Nama is hiding?" her daughter asked about the maid.

"Hopefully somewhere safe. But don't worry too much about her, nothing bad will happen," she said with a silent prayer.

"What's out there?" Florance pointed to the curtain wall.

Arrows arced and fell somewhere at the beach. "Is daddy winning?"

I hope so, she thought but couldn't get the words out. An evil melody of metal clashing against metal, chants and screams joined in. "Loose!" sounded over the chorus and arrows went flying, some with fire probably aimed at the ships.

It was too quiet for Flora. Being in the castle, away from the fighting, made her feel small. Useless. Not that she could fight off the attackers. So many of the men she saw would never return. She just hoped her father wasn't one of them. She needed him to come back. And when her daughter started humming a sweet melody, Flora needed her husband to come back as well. No matter how much they hated one another. No matter how sinful Flora was. Florance needed a father.

The world shook and a piece of curtain wall fell to the bailey below taking a dozen archers with it. Florance let out a scream and Flora saw a bolt larger than a horse crash into the ground. Another whipping sound then a crash and more of the stone wall exploded in rubble. This time the inner bailey was hit by the bolt. Anyone outside raced into the keep as more bolts began to fall from the sky and litter the castle grounds in stone and blood.

Screams escaped the castle as the keep itself was hit. Hit. Hit. Candles fell to the floor. Florance could hardly walk as the room shifted and dust and dirt fell on them. Another rip through the air and an explosion of polished rock echoed throughout the castle. Nama opened the door to the bedchamber and Florance ran to her. "My lady, I came to get you. They are loosing huge crossbows bolts on us. The cellar is the only safe place."

"Is anyone hurt in the castle?" She asked.

"So far only a few, but I ran as fast as I could to you so there might be many more."

"Will you take Florance to the cellars?" Flora asked the maid as another bolt shook the room. "As the daughter of the duke and lady of Woodrun it is my responsibility to help our people."

"Mama?" Florance's eyes welled with tears. "Don't leave me."

Flora bent down and kissed her daughter. "Nama will take good care of you and we'll meet in the safe place. I need to make sure others are alright. I promise by the Four and the Many I will see you again."

That didn't stop Florance from sobbing as Nama held her and they made their way through the halls and down the steps. The castle shook and shook and people let out scream after scream. Flora was kicking her dress while running. Random holes littered the floor with sunlight; candles and wax flooded the floors; and stone lay scattered with glass when she reached the great hall. There were a few dead servants and one old lord who had barely been able to walk. Their frozen eyes stared at her underneath the rubble.

A groan escaped from the stone below and Flora started to dig, a passing servant deciding to help as well. Under the rubble was a gray covered face, dust and dirt and blood pooled. It was Lord Toware's wife, Lady Lueva. She coughed and spat as Flora and the servant pulled her from the mess. The lady could not stand, a piece of wood in one side of her leg and poking out the other. Her back was covered in black blood, but not only hers, the blood of other women and children who died around her.

As a bolt pierced overhead they dropped to the ground. Her father's high seat was destroyed in the impact, sounding like the roar of a beast.

The servant, whose name was Lila, helped Lady Lueva as they made their way over fallen stone and broken glass and down stairs. Others joined them. Some healthy. Some limping and bleeding. Lila wept when she found her lover skewered with a piece of wood like meat. A few dakens had come with the many lords and they quickly got to work wrapping wounds and cutting out foreign objects.

Flora prayed to Meret as they made their way into the cellar, servants and ladies beckoning for them. Florence was sobbing and ran into her mother's arms. Nama tried to calm her but she just wanted Flora to hold her. "Is it over?" She cried.

"Almost," Flora lied.

"I need some help," a daken said as he examined Lady Lueva. "The wood is poisoning her, but I have a way to stop it, but it will be painful."

"What … is …" Lady Lueva struggled to speak as she sweated and withered in pain. "Do it."

"The leg must come off."

"No," Flora and the lady said at the same time. "There must be another way."

"Do … not …" Lueva clenched her jaw. She couldn't say anything else from the pain.

"Hold her," the daken said to Flora. "We've no time to argue. This is the only way to make sure she doesn't die and spread her sickness to us."

Flora was given a cloth and shoved it into Lady Lueva's mouth who tried to wrangle free. "I'm sorry, but we have to save your life. You must trust us."

The sawing of skin and bone and the blood and nerves that spilled out made Flora want to vomit, but she had to keep it together for Lueva. She was the one going through tremendous pain. Florance hid her eyes in Nama's skirts and Flora wished she could join. Lady Lueva cried and sputtered but the daken didn't stop, he couldn't any longer, the saw was already cutting deep. As Lady Lueva passed out from the pain and the blood splattered on Flora's dress, she began to doubt her husband would return. That her father would return. She prayed harder for the soldiers to win.

Tundavik

Blood spewed as his sword was pulled from a gap in the mail armor. Tundavik lifted his visor and spat blood onto the streets. The stream of men coming from the ships seemed to be never ending. They rowed to the beach, fought the men in the sand with poleaxes and hammers, then climbed the limestone stairs to the road in front of the castle.

Much to Tundavik's surprise, Barnet was doing well on the beach. His shield bore a tree that was chipped away by attacks, but the lord of Woodrun kept going. The men on the beach were using spears but that didn't always save them. Barnet had to pull out his sword and cut people down, filling the wet sand with blood and coloring the water red. Rickart the Crazed held two daggers, and with every whip of his long hair a man came crashing down in a heap of death. The crazed lord taunting them.

Mar and Pyre fought alongside Tundavik. Mar was quick as lightning with his sword. His silver plate armor protecting him from blows but the attackers' mail not able to withstand Mar and his sword. Pyre swung a warhammer and knocked men down one at a time. Crumpling their armor, shattering their bones. They would not let Ultiir take Storyah like he took Redington, would not let his forces raze the city like they did Greatbath.

Death surrounded them, but Tundavik was able to see Lord Rickart take a poleaxe to the leg and fall in a cloud of sand. Tundavik's armor rose with his breath and he jumped onto the beach, hacking and slashing his way to Rickart, trying not to hear the screams of his victims. He beat at mail and slashed with his sword at visible skin. Anything to stop the attackers from advancing. Rickart was swinging his daggers as men surrounded him. Barnet joined Tundavik in the fight to save the crazed lord.

All of my troubles would be gone if I let Barnet die. The lords already chose Devro. They won't turn their back now, he thought. But as a sword flew at the lord of Woodrun from behind, Tundavik parried it with his sword and knocked the man down with a red and yellow shield. All this fighting reminded Tundavik of training in the yards of Ritaeum, the war along the Bezir. He wondered if the sea would flow red with blood weeks after they've left like the river in the South did.

As men in plate began to disembark from the boats, Tundavik grabbed his sword by the blade and beat at their helms with the pommel. The helms caved in and he couldn't imagine what the heads inside looked like. Barnet was now being surrounded as Rickart's men took their lord, who was foaming at the mouth with rage, to the castle. Tundavik sighed as he jumped in again. His sword getting entangled in a battle of twisted steel. He beat with his pommel. He stabbed with the tip. His gauntlets blasted into faces, and his boots swept legs. Another man swung an axe and missed by an inch. Barnet cut the helpless man's head clean off.

"Up the stairs!" Barnet shouted to his men and Pyre from

the road echoed the call. The soldiers on the boats were coming and not stopping. Anyone on the stairs not of the Flewthlands was cut and thrown down. Tundavik knocked a man aside with his sword and drove a dagger into a weak spot in his mail by his neck.

"This is never going to end." Tundavik said to Mar as the knight fell beside him.

"Not with your old bones." Mar laughed as he danced with his sword and kicked men into the sand.

Huge bolts had been rippling through the sky. The castle walls were being obliterated and the archers with them. Stone was cascading down. Pyre had to be pulled away from the wall to not be crushed.

Arrows from the remaining archers were loosed as the stairs became overwhelmed with Ultiir's men. Tundavik and Mar and anyone else smart enough ran to find cover under the fallen stones as arrows rained down.

Pyre beat plated soldiers with his warhammer before finding cover near Tundavik. He was out of breath and he spat under his helm. "Why did I let you talk me into this again?" He chuckled.

"War is fun," Mar said as a boulder fell near him. "Well, the dying part isn't the best."

"How is Barnet holding?" Pyre asked as he scanned the commotion.

The lord of Woodrun was leading his men over the quay in front of the castle. The attackers were pulling the retreating men off the wall and beating them to death. "He's trying." Tundavik said not wanting to help him again, but remembering all the people trapped in the castle who would surely be killed. Even Little Flora. "Let's go." He called to the others.

They reached the quay and yanked the men to safety. Barnet was whacking at the mail and plate beneath him until Pyre came over with his warhammer and bashed heads in. Blood smearing his armor. Tundavik kicked and Mar dropped to the sand like an idiot. But the knight was agile and strong and was able to distract a few of the attackers with his sword and shield while Barnet's men climbed.

Pyre grunted next to Tundavik and a knife was pulled from the weak spot in his armor beneath the breastplate. One of Ultiir's men had stabbed the old duke. Tundavik pushed the man down and drove his sword through the slit in the eyes before grabbing Pyre. "Get out of here, find your men, and get help." *Just so your son-by-law can kill you later,* he wanted to say. Pyre limped away, blood running down his leg.

Tundavik and Barnet hefted Mar up and the men kept the quay free of attackers. "Go protect the stairs with Lord Toware," Barnet shouted, "we'll be fine."

They ran to the stairs and joined the dozens of clashing men. Tundavik sliced a young face and yellow teeth bounced off his armor. Mar appeared beside him ready to fight. There was a moment of calm when Tundavik looked at the knight. When he got off that ship in Gereduss he had no idea he would be fighting with knights of Viguran and trying to put a bastard on the throne. That he would be standing in the sand as dozens upon dozens of people died.

He gave his last nod to Mar and charged into the horde of men.

A shot rang across the silent ocean and echoed in the stiff air. One of the ships lurched as a hook from an approaching galley broke into the hull. More shots and wood breaking and ships emerging from the horizon had distracted almost everyone on the beach. *Not a part of anyone's plan,* Tundavik thought with a nervous smile.

"The gods send us a favor!" A young boy with a bloodied face yelled.

At first Tundavik couldn't make out the sails of the approaching ships, but as they got closer and he blinked his eyes clear of sweat and dirt he saw the rearing stallion of Rowan. Why the Rowai were all the way in Storyah he would have to find out later. Now, he was just happy Ultiir's forces were distracted.

More hooks shot from the ballista stationed at the front of the ships. The Vigurite fleet was pulled from side to side, closer to the Rowai fleet. Planks dropped, and the boarding began. Swords and knives glistened under the sun like diamonds.

Pyre shouted, "Charge!" through his pain. The men of the Flewthlands attacked the beach with their full might. Swords and spears and shields clashing, blood spraying. The tide was rising, but not from the water, from the hundreds of knights that dropped from the wall and the stairs and the path. A wave of steel swords, hammers, and axes, along with pointed and flat helms, black and silver gauntlets, and mail hoods crashed into the newly arrived knights.

It wasn't long until Ultiir's men were pulling back, racing to the water and trying to fill the boats without tipping them. Barnet and the men he led went to the small boats and stomped holes in them. The ships at sea with the owl masts that hadn't been boarded by the Rowai started rowing out to sea. The stallion masted-ships not following.

As the fighting raged at sea, the fighting became more

intense on land. Tundavik cut down one … two … three knights. He kicked sand into eyes and bashed heads with his pommel. He caught himself from falling on the uneven, shifting ground and lunged onto a defenseless man. Mar threw rocks and attacked his victims. Lord Blume yelled as he crashed through men with his warhammer carrying knights behind him.

***

Lord Ed of the Seeded Field called for the remaining attackers to be imprisoned in the dungeons and the men were stripped of their armor and weapons, the dead were thrown into a pile that would light the beach come nightfall.

Mar threw off his helm and put a tired hand on Tundavik's shoulder. "We fucked them. We did it," his laugh sounded like a cry. "I enjoyed that."

Tundavik patted Mar's cheek with a smile. "Live to see another day."

Pyre was holding his wound on his stomach, one of his men ripping cloth to tie on the lord. Barnet took his helm off and revealed a red and sweat covered face. His hair was soaked. He had a few cuts and bruises but he would be fine. Tundavik didn't like that for Pyre.

As Ultiir's ships fled, smaller boats started to come ashore from the Rowai ships. Men in gold and silver plate lined the beach as a small boy and a fat man disembarked. The men of the Flewthlands gathered to see who saved them. "Must be Bartel," Mar said before saying, "oh wait, he died. Bertin." Mar called and pushed through the group. Tundavik followed but they were stopped by an armored hand of a guard.

"How do you know that name?" The boy asked, his brown hair topped with a small crown.

"It's me, Sir Mar." The knight looked around for whoever this Bertin was until his face dropped. "Where is the king?"

"Right here." An older man said as he got off his boat and almost tripped in the wet sand. His velvets covered in sea salt. "This is King Baldewin of Rowan, and I am Caxton, a royal adviser to His Grace."

"And I saved you." The boy king squeaked. "I'm looking for the one you call king, Devro," he said like he had been practicing it.

"He isn't here," Lord Blume winced from behind. "He is in the Lands of Asara, a few hundred miles from here."

"Mind if we settle in your castle," Caxton pointed to the broken walls beyond the beach. "We've much to discuss."

Tundavik watched as the Rowai helped clean the beach and outer walls of prisoners of fallen men, the first battle won since setting out for Whitehall. *Perhaps our luck is changing.*

Sophie

Rain washed over the city and the farmland below as Swallow's Feast drew ever near. The pain of winter would be behind them with the joy of summer to look forward to. Mother Meret did everything right, except for feasting during the harsh winds and snows of winter. But the Mother knew once a year the world needed a fresh start, and death was as a part of life as anything else.

Sophie stood in the highest tower of the palace of Vigur, where the elves watched the city fall to humans those thousands of years ago. Where Valor the Iron watched the sunrise over his new kingdom. Where Valor the Betrayer took up arms against his allies. Where Sophie wished to jump from so many times.

It was different now. She didn't have the urge to plummet to her death as one last act of revenge against Hurvir or Ultiir, not even with a welt on the side of her face from where her husband hit her. "It is my duty to my family and ancestors. If I must be slapped then so be it," she said to no one. Her blue gown fluttered in the breeze that came from the Nokys so very far away. Her dresses of late were loose garments to hide her belly from her husband and all those who watched her. Lucky for her Sufar didn't seem to find out. Ultiir would never know.

"But I'm trying to change the inheritance laws. Not just so Lady Volles can claim Oceantree, but for my future daughters and granddaughters. Is it all a waste?"

There was a rap at the door, Lord Masson emerged, winded and breathing hard. "Couldn't have arranged a meeting in my bedchamber?"

"Ultiir already thinks we're having an affair. No reason to give him 'evidence' to bring before Maller in hopes for an annulment."

"Not like you're having his heir anyway." Tedbalt joked but Sophie didn't laugh. "Forgive me, my queen, I know how much thought you've put into this."

"Did you find some?"

"Some mite herbalist near the Eyes of Meret smuggled it to me." He held out a vial filled with a red liquid. "I went through the pleasure of grinding it and testing it. The orchid shriveled and died in seconds. You've nothing to worry about save for a possible headache and slight bleeding from your …"

"Yes, yes." Sophie took the vial and examined it. *One drink,* she thought as Tedbalt eyed her. "I trust the king will never know?"

"I would never betray you," the old lord bowed. "I've been telling you for months now that I am your ally. Your friend. Other than your ladies in waiting you don't have many. Though Lord Tylar seems to like you now. Don't let Ultiir catch you with him," he said with a wink.

"Will you leave me to be alone? I need to think."

Lord Masson looked over the edge. "Don't jump. Ultiir would win and some poor slave would have to clean you up."

When the lord was gone she hung the vial out the window, the palace grounds calling for it from below, to smash it into a million pieces. *The child of a monster. Of a man who beat me.* The red mixture scattered the light onto her face. Below, thousands of children would be waking for the day. Mothers would be mourning their dead babes, others would be rejoicing at giving birth, some would throw their child into the Ritae or leave them at the domaton because the babe would be born into poverty and hunger. *Mine would be born into opulence. Anything they needed would be taken care of.* Her welt burned. "Or they would be beat like Devro. Not cared for like Ultiir and his siblings. Killed in the war and I would be forced to watch."

Gripping the vile she placed it into a pocket in her dress before leaning out the window to feel the air on her face. Wandering birds chirped. Clouds parted above. Sunlight cascaded over the hills and valleys and villages that stretched beyond the city. The waters of the Ritae and Montla were brown and clogged with riverboats. A gaping hole of black soot showed the gods where the Rat's Nest once stood. The Noble Lands were full of guardsmen marching with spears and swords and bows. The city gates were teeming with refugees and pilgrims. Watchtowers were being constructed near Valor's Heights and the Cliffs of Iron on the other banks of the rivers as word just reached them of Drogue de'Vil's defeat.

Below the city was coming alive while she stood alone in a dark tower.

The rest of the day didn't bring her much joy either. Lady Rila was laid to rest and ready for all to see in the throne room. Sophie stayed in her bedchamber until the afternoon when most would already be gone. She didn't want to see anyone. Speaking up in court and dealing with the aftermath was bad enough. The lords in Udello were kind. The lords in Vigur were bloodthirsty. They would do anything to get their way and see their enemies fail which, in truth, helped Sophie in her quest to help Lady Volles and all the other women who wished for inheritance.

She touched her belly.

Sir Achen escorted her to the throne room while Sir Velle stayed at the bedchamber. Renna and Amalla had dressed Sophie in a black velvet gown. Her diadem balanced on her head.

The throne room was mostly empty save the High Doma, Maller, and her ladies in waiting, at least the ones still in Vigur. She wondered who would be the next to leave. Lady Ficca was especially devastated by Rila's death and continued to panic at the thought of being raped and murdered by the peasants. Baroness Mara denied her husband when he wished to leave the city. Countess Filra had to keep her husband, Firo, from recalling her back to his lands.

Sophie stood in a line with her ladies. Lady Rila looked peaceful in blue with yellow flowers in her arms. Vendo's eyes were red as he spoke with Maller. "How many came?" She asked the women.

Mara said, "a whole slew. I think the nobles just wanted to feel the safety of the palace one last time. His Grace is denying anyone but those closest to the king to stay here anymore. He believes it makes him less safe."

"And," Filra said, "I heard from a very reliable person that the king is upset at some of the lords discussing the laws of inheritance."

"The person she speaks about is the servant she's fucking." Mara said. "The one with the long, blond hair."

"We're supposed to stay composed." Filra glared.

"She's beautiful, isn't she?" Ficca wiped her teary eyes as she came over from the body. "Oh, how could they do this?"

Sophie rubbed a hand on the lady's back. "She is feasting with the gods and her ancestors now. A much better place than the palace."

Ficca rubbed her nose with her sleeve. "Some … some of the doma have said she will burn in Veltoora for adultery. That she was disloyal … that the rape was her doing."

"We don't concern ourselves with silly men." Mara said.

"High Holiness." Sophie called out to Maller. The old man waddled over and his breath smelt of wine. "Please tell the Lady Ficca that Lady Rila is happy with the gods, and make sure your lesser doma are not preaching hogwash."

"Hogwash?" Maller chuckled. "Whatever do you mean?"

"Preaching about Lady Rila's debauchery. It is not a sin to be raped."

Maller scratched his beard, flakes of skin falling off. "Yes, but that is a matter of debate, and since this is the holy city we have many theologians who come here and champion their side."

Sophie wanted to slap the old prick as Ficca started to cry harder. Vendo came over and comforted the lady. "What is going on?" he asked. "Why is she so tearful?"

"The High Doma is not being very friendly." Sophie said.

"Saying awful things about your wife." Filra added.

"Is that so? I've heard rumblings in the streets but thought a man of such esteem would know not to listen to fools." Vendo cracked his knuckles.

"Of course, fools know nothing," Maller blinked his faded eyes. "I was just telling them that some of my lesser doma are being awful and I was going to put a stop to it. Lady Ficca here just misunderstood me. Women are easily confused when in this state of being. I was just about to leave and see who is spreading these vile rumors."

The old man picked up his robes and left the throne. Servants were extinguishing candles near the body. "I buy the liquor that keeps him happy." Vendo said before his eyes fell on his wife's body. "We're about to leave for Cryton. Her family will be glad to see her like this, I mean in a better state then I found her. Shame His Grace wasn't able to see her today."

Sophie's eyes were welling up but that made her ears perk. "And where is he?"

Vendo bowed to Sophie and took her hand, kissing the rings on her fingers. "My queen, I fear His Grace has come down with a cold. May I hug you? For Rila's sake?" Sophie allowed the merchant to embrace her, forgetting what it was like to touch someone other than Ultiir. "His Grace couldn't be bothered to calm my grief," Vendo whispered in her ear, "so I shan't be bothered to fund his goals. If any of the lords who take my coin do not support the inheritance laws being changed then write to me and I will see to it that they support you."

Sophie kissed the man's cheek. "I will remember that, and I will always remember Rila. She was a close friend," she said as tears rolled down her face.

Vendo, one of the wealthiest merchants in Viguran, bowed and said goodbye to the other women. Ficca didn't want to see Rila go. Mara and Filra took Lady Ficca to the gardens outside to feel the coming of spring on their skin. Sophie made her way up the steps and down the corridors to her bedchamber.

"I'm glad we were inside the walls when the rioting occurred," she said to Achen.

"I would never've let what happened to Lady Rila happen to you."

"I know that, but sometimes I forget what safety these walls give us when Ultiir is always stalking. Sometimes I wish I could live as a peasant and the world would be so much simpler. Then the king comes around and burns half the town and incites a riot by killing Albon, turning the people into the monsters he fears. I like the walls more."

When the door to the queen's quarters came into view, she could see Sir Velle holding his head while Amalla rubbed ointment and Renna sneered. Other members of her household guard were standing in confusion. "What happened?" Achen ran over to Velle to see the bruise on the knight's head.

"Please, do not go inside, my queen." Velle said with agreement from the other guards. "It is no sight for a lady."

"What is it? Who did this?" She asked when she noticed the door handle busted.

"The king's men." Renna finally said. "Sir Velle wouldn't let them through as this was your quarters."

"They had no right." Velle said, holding his head.

"We were getting your bath ready when we heard screams," Amalla said. "I agree with the knight, do not go inside."

"And where were you all?" Sophie asked the other men.

"We were trading shifts along the wall," one said.

Another said, "His Grace wishes for all men-at-arms to take at least one shift."

"Well that's not going to happen anymore." Sophie stood tall. "And if *His Grace* has a problem with it he can write to my father and explain why he busted down my door. Now, I am going inside."

"My queen." Velle said.

"Enough," she waved her hands. "If it won't cause me harm then I'm going in."

No one stopped her as she pushed the door open. Her nose wrinkled as the smell hit her, she hadn't even made it passed her handmaids' room. The men outside her door whispered and worried but she went on. Whatever Ultiir ordered to be done to her room she didn't care. Even if they unleashed a dragon she would face it.

It wasn't a dragon she saw.

Atop her bed, hands bound by ropes tied to the canopy above, chest split open with innards and blood spilling out was a naked Atrice. The whore's mouth was agape. Her eyes rolled back. Her hair matted with blood and her knuckles bruised from fighting back. A parchment was attached to her bare stomach, red staining the words. "Treason."

Sophie held back tears once more. Her hands trembled and her head was in a daze. The smell of blood and shit made her nauseous. *A monster.*

She found the vial in a drawer, swallowed all of the contents, and vomited.

Tundavik

G o south! No more time to waste! Nhamcaryn is upon us! Upon us! This world will die in fire and war and you must stop it! South!" The lady was naked hiding behind decaying trees. Tundavik rubbed one of the dark, sturdy trees that grew to the heavens. The tree crumpled and blew to dust. The forest was dying all around him. Trees vanishing one by one. The lady touched the dotted swirls on her body and they began to glow bright red. It was as if she were bleeding. She cried out in pain and screamed words in some language.

Then gone.

Tundavik was alone on a flat plain. A sea of dark green choking his body. Pools were illuminated in the distance. Images of a dying world — rivers drying, trees falling, volcanoes erupting — filled the pools. Fires raged in the distance and Tundavik heard a voice from nowhere saying, "Ritaeum! Go south!"

***

When he woke with a fright he remembered where he was. His back ached from sleeping on the ground beneath the

357

tarps. Men snoring next to him. The castle grounds had been cleaned to make way for the hundreds of men who needed to rest after the battle, and the hundreds of men who accompanied the young king of Rowan on his ships, and the hundreds of women and children who had taken refuge in the castle walls. Great stones and glass had littered the baileys, but now raised tarps filled them.

Tundavik tried not to think about his sore and bruised body, but it was hard not to. His plate armor had given him protection from the worst blows, but his chest and arms still had purple bruises and his head ached. He wasn't sure if that was because of the battle or the lady who came to him. He slipped into new clothes that were laid out for him, gray and blue like Barnet, before making his way over the sleeping bodies to the dining hall.

The cooks had prepared rabbit stew and bread. He ripped the mold off the bread and dipped the good parts into the cold stew. The cooks hadn't been doing well since the battle, a few of them had died, and now they had hundreds of more mouths to feed.

The dining hall was silent save for birds singing their song of spring outside. Holes in the ceiling were covered with tarps but water still leaked in. He was happy to be alone. The chaos and noise of the battle had given him little sleep these past few days. Visions of death woke him. Visions of Panscar as well and the princess of Viguran. *How could I give in to Barnet like that? The only way he gets to be duke is by killing Pyre,* he thought as he sipped water. *Flora without a father and Florance without a grandfather. What have I done?*

"I needed men," he answered himself.

"Enjoying your breakfast?" The fat Rowai man said as he

entered the hall with the boy king. "I always loved rabbit stew." They sat across from him with their bowls and bread.

"Not very good, I might say." Tundavik said.

The big man swallowed the stew without chewing while King Baldewin picked at his bread before pushing his food away. "I am Blis," the man said between bites, "not sure if I've introduced myself. The king here has never seen battle before. I fear it has ruined his appetite."

"Not true," the boy whined before shoving a chunk of bread in his mouth. "See."

"Very well." Blis chuckled. "How have you been my lord?"

"Not a lord," Tundavik said, "but I've been as fine as one can be. I'm not dead. Just nightmares." *Nightmares of the world ending. Of whatever Nhamcaryn is.*

"I remember those days well." Blis said before adding, "I fought the mites in the Seler Bay. For the king of course, the People's Chamber had no say over me."

Baldewin rolled his eyes. "Have you fought in battle before?"

"I also fought the mites," Tundavik said. "Hopefully this war doesn't last as long. I haven't asked you how you found your way to Storyah. Usually the Rowai stay out of Vigurite business."

"Funny story," Blis said, "we set sail from Rowan to free Redington from Ultiir. When we reached the city the lord, I believe his name was Hank …"

"Henk," Baldewin corrected.

"Ah, yes. This Lord Henk fell to his knees and begged we not take the city from him and that he'd be a good lord to his people and the rest," Blis waved an annoyed hand. "He told us that Ultiir had sent the fleet north from the City of the Reds to threaten Pyre Blume into submission. His Grace here decided we needed to help his cousin, Devro. By the time we arrived you were already fighting."

"Ultiir's men must've not gotten the memo that they were just to threaten. The first men to land on the beach didn't do a lot of talking before deciding a fight would be better."

"You know how men can be, especially young ones." Blis said. "Always wanting to fight instead of using diplomacy."

"I'm not like that," Baldewin whined again.

"Of course not, Your Grace."

Tundavik ate a piece of cold rabbit and worried about food as the war dragged on. "So where will you go next? You could sail the Ters-Veck then the Montla-Ritae and help us in Vigur. We're to lay siege to the city."

"Risky," Blis rubbed the white whiskers on his chin. "But Lord Blume already had an idea. He thinks we should sail the Nokys and look for the remainder of the Vigurite fleet. He doesn't want any more surprises from them. We haven't decided. There is much debate between the king and his councilors."

"Going to scour the ocean for a dozen ships?" Tundavik shook his head as he took a bite of cold stew. "Good luck."

Blis laughed and nodded. "True, but war needs optimism."

"War is about surviving. It doesn't need anything else but men and steel. But if Pyre wants you to do it then so be it." Tundavik said with a hint of guilt in his voice.

"I'm too trusting," the boy king said as he rested his head on his hands. "We're going to do what the duke wants because Caxton says that's best. Aveline didn't want me to listen to the advisers but I can't help it, and now she's gone. If only Bertin were here. He'd know what to do."

"You're doing just fine, my king." Blis rubbed the boy's shoulder. "And you mustn't blame yourself for your sister's absence. She wishes to find your brother and you wish to help your cousin. Both are noble causes."

"Did you ever picture yourself as king?" Tundavik asked the boy. His dark hair reminded him of Guis.

"Maybe. Once my brother grew old and died and he didn't have any heirs. I thought I might serve for a short time." Baldewin rubbed his nose. "I never expected to lose my father and brother at the same time."

Blis looked sad as well before asking, "And you Lord Vandes? Did you picture yourself as king?"

"Never," Tundavik laughed

"But you share the same name as Viguran's first kings," Baldewin said. "You never thought of taking the throne back?"

"That was a very long time ago. Not many people even remember the Vandes name after Valor the Betrayer. I enjoyed ruling the Woodlands. However short it was."

A servant burst through the doors of the hall and bowed. "Your Grace." He turned to Tundavik. "My lord, the lord duke Pyre Blume wishes to meet with you. I shall take you there at once."

Tundavik stood and took one more drink of water. "Good luck in the open seas, you two. I hope you find what you're looking for."

"You too, Lord Vandes." Blis said as he and the boy waved goodbye.

***

Pyre Blume was standing on the road over the beach. The sand was still a mess of fallen swords and spears and armor and dyed with blood. Waves tried washing it all away. "You helped save us." Lord Blume said as Tundavik came from behind. "I give you my thanks."

"Thank the Rowai, not me. I brought the battle to you."

"I already did." Pyre smiled as he held the bandage on his abdomen. "And you didn't bring the battle. You didn't threaten us outside the walls with a sword and kill my people. Ultiir did all that. When I saw the approaching ships I couldn't help but be reminded of when I gave up my father's rebellion. My people must've been just as scared as I just was."

"If you didn't give up then who knows what the Flewth-lands would look like right now. Hurvir was vicious. The whole duchy would've looked like Ritaeum."

"Hopefully all goes well in Vigur and Ultiir won't follow in his brother's footsteps. And I'm sorry some of the lords and men are going to stay behind, but I don't want to leave the Flewthlands defenseless. We're going to have a fight along the border on our hands."

"I understand. I hope I don't lose too many men on the march to Vigur. You're sure traveling along the shore is a good idea?"

"As long as you cut west before Redington. I've received no reports of fighting along the shore, everyone is focusing to the west. That will change quickly as my men enter the foray. I'm going to write to King Leddo of Plajul, perhaps he can help in our defenses."

"Rowan joining the war, you want Plajul to join as well. Before we know the whole region will be fighting again. I pray this ends quickly."

"As do I." Pyre popped his knuckles. "I don't want my granddaughter to grow up in a war torn world like we did."

"Nice dream, but men always go to war."

"Maybe you can get the bastard king to change that. I wrote to Whitehall, the snow should be gone by now, so they should begin their march soon as well. I pray we see each other once you've won in Vigur. Invite me for the feast."

"Surely," Tundavik said before embracing Lord Pyre Blume. The last time he might ever talk to that old friend. He had to fight to keep tears from welling up in his eyes. *I could tell him. What could go wrong? The lords are furious with Ultiir now for attacking them and they won't change their vote.* Before he could get the words out, Pyre walked to the castle, leaving Tundavik to watch the red waves wipe the beach clean.

***

Over the next few days the men of the Flewthlands gathered their belongings and were ready to go south along the Nokys in hopes to take Vigur and end the war. There were even a few dozen men from the city who wanted to join. Wagons and carriages were full of armor and weapons. The cooks were hard at work baking bread and tack for the long journey.

Tundavik watched over it all. Any lords who were to stay behind and not fight relinquished their men to Tundavik's command for the time being. A few lords who had voted not to join the war snuck away in the night. Pyre claimed he would punish them when the war was won. The Rowai were readying their ships to leave as well. They had come to a decision. They were to hunt the Vigurite fleet and hopefully take the ships in the name of Devro. With the Flewthlands and possibly a fleet of his own, Devro had a chance to win.

Mar, guiding Brun and Bera through the crowd that amassed near the harbor gate, found Tundavik sheathing his dagger. "Just sharpened," Tundavik said after thanking the smith. "Ready, Mar?"

"I'm ready to fight my way through the Eastlands, yes. Maybe Reran will bring some men to help."

"We can only hope. Are you worried for Ruwy?"

Mar shrugged and said, "what can I do? At least Reran's wife and son are safe. I told the men to go easy on Ruwy if they find it. Rickart the Crazed is leading an expedition in the north of the Eastlands, showing them he won't let them cross the border."

"Let's hope all goes well."

As Tundavik saddled Bera, Flora and Lord Barnet found him. "Ready for war?" Barnet said. Flora was the obedient wife, not even looking at Tundavik.

"Of course, what will you do in Storyah?" Tundavik knew the answer, but he wanted to see Barnet sweat. Taking over his own wife's lands. He couldn't imagine betraying those closest to him. *Yet I still betrayed Pyre.*

"I will protect my family." Barnet smirked.

"Will you come to Storyah after the battles?" Flora said meekly before she swallowed and stood up straight. "You did our city a great service by saving it."

Tundavik ignored Barnet who rolled his eyes. "I hope to come back, but first I have a war to win. Once that's over, who knows what I'll do."

"I pray to the Four and the Many that you win." Flora said with a smile.

"Time to go," Mar called from atop Brun.

"Stay safe," Tundavik told Flora, even though he wanted to tell her so much more. Barnet standing beside her like nothing was going to happen. *I can take Vigur and march on Storyah just like Mar said. Kill Barnet before he turns on his family.*

Tundavik climbed his mare and rode beside Mar as the world lurched behind him. Hundreds of men and weapons, dozens of horses and wagons, and armor of leather and steel shook the roads and the ocean as peasants watched them depart the city.

The fields beyond the city of Storyah rumbled. Tundavik had one last look at Flora and Pyre. He couldn't worry about them at the moment. What's done was done. Tundavik looked into the fields and saw small boys holding wooden swords, pretending to fight a die, running alongside the train of warriors.

Tundavik had a war to win.

Bertin

He watched as the elves and the mites fought beneath the canopy of Anha Jorbstah. The mites had crossbows that exploded every time they loosed a bolt. Elves were dead everywhere. Thatar swung his sword and protected Bertin from the worst of it. Ariad was almost as good as Vhistela with a bow.

Dwarves swung hammers and hacked at knees, fairies attacked faces, and the gnomes lunged for ankles. At first Bertin wasn't sure how the mites thought they'd be able to win. They were outnumbered by creatures that had lived on this land thousands of years longer. And the few elvish mages, rainík, were using fire or water or wind or calling on the trees to help. But the crossbows with smoke that rose from them worried him. A gnomes face was completely gone as a fast flying bolt teared through it. Fairies were shot out of the sky without a chance to flee. A rainík with her fire didn't stand a chance as her insides were blown open. Even the little elvish children were pierced with a bolt by the mites as if they were monsters. He had never seen anything like the exploding crossbow, and wondered why the mites didn't use it during the war all those years ago, but he was thankful they didn't.

Bertin had almost never held a sword, only a few times when he practiced with the swordsmen in Rowan. His father always wanted a fighter, but Bertin liked running more. Except Ariad and Thatar wanted his help. And seeing all the killing around him made him grip his sword harder, his knuckles turning white.

Thatar's slender sword was like an extension of his arm. He cut down as many mites as he could reach, any that came near him died. Bertin hacked as if he were cutting through a jungle. Occasionally he would feel his blade cut into clothes and skin and see blood. But he was lucky to be alive. Lucky the elves were protecting him.

"Back you beasts!" Vhistela yelled as she jumped from a tree canopy and shot four or five or even six arrows at once into the mites below. Bertin lost her in a crowd. Kelltar was nowhere to be seen. *Probably cowering.* He thought before remembering it was Kelltar who killed Ioelena. Sliced her back open. *He's someone out there, killing ... protecting me as well.*

The entirety of Anha Jorbstah was drowned in a chorus of steel against steel, with the occasional drum of an exploding crossbow. "Not how I imagined my return," Thatar shouted over the noise as he kicked a mite into a jumble of rocks. "Not much different from Telemaw is it?"

Bertin didn't say the biggest difference was that he was now fighting with those who took him hostage. The ones who starved him. And Ioelena wasn't here to save him this time, now he had to save himself. But the blow to his head by a fist stopped that thought.

***

Bertin could barely see out of his right eye when he came to. It bulged and twitched and he tasted blood. Thatar was on the ground next to him. He withered as a steel boot left his stomach. Ariad had tears as the hunters used their swords and spears and killed the elves in a line. A group of elven children huddled together. Hugging. Crying. The mites kicked them apart and yelled in their language to horrified screams.

"Why?" Ariad said in the common tongue and the nearest mite seemed to understand. "Leave them alone. Leave us alone."

The mite, whose hair was thin and skin tight, bent over her to grab her chin and squeeze. "You all are monsters. We kill monsters. You have attacked us time and time again. If we are to win then we must punish you all."

"But the little children have done nothing. Killed no one. Spare them and kill the rest of us, but send the children away."

The mite looked at the children with sorrowful eyes before they turned red with anger once more. "No tricks from you, you elven bitch," he slapped her cheek. "You try to hide behind them. Make them your shields. What do you think these monsters will grow up to be?" He shook his head and two other mites came over with swords and began to cut the children down. Ariad yelled and cursed, Thatar could barely move. Bertin's eyes watered at the sound of dying, afraid, elvish babes.

Then an axe flew from the trees and split the mite's face in two. Kelltar emerged. A dozen elves with bows followed. The mites turned their attention to the attackers and Ariad ran to Thatar and whispered in his ear as she tried to help him up. *"Righi fi giriad. Ein paista. Ein paista."* A sword flew down into her spine and cut her innards out.

"No!" Thatar seethed, but he couldn't do anything as Ariad fell atop him and an arrow from a mite shattered his skull.

Bertin's stomach lurched and the stone path was covered in vomit and blood. He wiped his face clean and sat near the two dead elves as Kelltar ripped his axe free of the dead mite and used it on perhaps a dozen others. Bertin couldn't be sure. The world was as still and quiet as it had been when Ioelena died. When his mother died. He thought he had outrun the death that followed him, but it found him in Anha Jorbstah, and it brought about the end of all the living things in the ancient city.

As the world came back to him with the sounds of fighting he once again saw Thatar and the arrow poking through his skull. Ariad's black hands over her husband's face, dead, sprawled over him. Kelltar pulled Bertin to the trees as screams echoed in the mountains. "Come." The elf said. "We've only one way to defeat these hunters."

"I'm not going anywhere with you," Bertin said as he yanked free of the elf's grip. An explosive force brightened the world and he heard Vhistela's screams as she lay in a pool of blood and bones. Bertin needed to stop walking. He needed to find a place to lay down and cry and breathe and sleep. But everywhere around him was death.

"We cannot fight them all." Kelltar pulled once more. "Come."

Bertin didn't have a choice. It was either go with Kelltar or end up like the others. He didn't want to die in Anha Jorbstah just like he didn't want to die in Telemaw. *I will die old and gray atop my seat in Rowan,* he told himself, *with my family by my side.*

They ran over the paved roads, dodging bodies of elves, some of them children, most of them little elven children. Rainvealandians tried to attack them. Kill them. But Kelltar was far too good with his axe to let that happen.

The elf hunters who didn't attack them were too busy destroying books and paintings and vases; the more insidious ones were raping and killing and laughing. Bertin wanted to vomit again, but any hesitation and he would be the next to die.

Kelltar pushed a huge, stone door open beneath the great tower of stone above. He ushered Bertin in before slamming it shut. "We'll be safe in here for the time being."

Bertin's hands went to his knees as he panted. "Why are they doing this?" Tears filled his eyes then streamed down his face at the thought of Thatar and Ariad dead. Together. "Why are they attacking all of the sudden?"

Kelltar grabbed Bertin by the collar and brought him up close. "No tears. This is how we always live. You think this just started today? My brethren have been getting killed by your kind for centuries. No matter what we do. Where we go. They always find a way. Even when we say we want to live peacefully. Even if we take cities back, our cities back, by force. There is no pleasing them until we are all dead." Kelltar threw Bertin toward a wall. "Now," he said as he found a torch to light their way down a dozen steps, "help me avenge those who have died."

"Did we do this?" Bertin didn't follow as the realization hit him. "We decided to use the dwarf tunnels instead of going around the mountains. Did we show the hunters how to get in? The words to use?" He couldn't breathe, he wanted to claw at his chest.

Kelltar rolled his eyes but they almost looked sad in the firelight. "Maybe," the elf started down the stairs again. "Are you coming?"

Bertin nodded and followed the light. What happened couldn't be changed. No matter how hard he willed or prayed or anything. Ariad and Thatar and Vhistela and Ioelena and his guards and his mother weren't coming back. All of them his fault. The elves and guards were trying to protect him. His mother jumped from the rumors of his birth, or so he heard. But he was the son of King Bartel and Queen Rouna of Rowan. He would do everything in their power to make it right. To avenge the fallen.

Kelltar stopped at a giant wheel made of stone. It looked like the wheel of a ship. Dwarvish runes, he guessed, were etched into the stone, glowing white in the darkness. Kelltar dropped the torch, gripped some handles, and his muscles bulged as he turned the wheel the best he could. A low rumble escaped from the mountain underneath as the elf turned and turned. "Help me," Kelltar said with a strained voice. "I can't do it alone."

Bertin found a handle, the stone rough, scratching his hands, and pushed with all his might. His legs and arms felt like breaking as he clenched his jaw and turned the wheel. The rocks shook, small ones falling on their heads as they turned in sync with each other. The white runes glowed ever brighter. Bertin had to squint his one good eye to protect it from the light.

Then the whole chamber lurched as if a heavy door was shut. The wheel couldn't be turned anymore. "Now we wait. We'll be safe in here." Kelltar said as he wiped his bald head of sweat.

"What did we do? Some magical thing? Summon all the rainík?"

"Dragonfire." Kelltar said as screams began to flood down the stairs. "The dwarves had dragons help them build this city. The stones will withstand the fire that pours from the top of the tower, but the trees and the hunters and all the dead will burn away."

"Then what?" Bertin asked. He swallowed as he looked toward the steps to the large stone door. His only way out. Blocked by Kelltar and now by some magic fire. *If I distract him I can run. Then I'll deal with the fire.*

"Then we go to Mi'rallen. We still need your kingdom to give us coins and whatnot."

I helped you and this is how you repay? is what he wanted to say. He wanted to slap Kelltar or push him. Bertin had seen every semblance of friends die. And the evil elf still wanted to keep him hostage. "And these runes? What do they mean?" Bertin asked, trying to get Kelltar to lean into them.

"Who cares?" The elf shrugged. "They've done there work. If a dwarf survives you can ask them, it's their old writing."

"But it's glowing red," Bertin shook his head, not thinking that would work. But Kelltar squinted and leaned his head just enough to be close to the stone handle. Bertin mustered all the strength he could find and grabbed the elf's head and slammed it into the stone. Kelltar groaned and blood spilled as he fell to the ground. Bertin was already running up the stairs.

His arms didn't have much strength left, but he opened the stone door just enough to squeeze though. He panted as he emerged to a world on fire.

All the trees looked like a thousand candles as they went

up in flames, the canopy shredding. Dead elves and dwarves and gnomes and fairies all melted away. Bertin looked up at the massive stone towers and the tallest one in the center had a gaping hole in the top. Slow streams of thick fire poured. It was as if a volcano on the Saipta Isles had erupted. He had only heard stories of those, never seen one with his own eyes. The stone was unscathed but everything on the ground was not. There was a yell behind him and he knew it was Kelltar coming to get him, or this time finally kill him.

He ran over the stone path, but eventually hit a river of fire that streamed toward the water below. He jumped to a stone fence just high enough to escape the flames. He didn't want to turn around, but his head didn't listen. Behind him was Kelltar. He had thrown the stone door open and raged toward Bertin. His face redder than the slow-moving flames.

Bertin leapt to another stone wall that acted as a railing. Below was the path they had used to come into the city. In the distance the surviving mites were running toward the dwarf tunnel, still open. The ancient creatures that lived were all running inside the stone walls, throwing off any person who tried to find refuge. Thatar and Ariad's bodies were off in the distance. Flames crept up before engulfing them. The smoke rising to the night sky. He couldn't see any stars due to the haze, but he remembered that Ioelena said they were the Dragon's many eyes. *I wonder if the Dragon is watching now. Crying.*

He dropped down and ran toward the bridge that would carry him over the water and to safety. But Kelltar got him first. The elf wrapped his arms around Bertin's legs and brought him to the ground in a smash. Bertin kicked and kicked but Kelltar was too strong to let go. "You wretched human," the elf seethed. "You watch my brethren die than run away? I thought they were your friends."

Bertin tried to crawl away but he couldn't. "They were my friends. You … were … never …" He strained to get the big elf off of him, and for a slight moment he felt Kelltar's hand relax. He took the opportunity and wrest free his right leg and kicked his boot over and over on the new, bloody scar across the elf's head. Kelltar shouted in agony. Fire was now pouring over the stone wall above them, any longer and Bertin would be dead.

He stood and thought about running. But the image of Kelltar slicing open Ioelena's back and leaving her for dead in the desert crossed his mind. He turned to the big elf, who was just now standing, the flames behind him. Bertin cried out and pushed Kelltar back. The elf went stumbling, tripped over some rocks, and fell in the fire. He screamed and thrashed as his body was engulfed instantly.

Bertin didn't have time to react. Instead, he turned and ran with the mites toward the unknown as Anha Jorbstah burned behind him.

Yvanne

Yvanne sat on the cool, dark, stone chair of her ancestors. For hundreds of years the Relys have ruled in the Asara Mountains. And now she was the duchess. The queen. The regent. With Devro gone, taken by Drogue on the lord's retreat toward Blackrock, Yvanne was in charge. She was the ruler now. The councilors looked to her.

"What do you think, Your Grace?" Arold asked her. The swordmaster stood in front of her, the other councilors near him. The keep was quiet other than that. No coughing from her father. No battle outside. No Devro muttering and trying to make sense of everything. "We cannot wait in the mountains forever. It could take months just to cross the lowlands with the heavy fighting they're seeing, and the usurper has the king."

Yvanne didn't say anything as her fingers pricked the throne. *How many more battles can we win before Ultiir unleashes all his might on us?* Lord de'Marisco stepped forward. The lord had hid during the battle, not wanting to be captured by Drogue. Yvanne was thankful for that. The man was scheming, but he offered her good advice. She hoped.

"I think leaving the safety of the mountain would be a mistake, especially without word from Tundavik and Lord Blume. If the Flewthlands don't join your side, then the Eastlands can put their entire weight on us. At least the mountains protect us."

Lord Cul nodded, he, like Lord Aimora, was a new member of the council. Chosen because of the exceptional prowess of his warriors, and because he was supposed to defend Whitehall from a Terropian attack once spring set in. "If the Lords of the Peaks are to teach you anything," Cul said, "it's that the mountains are unbreakable. And it would be far too risky for you to only take your small army toward Vigur."

"Why don't you go too?" Cada asked. She stood next to Sidoro, both dressed in blue robes with a red snake slithering around them. "Most of the van survived the battle. Obviously the dukes of the Asara have long neglected those of the peaks. I think each of your fighters alone could best ten men."

"Twenty," Cul spat. "I was told my warriors would stay here. Terrop is an ever-looming shadow that could attack the moment the last snow melts, I pray not before. Who would defend Whitehall? Who has my strength?"

Yvanne rubbed her face, still not believing she was regent. *All of these people below me are hoping I answer their questions. Now I know how much weight was put on Devro,* she touched her belly as she thought, *and what will be put on my son.*

"Well the Lodean will attack Vigur with the queen," Aimora said with a puffed chest. "That's been our mission all along and we plan to carry it out."

"You don't think my husband's sea snakes can protect the town?" Cada asked to Lord Cul. "My Sidoro is a great commander, and maybe if King Anvrin knows a Terropian sits in Whitehall he'll think twice before attacking."

"King Anvrin doesn't seem the type to care about others," Aimora said, "just look at the Rainvealandians he holds captive in Tharet."

"We are not mites." Sidoro said in his deep voice with a stern face. "We are as much Veck'kop as he is."

As the lords continued to argue Yvanne saw the streams of energy being pulled to the back of the room. Helge, the old doma, was standing as still as a statue. *She must be seeing the future. She has the answers.* Yvanne cleared her throat when Arold started going on about the bad swordsmanship of the Sea Snake men. "Helge," she called to the back, "come forward." She didn't like commanding the old woman. Helge was her teacher, her confidant, her spiritual guide, but as queen Helge would obey her. "What do you think?" Yvanne gave a knowing look. *We both know what you can do.*

The old doma shook her head and closed her eyes before saying, "I think your sister is right. Lord Cul's fighters would be better in Vigur and whatever lays beyond." The old woman wiped her eyes but there were no tears.

"We're supposed to listen to an old hag?" Arold laughed. "What does she know."

Pollard straightened his back. "That *old hag* can communicate with the Four. She holds the power to your afterlife, whether you'll see Veltoora or the gods. I would hold your tongue."

"Enough," Yvanne said, though she was thankful for her brother. "I have listened to you all, not just Helge, and I think bringing Lord Cul with us will do wonders for the war. Sidoro and the men of Sea Snake can stay here and protect Whitehall, I have faith. And Arold," the swordmaster's face twisted like he was about to get thrashed, "you will also stay. Help the men learn new ways with the sword."

"Yes, Your Grace," he bowed.

"If I may, my queen," Urses de'Marisco said. "I would also like to stay in Whitehall. If King Anvrin were to attack maybe I can use some of our shared history to dispel him."

"Afraid the false king will name you a witch if he captures you and hang you as well?" Cada asked with pursed lips. Urses only smiled.

"Very well," Yvanne answered. "Stay here and advise Sidoro on the best plans. I assume you're well acquainted with the caverns behind the keep?" Some of the councilors snickered at Urses for hiding during the battle. She didn't mean it as a slight, and hoped Urses wouldn't take it that way.

"Of course, Your Grace, protecting the women and children was a tough job," he smiled and more snickers filled the air.

"So we should be ready by week's end?" Yvanne asked to quiet the laughs. "Even if we hear nothing from Tundavik and the Flewthlands?"

"I think that wise." Aimora nodded and the other councilors did as well.

***

"I don't trust him is all," Cada told Yvanne as they walked the stone corridors of the keep. "Urses is a cunning, conniving man, and we all know how people from Keeland act. They don't call it the city of bandits for nothing."

"Because of all the bandits that hide there," Yvanne said with a confused look.

"Because the people act like bandits." Cada and Yvanne's

arms were intertwined as they passed the rooms on either side of them, the keep much emptier than it was just a few months ago. "You don't find it odd that he travels to Whitehall with a severed head then wishes to stay here instead of face Vigur?"

"He isn't much of a fighter."

Cada rolled her eyes. "Convenient excuse." They stopped in front of Yvanne's bedchamber, Helge and Jacka inside fluffing the bed and cleaning the cobwebs. "Just think about. He won't have much use in Whitehall anyhow, and if he goes with you then Pollard can watch over him."

"You're not very trusting," Yvanne said as she hugged her sister. "I'll think about it." Cada bowed away and Yvanne went inside her room. She sat at her vanity. Her red hair was a mess from her rubbing her hands in it as the councilors spoke. Her eyes with dark circles from a lack of sleep. How her father and Devro did this she didn't know.

"How do you think father would react if he saw me?" She asked Helge as Jacka came over to brush the tangles from Yvanne's hair. "How would mother have reacted?"

Helge put down the Book of the Swallow, the tome described the god's journey across this world, using birds to help guide him to the heavenly places. Yvanne always wanted to follow in Swallow's footsteps. But the god had gone west at one point, and Yvanne new nothing of what was west. Besides, she wasn't a queen beyond the Western Ocean. "They would be thrilled to see how far you've come," the doma answered.

"They wouldn't believe their eyes," Jacka beamed. "I do have a question, Your Grace." Yvanne raised her brow. "Am I to come with you? I know you're leaving Helge behind, but what queen travels without a handmaid?"

"I won't need my hair in braids if I'm leading the men." Yvanne chuckled.

"The baby," Jacka said meekly. "You'll need someone to attend to you when the pregnancy gets harder, and what if we're in the field when you go into labor? I think it's very important I be there to help."

Yvanne hadn't considered that. Other than being pregnant, and her belly growing every day, she didn't think much about the future. She knew she would have an heir one day. But actually giving birth? As she thought about the pain she would have to endure and swallowed hard. "Yes," she gave a quick nod. "I think you're right. I'd love to have you by my side anyhow," she stood and squeezed Jacka's hands. The handmaid had always been so kind to her. "Without you there wouldn't be many familiar faces." She looked to the doma. The old woman's eyes were glossy. "May I speak to Helge alone?" Jacka curtsied with a smile and left Yvanne to her chamber. Helge fixed her gray hair as she watched herself in the mirror. "What is it?" Yvanne asked.

"I see a stone crushing a flock of birds," Helge shrugged. "It's a terrible sight and I'm not sure what it means. I wish the Four and the Many would've given me clearer sight."

"You think that has to do with me?" *Who here has anything to do with birds?* "What did you see that made you think Lord Cul coming to Vigur was a good idea?"

Helge scratched her head. "I saw a marble crown rolling off a peak to a fiery death below. A sign I took for Ultiir and the marble palace."

Yvanne pinched the bridge of her nose. "I wish the gods were clearer too." They laughed together, though Yvanne knew the battles to come would be nothing funny. "I don't plan on losing out there. Even if Ultiir can get the Terropians involved. I want to be there for my child."

Helge took Yvanne's hand, "I have full faith in you, but …" the old doma finally let tears fall. "You've been like a daughter to me for so long, so many wonderful years, and you've learned so much." Helge sniffled. "War is a deadly business. Many I knew never came back when Hurvir crossed the Ters-Veck. I don't want to — no — I cannot lose you."

Yvanne wiped the old woman's tears and kissed her cheek. "You will see me again, I swear it on the Four and the Many. You will see me in Vigur with the queen's crown atop my head."

"I hope I do," Helge said as she hugged Yvanne and they cried together.

There was knock at the door and Helge, wiping her tears, opened it to Tiro. The young boy was out of breath from running. "Your … Grace … we've a letter … from Lord Tundavik …" Tiro wiped his brow from sweat.

"What did it say? What did Lord Blume say?" She prayed while holding Helge's hand that the Flewthlands would join the war. If the duchy stayed neutral, or worse, sided with Ultiir, that would spell trouble for Yvanne ever being queen in Vigur, and Devro would be lost forever.

"I was told to not say anything," Tiro took deep breaths, "but," he whispered, "Lord Tundavik has said to start marching on Vigur. He has a whole host of Flewthmen behind him."

Yvanne didn't know if the tears in her eyes were from when she said goodbye to Helge or if they just formed. The two northern duchies joining together to counter the weight of the Kinglands and Eastlands. She could actually see the path to victory now. *I'm going to give you a kingdom,* she thought as she rubbed her stomach.

"The councilors are waiting for you near the throne," Tiro bowed and began to back away but stopped himself. "My queen," he bit his cheek, "I was wondering if it were possible I could go with you. I wouldn't have to fight," he said quickly before Yvanne could protest, "but you might need a messenger and I'm perfect for the job."

Yvanne giggled, but then she remembered what he did for her during the battle. Killed for her. The young boy. A murderer. Or a savior. "Well, you can't go unless you're a knight or a squire. I'm afraid we've no more room."

Tiro's eyes dropped. "I understand." As he went to leave Yvanne imagined the boy in Whitehall when the Terropians invaded. Hanged with the rest of the village. *At least if he's with me I can look after him. Have Pollard keep him close.*

"Wait," she said and the boy hopped to turn around at attention. "Perhaps I can make more room. But I'd have to knight you first for saving my life at the battle."

Tiro's face was wide with a grin before he dropped to his knee like he must've seen so many do before him. "Of course, Your Grace. I would be honored."

"We can do it right now," Yvanne said. "The law says a doma must be in attendance to oversee the oath, and Helge is right here. Are you ready, Tiro?" The boy nodded and stayed on his knee. Helge gave a shy smile while Yvanne found a small knife she had used to cut cheese a while ago. "This will be our sword." Tiro nodded before bending his head. He probably watched a dozen ceremonies that her father had conducted just as Yvanne had. Tiro would be the first person to be made a knight by her.

"Do you swear to follow these commands under the Four and the Many?" Helge asked, the start of the ceremony.

"I do." Tiro answered.

Yvanne tapped his right shoulder with the knife. "As your liege lord I command you to pass judgment in accordance with Vigura," then she tapped his left shoulder, "to answer the calls of the people in accordance with Meret," his right shoulder again, "to help the lowly travelers in accordance with Samosay," left, "to protect the nature of this realm in accordance with Swallow." She bent and kissed both of Tiro's cheeks. "Do you promise to stay loyal to your oaths so long as you live?"

"I do."

Yvanne helped Tiro to his feet and handed him the knife. "Then I name you a knight of Whitehall, a knight of the Lands of Asara, a knight of Viguran. Sir Tiro."

Tiro hugged her, which wasn't usually part of the ceremony, but she allowed it. "I shall make you proud, make my father and mother proud."

Yvanne smiled and said, "stay close to Sir Pollard. He can teach you everything you need to know." Tiro nodded, his face was giddy. "Now," she looked to Helge then the young boy, "shall we go save Devro?"

Raimund

Snow beat at them as they trudged their way through the white powder and the screaming winds and the jagged rocks. Raimund didn't need a fire to warm himself though, his anger was all he needed. Sile was dead. Burned. Charred. Potter and Raimund had dug as best they could in the hard ground of winter, but it was only a foot or so deep. Sile's body was wrapped in some cloth that hadn't burned. Snow covered her. Eventually her body would be pecked by ravens and crows, but Raimund tried not to think about that.

They had set out for the peak the monster had flown to. Raimund watched it disappear in the distance. Even if this potvoryn wasn't there, he was glad to be hiking, it gave him something to focus on other than Sile. That woman was to go south with them, see Whitehall, see Yvanne. That was the reason he had even found her in the mountains. To reunite a family. The gods played cruel jokes.

As the days went on the storms started to die down. He was glad for that. Now, the snow was hard making it easy to walk on. Parts of the mountainside were freshly shaven. The black rocks gleamed in the sunlight.

Potter was the first to slow. Raimund was exhausted but

tried to hide it. "We can rest here for a moment, but we need to keep moving." The sun was starting to set. The shadows moved and danced for miles down the mountain. "We'll start a fire, get water, then be ready by first light." The mountain tops seemed to be on fire with the orange rays of the sun. Farther down the black rock and white snow danced their way across the mountain. Trees swayed miles below as a cold northern breeze swept through. It looked like a painting he would've found in Gereduss.

They spent the night huddled together. Raimund could only get a couple branches burning so the fire was low. He gripped his sword as they slept. Wolves howled. And the potvoryn was somewhere.

They continued up the mountain, luckily it wasn't too steep. In the summer the valleys were probably covered in flowers. Reds and yellows and blues and pinks would light up the mountainside. Now it was just white and gray and dead.

"Oh my," Potter said as Raimund came around the corner of an outcrop of rocks. A river was frozen in front of them, fresh snow covering the ice, but a waterfall farther up was leaking water.

"We can't go around," Raimund said. The ice sheet went for miles in either direction. On the other side of the river was a mix of evergreen and dead trees. The mountain peak that the large, shadowy monster flew to was just ahead.

Potter was to go first across the frozen river. Raimund stood on the ground watching as the big man slowly stepped on the ice. There was no telling how thick or thin it was. Every step could be Potter's last. Then Raimund would've attacked the prison with Sile for nothing. "It's alright, Potter, one step at a time." Raimund tried encouraging the boy.

Potter continued to make his way across. The ice cracked and screamed. Water shot out and hit Potter. The large man jumped from shock and fell onto the white glass.

"Stay still, Potter. Take it very slowly." Raimund yelled.

Potter wiped tears and flipped over to push himself up. Water gushed through the cracks surrounding him. With one push he was standing. Then the ice broke and Raimund watched in horror as he fell into the freezing water.

Raimund had no choice but to rescue the boy. He patted the ice with his foot and took his first steps. Potter was flailing in the water throwing the cold liquid all around. Raimund reached his arms out and pulled with all his might, the water freezing his gloves as it hit. Potter climbed as best he could, his legs kicking wildly. Together, they were able to hoist Potter back onto the ice, the sheet bobbing with every step. They panted as they made their way across. A trail of water and cracking ice left behind them. The white grass was a welcome sight as they stepped and fell onto the earth.

"I thought I … I was going … to die," Potter said through pants and chatters.

"Are you okay otherwise?" Raimund shook the water from his gloves the best he could.

"Fine," Potter's teeth chattered and he used Raimund's cloak to dry his wet clothes. "Dangerous out there."

"It is," Raimund agreed. "Sorry for bringing you along. Should've sent you down the mountain instead."

Potter raised an eyebrow. "I chose to came along. I want to find that monster just as much as you. 'Sides, I'm having fun," he laughed. "Ma and pa would be proud."

Raimund made a small fire. The damp and snow-covered logs and sticks didn't make much flames, but it was better than the ice. Potter wringed his clothes, letting the water freeze on the ground below. Raimund held his knees close. His stomach churned. His insides were cold. He didn't want to get frostbite, but they were slowing, and this potvoryn showed no signs. All he knew was that it was had flown to the mountains. Flown. *Just a griffin ... but the fire,* he argued with himself. He didn't bring it up to Potter and rarely to himself. But only one thing in legends could fly and breath that much fire. *But that's only a legend,* he thought before leaning against a rock and teetering to sleep.

Then the growl ripped through the air.

Raimund's eyes shot open and his hands found his ears. Potter was doing the same. The fire had gone out, the only light from a sliver of the moon, the snow reflected the light, but the snow had started to blow around, blinding as it hit his eyes. The earth shook. Another growl. It was nothing like the low sound of the griffin. It was loud enough to shatter the stained windows of a domaton. "Run!"

He grabbed Potter and helped him up. A large shadow grew around them, choking them, but Raimund headed to a batch of trees. As they raced through the trunks and over logs, the trees behind them were being uprooted. They tripped and clambered through the flashing of snow. Raimund held onto Potter so he wouldn't lose him. They ran together, sword in hand, from the never-ending roar that echoed through the mountains.

Raimund jumped over a jagged rock and Potter ran around it. He pulled the large man with all his might to make sure he kept up. They ran toward another shadow, but this one wasn't moving, and as they got closer Raimund could see a rock face and a hole.

Raimund stepped in a puddle. The moonlight just enough to make out his surroundings. They had entered a long serpentine cave. Potter dropped to his hands and knees to recover from the run.

Black marks and twisting shapes ran the length of the cave. The mouth they entered was wide, rocks chipped and falling. "We're in it's lair," he whispered.

"How can you be sure?" Potter shuddered. "I think I'd rather be outside now."

Raimund made a small flame with his finger, it blew toward the mouth which meant air from somewhere else was pushing it. "Follow me." He said as he went deeper into the cave."

"I don't know," Potter started but he stopped as Raimund didn't wait to hear any objections. They followed the bumpy rocks through the twists and turns. It looked like scales were all around them. Potter rubbed his hand along the walls. "What's this?" He said in his Western accent. "Bumps on the cave."

Small bumps made in patterns protruded from the rock. Raimund followed each one with his finger. "Is it an ancient tongue? I can't make anything out." He used his flame to follow the twisting marks, but there were no words to gleam. "Think this monster writes?"

"I hope not," Potter rocked on his ankles.

They went deeper into the confusing cave. It twisted and turned and slithered, but Raimund kept the small flame going and followed where the wind was coming from. His fingers were sore from gripping his sword. He expected the monster to burst through the cave at any moment, wrap them in claws and rip their heads off. Or burn them like Sile. If only he had

Valkyr. The monster wouldn't stand a chance and Raimund could get revenge.

Pebbles and rocks fell from the top of the cave as the world shook. "What's that?" Potter asked as it shook once more. "The monster is walking."

"We'll be alright as long as we're in here," Raimund hoped.

The cave split into more and more tunnels. Raimund used the flame on his finger to make sure they were going the right way. *Hopefully this isn't too much farther, we need to escape this beast.* The sword on his hip called for him. He didn't want to just escape, he wanted to kill it. Kill the monster for Sile.

"Potter," Raimund stopped and the big man did as well. "Do you think you can find the Drewogh? Find a ship?"

"It's east isn't it? I at least know how to follow the sun." Potter scratched his hair. "Why? You want to go that way instead of deal with whatever this is?"

"No," Raimund shook his head. The flame on his finger was blowing slightly more and if he squinted he could see the opening, a small hole that looked just big enough for a person to slide through. "I think we need to go our separate ways." Before Potter could protest, Raimund said, "think of the monster. I would rather it not kill us both. I have a sword," he patted the steel at his side, "I can fight it or at least distract it. You get down the mountain and find the sea and a boat and get south. If I make it out we'll see each other again. We'll meet at the docks in Redington. Sound good?"

Potter rubbed his nose, frozen snot clung to his glove. "No. I think that is a horrible idea. How am I going to get down the mountain alone? How am I going to find the sea? Then I have to talk some Northerners into takin' me south? I will die out there."

A growl pierced the cave and it shook. "The beast is looking for us, hunting us." Raimund said. "You have more of a chance if you leave. I promise I won't die," he rested a hand on Potter's shoulder. "I'll find you."

Potter's eyes filled with tears, but another growl spooked him. "Fine," he said as he wiped melted snow from his hair. "But you better be in Redington."

Raimund nodded and they embraced. "When you hear the fighting make sure to run."

Raimund went to the opening while Potter looked on. He put the flame in his fingers out and pulled himself through the hole. Ice and jagged rocks clung to him, but he was back outside on the other side of the forest. Snow had started to blow in from the east. As he stood the white began to blind him. But a black shadow grew taller and dwarfed him, and he saw strings of orange start to lick. So he began to run.

Need to keep it away from Potter, he thought as he ran blinding through the storm. Ice and snow attacked his face. He held a hand in front to keep the stings away. With every step the world jumped. The monster was gaining speed and not slowing down. Raimund stopped what he was doing. He was all alone. He lifted his sword and turned to face the beast. The shadow neared him, and he knew it was the end. He started swinging, but a claw hit him and he was thrown ten feet across the snow, his sword falling behind rocks.

He pushed himself up, lost in the snow, lost with no sword. *Potter can at least run down the mountain. The monster should be fine with just me, but I need to keep moving.*

Raimund kept running. He was defenseless. The snow was too thick for him to find his sword. He found a rock and hid behind it trying to catch his breath. The beast sniffed all around. Raimund saw the snout reach around the rock and he took off running again. Always running.

The beast chased after him through the snowstorm. Whenever he turned he saw the giant shadow ready to attack. No matter how far he ran he would die. So why run at all?

He stopped in his tracks and turned to face the shadow of the beast that would kill him. The snout burst through the snow first. Then came the yellow eyes. Raimund stared at the beast, and the beast stared back.

The snowstorm stopped abruptly. The beast huffed before giving a roar to the world. A roar of strength.

End of Book Two

List of Characters

Kinglands:

King Ultiir de'Tro – King of Viguran, lord of Goldfield, and Sophie's husband

Queen Sophie Margia – Queen of Viguran, Princess of Terrop, Duchess of Aele, Hurvir's fourth wife before his death, and now Ultiir's wife

Hurvir de'Tro – previous king of Viguran, Sophie's husband, the father of Devro, and was killed

Rila de'Tro – Queen Mother of Viguran, mother of Hurvir, Ultiir, and Analere, and was married to King Ferrick of Viguran

Lord Tedbalt Masson – chief consultant on the King's Council

Lord Edel de'Viere - chief informant on the King's Council

Lord Alan Hirons – chief commander on the King's Council

Lord Serle Verrier – chief ambassador on the King's Council

Lord Dovi Lyons – chief collector on the King's Council

Lord Henk Zazí – lord of the recaptured Redington

His Most Holy Maller – High Doma of Viguran

Lady Abre Volles – lady of the Queen's Council who went back to Oceantree

Countess Filra - lady of the Queen's Council

Lady Betal - lady of the Queen's Council who was recalled to Ghostfield by her husband
Baroness Mara - lady of the Queen's Council and wife to the Baron of Sheplan
Lady Ficca - lady of the Queen's Council
Lady Rila - lady of the Queen's Council
Lady Alba - lady of Midriver
Lord Drogue de'Vil - lord of Blackrock
Lord Tyter - a lord in Viguran
Tylar - Lord Tyter's son and heir
Count Ompter - lord in the royal court in Vigur
Sir Achen – chief knight of Sophie's guard
Sir Velle - member of Sophie's guard
Sir Lovis – chief knight of Ultiir's guard
Sir Ard - member of Ultiir's guard
Sir Gid - chief knight of Rila de'Tro's guard
Amalla – Sophie's handmaid
Renna - Sophie's handmaid from Zhepatev in Masa Naq
Sufar – Ultiir's chamber slave
Albon - former High Doma of Viguran
Clava - slave in Goldfield
Master Ayter - slave master of Goldfield
Master Vachen - slave master in the palace of Vigur
Rou - the royal executioner
Olier - the palace jailer
Atrice - a prostitute in the King's Brothel
Madam Taire - owner of the King's Brothel

Eastlands:
Duke Adyn Gallient – Duke of the Eastlands
Lady Annue Gallient – the Duke's elder sister and first wife

of King Hurvir

Lord Delan - lord of Ruwy and Reran and Mar's father

Lady Memi - lady of Ruwy, wife of Delan, and mother of Reran and Mar

Reran - heir to Ruwy and Mar's brother

Luxe - Reran's wife

Orson - Reran's son

Burt - farmhand in Ruwy

Gilfred - regent of Montlahead for the young Gerold Geary after Lord Gofrei Geary's death

Flewthlands:

Duke Pyre Blume - Duke of the Flewthlands

Tundavik Vandes - once a duke in Viguran who came back after living in Baragio

Sir Mar - knight of Viguran and member of Devro's guard

Lady Flora - lady of Woodrun, Pyre's daughter, Barnet's wife, and Florance's mother

Lord Barnet Lovell - lord of Woodrun, husband of Flora, and father of Florance

Florance - daughter of Flora and Barnet

Tedbalt Ver - Flora and Barnet's carriage driver

Lord Umid - lord of Grayfield

Lord Toware - lord of the Riverend

Lady Lueva - wife of Lord Toware

Lord Ed - lord of the Seeded Field

Lord Rickart - lord of Uphain, known as the Crazed

Lord Arnate - lord of Grass Ridge

Lord Olette - lord of Meadowton

Nama - maid in the service of Flora and Barnet

Lila - servant in the Storyah castle

Lands of Asara:

Yvanne - the young queen of Viguran and daughter of David Rely

Devro - the young king of Viguran, bastard son of Hurvir de'Tro, and nephew of Ultiir

Duke David Rely - Duke of the Lands of Asara

Sir Pollard - knight of Whitehall, David's youngest son, and Yvanne's brother

Lord Urses de'Marisco - lord of Keeland, once the chief informant to Hurvir and chief consultant to Ultiir

Cada - lady of Sea Snake, Sidoro's wife, one of David Rely's daughters, and Yvanne's half-sister

Sidoro - lord of Sea Snake in Terrop

Helge - local doma of Whitehall

Sir Loc - knight of Whitehall

Sir Groel - knight of Whitehall

Sir Rye - knight of Whitehall

Sir Rickart - knight of Whitehall

Arold - swordmaster of Whitehall

Jacka - Yvanne's handmaid

Tiro - a young man in Whitehall

Dera - daken from Midvalley

Lord Aimora Dore - lord of Lodeanhold

Besta - a Lodean man

Orra - a Lodean man with red hair

Achi - dwarf in the tunnels of the Asara

Lord Cul - lord of Mount Meret

Lord Plantan - lord of Mount Swallow

Lord Emni - lord of Mount Samosay

Lord Aute - lord of Mount Doma

Rowan:

King Bartel Thomas - King of Rowan

Queen Rouna - Queen of Rowan who committed suicide

Princess Aveline - Princess of Rowan, the eldest child and only daughter of Bartel

Prince Baldewin - Prince of Rowan and Bartel's youngest child

Blis - teacher to the royal family

Mari - Aveline's handmaid and close confidant

Aida - another of Aveline's handmaids

Caxton - leader of the king's council

William - a member of the king's council who has no tongue

Wycleaf - a member of the king's council

Jac - a member of the king's council

Zoell - one of Aveline's guards

Bert - one of Aveline's guards

Ivlin - one of Aveline's guards

Tomas - one of Aveline's guards

Dern the Third - one of Aveline's guards

Lord Darry - Lord of the Sunrise (eastern Rowan)

Lord Rean - Lord of the Sunset (western Rowan)

Sir Delmar - household guard for the king of Rowan

Hecher - the High Chancellor of the Royal Chancellery in Rowan, an elected position

His Most Holy Emmett - the High Doma of Rowan

Neşe - an old friend of Aveline's

Kari - Neşe's wife and friend of Aveline's

Celat - child of Neşe and Kari

Nico - the royal painter

Captain Pitor - captain of the king's ship

Awaran:

Grand Duke Peliz Fonds - leader of the Upper House of Awaran

Grand Duchess Lue Sant - leader of the Lower House of Awaran

Caral - a representative for the House of Awaran

the North:

Raimund - a knight of Viguran who was captured and taken to the North, best friends with Mar and Devro

Sile - a woman who lives a hermit lifestyle in the mountains

Potter - a young man from Verva in the West

the South:

Bertin - Prince of Rowan

Kelltar - the elf who killed Ioelena

Thatar - an elven fighter

Vhistela - an elven fighter, and a very old elf

Eyln - an elven fighter

Ariad - Thatar's wife in Anha Jorbstah

Blaenda - an elven leader, part of the Circle of Elders

A Song of Triumph

Blis

Men untethered the boats, hoisted the anchors, and dropped the sails. The great masts of a rearing stallion would race through the ocean once more. Blis stood at the bow of the monarch's grand ship, the *Sea Glider*. It was a newer ship, built just after Queen Rouna's death. Her love of ships almost matched his. Blis loved the scent of the ocean, the salt and fish. The sound of gulls was music to him. "Ready to take to the seas once more?" A short worker said to him after unfurling a sail.

"Of course. I wasn't always this old or this fat. I captained the *Red Ember* during the war with the Rainvealandians and worked as crew for the *Sea Mare* much earlier when the Nowexerts were in Therirock. The salt of the sea is in my blood," Blis said.

"My father was on the *Red Ember*. He always said how the captain was the best in Rowan. Knew everywhere to go and the best practices for blocking mite ships. He also told me the captain knew the best whorehouses when they took to land."

Blis laughed. "As I said, that was long ago. What was your father's name?"

"Raimund, a knight of Fairgrove. He fought to keep the mites from blockading the Ters-Veck. Unfortunately, he was killed some years later during a storm."

"A knight of Fairgrove does sound familiar." He lied. "What's your name, sailor?"

"Ormin, knight of nothing." Someone yelled Ormin's name and beckoned him over.

"That makes two of us," Blis said as the young sailor went back to work. He tried to think back to the *Red Ember* and all the crew aboard. The deaths of his friends and the bruises his ship took while fighting the mites. The great red sail with a yellow and orange flame plastered across. It was his favorite ship, given to him by royal decree, before the monarchy collapsed. But he couldn't remember any knight of Fairgrove. His old age had muddled his memory.

A commotion rang out on the gangplank. Blis turned and saw a young fellow with ragged clothes and the boy king being led by a royal guard. He sighed and sauntered over to the boys.

"Is there a problem with His Grace?" Blis asked the knight.

"These two were found in a brothel at the far end of Liari. Apparently, His Grace was escorted by this lowborn, Torbet. I was worried the king would miss our departure."

Blis doubted that. "I will deal with this nonsense." The knight bowed and worked his way to the stern. "You, Torbet, I will have you go to the *Fair Fellow*. Enjoy your work." The worst ship in the royal fleet. Blis was glad to never step foot on it. Torbet gave a slight bow and raced off the gangplank. Blis put his hand over Baldewin's shoulder and walked with him. "Should a king your age be found in a brothel?" The boy shook his head. "Then why were you there?"

The boy's eyes of honey grew wide. "Torbet told me a king needs a queen. We hoped to find one in the whorehouse. Torbet said to look for large breasts and wide hips."

"A child as young as you should worry about other things. And as king, you will have an arranged marriage. Your father, may the Four watch over him, was meant to choose, but the gods wanted to feast with him."

"Will this arranged wife have wide hips?"

Blis rolled his eyes. Baldewin never cared for girls or 'wide hips.' He knew that was Torbet talking. "I'm sure," he said anyway. "I'm also sure the people of Rowan would not like a Vigurite whore as their queen. Lords and ladies across the realm would question it, and men have gone to war for less."

"I don't want to start another war." Baldewin's voice was shaky.

"Good thing I'm here to stop you." Blis led Baldewin into his royal chambers with a laugh. Mari, Aveline's handmaid, pretended to clean. Baldewin and Blis were to keep her safe while the princess was away.

The room was fit only for a king. Purple drapes, gold etching, and a feather bed large enough for Blis himself. The king sat on a velvet chair and Blis admired the wide window at the back. He could see the people of Liari. They differed from people on the continent. Fish and shipping dominated their life. They wore hats to keep the sun and salt away. The roads were lined with open shops and tents selling goods from as far east as the maps went. It differed from the wool coats the Rowai had when they landed in Anhar. The people gave them strange looks, and they returned the favor.

"How are the councilors doing?" Baldewin asked as he plopped onto his bed. Mari went back to 'cleaning,' but Blis knew she would listen to every word.

Why else would Aveline leave her here? She'll report everything she knows once the princess comes back. Blis stretched his arms and said, "they wish to leave sooner rather than later."

"And where did *they* decide to go?"

Blis sighed. "If you want to make decisions for our course of action, then I suggest you meet with the councilors instead of hiding in your cabin or whorehouses." Baldewin had done little since Aveline left, and after they won in Redington and Storyah, he was even less interested. He thought battles would bring him glory, but he never fought to gain any.

"You know they don't listen to me," the young king whined. "They didn't listen to Aveline either. They do whatever they wish and I have to put up with it."

"Your Grace," Mari said with her head lowered; her words were soft. "If I may, why don't you show them some force? You are the king, after all. Aveline wouldn't want to see you isolating yourself."

Baldewin threw himself back on his bed. "Now even a handmaid is telling me what to do."

Blis nodded at Mari and cleared his throat. "Yes, but the handmaid is, of course, correct. You are king, and even though your regent is off somewhere else, you still have power, even if the councilors have a bit more now. Your father made sure of it when he healed the kingdom."

"And what do I tell them?" Baldewin traced the air. "'If you don't listen to me, I'll sic my hounds on you?' That will go over well." The young king sat up, his brown hair a mop on his head. "I don't even have hounds."

"You have knights," Mari said before bowing and wiping dust from her loose clothes.

"Shall we find Sir Delmar?" Blis asked. Baldewin, much to Blis' surprise, nodded.

As they left the king's quarters and made their way up

one deck to the captain's quarters, shouts rang out from below and the ship lurched forward. Blis had to hold on to a railing to keep from falling into the sea below. Sails and oars worked together to pull the *Sea Glider* from port. He watched the window to see the other ships leave Liari. The *Queen's Tear* and the *Silent Kraken*, holding the lords of the east and west, followed closely behind as they moved further from the island. He could see the painted masts of the forests of Lord Arin, the twin fish of Lord Monir, and the hills of Lord Ridas. Dozens of other sigils stared back at him, but his eyes were too old to see.

Delmar was wiping sweat from his brow when Blis found him. "Your Grace," he said to Baldewin, who was distracted by the ships cutting through the deep blue water. "What is it?"

Blis answered for the young king. "My good sir, we need you to come with us to the council meeting. Also, we must talk later about you forgetting your duties and letting the king here gallivant around Liari like a common lout."

The knight tensed, but bowed his head and followed them into the captain's room. Captain Pitor was busy at the helm, but the councilors were already discussing matters round a small table. As the door closed, the lords' voices dissipated.

"Your Grace," Wycleaf said in almost a whisper. "What brings you to a council meeting? You've missed quite a few in recent weeks."

"The king may go where he likes," Delmar said.

"Naturally," Jac chimed in, "we just weren't prepared for you is all."

Baldewin's voice strained as he said, "I ... I want to ... join this one." Whatever force he was trying to convey certainly didn't come through. "I hope, my lords … that you don't mind."

"Never," Caxton said with a smile as his black hair fell to his face. "Stand by my side." He ushered for Baldewin, who took his place at the right of the councilor. Caxton worried Blis the most of all the royal councilors. He never knew what King Bartel saw in him, but Caxton had been a loyal servant to the crown for decades. He also wished for Blis to leave the *Sea Glider.* "I think you'll be better help to Lord Rean as he sails south. He'll need your knowledge of the seas. Plus, the North is far too cold for you," Caxton had told him as they docked in Anhar.

"I must stay near the king," Blis had said. "You already know I have advised his family for dozens of years. I cannot stop when I am needed most." And Blis never let Caxton bring it back up. *Why do you want the king alone?* Was all he thought.

"So, what have you been discussing?" Baldewin asked as he looked over the maps. Blis could see the finger of the Flewth-Vet, where they would head; the city of Storyah, where they came from; and the many Glybelm Islands to the north.

Caxton pointed to the Nokys Ocean on the map. "We are discussing how the ships should be divided. We believe half of our fleet must search the southern waters, with a few ships following Lord Darry to the Island of Meret. The rest will follow us as we search the Glybelm."

"You think the fleet is there?" The young king asked. "Why would they go to frigid waters?"

"To hide and repair, of course," Wycleaf said as he slightly rolled his eyes, but Baldewin was looking at the map, not paying attention to the councilor's face. Blis crossed his arms, not able to say much.

"You don't think they went south?" Baldewin asked, tracing the coastline and up the Ters-Veck. "Perhaps back to Vigur? If my cousin's armies are heading to the capital, the usurper may want ships to defend it."

"Possibly." Caxton rubbed his chin. "Though north makes more sense to me. It's a perfect place to hide, and Viguran has controlled the Glybelm for centuries. So far, the islands have stayed out of the war."

"And we should bring them in?" Baldewin chewed on his lip. The ship moved with the waves of the open ocean as the wind carried them out. "Aveline would want that," he said as his eyes lit up. "She didn't want anymore of our people to be hurt in the war, but if the ships are in the Glybelm, maybe the raiders will take care of it. Isn't that right, Blis? The islanders hate the Vigurites. Maybe we can convince them to fight."

Blis didn't want to answer, but he gave a nod because His Grace was correct. But Aveline would surely want to return to Rowan.

"Perfect," Wycleaf said with a smile. "So to Cahlun? That is where the largest port is in the islands. Might be the best place to start, Your Grace."

Baldewin nodded, and they discussed where the other ships were going, the plan once they reached Cahlun, and how Baldewin could help. The king was all smiles. Sir Delmar and any use of force wasn't needed. Baldewin was happy to help. The councilors giddy for his involvement. But Blis couldn't shake a creeping feeling.